The Minerva System

By Simon Leighton-Porter

Published by Mauve Square Publishing Ltd
http://www.mauvesquare.com/

ISBN: 9781909411180

By the same author:

The Seven Stars

The Manhattan Deception

This book is for Wendy

Chapter One

The automatic gates swung open and the silver Mercedes coupé turned into the lane where it was briefly lost to sight behind a stand of cypress trees.

From the scaffolding on a building site, five hundred metres further up the lane towards the village of Mirepech, a nineteen-year-old building worker watched the car emerge from behind the trees and turn in the direction of Béziers. He got out his mobile phone and dialled. 'Five minutes to eleven. They haven't closed the shutters. At twenty-five past then? OK.'

Up the reverse slope of the hill which faced the house to the south east a man struggled under the weight of a bulky rucksack. Although it was not yet eleven o'clock, the sun was beating down on the back of his neck as the temperature neared thirty centigrade. The journey from Marseille had taken far longer than expected and to his great annoyance he was now running late. He stopped, wiped his brow and, making sure he was well concealed from any casual observation, put down the rucksack and took out a hand-held anemometer from the side pocket. He checked all around once more, held the anemometer above his head for 30 seconds, then pressed and held a button in its base. He looked at the small digital screen on its side: 325 degrees, 19 kilometres per hour with gusts to 28. A further 100 metres further up the slope he repeated the exercise: similar readings. Always windy there, they'd warned him: today was in fact one of the Languedoc's calmer days.

He stopped just short of the summit of the hill and, making sure not to skyline himself, set down the rucksack and took another reading. Further along the ridge was a small dip, overgrown with rosemary, holm oak and juniper. Behind it was a rocky outcrop. Perfect: he eased himself into cover and dropped to one knee. From the other pocket he took a small metal box and flipped up the lid. Using the keypad, he entered the wind readings: a GPS display confirmed what his trained eye had calculated – 47 metres above – he'd estimated 50, so not bad. He removed the rubber cover which protected the lens and pointed the box at the house. The laser rangefinder confirmed his estimate too: 487 metres, only 13 away from the likely distance he'd calculated from the 1:10,000 walkers' map.

With practised hands he assembled the Russian-made VSSK *Vychlop* rifle, and clicked the integral lightweight bipod into the down position. He slotted the five-shot box magazine of 12.7mm subsonic, low-drag rounds into place, cocked the action, checked the safety catch and settled down to wait. It would not have been his choice of weapon for a job like this, but it would certainly send the right message. If the reports were correct it wouldn't be long now.

He'd only been waiting a matter of minutes when a dark-haired young woman emerged from the house. Same time, same routine as he'd been told to expect he noted with satisfaction. She was wearing sunglasses, a bikini and carrying a sunbed cushion. The woman moved one of the hardwood loungers by the poolside to face the sun, propped the backrest up into the sitting position, attached the cushion and went back into the house. Moments later, she reappeared with a towel, a book and a bottle of sun cream which she began to rub into the front of her legs, her face and upper body. She spread the towel out over the cushion, slipped off her bikini top, applied a little more sun cream and settled herself down. Evidently at ease with the world, she picked up her book and started to read.

He checked his calculations for the last time, brought his eye to the sight and slipped off the safety catch. As the squeeze of his index finger overcame the trigger's second pressure there was a sound little louder than a cough and he felt the slight recoil of the VSSK against his right shoulder. Through the telescopic sight, he checked his handiwork and, evidently satisfied, applied the safety catch. For the next few minutes he remained motionless – after years of training it was as natural as breathing – the human eye detects motion: keep still and nobody will see you. Then, without hurry, and making slow, deliberate movements, he checked all around. Not the time to run into an idiot dog walker, he thought. But if anyone was so foolish to disturb him, he had a 9mm pistol with a round in the chamber and the hammer back, ready for any such eventualities – one more wouldn't make a scrap of difference now. Retreating soundlessly to the back of the wooded hollow, he removed the magazine, ejected the live round from the breech, picked up the empty brass case which he put in a plastic bag, sealed the bag, released the rifle's action and soundlessly fired it off. Once the weapon was stowed in his rucksack, he returned the way he had come and rejoined the way-marked *Grande Randonnée* footpath – just another hiker on a nice day out in Southern France.

At twenty-five past eleven, the young man slid down from the scaffolding and collected his toolbag from the back of the van. He made another quick call on his mobile and set off on foot down the lane. As he approached the corner of the tall hedge in front of the house he was joined by his two friends.

'The hydraulic ram on the right hand gate panel is weak. You can push it open.'

'Are you sure they're not going to come back?'

'I told you, didn't I? Last three Tuesdays they've gone out between eleven and quarter to twelve and they return anywhere between two and just before three. They're obviously going out to some restaurant or other every week so we've got loads of time. We can't be seen from the road and we can be in and out in under ten minutes. Not scared, are you?'

'Course not.'

'My arse you're not! Right. Stay here, stay out of sight, keep your eyes open and if they come back, three rings on the mobile, hang up and run. *Cassos, d'accord?* We'll look after ourselves. If it's the postman, anyone on foot, anyone else but them just sit tight. Got that? Good.'

As predicted, a hefty continuous shove with a shoulder was enough to overcome the mechanism of the right-hand gate. They closed it behind them in the same manner and followed the curve of the drive towards the house. They stopped dead in their tracks.

The younger boy, turned away and vomited, the other dropped his toolbag and stared in blank disbelief. On a sun lounger lay a young woman with a book in her lap. Of her head there was no sign – some of it was spread against the wall behind her and the rest, in a long obscene spray, covered the tiles of the terrace that surrounded the pool.

Chapter Two

Eighteen months earlier

Sally Mansell considered her options: a soggy, freezing walk back across London Bridge, or trying to fight her way onto a Northern Line train at the height of the rush hour. Neither was an attractive proposition, but she decided that walking, even under the driving rain, was the lesser evil. Craning her neck for a gap in the traffic, she waited to cross Tooley Street but then jumped back from the edge of the pavement a fraction of a second too late as a bus sped through a puddle, showering her in cold, dirty water. Bugger the company's expenses policy, she thought, I'll get a cab. It was only five o'clock but the sky was almost completely dark. She spotted one with its amber lamp on and the driver slowed down in response to her wave.

'Sorry, love, can't pick you up here. Not allowed on the approach road to London Bridge, not fair to the people waiting at the cab rank. You'll have to join the queue at the station – shouldn't be too long, even at this time of day. It's just round here to the left.'

'Thanks.'

From behind came the sound of running footsteps but she thought nothing of it; probably late for their train. As the three youths drew level with her, one of them shoved her hard in the small of the back and another grabbed her handbag. She fell towards the gutter and swung round to try and hold on to the bag. This spun her onto her back, half lying on the ground but being held up by the violent tug of war she was now engaged in. She opened her mouth to shout for help but the youth holding the bag stamped his foot hard down into her stomach, forcing her to release her grasp and sending her sprawling and winded into the filth and wet of the gutter. The three of them then loped off towards the station and just before they disappeared round the corner, the one who'd kicked her in the stomach, turned round and spat contemptuously. For some reason, the thing that caused the red mist of rage to come down was that in the struggle, the heel of one of her shoes had broken off. Her best shoes.

Under the influence of a massive release of adrenalin, people are likely to do things that, depending on the outcome, can be seen with hindsight as anywhere between heroic, suicidal and just plain stupid. My shoes, my best sodding shoes, she fumed. Right, you little fuckers, you're going to wish you'd never been born.

Getting to her feet, Sally took off her shoes and ran full tilt after the youths in her stockinged feet.

'Help! Stop, thief. Somebody stop them, they've got my handbag. Somebody help me. Police, help!' Without exception, all the passers-by averted their gaze and hurried on. Whatever you do, don't get involved.

Alerted by her shouting, the youth who'd taken the bag passed it deftly to the larger of his two companions and set off alone at a run towards the station concourse. The one who now held the bag tucked it under his jacket, and together with his other accomplice, ran across the road and disappeared down the station ramp towards Borough High Street.

The chase careered round the corner and into full view of a bemused crowd on the station forecourt that was suddenly treated to the spectacle of a wet, bedraggled, screaming, five foot three, barefoot, female divorce solicitor in hot pursuit of a lanky seventeen-year-old boy.

'Stop him, he's got my handbag. Help!'

As the boy turned round to assess his lead on this avenging harpy, a middle-aged man in the taxi queue stuck his foot out and sent the boy sprawling. Two other men moved to grab him, by which time Sally was closing fast.

She hurled one shoe at her assailant and then the next. Both missed. 'You pig, you fucking bastard. How dare you?' she gasped.

The youth recoiled in fear.

'You bloody people make me sick. You dirty, thieving black bastard.'

A pin dropped and its deafening reverberations set the pigeons roosting on the cast-iron roof girders of the station into clattering flight.

A voice broke the silence. 'What did you just say?'

As if from nowhere, a policeman had appeared. The crowd recoiled from Sally as though she were radioactive.

She struggled to get her breath. 'He stole…he stole… he stole my bloody handbag and broke my shoe,' she said. As a little of the adrenalin began to wear off, the sheer awfulness of the situation overwhelmed her and she felt the tears welling up.

The youth was grinning now, despite still being restrained on his back with each arm pinned firmly to the ground. 'No I never. I never stole nothing.'

'What did you just say, Madam?' asked the policeman.

'I said he stole my handbag.' Sally was still panting from the chase and shaking with rage and fear. Her make-up was streaked with tears and she could barely stand upright.

'No. Before that. I heard you use a racially offensive term.'

'What?' she sobbed. 'For God's sake, you idiot, he's just stolen my handbag and all you care about is that I called him names? Right!' And she made towards the youth who recoiled in mock fear, with a grin from ear to ear.

The policeman stepped between them and violently body-checked Sally, spun her around and pinned her arms behind her back. As he handcuffed her he said, 'I am arresting you for the use of racially aggravated threatening words and behaviour. You do not have to say anything, but it may harm your defence if you do not.....' The rest of the caution dissolved into a blur of noise and Sally was now sobbing uncontrollably.

Summoned by a brief radio call, two other policeman arrived, one of whom freed the youth from his captors, helped him to his feet and informed him that he was going to be searched on suspicion of being in possession of stolen goods.

Streetwise and cocksure, the Police held no terrors for him. 'Fine by me. I ain't done nothing.'

After giving the youth a thorough pat-down, the Constable

gestured to his colleague who now held Sally by the upper arm. 'Nope, nothing. Clean as a whistle. Right, son, come with me and tell me what happened.'

The third policeman worked his way through the crowd asking for the names and addresses of those who'd seen what happened.

'…well, this mad woman, she starts chasing me for no reason, right, and yelling an' stuff, so course, I ran. Thought she was gonna stab me or something. Then this bloke trips me up, right, yeah, that one, the one with the umbrella. Yeah that's him – look, my jeans are all torn and they was new too. And them two blokes there, they grabbed me – really hurt it did…An' I am very upset and traumatised by what that lady called me.'

'Just a minute, please, son. Just stay here would you.' He returned to the taxi queue. 'Excuse me, sir. Yes, you, sir. And you two gentlemen. Please go and wait over there and do not attempt to leave, I'd like a word with you in a moment.'

Sally was left in handcuffs and forced to sit on the pavement outside the station with her back against a wall. A policeman stood over her but did nothing to disperse the crowd of gawpers that shouting and arrests inevitably attract. Some of them were taking pictures with their mobile phones, but still the policeman remained impassive. Sally put her head down between her knees to try and hide her face and her tears, but that only forced her hands and wrists hard up against the unyielding Victorian brickwork of London Bridge station.

After what seemed like an age, a police car arrived. The policeman pulled her none too gently to her feet and led her over to it. Once again, she had to run the gauntlet of flashes from mobile phone cameras, but with her hands still cuffed behind her back she was unable to hide her face: even after she'd been bundled unceremoniously into the back seat and wedged in next to a stern-faced policewoman, the flashes went on and yet more contorted, gargoyle faces pressed against the car's windows.

'I am the victim of a robbery and I demand that you release me at once.'

Residual spikes of adrenaline were still coursing through

Sally's system. No longer the frightened, cowed little figure she'd been earlier, she was now angry again: raging, spitting, furiously angry – angry with the verminous low-life who'd robbed her; angry that he'd lied about it; angry with the other two little shits who'd got away scot-free; angry with the police for treating her like a criminal, and above all, angry with herself for saying something that she'd never even thought, let alone said to anyone in her entire life. All those years of what she had always taken for instinctive, rational tolerance had been obliterated by something deep-seated, visceral and thus far hidden even to her, that the attack had unleashed.

'Madam, I am the Custody Sergeant and before we deal with any allegations you wish to make I am obliged to inform you of your rights under the Police and Criminal Evidence Act 1984.' He handed her a leaflet entitled "PACE – Your Entitlements While in Custody." 'Please sign here – this is the custody record and it shows that you have read the arresting officer's account of the events at the time of your arrest.'

She signed the record and exercised her right to add a written comment to what the arresting officer had written – it wasn't flattering.

'No, I don't want a solicitor, thank you. I *am* a solicitor and I wish to report a robbery. Kindly inform my husband of my arrest: here are his contact details. I do not require medical attention, nor an interpreter, nor help checking documentation. Oh, and before we get to the bit about the "detainee's property" please don't worry about that either; I haven't got any, because the low-life your people have no doubt released by now and his thieving friends have got it.'

After being cautioned, searched, DNA sampled and fingerprinted, Sally was put into a cell where, once again, time seemed to stand still. Somewhere in the struggle her watch strap must have broken. It was only a cheap watch but its loss was further proof to her of life's unfairness.

"Bonfire of the Profanities," shrieked the tabloids, "High Flying Lawyer Brought Down," "The Legal Profession -

Institutionally Racist?" "Strike Her Off!" "Racist Scum!" She'd made headlines nation-wide and even her husband, Tom, was under siege from the media. He'd decamped to his colleague, David Liebowitz's house in North London and, along with Caroline, Liebowitz's girlfriend, they watched the TV news with a sense of mounting disbelief.

'I'm coming to you live from leafy Betchworth, deep in the Surrey stockbroker belt...' panted the reporter.

'Won't see a lot of leaves this time of year,' growled Tom Mansell, his features taut with anger.

'...coming to you exclusively live from outside the luxury mansion of top divorce lawyer Sally Mansell, who tonight is in police custody after what appears, according to news just coming in, to be a racially-motivated attack on a star pupil of the Jacob Zuma City Academy in South London. Eye-witnesses report that Ms Mansell had chased the youth, who for legal reasons, cannot be named, onto the forecourt of London Bridge station where she tried to attack him and subjected him to a barrage of racist abuse and accusations of theft. Other witnesses report that the youth was searched by police and her allegations of theft seem to have been groundless. He is said to be seventeen years old and a spokesperson for the family earlier told us that he is considering legal action.'

The camera panned away to show a stout, Victorian, four-bedroomed detached house behind a yew hedge.

'The house, said to be worth over one million Pounds, is, as you can see, in darkness this evening and Mr Mansell, who, sources tell us, is a millionaire City financier, was reported to be staying with friends and is not available for comment. Condemnation has been coming in from minority and anti-racist groups all over the country and also from the government's flagship Community Diversity Unit, whose director, Bernie Collingwood, has already made demands for a custodial sentence. A police station in South London is said to be under siege from at least five hundred anti-racist protestors where Ms Mansell is rumoured to be held following her arrest and the BNP have been forced to remove what the police are describing as "inflammatory content" in support of Ms Mansell from their website. That's all the information we have for the moment, so back to you in the studio, John.'

'Thanks, Jenny. Now, other news. Reports are coming in from our Africa correspondent of renewed fighting in the embattled republic of...'

'Great, that's all we bloody need,' said Tom. 'That makes her sound like a member of the BNP. These media people really are the lowest of the low. Let's see what they're saying on the other channels.'

It wasn't any better.

Over the following days, the Sally Mansell story slowly migrated to the middle pages and then downwards to the footnotes and by-lines at the bottom of the page until it finally disappeared. She took unpaid leave from work and stepped down from the divorce case she'd been handling. If the Mayoress of London had been more discreet, then her husband would never have found out about the affair, divorce proceedings would never have started and Sally would have had no cause to be walking from City Hall to London Bridge that afternoon: if only...

Eventually, even the reporters and the TV crews gave up hanging around the house and pestering the regulars at The Dolphin for gossip about the Mansells.

Paul Wilson, a colleague at Sally's law firm had taken on her case and agreed to waive his fee. Tom fielded his call – for days Sally had been too depressed to do much more than stare out of the window or occasionally wander round the damp, lifeless garden. Spring seemed very far off.

'It's good news. They've got some information on the gang that robbed you. Seems that the one you chased is called Duwayne Fisher and, far from being a model A-Level student, young Mr Fisher has a form sheet as long as your arm: possession of an offensive weapon; dealing class-B drugs; breaking and entering and robbery with violence. He was sent to Feltham for six months but let out after two to "ease overcrowding" three days before he robbed you. Paul also said he's been on to that scumbag publicist that Fisher's people hired and has threatened to spill the beans about his angelic client if they don't back off and, better still, he's managed to call in some favours from a friend who does police solicitor work. Yesterday evening the police nicked someone for trying to use your card at a cash dispenser in South London. Paul couldn't give me a name, but apparently the kid they've got lives in the same council block as Fisher and was in the same class at school. According to the contact, it's almost certainly one of the three who mugged you but they haven't got conclusive proof yet. He claims he found the card in a purse that just happened to be lying about in the street, but that gives far more credence to the fact that you were robbed.'

Sally's face brightened momentarily. 'Thank you, darling. Next time you speak to Paul, please tell him I think he's wonderful. I know nothing can excuse what I said, but I just want to get this all over and done with and then…' She paused. 'And then leave this horrible country for good.' At this last remark, Tom's eyebrows rose but he didn't make any comment.

Later that evening, after making sure that the fire was drawing properly, Tom went through into the kitchen and came back with two tumblers of whisky. 'Here you are, this'll make you feel better,' he said, handing his wife a glass. He sat next to her on the sofa and she put her head on his shoulder, drew her feet up and snuggled up next to him, her thick, dark hair falling over his shoulder. He put his arm round her and pulled her tightly to his side. For a while, neither of them spoke as they sat watching the flames dancing in the fireplace. Sally broke the silence.

'Darling, how would you feel about moving abroad, you know, leaving this country for good?'

He recoiled slightly and turned to face her. 'Wow, that's a bit of a fastball. I don't know, really, I'd never given it much thought: I didn't realise you were being serious. Has it really affected you so much that you'd sell up and go?'

'Yes, I think it has.'

'And if we did,' he continued. 'Where would we go and how

would we earn a living? We can't afford to retire yet and the only place where I'd find another job would be in another big city unless I took a huge pay cut, so we could end up facing exactly the same problems somewhere else. They have street crime everywhere. I know it doesn't help, but you were just unlucky.'

'I know, but it's not just that, I'm fed up with the job too.'

Tom stared at his wife in amazement. 'That's news to me,' he said. 'I thought you loved it. Why the sudden change of heart?'

'I don't know. It's just the robbery and everything that's happened since has made me feel so…' she searched for the right words, 'well, bitter and resentful really. Just think about it: every single aspect of my job is based upon people making a mess of their lives, and often as not, the lives of those around them too. So once they've buggered up their own lives, they call me in with the sole aim of reducing the misery for themselves and increasing it for the other party.'

'But you always told me that you didn't see it that way; that it was dispassionate and all about who had a better knowledge of the law and could use it to best effect, that it wasn't personal. And anyway, you know you love a good scrap.'

'I do, but it's lost its appeal.'

Tom looked away. 'I don't know what to say – I thought you were happy. The job, this house, the village and everything we have here, and now you want to chuck it all up and move to somewhere else.' He stroked her hair. 'Sally, darling, I know this is bloody awful for you – it's not great for me either – but don't let one worthless little yobbo make you think that everything's changed for the worst. If you do that, then the yobboes win.'

Sally took a pull of her whisky. 'It's more than that, Tom, and it started before the mugging if I'm honest: long before. I assumed it would go away and I didn't want to worry you. I thought it was just the long hours, commuting, winter, the cold and the gloom getting me down and that I needed a holiday. On top of that I've had a run of clients lately who should've been strangled at birth to prevent them ever marrying and inflicting themselves on other people, so I thought it would just pass, but it didn't and it hasn't. I know this sounds like something that men get when they hit middle age, but it won't go away. I hate myself for what I did, but every time I step out of that door now I'm frightened: I feel like an unwilling tourist in a vile foreign land.' She snuggled closer. 'I'm sorry, darling, this is all so bloody selfish and whiney of me. I don't want to muck things up for you at work, it's just that I really, deep down do want to leave.'

He stroked her hair. 'Work's ok, I suppose,' he said. 'But I'm not crazy about what comes with it. Big bank equals big politics.'

'But you said they've talked about you making desk head,' she said.

'Sure I will one day if I kiss right arses. The extra money would be nice, but David's ahead of me in the queue. And do I really want to swap something I enjoy for something I hate?'

'I see your point.'

Tom thought for a moment. 'You know, you might be on to something. I don't need to be on the trading floor all the time. I could do my work from anywhere and be more productive into the bargain.' He paused again before turning to face her again. 'Are you serious about this?'

She nodded and bit her lower lip.

'All right then. How would you feel if I took a look at the bank's working from home policy? You realise I'd be under your feet all day and after three weeks you'll be so sick of the sight of me that you'll be pleading me to go back to the office.'

She turned her face to look at him, her eyes shining. 'You'd be giving up a hell of a lot for me – I know you don't like the office politics, but if we did go, you wouldn't see your friends at the rugby club any more, no more flying with Hutch at the weekends, lots of other things too.' She stopped suddenly, her voice trailing away. 'I'm being a selfish cow, aren't I?'

'No, you're just being honest,' he replied. 'If you're not happy here, then nothing else matters. Listen, they have flying clubs and rugby clubs in France. We'll go.'

'But would you really do that for me? Would you? We could go and live in the France house. I could be happy there. I'm always happy there, we both are.'

His smiled affectionately at her. 'Why not? It's in the same time zone – all bar one hour – and not too far that I can't spend the odd week in the office if they need me. If that's what you want, then I'll do it. But before we start getting carried away you do realise that there's a very high probability they'll say no?'

'Let's cross that bridge when we come to it,' she said.

***

Despite every instinct of her combative nature telling her otherwise, Sally took her colleague's advice and entered a plea of guilty. The presiding magistrate fined her £1,500 with £500 to be paid in compensation to Fisher. She was also given a three-month suspended sentence.

His words made her want to scream out loud at the injustice of it all. 'It is only because of the fact that it appears that you were indeed robbed, Mrs Mansell, that you sincerely believed your assailant to be "boy X" and because of your previous good conduct that we have decided to give you a suspended sentence rather than jailing you.'

Her resignation letter was answered by someone she'd never heard of from the HR department and the Solicitors' Disciplinary Tribunal struck her off for "disgraceful behaviour" and "bringing the profession into disrepute." The press were not slow in underlining the irony of this last pronouncement.

To paraphrase Thomas Hardy: justice was done, and the president of the immortals had finished his sport with Sally – for now, anyway.

***

Tom's immediate superior and head of the Alternative Execution Service trading desk, Denise Evans, peered at him from under her shock of badly cut, bright orange hair, suspicion and mistrust written all over her face.

15

'Aren't you a bit senior for this sort of thing, Tom?' she said, indicating the application form that sat on the desk between them as though it were something vaguely toxic.

'Well,' he replied, fighting the urge to make the barbed reply that such a question deserved, 'As I told you when we first discussed the idea, I've read through the relevant sections of the employee handbook, gone through all the steps on the HR website, my job meets all the relevant criteria for portability and so I think I've got a pretty good case, don't you?' He did his best to smile at her, something that no one found easy, least of all Tom. 'I don't recall it saying that directors couldn't apply or that people over a certain age couldn't apply either – that would be...,' he smiled, relishing the opportunity, '....unfair discrimination and we're all utterly opposed to that, aren't we?'

She tutted and drummed her fingers on the desk, 'Yes, all right, Tom. Get to the point.'

'Look,' he continued, 'Most of what I'm doing now is quant development work which I can do from anywhere and if I'm working from home I'll be far more productive without all the noise and distraction of being on the trading floor.'

'Yes, I know, you said all that on the application,' she said, prodding at the toxic waste on her desk with the chewed end of her pen. 'I've spoken to Matt of course and to HR and they were a bit surprised too, so I just wanted to be sure that you wanted to go through with it.'

'Oh, definitely.'

'And you've put down an address in France as the location you'd be working from. I presume that's the place you've been doing up?'

'Correct.'

'Well, if Matt says yes, we'll be sorry not to have you on the desk all the time,' she said with what passed for a smile.

Liar, thought Tom and smiled back with even less genuine feeling than his desk head. I'll see your bogus concern for my wellbeing and raise you five – you're up to something, it's written all over you.

Chapter Three

Several thousand kilometres east and slightly south of London, in Novi Bar, the capital of the former Soviet republic of Nashyastan, a large personal black cloud was descending. To be specific, it settled right on top of Igor Kaliski, head of Noviprom, the country's sovereign wealth authority. The president was his brother-in-law, but that wasn't going to make the conversation he was about to have any easier. Kaliski straightened his tie, smoothed down his crumpled shirt-front, took a deep breath, knocked and went in.

The president addressed him in Nashyastani, a Turkic language they had both grown up speaking at home and which the Soviets had tried unsuccessfully to supplant with Russian. 'Come in, my dear Igor, do come in. Please sit down. And how is my dear little sister? Well I hope.'

'Very well, sir, and she sends her love.'

'Excellent, do please return her kind wishes. Now, I believe you have some news for me.'

The president's office was on the top floor of the National Government Centre, a building that had served as the headquarters of the Communist Party during the Soviet era. A grim and now crumbling concrete slab, it was by far the tallest building in a city comprised almost exclusively of other grey concrete buildings, laid out in a planned geometric grid, and which were only differentiated by their size and state of decay.

Kaliski had taken the one working elevator from the sparsely furnished offices of Noviprom up to the presidential suite.

The president was in his late seventies and his bony frame felt the cold intensely, so he kept his office stiflingly hot throughout the year. Beads of sweat ran down Kaliski's back, and the unaccustomed constriction of a tie around his neck made the level of discomfort even worse. If truth were to be told, the president's younger sister was making his life a non-stop misery.

'Mr President, sir. The news remains mixed. Total annualised returns are positive, that much is good, but we are barely making 2.5 percent.'

The president's gaze hardened as it fell on Kaliski.

'My dear Igor, I am getting tired of saying this. You were brought in to turn things around. Two point five percent is hardly spectacular and, might I add, well short of your own predictions – yet again. I haven't spent all this money on people and technology for the sort of returns I can get from buying and holding government bonds. I am sure you will recall what happened to your predecessor, so please tell me what is your explanation and what do you intend to do to improve matters?'

He tugged at his collar. How can I put this tactfully? thought Kaliski. Another deep breath. In the past, the president had never hesitated to eliminate anyone, including members of his extended family when it suited his ends. 'Well, sir, I'm afraid, the downside risks I identified when we created Noviprom are just as big a problem today, if not bigger.'

'Which means?'

'Although we have some of the best programmers, mathematicians, theoretical economists and intelligence-gathering people in the world, they do not yet have that feeling for the markets that comes with experience, and it is proving every bit as difficult as I predicted to develop and improve our expertise. Furthermore, you cannot get that experience and expertise by watching from the sidelines, which is effectively what we are doing. This factor is also holding back our systems development. Our algorithmic and high-frequency trading capabilities are at least three years behind the market leaders.'

'So what do you suggest, dear Igor?' said the president, his voice heavy with sarcasm.

'That we buy in a team from an established financial centre; ideally one that can bring its own software.'

'As simple as that?'

'In theory, yes.'

'So why not just get hold of the software? I thought modern proprietary systems were supposed to do away with the need for more than one or two traders and support people?'

'Well, yes and no.' Kaliski was taken aback by the old man's knowledge: a timely warning that pulling the wool over his eyes had just got harder. He was on thin ice. The president had been a child during the Great Patriotic War and had grown up confident in the superiority of the Soviet system over the West and above all he loved his country to the very last atom of his being. To him, Nashyastan and its capital, Novi Bar, with its ring of snow-capped mountains, was an earthly paradise. 'I'm not sure that's feasible, sir. We'd still need developers and support people but we don't have any overseas offices.'

The president beamed, showing a mouthful of yellowing Soviet-era false teeth. 'Why should that be a problem? They can work here, we will pay them well. We can offer them everything they need.'

'If you'll pardon me, sir, I have travelled and worked extensively among these people and they are not like us. Much as it may seem illogical, irrational, even, there will be westerners who would not want to come and live here.'

'Do not treat me like a child. I'm not stupid,' snapped the president. 'I am perfectly aware that people prefer things and surroundings that they know best, but how do you know that we can't offer the sorts of rewards that will tempt the sort of people you're looking for to come here. Have you asked any of them, Igor?'

'Well no, sir.'

'Then do so. I trust you to do your research well and to find the best systems and the best people. When you are ready to recruit your team, make it happen. And you have my permission to be as generous as you see fit. All I would recommend is that you do not fail me.'

Kaliski swallowed hard and did his best to smile. 'Yes, sir.'

'Good. I expect you to pay the market rate for these things. Do not cut corners when it comes to spending, and above all, just in case you didn't hear me the first time, do not fail me. That will be all.'

As he left the office, he felt the old man's eyes boring into the back of his head.

He took the rickety, malodorous elevator back down to the Noviprom floor. Shoving open the one side of the electric doors that wasn't jammed, Kaliski loosened his tie, pushed it clear of his bull-like neck and strode purposefully across the small trading floor. His shirt was too tight and his suit trousers were digging in. Since passing fifty he'd started piling the weight on and it wouldn't seem to budge. He stuck his head round the door of the office next to his and called out, 'Come on, Ursk, I'm starving. Let's go and get some lunch.' He did a double-take. 'Christ, man. What have you done to your hair?'

Vladimir Ursk, Kaliski's fellow managing director at Noviprom, frowned, sending his single, long, dense eyebrow into a v-shape. 'It's cooler in the hot weather, and I like it anyway,' he said petulantly.

'Makes you look like a lavatory brush. Still, come with me, I've just spoken to your uncle. You and I are going fishing.'

'Fishing? What the hell are you talking about?'

'Uncle says we're going fishing, you and I: head-hunting if I'm strictly accurate. But either way we're going on a little trip to Europe and the US.'

'Sounds fun.'

'Well it won't be. It's going to be a lot of hard work. Ever heard of a system called "Minerva"?'

'Don't think I have.'

'It's an algorithmic trading system being used by the London office of an American bank. If we can get hold of it, our problems are over.'

'Do you think they'd sell it to us – just like that?'

'No. But they don't own it, that's the beauty of it.'

'I'm not with you,' said Ursk.

'Didn't think you would be. Minerva is owned by the man who designed and built it. We offer him a big chunk of cash for the system and to work for us. Job done.'

'What if he says no?'

'Then we frame the offer in such a way that he can't possibly say no.'

Ursk smiled. 'I like the sound of that,' he said.

Chapter Four

In the Languedoc region of southern France at a house not far inland from Béziers, the telephone rang and Sally Mansell answered it. 'Tom, can you take it? It's Denise, she says it's urgent.' She made her lemon-sucking face.

Tom Mansell got down from the ladder, wiped the paint off his hands, took the phone from his wife and spoke to his desk head. The conversation was brief and Tom's face gave no hint of what was being said on the other end of the line in Canary Wharf. He hung up.

'Bad news?' she asked.

'Well, yes and no. The bad news is that Denise wants me to come back a day early for a meeting.'

'Yes and no?' Sally exploded. 'For Christ's sake, Tom, can't they do without you for two whole weeks without dragging you back early? And for a bloody meeting too. Why didn't you tell her this is the first proper holiday you've had in over a year and that we've got work to do on the house? If there is any good news, then it had better be pretty good.'

Sally slammed down her brush sending paint splatters flying into the air, and with a heavy sigh, sat back on the stepladder and looked at their handiwork. The floor and worktops were festooned in old sheets to protect them, and although there was still a good week's work to do to downstairs, the kitchen at least was looking brighter and less dowdy than when they'd first seen the house at Mirepech over a year ago. She leant forward with her chin cupped in her hands and a face like thunder. Tom's job pays for all this, she thought. And thanks to Tom's bloody job we never get to see the place.

'Hold on. It's not all bad,' he said. 'It's a meeting with Denise, Matt O'Reilly and some girl from HR called Vanessa something. Matt's going back to New York on the 7th for an MDs' strategy meeting or some BS talkfest or other and he wants to see me before he goes.'

'A meeting with your boss, your boss's boss and someone

from HR – isn't that what happens when they're going to sack you?'

'It can be, but not this time.' He walked over to where Sally was sitting and took both of her hands in his. He looked into her eyes and asked, 'Are you ready for this?' She nodded. 'No, they're not chucking me out. It's about my application to move to remote working.'

Sally let out an excited squeal and, jumping to her feet, threw her arms around his neck. Once he'd got his breath back, Tom continued. 'Just think, no more commuting, no more idiot meetings all the time. I can work from here and we can pop back to the UK whenever we feel like it.'

Sally couldn't stop grinning. 'This is just so wonderful. Have they given you a date?'

'Not yet. They haven't even said yes for certain either. All she said was they want to talk to me about it.'

She treated him to one of her looks. 'Well, just so long as you're not getting my hopes up for nothing. You put the application in ages ago and if Denise is involved it could just be a bollocking for trying to step off the treadmill.'

'Possible, but unlikely,' said Tom. 'I think they're a bit worried that I'll resign if they say no. And if I do go, I don't think David will stick around either.'

'I thought everybody was hanging on to their jobs for dear life right now.'

'Well they are, but there are still other outfits that are interested in us as a team – remember what I said about Citi sniffing around a while back? Although as things turned out it was a good job for us they got cold feet. While we're making money, I think our desk is safe – and we're still one of the most profitable teams in the whole equities business. The downside is that Denise takes all the credit –'

'As usual,' said Sally.

'True. But I think the idea of letting me work from out here suits her just fine: I still produce the goods but won't be around to wave the flag when she starts talking bullshit. No I'm optimistic.

Anyway, I'll call and change our flight.'

They'd bought the house on a whim just over a year earlier – more than a whim really – they fell in love with the place just like they said they wouldn't. Just a reconnaissance mission, they'd promised themselves. Only mugs fall in love with old ruins and buy them without doing any research, they'd said. They'd both seen the voyeuristic TV shows with their seemingly never-ending cast of hopeless Walter Mittys who give it all up to live the good life in the Mediterranean sun, but end up broke, jobless, arguing and lonely, living in a cold dark ruin miles from nowhere in a country whose language they've never attempted to master. So, Tom and Sally Mansell thought they were well-prepared for their little look-see – just to get the lie of the land of course, and, as they repeated to themselves, we're definitely not buying anything, however tempting. That was until they saw Le Mas des Oliviers.

It was a long, two-storey structure, built, like most of the farmhouses in the area, with its back to the prevailing north-westerlies. It was a short walk from the village of Mirepech and stood between two small wooded hills, the one to the north west affording it some protection from the wind. Its previous owner, a man with "a past" according to some in the village, had bought the place as a semi-ruin and had spent the next two years and a small fortune having it renovated. Unfortunately for him, one day, some of his past, in the form of his ex-wife and a posse of creditors and lawyers, caught up with him, thus putting an end to the renovation work and precipitating a hastily-planned move overseas "for health reasons." He left the house in the hands of the local *notaire* with instructions to sell it and was never seen again.

Not all of his renovation work had been entirely successful, however. The national passion for gloomy, dark-wood kitchens had been expressed with a master's touch. The result was positively sepulchral. Just in case any of the light from the two 5-watt bulbs in the brown wooden light fitting should be reflected from the brown units and the brown fittings, the kitchen was decorated to half height with tiles whose only distinguishing feature was their brownness – that and their ability to absorb light.

The walls and ceiling had started life at the gloomier end of beige and had been darkened further by nicotine – the previous owner's suspect past was said to include the illegal import and sale of duty-free cigarettes from Andorra.

Leaving aside the kitchen and its overwhelming brownness, the other rooms were vast and the interior stonework had been beautifully renovated. Throughout were exposed beams which had been stripped, treated and re-stained. The garden too had obviously once been cared for and had been expensively landscaped and planted. All had been overgrown when they bought it and the swimming pool had looked as though new life forms were probably evolving in its green, murky depths. There was still much to do, but things were taking shape.

Tom and Sally Mansell had been married three years when they bought the house. Tom was thirty-five, tall and broad-shouldered with a mop of mousy hair that seemed to have a mind of its own and gave him, in the words of one of his former girlfriends, the air of a perpetually startled haystack. Shortly after university he'd been offered professional terms to play rugby for Wasps, but after much soul-searching, he decided that he was neither good enough nor big enough to make it to the top and that professional Rugby Union was too precarious a calling anyway. Much to Sally's concern, he still played for his local club side and from which he usually came home battered, bruised, not very sober and beaming from ear to ear. His unpretentious charm meant that he'd never been short of female company and unlike many attractive men, he was totally unaware of the effect he had on women which often rendered him all the more alluring to them. Less so was his tendency to wander which had earned him a rather bad reputation among his circle of female friends.

Sally pulled on an old jacket against the biting *Tramontane* that was howling out of the north west, crossed the garden to the gate in the back fence and climbed to the top of the rise behind the house. Through the wind-blown, consumptive pine trees she looked down over the roof of their lovely house and along the Mirepech valley.

The village of Mirepech-lès-Cazouls lies in a side valley to the west of the river Orb, on the road from Cazouls-lès-Béziers to Puisserguier. All around, the views were to die for – to the east the folds in the land hid the sprawl of Cazouls-lès-Béziers from sight and to the north, the steep slopes of the Minervois looked close enough to touch. At the western end of the wooded rise was their favourite spot. It was secluded, sheltered from the worst of the wind by a circle of rocks which formed a small natural amphitheatre beyond which was a spectacular cliff which dropped sheer to the river a hundred or so feet below. On summer evenings they would often come up here with a bottle of wine, spread a rug out on the flat rocks and watch the sun go down.

A jumble of emotions went through Sally's mind. She was cross with bloody Denise for mucking up their holiday, but if they could come and live out here, just the two of them, well, that would be worth any amount of short-term inconvenience. As she walked, she thought about all the events that had brought the two of them to where they were. The terrible aftermath of the mugging and the catastrophic results of a split-second of stupidity still haunted her, but perhaps this was the silver lining that people always talked about. And she had Tom: that was more important than anything.

When it came to their marriage, Sally often wondered what she'd done right. During her career as a solicitor specialising in divorce, she'd seen just about every possible facet of humanity's shortcomings, and had lost count of the times she'd heard the familiar tale of adoration transformed into loathing by a thousand petty squabbles. Yet she and Tom had something special, and despite her expertise on the many forces driving other people apart, she'd never quite been able to define what it was that bound the two of them together so tightly. She thought about his willingness to put up with her short fuse and fiery temper – the storm always blew over as quickly as it had begun – and he never rose to the bait. In return, she put up with his untidiness, scruffiness and general blokeishness. But most importantly, each delighted in the other's company, so all-in-all, she reckoned, they had a pretty good thing going.

They'd met at a dinner party in Fulham five years earlier, and whenever she related the story in company, Tom used to rib her, saying that meeting at a dinner party – especially in bloody Fulham – was such an awful cliché and why wouldn't she admit the truth that they'd met while they were both in rehab? On the evening in question, however, Tom was for once genuinely single and, as is often the way with these things, spare man was placed opposite spare woman and by the end of the evening, things had progressed well beyond a simple exchange of phone numbers with this rather handsome chap – despite his crooked nose and the wild hair – who actually listened to what she was saying and didn't butt in before she'd finished speaking.

He'd explained that he worked in banking, which had put Sally off at first, given that she'd recently split up with a banker boyfriend following a stormy six-month relationship during which he'd cheated on her almost from the first. But as the evening wore on, Sally's prejudices evaporated, and although she was still a bit baffled by what it was he actually *did* and his worrying tendency to talk about exciting mathematical models, she was definitely warming to him. He offered to take her flying too, which she thought sounded a lot of fun.

As for Tom, although he did his best to disguise it and to maintain an air of detached *sang froid*, he found Sally absolutely stunning: she was small and dark with pale blue eyes and a face that he thought of as cute rather than classically beautiful. But what Tom found most alluring was the way that the little black dress set off her figure. He'd always been a man for girls with curves rather than "boys without willies" as he called them, and as the evening wore on he found his gaze being drawn irresistibly towards her cleavage – he hoped Sally hadn't noticed, but she had and was secretly pleased with the effect she was having on him. Towards the end of the evening, she leant over to him and said quietly in his ear, 'Do you like this dress?'

'Er, yes, very much.'

'Good. Do you know what I'm wearing underneath it?'

Tom blushed. 'Um, er, no.'

'Nothing. Absolutely nothing... I don't suppose you'd like to see me home, would you?'

They started seeing more of each other, despite the warnings of Sally's girlfriends about his tendency to wander. And after a long heart-to-heart about Tom's track record of infidelity – or parallel monogamy as he called it – and what would happen to him if he cheated on her, it became pretty obvious that they were going to remain a couple.

***

The flight back to the UK was late, so by the time Tom and Sally reached home, it was very nearly midnight.

Despite being a seasoned veteran of the red-eye from New York – only wimps don't come straight into the office – Tom felt gritty-eyed and drained when he walked on to the trading floor the following morning. Although it was barely seven thirty, the noise level was high – sales and sales-trading teams were relaying the morning briefing and the latest research notes to their clients. From a dozen wide-screen TVs a new Money Honey was doing her best to keep up with the autocue on CNN, and Bloomberg Radio was blaring from the loudspeakers built into the dealer boards in front of every trading position. Over to his right, some of the market-makers were joshing their new desk assistant and hitting him with rolled-up copies of the Sun. Others were arguing about last night's football. He dumped his briefcase under the desk and slumped down in his seat. His battery of four blank screens stared at him reproachfully. Years of tuning out this familiar background din reduced his awareness of the cacophony that so shocks the casual visitor to most trading floors, so much so that he felt he could just doze off. A familiar voice and a hearty clap on the shoulder dragged him back to the reality of a wet, monochrome morning in London.

'Well look at what the cat dragged in. And what the hell are you doing back anyway, you're not due in till next week?'

It was David – Dr David Liebowitz: Caltech, Cambridge, and one of the best financial mathematicians in the business. His work in the field of non-linear dynamics and its application to the financial markets had made him a highly-respected figure on the conference circuit for his ability to make a highly complex branch of mathematics not only comprehensible but entertaining to a lay audience.

'Denise,' said Tom flatly. 'That's why.'

Liebowitz's face lit up. *Reeeeally*? Now who'd have guessed? I never knew you two were so close. You broke your holiday because you couldn't bear to be separated for a day longer, huh? Have you told her how you feel? Well have you, lover man?'

'Fuck off, David. I feel like shit.'

Liebowitz recoiled in mock indignation and clutched his chest. 'Wow, you sure know how to hurt a guy. I'll bet you were captain of your high school debating team.'

Tom looked at him, shook his head and smiled. It was impossible to be cross with Liebowitz for very long. Nor was he ever going to win a contest of smart-Aleck repartee against him – not at that hour of the morning, anyway.

'If you must know, I have a meeting with Denise, Matt and HR at eight.'

Liebowitz raised an eyebrow. 'Interesting. Do tell,' he said, his tone now serious.

'It's about moving to remote working, you know, all that bullshit in the employee handbook about work-life balance, respecting the well-being of the employee and promoting diversity? Well I decided to call their bluff. We've nearly finished doing up the place in France and I figured that I could do the job just as easily there as from here, so I put in an application. You know, work from home – the quality of life thing. It's all Sally's wanted since the mugging.'

'You never told me about this.'

Tom shrugged. 'Guess I never thought it would ever happen.'

'Guess you were wrong.'

'I applied a few months ago and I'd almost forgotten about it, but the rules state that your manager has to forward it to HR and so on up the food chain, and it looks like it's finally arrived on Matt's desk because he wants to see me before he goes to New York – I think Denise said he's flying out later today.'

'From your point of view I can see that working from home makes sense,' said Liebowitz. 'We'll miss having you on the desk though.'

'I don't think Denise will miss me.'

Liebowitz perched on the desk, swinging his legs in the space underneath it and looking at Tom attentively. Sitting like this, he looked like a gnome – a small, dark, wiry, Manhattan Jewish gnome and one with a face that exuded a shrewd and penetrating intelligence.

'Shit, Tom. You're the only one of us she even vaguely tolerates. With the rest of the desk she communicates by screaming.'

Tom laughed. 'Christ, I always thought she hated me. If that's what passes for toleration, I'd hate to see what happens to people who really piss her off.'

'Yeah, tell me about it. So when you put the application in, she didn't go crazy? Didn't try to talk you out of it? Didn't boil anyone's rabbit?'

Tom shook his head. 'No, I suppose she didn't seem desperately pleased and, if I read her right, she seemed to be trying to imply that the remote working scheme was really just a bit of corporate window-dressing for dealing with junior level under-achievers who it was cheaper to keep out of the way than sack.'

'She's up to something, Tommy boy. If that'd been me, she'd have gone postal. Woulda called me disloyal, no commitment, not a team player, y'know, all that kind of shit. The desk is making good money and she wants us here so she can keep on taking the credit. If you think about it, apart from the guys who need to screen trade or work directly with one of the other desks, most of us could work remotely but then she'd have nobody on hand to blame when she screws up, or to pull her out the holes she digs for herself.'

'Sounds like she's ideal management material,' said Tom, with a nod towards the corner office.

'Don't joke. She's definitely up to something: she's spending more and more time in her office or cosying up to Matt than she does out here on the desk. You remember I wanted to bring down those two guys from fixed income for the cross-product stuff we're doing with them?'

'Course I do. It's a licence to print money. You don't mean to tell me she's being difficult about it.'

Liebowitz snorted in exasperation. 'Difficult?' he said. 'We should be so lucky. Last week while you were away she blocked it – some crap about having to take them on to our cost code. I think she's angling for a move into management, in fact I'm sure of it. We know we're carrying her, she knows we know and she's smart enough to realise it'll catch up with her sooner or later. So what's her best way? The last refuge of the inept – management. And what gets you up the management tree the fastest in this bank? Saving money – saving money at all costs even if it screws the business.'

'You're probably right,' said Tom wearily. 'But, you know right now I couldn't care less if they make her Prime Minister; all I want her to do is to get Matt and HR to rubber-stamp that application and let me get the hell out of here so that I can have my life back, give Sally what she wants and actually get some work done rather than sit in meetings all the time.' He narrowed his eyes and looked hard at his old friend. 'You whinge like hell, but admit it, you love it here, don't you?'

A crooked smile lit up across Liebowitz's face. 'But I've got nowhere else to go – I mean, I can't go back to the States can I?'

'Why ever not?'

'Because of the Draft – I don't want to serve in the Army.'

'The Draft? David, what are you talking about? The Draft ended in 1973!'

'It did?' said Liebowitz slowly, 'It *did*? Like there's no more Draft? You mean my parents have been lying to me all this time, my own stinkin' parents have been lying to me just so they can rent out my room? I just *cannot* believe they'd do that.'

Tom rolled his eyes. 'You are a mad bastard, David, you really are. Do the rest of us a favour, will you, and stop skipping your medication.'

***

Matt O'Reilly's was, of course, a corner office. It had views of the western loop of the Thames as it bends its way round the Isle of Dogs and of the Gotham City skyline of Canary Wharf. On his desk was a picture of the obligatory trophy wife and their three straight-toothed children, ranging in age between three and ten years old. On the walls were pictures of his college football team and various nautical charts showing the waters round Nantucket and Cape Cod, where the O'Reilly family had a summer home and where he loved to sail. He looked up and spotted Denise Evans outside the office. Turning to the HR rep with whom he'd been talking, he said, 'Vanessa, could you just wait outside a second? I've got a couple of business-related things I need to discuss with Denise.'

'Sure, Matt. No worries.'

Matt O'Reilly, head of European equities, late thirties all-American boy, blessed with good looks, straight teeth and good hair, put his hands behind his head and leant his large frame back in the chair. He looked even more pleased with himself than usual and was positively basking in the wonderfulness of being Matt O'Reilly.

'So what's happening, Matt?' said Denise. 'Why the secrecy?' She nodded towards Vanessa who was now in soundless conversation with Scary Mary, O'Reilly's secretary, on the other side of the glass partition. She was expecting some juicy tit-bit about a so far undiscovered indiscretion of Tom Mansell's, but O'Reilly's words came as a bolt from the blue.

'Looks like I'm going to be re-locating back to New York. It's not been officially announced yet and won't be for a few weeks,

32

so for now the fewer people who know the better.' He got up and crossed to the corner of the office and stood with his back to Denise, looking out over the river through the rain-streaked windows. 'I'll miss it here. It's been a good four years but I'll be glad to get back home. Molly's keen to go home too. She doesn't want the kids to go through school here either, that's another factor. They'll get to see their grandparents more often, so that's good too.' He paused for effect. 'The reason I'm going back is that I'm moving to a new role - obviously I can't tell you what that is yet, but that announcement will be coming out in a couple of weeks as well; that's one of the reasons I'm going over today. But that's not what I wanted to talk to you about.' He paused, turned back to face her and smiled. 'How do you feel about taking over from me?' he purred.

Denise looked as though she was going to choke. Her pallid features flushed and her eyes went wide with surprise. 'What, take over from you? Me? Are you sure? I mean… well… of course I'd love to but isn't it…?'

'An MD role? A big jump up? Unexpected? Yes, Denise, it is – all of those,' his face creasing into a grin. God, he was loving this. 'And if we didn't think you were capable of it, we wouldn't be having this conversation. Sam Bortoleski's very pleased with the cost-savings you've made and he's given your appointment his seal of approval. He's also approved an out-of-phase promotion for you to move up to MD so that you'll be at the same level as the desk- and section-heads who of course,' he added with the charm of the consummate salesman he was, 'will be reporting in to you.'

Denise continued her life-like impersonation of a goldfish.

'So what do you say, Ms Evans? Want the job or not?'

'Well, Christ, Matt,' she gasped. 'Yes. Of course I want it, but it's just such a shock.'

Not as much of a shock as it's going to be for everybody else, thought O'Reilly. This is Sam Bortoleski's train wreck, not mine, and I'm not going to be anywhere near it when it happens.

'Good. I hoped you'd say that,' he said. She began to talk again but he held up a hand to silence her. 'We can talk about this in more detail when I'm back next week. I'll tell Bortoleski the good news when I see him tomorrow, but for now not a word to anyone. Got that? Good. Now, let's talk about Mansell. Can you get Vanessa back in here, Denise and then remind me what it is he wants exactly.'

At eight o'clock Tom went over to Matt's office which was guarded by Scary Mary. Secretaries sometimes assume the power and influence of those they work for, leading them to treat lesser mortals from lower down the food-chain than their boss as inferiors. Mary fell into this camp and was legendary for her rudeness.

At his approach, Mary's face creased into what Tom took for a smile – clearly not one of her Broadmoor days today, he mused – and motioned for him to go into the office.

'Sit down, Tom, please,' said O'Reilly. 'I believe you know Vanessa from HR. Tom, I'll come straight to the point. It's not going to make life easy for the team not having you on the desk full-time, but I've discussed your application with Denise and,' he paused for effect, 'we've agreed to let you work from home, subject to all the usual conditions which I believe you're aware of, and I wanted to be the one to tell you.' He turned to look at Denise, 'I hope you don't mind my pulling rank.'

'Not at all, Matt,' she simpered.

It was clearly a good morning for surprises.

Tom's face lit up. 'Matt, that's fantastic. I can't thank you enough and you too, Denise. I'm totally lost for words. Sally will be delighted – this is simply wonderful.'

O'Reilly continued. 'There are of course some special conditions because of the fact that you're going to be working from abroad and that's why Vanessa's here. Vanessa, over to you.'

'Thanks, Matt,' she said and started to read from her prepared script, the twang in her accent betraying her Kiwi origins. Tom's observations had led him to the theory that there was an unwritten but scrupulously-observed, secret rule in the City that 95% of HR staff must be female and come from Australia, South Africa or New Zealand. From what he could deduce, high levels of intelligence, possession of a degree in a serious subject from a proper university, empathy, knowledge of banking and any useful grasp of UK tax and employment law were all absolute bars to employment in HR, however. The most sought-after quality, according to his theory, was a willingness to defend the firm's interests against those of the employee at every opportunity, even at the expense of putting the firm on the wrong side of the law. He was, perhaps, being a little harsh because, in fairness – even he had to admit it – one or two bright ones with high standards of integrity did occasionally slip through the net, but as far as he could see, they were few and far between. He'd soon find out into which side of the divide she fell.

'As you know, Tom,' said Vanessa, 'there are tax implications of any move abroad and once you become a French tax resident, you'll have to pay French tax and social security charges and the London payroll department is only geared up to pay UK tax. We spoke to HR in Paris and asked if they could take you onto their payroll system but they weren't able to do so.'

'Why was that?' asked Tom.

'Er, they, um...' She looked at Denise for support.

'Refused,' said Denise. 'Cost saving.'

Good old HR – no exception to the rule then, thought Tom, but said nothing.

Vanessa carried on. 'So, Tom, the only way we can support you is for you to resign as a full-time employee and we will then pay you as a self-employed contractor in France. Legal have drawn up a draft contract – you'll need to take professional advice from a French accountant on how you structure your affairs over there as we don't have the expertise here.'

Support me? He thought – Christ, I'd hate to see what happens when you leave someone to their own devices. Tom raised his eyebrows. 'Wow. Rather a lot to take in there. From our earlier discussions, I'd hoped that if the answer was yes, then I'd simply go into the French system as an employee.' He quickly scanned down the draft copy of the contract that Vanessa had given him. 'I think the best thing for me to do is to take the contract and let my solicitors have a look at it – I will say though that I'm happy with the daily rate – I can see a couple of things I'd like to discuss changing. I'm just very, very grateful to you all. Vanessa, if you could let me have an electronic copy of the contract, please, I'll get them looking at it today.'

Chapter Five

Samuel J Bortoleski, Head of Global Execution and Brokerage Services, was not a happy man. The novelty of business travel had worn off so long ago that he couldn't even recall a time when he'd enjoyed it. The flight from New York to London was delayed – again, he couldn't remember the last time when one had been on time – and his mood wasn't improved by lack of sleep. Scotch was the only thing that worked, but he had to ship industrial quantities of the stuff to put him out and then he felt like death the next day.

Denise Evans looked at him across the desk, her pallid complexion drained of what little colour it had. He was in his late fifties: short, muscular and squat with the broken face of an unsuccessful boxer and the broken veins of a highly successful drinker. What Bortoleski lacked in inches he made up for sheer presence and his small, hooded eyes burned with anger at what his new head of European equities had done. He thumped the table yet again, causing her to jump in her seat. 'So why didn't you run this past legal counsel?' he shouted.

'But I did, Sam. I already told you that,' she said, gripping her notepad as though her life depended on it.

He rolled his eyes in despair. 'For Christ's sake, Denise, I'm not talking about the in-house people – do you really think they'd know an intellectual property agreement from a hole in the ground?' Denise remained silent. 'Well do you?' he bellowed. Even with the office door closed and on a busy trading day, his side of the conversation was clearly audible half-way across the floor.

She broke eye-contact and looked down. 'No, Sam. I realise that now, but at the time I thought because they were lawyers they'd know about contracts and intellectual property rights.'

'So you'd use a real-estate lawyer for a tax case would you? It makes just about as much sense.' He paused, running a beefy paw over his perspiring scalp. 'Have you asked him to reconsider?'

'Yes. Several times.'

'And what did he say?'

'He said no. Without ownership of the IPR and source code within Minerva, he says the bank could terminate his contract tomorrow and walk away with a system worth millions. I don't think he trusts us, Sam.'

'No shit, Sherlock. Tell me, who do you trust in this industry?'

She hesitated and looked away once more. 'Well, it's not so much a lack of trust –'

Bortoleski banged the table again and went puce in the face. She thought for a moment he was going to burst. 'Denise,' he said, regaining a fragment of his calm. 'If you trust anyone in this goddam industry, then you're a bigger idiot than I thought you were. In God We Trust – everyone else pays cash up-front. Now go and tell Mansell I want to see him. And remember in future, anything other than boiler-plate trading agreements and client classification work, you take it straight to outside counsel. Got that?'

'Yes, Sam,' she said, her voice sounding like a child's.

The Alternative Execution Services, or AES, desk where Tom worked during his trips back to London was within earshot of the corner office and although he was confident of his legal position as owner of Minerva, he still wasn't looking forward to meeting Bortoleski when he was in this sort of mood. He spotted Denise Evans striding towards him, trying to pretend that nothing untoward had happened, and turned his attention once more to his screens. He heard her approach. 'Tom, Sam wants to see you in my office.'

'Oh really,' said Tom over his shoulder, affecting an air of nonchalance. 'Did he say what it was about?' All heads turned towards her as the AES team awaited her answer. Bitter memories of Denise as their desk head made the spectacle of seeing her on the receiving end all the more enjoyable.

She went red in the face and said. 'Something about your contract, I think.'

Tom wasn't going to miss an opportunity like this. 'You *think*? Was he too busy shouting at you to say?' The other members of the AES team laughed behind their hands, and realising perhaps this was rubbing it in a bit too much he relented. 'OK, Denise, I'll take a wander over and see what he wants.'

'Tom, good to see you again,' said Bortoleski, rising to shake his hand. 'How's life in France treating you?'

'Oh, not bad thanks. The bureaucracy's pretty bad, but you get used to it.'

'And you're managing to get plenty of work done?'

'Oh, sure. More than I did when I was on the desk.'

'Fewer distractions, I guess,' said Bortoleski.

'Something like that,' he replied, and the small talk continued as Tom waited for Bortoleski to make his move. Gone was the red-faced, shouting monster and in its place something far more affable, but he wasn't going to let his guard down – not where Sam Bortoleski was concerned.

At last he made his opening move. 'Denise tells me there've been a few problems with your contract.'

'Oh, I wouldn't say that,' replied Tom. 'I made a few changes to the one the bank drew up and both Denise and internal legal signed them off.'

Bortoleski looked at him sideways. 'Come off it, Tom. It wasn't a case of just a few changes, was it?'

'Depends how you look at it I s'pose.'

'Well, the way I look at it, Tom, is because of those "few changes" you own the intellectual property rights in the system and the source code.'

'Correct. It's got nothing to do with the original system I developed when I was a full-time employee, I developed and built it on non-bank servers, it's not specific to any one institution so I don't see why I should convey the IPR to the bank for free.'

Bortoleski took a deep breath and pushed his fingers together, deep in thought. 'Are you angling for us to buy you out?' he asked.

'Not at all. I'm happy how things are. The contract stipulates a multi-user annual licence of £0 and in return, I'm guaranteed a minimum of ten days' work per month at the agreed consulting rate.'

'And what if you get run over?'

'Then the bank has first refusal on buying it from my estate.'

Bortoleski smiled, 'Sounds like our best option is to kill you then.'

Tom laughed. 'Already thought of that, Sam. My executors are well briefed on what it's worth.'

'Should've guessed as much. So what would you take for it, assuming we don't kill you?'

'I'll tell you what, Sam. You look at the profit figures – and I'm not talking about using it as a client-facing system – calculate what the cash flow would be if we used it for proprietary trading and then make an offer –'

Bortoleski held up a hand. 'Whoa, Tom, you know as well as I do that management won't let us use it for prop trading. I can only value it on the basis of what it's generating doing agency trades. I'm sorry, I'd love to help you but my hands are tied.'

'By whom?'

Bortoleski spread his hands in a vague gesture of helplessness. 'Senior management, the Board, you know how risk-averse those guys have to be these days,' he said.

'And they've given you a remit to make me an offer: to buy the IPR and the source code?' Tom noticed that Bortoleski wouldn't look him in the eye. 'How much, Sam?'

'Like I said, Tom. Based on the net proceeds of what we're making on the agency trades – and don't forget, we've got some chunky overhead charges on the AES desk – one year's net earnings.'

Tom churned the figures rapidly in his head. 'So three years of what I'm making now? Have you checked the date, Sam?'

Bortoleski frowned. 'What's the date got to do with it?'

'Because it's not April fool's day,' said Tom.

'Aw, c'mon, don't be like that. I went in there and pitched for you, I really did.'

A likely story, thought Tom.

Bortoleski continued, 'And the bastards fought me every inch of the way: they wanted to offer you six months till I talked them round.'

'Sam, do you know how much the bank could make using Minerva for prop trading?'

'About three-fifty to five hundred million a year.'

'Close enough,' said Tom. 'And so could any other outfit with a big enough balance sheet to handle the risk. I can think of half-a-dozen banks that would happily pay one year of that sort of money for it, so now do you see why I don't like the offer.'

'But, Tom, it's still a lot of cash.'

'Sure it is, but why should I take less than it's worth? Try going to a major art dealer and saying, "Yeah, I know that Picasso's worth millions, but hey, two hundred and fifty thousand's still a lot of money, so what do you say?" They'd laugh you out of the door.'

'So is that your final answer?'

'No. My final answer is pay me somewhere near its market value and you've got a deal.'

'And that's it?'

'No. You've forgotten someone.'

'Who?'

'David Liebowitz. Without him, Minerva wouldn't be what it is today. He gets 40% of any deal.'

Bortoleski shook his head. 'No dice. He's a full-time employee. Any IPR he creates on the bank's time belongs to the bank. And he's not mentioned in your contract.'

'Doesn't matter,' said Tom. 'Those are my terms – 60:40 split and a sensible offer. When you can put one on the table, we'll talk. Until then, no deal.'

'Be reasonable, Tom, you don't know what sort of pressure I'm under from on high. Let me talk to them, maybe we can squeeze out a little more.'

'You think they'll agree to a price based on the prop trading value?'

'No, Tom, I know they won't, but you've got to be realistic –'

Now it was Tom's turn to hold up his hand, stopping

Bortoleski in mid-sentence, 'I am being realistic, Sam. Not only that, I'm being generous. Any company making a regular profit has to be worth ten times annual earnings and what I'm asking represents just a few months' worth. The bank's trying to screw me, isn't it?' Bortoleski made no reply. 'Come on, Sam, they're trying to screw me, admit it.'

'Yeah. I guess they are. I'll tell them you said no.'

'Thanks. When are you headed back to the States?'

'Tonight.'

Chapter Six

Andrew Chivers was English but had spent most of his working life in America. New York was home now and he rarely went back to the UK except for business trips and the odd visit to his widowed mother in Godalming. She was well looked after by his older sister and her family so his conscience was clear on that score.

Someone had once said of Chivers that he would have made a perfect secret agent because of his ability to melt into a crowd. He was in his mid-forties although looked younger, having caught the New York bug of working out and faddy eating. He rarely drank. Of medium height, he had a full head of neatly trimmed mousy-brown hair that was greying at the temples; narrow, rather sloping shoulders and slightly angular, but unremarkable features with a pale complexion and pale, close-set eyes.

He left his apartment on the Upper East Side and walked the few blocks to Central Park in the hope that a stroll in the fresh air would give him inspiration or even a vague idea of what he should do next. It was a glorious Spring morning, but he was in a foul mood. "April is the cruellest month," he mused bitterly: they weren't kidding. He needed to get out of the apartment and away from the omnipresent reminders that he was on his own now: ghostly outlines on the walls of the pictures that had until recently hung there, the indentations in the carpet where her furniture had once stood, the blank shelves on the bookshelves and the gaps in the CD rack.

Six weeks ago, in the midst of all the panic from senior management, he had done as he'd been advised and tendered his resignation, in the full expectation that it would be refused, that he'd be patted on the back, told that his noble sacrifice was after all unnecessary, that he had done nothing wrong and that although, yes, he was vicariously responsible for what had happened, he couldn't be expected to oversee and monitor every keystroke made by every desk assistant and trade booking clerk. And all because some worthless, hick, mutual fund from Nowheresville Montana had gone screaming to the SEC. Then on Sunday, after another stupid argument about Christ knows what – it was so stupid he couldn't even remember what had started it – Stacey had finally carried out her threat to leave him and had gone back to her parents.

Sod it. I'll call Sam. Worst he can say is no.

***

'Mr Chivers for you, Mr Bortoleski.'

'Thank you, Mandy, show him in please.'

At the press of a button on Mandy's desk the door swung open and Sam Bortoleski stood to greet his visitor, shook him warmly by the hand and enfolded him in a bear-like embrace.

'Andrew, good to see you as always. It's been too long. Come and have a seat.' Bortoleski motioned him towards the sofas by the window. 'Sorry to hear about what they did to you at Citi. Those guys, shit….say, why don't you sit down and tell me what really happened.'

Chivers shrugged and lowered himself wearily into a chair. 'Nothing to explain really, Sam. We had a large program trade with a guaranteed element. We'd won the bid on very low commission and stood to take a major loss because a lot of what we were buying was very illiquid and volatile. So, to help the client, we pre-hedged some of it and when it came to allocating the executions, we made a screw-up and it looked as though we'd taken the better prices ahead of the client.'

Bortoleski snorted. 'So I take it you killed your head of trade processing on the spot?' he asked.

'Tempting, but the damage was already done. We should've spotted it earlier, but we didn't. The client picked it up before we did, promptly screamed blue murder, and management, as you'd expect, panicked. As desk head I was vicariously responsible and although no one actually levelled any specific accusations, I was told that if I resigned, that would do the trick; client happy,

44

management being seen to crack down on trading abuses. They dropped a whole bunch of hints to the effect that they'd take a good long time to consider my resignation and then it would be refused. I've been in this industry long enough to know that if you put yourself in a position of vulnerability when management is looking to save its collective arse, you're taking a very big risk, but I had no choice but to trust them.'

Bortoleski shook his head in disbelief. 'How long did you say you've been in this industry, Andrew? All day? That was a beginner's mistake.'

'Yeah, you're right. Huge mistake. Result, me out on the street. Management's still living with the after-effects of dealing ahead of research and all the stuff that happened with the Japanese private bank, even after all these years, and so they wanted to be seen as purer than pure.'

'It played a lot worse in the press,' said Bortoleski. 'The way they spun it, you were caught, given a bottle of whisky and a revolver and told to do the decent thing. Funny how screw-ups can be made to look like irregular trading.'

He ignored the irony. 'Yeah, I know. The bit about me having been investigated by the SEC and completely exonerated of any wrong-doing, acting honourably by resigning and so on never quite made it into print. And I can guess why not.'

Another shake of the head. 'You should've called me earlier, Andrew. Could've helped you, maybe. Called in a few favours. Still, it's too late now I guess.'

'Way too late. My name stinks because I did the decent thing instead of blaming someone else. Nobody's hiring and I'm not ready to retire yet. My last four bonuses were largely made up of deferred shares and share options, and with a strike price anywhere north of thirty five and the share price stuck below five Dollars, I need a job. And before you ask, yes I am bitter and twisted about what happened.'

'Eleventh Commandment, Andrew. Never forget the Eleventh Commandment. Anyway, it's done now, but you called at a very good time as it happens, which is why I asked you to come and see me. How would you like to come and work for me again? It'll mean a move back to London. How would you feel about that?'

The Englishman tried desperately to hide his surprise and delight. Don't seem too eager, comes across as needy. He paused, trying to give the impression of weighing up his options. 'Sure, it'll be a big upheaval to leave New York after all this time, but I need a job and I guess the timing's not bad for either. What've you got in mind, Sam?'

'I want you to head up the London alternative execution services desk. It's a strong team and we've got the best algos and systems guys in the business.'

'Yes, I heard they were good. So who was the previous head? Where did he go?'

'It's a she. She's called Denise Evans. She couldn't work with the team we've got on the desk. They think she's an idiot, so I've kicked her upstairs into Matt O'Reilly's role – you do know Matt, don't you?'

Chivers nodded.

'O'Reilly is coming back here because I want to centralise control of Execution and Brokerage Services in New York and leave the overseas offices acting more like remote trading desks rather than independent functions in their own right. O'Reilly can drive that through and I wanted someone in his old role who'll do as they're told and shut the fuck up. So the fact that most people hate her on sight doesn't bother me in the slightest. We get good marks with the diversity jerks for putting a woman into a key management role and we have someone O'Reilly can run from here with minimal pushback, given a little local help from you.'

'But if I take the AES role, that means I'll be reporting in to her, right?'

'Right first time, Andrew, ten out of ten. You've known me long enough to know that there's always a "but." Still want the job?'

'Sure, Sam. Course I do.'

'Right. Beggars can't be choosers, eh, Andrew? Who wants tainted goods? Now, here's the angle,' Bortoleski continued. 'This is the good news: the AES desk has the best quant guy and one of the best developers in the market, like I just told you. We have a system called Minerva that is at least three years ahead of the competition, maybe more – I expect you know our profile in the market as well as I do.'

'So what's the bad news?' asked Chivers.

'The bad news is that, instead of using Minerva for proprietary trading and taking the competition for millions, if not billions, we're stuck with using it as a client-facing system. My hands are doubly tied. First, since the markets went bad in 2008, the board have been scared of their own shadows and the word from on high is risk-aversion. So, proprietary trading, risk-taking and anything that leverages the balance sheet has to be kept to a bare minimum. And second, the schmuck that you are going to be reporting to only went and let the dev guy, who is now an outside contractor, keep ownership of the intellectual property in the system and the source code when he moved; so effectively he now has our balls in a vice.'

'Shit. So why did you promote her to O'Reilly's job, Sam? That doesn't make any sense.'

'All in good time, Andrew. It makes perfect sense for a number of reasons as will become clear.'

'So, this dev guy, the contractor, why don't you just buy him out?' asked Chivers.

'We tried. You know what this lousy bank is like, Andrew. For stuff that's not worth a damn, they'll hose millions out of the window. Do you know how much our "Diversity Outreach Program" and all the associated extra hires cost us? No? Believe me, you don't wanna know. Like we haven't got enough dead wood on the payroll as it is. But when it came to buying Mansell out of his system, the amount we were able to put on the table was a fraction of what it was worth and he damn well knew it.'

'So what did he say?'

'Well, being the well-brought-up Englishman that he is, he very politely suggested that we should go screw ourselves. Not in those exact words, you understand, but that was the general drift of what he said.'

'We'd both have done the same, Sam.'

'Damn straight we would. Now, here's the hard part for you, Mr Chivers – told you there was always a "but" didn't I? I want you in post two weeks from now. You have no budget over and above what the bank has already allocated for this year, but I want that system. I want Minerva and I want it back in the firm's ownership. Once we own it, we move it from the AES desk which can carry on making 2 basis points on agency crap for all I give a shit, and we use it to set up a new proprietary trading desk which you will head up.'

Chivers nodded. 'Sounds ok so far,' he said. 'Where's the catch?'

'I'm coming to that. The next stage is harder still, and this is where you get to earn your pay. We're going to have to be very creative about where we source the capital to get the prop trading operation going. Correction, *you're* going to have to be very creative – just think of it as a hedge fund without a prime broker – nothing you can't handle I'm sure. Just speak nicely to the equity finance desk and tell 'em I sent you. Get it right, you get rich; screw up and it's "rogue trader up to his old tricks again" and we'll feed you to the authorities so fast it'll make your eyes water. We won't even come and visit you in jail. Still want the job?'

'Do I have a choice?'

'Sure you do. You can trade in your bonus shares and go live in a trailer park in New Jersey. There's all kinds of stuff you can do rather than come and work for me. I hear Burger King are hiring and food stamps have been replaced by a kind of credit card so they tell me.'

'You don't change, do you, Sam?' He shook his head and smiled. 'Course I'll take it. Now, fill me in about the personalities and then we can talk about money.'

'OK, let's take it from the top down. Matt O'Reilly you already know. Matt's good at his job but spends too much time with his head up his own ass and listening to his own publicity, although not at the same time I guess, or maybe that's where it comes from, I dunno. Anyway, he moves back here. That way I have more control over what he does. Job done. With me so far?'

'Yes, Sam.'

'Good. Once his move is announced and Evans takes his spot, your reporting line will be Evans-O'Reilly-me: that's the official version. The reality is that you report direct to me. With Evans out of the way in the corner office, that should make your life easier, but you'll need to manage her and, naturally, do so without her knowing it. Do *not* let her go anywhere near contract negotiations and just keep a close eye on her in case she tries to do anything stupid again.'

'Like what?'

'Who knows? That's the trouble with stupid people, they're endlessly creative. When she's told about the move, it'll be made clear to her that she's to concentrate on the day-to-day stuff: make sure we keep trading errors down; keep on top of operations to make sure we get no more corporate actions and settlement screw-ups; keep the interest claim level down; sit on the equity finance desk to make sure they're not over-borrowing again – all the crap that O'Reilly wasn't so great at because he thought it was beneath him.'

'I reckon I can handle that,' said Chivers.

'Sure you can. You keep her to the basics – even *she* shouldn't screw that up – and stop her getting stupid ideas into her head and trying to do any big-ticket corporate re-engineering shit that's out of her pay grade, or anything else that's out of her league intellectually – like buying pencils or negotiating fucking contracts for example. You got that?'

Chivers nodded.

'Next is the AES desk itself. We have three traders and they have a desk assistant each. They're good people and revenues are ok, even in these markets. I hear nothing about them day-to-day, which is usually a good sign. However, the two characters who are going to be of most immediate interest are an American called Liebowitz and the contractor dev guy – he's a Brit, like you – who's called Mansell.'

'I think I know both those names.'

'I thought you would. They do a lot of time on the conference circuit. They're a good double act and it brings in the business – the audiences love them. Liebowitz writes a lot of stuff for the trade press on some of the scary math he does, so I'd have expected you to know the names.'

'If they're the guys I'm thinking of, then they're pretty good,' said Chivers.

'Yeah, Liebowitz is a smart guy and it's the power of his algos plus some of the stuff he's done on modelling tipping points in human behaviour that lies at the heart of what Minerva does and why it's out there on its own. He's got his own outside interests and we let him get on with those because it keeps him happy and stops him wanting to go someplace else. He's talked about going back into academic life one day and we just want to keep "one day" a nice long way off into the future.'

'So what about Mansell?'

Bortoleski continued. 'Mr Mansell is a smart guy. Started out as a bond trader years back and found he liked the under-the-hood stuff better than the actual trading. Guess you could say I stole him from the fixed income guys – that's what they say, anyway. What he's good at is being able to understand complex trading ideas, Liebowitz's scary math, anything you want, much faster than anyone else I've ever come across, and then turn it into usable software. Code monkeys are a dime a dozen for chrissakes, but someone who knows the markets right from pre-trade through to settlement and accounting, and can also turn weird ideas into stuff we can make money with is worth keeping. He does the user interface, the application and database layers, the security, the networking: the whole damn thing.'

Chivers raised his eyebrows. 'Sounds impressive.'

'He is, but we've had to tread pretty careful around him recently. About a couple of years back – maybe a bit less, I don't remember – his wife was mugged in some shithole part of London. Gang of young punks stole her handbag and for some crazy reason she ran after them: try that in Queens and you're dead. I don't recall the exact story, maybe the kid threw the bag away, I dunno, but when the police got there he was clean and in the meantime she'd called him a dirty nigger in front of half the population of old London town.'

'Ouch.'

'Yeah, dead right, ouch. So she's some kind of attorney, divorce lawyer I think, and it turned into one of those Bonfire of the Vanities things, right? She loses her job, damn near goes to jail and all that either of them could think about after that was getting the hell out of Britain. The desk was making a shit-load of money, and at that time we had fully-funded plans to move Mansell and Liebowitz over to prop trading and to let them try out some ideas they had for trading credit instruments – they were crazy mad to start shorting the CDO market, ironic, huh? Since then we've hit a spending freeze and the move got nixed from on high. So for now we're doing what we can to keep them sweet: we've been lucky so far that nobody's been able to poach them off us.'

'Has anyone tried?' said Chivers.

'Citi were nosing around just before all this stuff with his wife happened but I chased them off.'

'How did you manage that?'

'Don't ask, you don't need to know. What you *do* need to know is that a few months ago, Mansell applied to work from home under the firm's flexible working policy. That came as a bit of a surprise since it's something that's really just for working moms who we can afford to cut a bit of slack and at the same time make nice to the feminist lobby.'

'Yeah, it was the same at the last couple of places I worked. Diversity's the new big thing.'

Bortoleski turned his nose up as though he'd just stepped in something. 'Yeah, tell me about it,' he said. 'Anyway, the application had to go via Denise Evans who was going to tell him to take a hike, but happened to mention it to O'Reilly, who in turn had the sense to tell me. So then I told Evans to make it happen because I didn't want Mansell leaving the firm.'

'Makes sense.'

'That's what I thought. Anyway, just before this happened, IT found out that a business-critical application – Minerva in this case – was being run on an unauthorised server that Mansell and Liebowitz had rigged up under the desk. It wasn't bank-compliant software either, so they made them shut it down but, being the dumb fucks they are, without offering any alternative hosting or budget. It seems that Mansell was able to get space in a data centre somewhere and moved Minerva there at his own expense so that they could keep going. Loyalty, see? I like that.'

'I'm impressed,' said Chivers.

'See, told you Mansell was a good guy. But now here's where we really screwed up big time. Because Mansell was going to be moving to France, the jerk-off artists in HR either couldn't or wouldn't help him move onto the Paris office payroll, so they made him resign and come back as a self-employed consultant. They gave him a boiler-plate contract and I made damn sure they gave him a decent rate – Evans had wanted to nickel-dime him of course – and left the rest of the contract to London to sort out.'

Chivers' jaw dropped. 'Please don't tell me they used in-house legal counsel?'

'Afraid so. Mansell's not stupid and he'd got his lawyers to add various clauses, ensuring that the intellectual property rights to anything he developed on his boxes outside the firm's data centres belonged to him. Evans didn't understand what that really meant and without checking her facts told our London in-house counsel that everything was ok.'

'Sneaky.'

'No, Andrew, not sneaky. He was covering his ass. Would you trust this bank, any bank for that matter, to deal straight with you as an employee, let alone as a contractor? No, me neither, they'll screw you in a heartbeat soon as look at you. So what do you do? You make sure that if they've got you by the balls, you grab theirs too and that's what Mansell did.'

'So want do you want me to do?'

'Like I said, I want you to keep Evans from screwing up. Next, I want you to make damn sure that Liebowitz and Mansell are happy, and if it even looks like they might be thinking of going someplace else, you are to know about it before they do, and tell me. Lastly, get the IPR for that system back into bank ownership by whatever means you see fit. However, do not screw things up by rushing at it. Remember, if you need to step over the line, make damn sure it's got Evans' name on it – that's what she's there for.'

Christ, you are a ruthless bastard, Bortoleski, thought Chivers.

'Reckon you can do all that for me?'

'I'll give it a go, Sam.'

'Glad to hear it and remember: once you start working for me you are a colleague and an employee, no longer a buddy. Once on board, same shit as everyone else. Got that?'

'Yes, Sam.'

'Good. Now, how much are we going to pay you?'

Chapter Seven

The atmosphere in what had been Matt O'Reilly's office in London and which now belonged to Denise Evans, positively crackled with indignation. As O'Reilly had predicted, her appointment as his successor had not been well received: the head of equity derivatives, who had been widely tipped for the job, had resigned to join a hedge fund. Several other desk heads were in close and regular contact with their head-hunters.

It had started as just another weekly product heads meeting, but the pressure that had been building over the last few weeks had finally reached bursting point. The head of operations, Lydia Shaw, was trying to make herself heard over the noise of several agitated people all trying to speak at the same time. She and Denise had had a blazing row the week before and now the dispute was about to go public.

'Denise, I simply cannot support the business with the number of people I have as it is, let alone with twenty percent fewer.'

Denise's voice took on a condescending and shrill tone. She'd had a lot of practice. 'Lydia, I hear what you're saying,' she said in an exaggerated manner, just in case anyone had missed the unspoken sentiment that the "back office" were a lower order of beings to be treated as slightly backward children, 'But the simple fact is that we, as a business, are doing twenty percent less in revenue terms than we were this time last year.'

'Christ, Denise.' Lydia was almost trembling with rage and frustration – why wouldn't this damn woman listen for once? 'We went through all of this last Friday. I agree, the value of the business we're writing is down by twenty percent, but transaction volumes are up – we're doing far more trades, it's just that they're smaller in value. The number of manual tickets, reconciliation breaks, cancel-corrects – everything that requires us to touch the trades, is up by thirty percent and that's what's killing us. My people are already working shifts and nobody is doing less than twelve-hour days. This isn't a sob-story, we're all big boys and girls and we're glad to still have jobs after all that's happened in the market, but the simple fact is that our workload has gone up, we haven't got enough people as it is and if I have to cut, then I dread to think what'll happen.' Evans made to interrupt, 'No, Denise, let me finish, I'll tell you exactly what'll happen. With the best will in the world, someone will make a mistake and we'll end up wearing yet another big loss that will outweigh any savings you're trying to make, several times over.'

Denise began to bluster, but Lydia Shaw cut her short again. 'Denise, our systems are not fit for purpose and for every dollar we make in revenue, my calculations show that processing issues and overheads are eating up an unacceptable percentage.'

'Then the trick, Lydia,' she said with her trademark sneer, 'is to stop being an overhead and start making a contribution. The solution is in your hands.'

All eyes in the room turned towards Lydia to see how she would react. "Overhead" to an operations professional is up there with the n-word and Denise Evans had meant her words to hurt. However, she did not get the result she expected. I'm not going to rise to this, thought Lydia. I'm not going to let her turn this into a problem of my making. Don't let the Lizard Brain start talking. Stay calm and *think*.

'Denise, I've got a report here that shows the corporate action losses, interest claims and over-borrow charges that we've taken in the last quarter because of system issues and, more importantly, the return on investment we gain from fixing them. I'll give you a breakdown…'

'Just mail it to me, Lydia. We've got a lot to get through today.'

Lydia had already sent it to her as an attachment to an e-mail following their previous meeting. The return receipt said, "Deleted Unread."

She made no further headway. The meeting continued and the level of acrimony returned to a high simmer. Skilfully and imperceptibly, Denise Evans managed to turn every demand for more staff, every well-argued case for more funding, every plea for more IT investment into evidence that the person requesting it was not doing their job properly and thereby letting their colleagues down. When divide and rule was not practical she invoked higher authority, blaming New York and their policy of tightening the purse strings, which of course she deeply opposed.

When each of the desk heads had submitted their weekly update and the meeting was about to come to an ill-humoured close, Denise motioned for silence and stood up. She opened the door and spoke to Scary Mary. 'Ask Andrew to come in, would you, Mary.'

A very ordinary-looking individual came into the office and stood, looking rather nervous, next to Denise's desk. Everything about his appearance could be described as average: average height, slightly pointy, average-ish sort of face, grey suit, pale grey eyes, white shirt, red tie; Joe Soap and Jane Doe had a child. She smiled benevolently at her assembled desk heads and clasped her hands together. 'Ladies and gentlemen, I would like to introduce you to Andrew Chivers. As you know, since the recent reorganisation, the Alternative Execution Services trading team has been without a desk head, so we are very fortunate that Andrew has agreed to join us to take on the role.'

David Liebowitz looked as though he was going to choke.

She continued unabashed but avoided all eye-contact with Liebowitz. 'Before coming here, Andrew worked at Citigroup where he was responsible for setting up their proprietary trading desk, prior to being promoted to head of program trading. And before that he worked at Lehman Brothers where, again, he was responsible for equities proprietary trading. Andrew, perhaps you'd like to say a few words and introduce yourself to your new colleagues.'

To his credit, Chivers realised at once that something was horribly wrong and that he'd been made an unwilling accessory to a mugging. He mouthed the usual platitudes about being glad to be part of such a highly thought-of team and that he was looking forward to getting to know them all better over the coming weeks. He threw the hospital pass back. 'Over to you, Denise,' he said, trying his best to smile.

The meeting broke up in shocked silence. When the others had left Liebowitz came over to her and said, 'Denise, could I have a private word with you please? Now.'

'David I'd simply love to, but I have another meeting straight away. I promise I'll explain everything to you in due course – ask Mary to slot you in to my diary. Please excuse me.' She stood up, turned her back on him and walked out of the office.

***

Later that evening, Liebowitz called Tom Mansell in France.

'She did what?' Tom couldn't believe what he was hearing. 'Look, mate, if this is one of your jokes, it just isn't funny.'

The tone of his friend's voice made it clear that he was not joking.

'No, Tom, it's for real. I've been her deputy for two years and Matt himself told me that the desk head job was mine just before he went back to New York. I just cannot believe that even she would stoop so low and that Matt let her do it – he must've known. You want to see what she's doing to the business – the head of equity derivatives has walked out, everyone's at each other's throats and now she does this. I just cannot fucking believe it. Oh, yeah – and Matt's not returning my calls either. This whole thing stinks to high heaven.'

'Who's the new guy?'

'He's called Andrew Chivers. No, I hadn't heard of him either – seems he's spent the last few years working in the States. Seems nice enough at first sight – turns out he knew nothing about what she was playing at and I think, for now, I believe him. Apparently they told him the job was vacant because of a promotion and that he'd just be slotting in where she left off. He was very apologetic about it – like I said, seems like a regular guy – and said he'd ask Denise why I hadn't been told. Don't hold your breath, eh?'

'This is crap, David. They can't do this to you.'

'Too late, they just have. Anyway, we tried to get Chivers out for a beer after work but he made some excuse. He's playing

57

things very tight to his chest and even if he didn't know what was going on, he's certainly been given an agenda. I don't know what it is, and God only knows what else Denise has told him, but it can't be good. She won't even talk to me – all today she's either been in meetings or she keeps the door shut with Scary Mary playing defensive end.'

'What else?' asked Tom.

'Chivers has been asking about you. Why you're not on the desk full-time, what Minerva does, why we don't run it on the bank's servers, how much you cost, what we're paying for rack space in the data centre. Stuff like that – a whole bunch of questions he wouldn't have known to ask day one if he hadn't been briefed. Know what I think? I reckon they want to move the whole Minerva system in-house and then get rid of you to save the cost.'

'Well, they won't have much luck,' said Tom. 'They can't get rid of me for the first eighteen months of the contract – I made sure I got that one in. And while the system sits outside their data centres I own the intellectual property rights and the source code – that's in the contract too – and the only proviso is that they have first refusal to buy it off me if and when the contract ends. I don't trust the bastards any further than I could throw them and, luckily for me, in-house legal don't know the first thing about application hosting, that's how I got those clauses in. Serves them right for being too mean to use decent outside counsel for stuff they don't understand. So what are you going to do, David?'

'Nothing much I can do, is there? Not in these markets.'

'Look, I'm coming over to London next week, we'll talk about it then. I'll let you know if Chivers contacts me.'

Chapter Eight

Not everyone adapts well to working from home but, for Tom Mansell, it was a dream come true. He was usually at his desk by seven o'clock (6 AM in the UK) and could accomplish in seven undisturbed hours what had taken him ten when he was working on the desk. If the weather was lousy on Saturday he would spend the day working and then take Monday off. But for him, the biggest treat was to be able to spend time with Sally.

Nowhere is perfect, however, and during Tom's most recent trip to London, Sally had become convinced that someone was following her. She felt embarrassed about voicing her concerns, and breaking the news on his return wasn't easy.

His face fell. 'Why on earth didn't you call the police?'

'Because I don't have any proof.'

'So how do you know someone's following you?'

She sat down on the arm of a chair and cupped her chin in her hands. 'I know it sounds silly, but I just do. The first time, I was out on my bike and there was a chap coming the other way on his. As I got closer, he stopped, took out a camera and as bold as you like, took a picture of me as I cycled past. I was going to say something to him but there was nobody else around and, you know, I didn't feel safe.'

'OK, I agree it's a bit creepy,' said Tom, joining her on the arm of the chair and slipping his arm around her shoulders. 'If you were concerned, you should've called me, silly.'

'I didn't want to worry you.'

'Well you've got to if it happens again.'

'But that's just it. It did.'

'What?'

'Happen again. I'm sure I was followed back from Béziers by a dark blue Renault.'

'Did you get the number?'

'No I didn't, he was too far back. And then I saw something on the hill, you know the hill opposite the house. I know you'll think this is daft, but I've seen people hanging about up there on the crest of the ridge like they were watching the house. And there were flashes, like reflections from camera lenses.'

Tom thought for a moment. 'But we've seen people up there before, it's not far from the footpath: it could've just been someone admiring the view or even bird-watching. I'm sure it's nothing to worry about.'

'I'm sorry, Tom, but the chap with the camera got me worried and, with you being away, I suppose I let my imagination run riot.'

He stroked her hair. 'It still hasn't gone away, has it?'

'Mostly,' she said. 'But it doesn't take much to bring it back.'

'And if it happens again when I'm not here, promise me you'll call the police.'

'I promise.'

***

Tom knew that he would be commuting regularly to London and although it was pleasant to see old friends, catch up on all the latest gossip and to feel part of things again, the novelty wore off very quickly. The wrench of giving up the comfort of setting his own timetable, deciding his own priorities and working at his own pace, to set off on what was now just another business trip, became increasingly hard to bear. What Sally had said about being followed didn't make it any easier either.

Getting from France to the UK was relatively straightforward. There were airlines offering direct business class flights, but that meant a two-hour drive to either Toulouse or Marseille, so for this trip Tom decided to try one of the low-cost operators. There was no shortage of choice: the usual suspects operated from the airports within an hour's drive of Mirepech and he'd flown with most of them before, an experience that had ranged from just-about-ok to, I-can't-believe-they-can-get-away-with-this. So he thought he'd try Jetaway Airlines who had recently opened a service from Béziers to Southampton, from where he could get a train to Waterloo. After all, they couldn't be worse than the last lot he'd flown with, could they? They were.

On that last low-cost occasion, Tom had flown out to join Sally who had already been down at the house in Mirepech for a week. As usual, the Tramontane was blowing and as the aircraft continued its approach to the small regional airport, it was clear that events were getting well ahead of the pilot's limited flying skills. So unused was he to hand-flying the aircraft in a strongly gusting crosswind (and without the assistance of autopilot and autothrottle), that he was being led, towed almost, behind the aircraft like a water-skier, to the scene of the accident. At about 300 feet on short finals, with the airspeed varying wildly and the aircraft 30 degrees off runway heading, survival instinct kicked in, he abandoned the approach and initiated a go-around. This wasn't handled well either but somehow, after another agriculturally-flown approach, the aircraft landed after a fashion and began to slow down on the runway, at which point a group of passengers burst into a loud round of applause.

'What are they clapping for?' Tom, who hated flying unless he was at the controls, asked the man sitting next to him.

'That's not clapping, mate,' came the reply, 'that's the sound of buttocks unclenching.'

At first he'd thought the Jetaway fare was quite reasonable: it was advertised at £70 return, so at least the bank couldn't accuse him of not doing his bit to keep costs down. However, as the booking proceeded, the costs began to mount up:

Item	
Basic fare	£35
Fees and taxes	£35
Credit card charge	£8
Cabin baggage fee	£10
Hold baggage fee	£30
Privilege boarding	£10
Online booking fee	£5
Check-in fee	£10
Total	£143

Two hundred and eighty six quid return! Funny old £70 he thought. He also couldn't work out why "Privilege Boarding" wasn't an optional item.

The flight itself was a nightmare. Funny that, thought Tom, why is it that whenever a company puts up notices telling you not to assault their staff, you can be sure that the level of service will make you want to thump somebody?

Not having children, Tom hadn't realised that the date he'd chosen to fly to the UK coincided with the end of the school holidays. At the airport, one bored, slow and not very competent check-in girl was trying to process a huge scrum of humanity, all of whom, it seemed to Tom, were behaving like typical, badly-behaved, loutish British children, but most of whom were adults. After about half an hour of queuing he was two from the front when with much shouting and barging an extended family group of about ten people joined the person in front of him. He was going to say something but thought better of it.

Security procedures followed their usual course of ritual humiliation and he eventually found his way through to an overcrowded, stuffy waiting room with one lavatory for nearly 200 people.

The incoming flight arrived and was duly unloaded and refuelled. Three of the flight attendants, grumpy eastern European girls who spoke very little English and no French, came into the departure lounge from outside. As they opened the doors there was a stampede towards the departure desks which, to their credit, the Poland select XV front row halted with remarkable efficiency. While one of them stared down the charging herd, her colleague picked up the microphone and made a barely comprehensible announcement that passengers with privilege boarding cards (almost everyone) should board now, followed by families with children (everybody else). The stampede re-started and Tom was swept to one side by a burly woman with tattooed arms who was clutching two whining toddlers. By the time he had fathomed what was going on, he was almost at the back of what passed for the queue. When he finally managed to find a seat on the aircraft, all the overhead lockers were full and he had to put his laptop bag under the seat in front of him which restricted what little legroom there was. Other eastern Europeans wearing cheap polyester uniforms in Jetaway colours were now stamping up and down the aisle and attempting to make the remaining passengers hurry up and sit down. The cabin crew had to shout to make themselves heard over a deafening cacophony of advertising and thudding pop music blaring over the aircraft's PA system – not that anyone could have understood what they were saying anyway. There followed the usual announcement from the flight deck, and as far as Tom could make out from the few words of broken English he could catch, the captain on today's flight was Yuri Unpronounceable who was going to be ably assisted by first officer Boris Unpronounceable. Let's just hope French air traffic control understand them better than I do, he thought.

Sitting just across the aisle from Tom was a French family who seemed absolutely petrified and bewildered. The father looked across at Tom as though seeking his help. You wait till you get to the UK, chum, thought Tom, this is only the start.

As soon as he arrived in London that evening, the first thing Tom did was to book a business class single back to France. The following morning he took the Tube from Canada Water to Canary Wharf. His friend, Brian, kindly let him use the spare room in his flat when he was in London. The flat, although relatively modern, had been rendered utterly squalid by Brian's lack of basic domestic hygiene and although it was "handy for the office," a week at the Cockroach Hilton was not something Tom relished, so he spent as little time there as possible, using it just to sleep.

He left the flat early to avoid the morning crush on the Jubilee Line, arriving in the office shortly after seven. That left him three clear hours before his meeting with his new desk head, Andrew Chivers.

David Liebowitz came in about ten minutes later and the two of them went out for breakfast.

'You feeling any better? asked Tom.

'Yeah, I suppose. Still mad as hell but what can I do about it?'

'So what did Denise say? Did you even get to talk to her?'

'Yeah, but she just blanked me. Said that Matt had said nothing to her about my taking over as desk head and that Sam Bortoleski had approved the hire. So either Matt lied to me, Denise lied to me or both – and my money's on "both." There is no way in hell that they could get the sign-off and funding through for a senior hire like that, do the hiring trawl and all the interviews, find the right candidate and get him on board so fast – it must've been in the pipeline for months before Matt left, but I just can't work out what they're up to. This has Bortoleski's fingerprints all over it, that I'm sure of, and I'd be very surprised if he hadn't told Matt or had over-ruled him.'

'So have you changed your mind about Chivers?' asked Tom.

'Not really. Still seems just about ok, I guess. He knows the product, makes sensible decisions, asks intelligent questions and, most important of all, he lets me get on with my job. Maybe I'm being bitter and twisted and unfair on the guy, but I just get that nasty sneaking feeling he's got an agenda that we don't know about. I'd like to trust him, but I can't.'

'Well, I'm seeing him at ten. I'll let you know how I get on.'

***

The two men shook hands.

'Andrew Chivers.'

'How d'you do, Andrew? Tom Mansell.'

'Shall we go over to my office?'

Chivers closed the door behind him and asked Tom to sit down. The office looked bare and spartan. Chivers had cleared out much of the clutter he had inherited from Denise and had yet to stamp his personality on the place.

'Tom, first of all let me apologise for not getting in touch with you earlier and for the way in which my arrival was handled, but I prefer to do these things face-to-face. I only found out after Denise's announcement at the section heads' meeting that all of you were expecting David to take over as desk head. I now realise that the news must have come as a bombshell and can't have left anyone terribly pleased to see me. I've cleared the air with David now and I can see that it could've been handled more sensitively, so all I can do is to apologise.'

Apologising for something that's not your fault? thought Tom. Chivers was either a consummate politician or he really was a nice guy after all. We'll have to see.

'I've had a look at Minerva,' said Chivers, 'David's set me up with a log-in and has gone through pretty much most of what the system does. Before we go any further, can I just say how impressed I am with what I've seen. And you wrote it from scratch yourself?'

Tom nodded in affirmation.

'I think I follow most of the high-level functionality but I'd like you to fill in some of the gaps for me. I'm also concerned as to why we're using external software for mission-critical work and who would support it, if, Heaven forbid, anything were to happen to you.'

'OK,' said Tom. 'I'll give you a bit of background. Firstly, we called it Minerva after the Roman goddess of wisdom, which was a terrible act of hubris on our part, or whatever Latin for hubris is, but we did so because we knew we were doing stuff that the competition couldn't do, not even Goldmans, and therefore we saw ourselves as being just a tiny bit brighter than some of the big-budget shops out there. In mitigation we were very drunk when we thought of it, and now if anyone asks us why we used the name we just tell them we can't remember.'

Chivers scribbled a brief note before looking up once more. 'What about the core functionality?' he asked.

'OK, let me back up a bit,' said Tom. 'When they set the Alternative Execution Services desk up, we already offered electronic trading, program and block trading and a basic algorithmic trading service – nothing fancy, just basic VWAP, iceberg and time-slicing stuff. Then David and I started working on some ideas that we'd had around access to dark liquidity pools and going way beyond what the second-generation smart order routers were doing. That led us on to trying out some ideas on how to detect and arbitrage dark liquidity using the algos we'd written. Initially, we were using Fourier analysis and most of the other mathematical standards from the quant toolkit…'

'Hold on a second, I'm not a quant,' said Chivers. 'Just take it easy.'

'Sorry. Fourier analysis is just a way of taking a flow of complex information that can be expressed as a wave-form – price, volume, volatility and so on, for example, and breaking it down into bite sized chunks of trigonometric functions that are much easier to understand. It's a branch of maths that's used in radar signal processing to transform all the mess that comes back when a signal is reflected back off something so that the operator can clearly see whether there's a ship, an aircraft or whatever out there.'

Chivers raised his eyebrows. 'And do we have many people attacking the building with aeroplanes?' he asked.

'None so far,' replied Tom. 'Which shows how effective it is.'

Chivers smiled. 'Fair point. Please carry on.'

Chivers scribbled furiously, trying to keep up with Tom's explanation of Minerva: how they tried and failed to get anyone to understand its potential; how the IT department tried to block their way when they used their own server under the desk; how Tom and David had spent their own money rebuilding the system and having it hosted in an external data centre. At last, when Tom stopped speaking he looked up from his notes and said, 'I think I've got all that, but I do have one last question. You said you own the intellectual property rights in Minerva. Are you sure about that?'

'Yes, completely.'

'I don't get this,' said Chivers. 'Surely your contract states that anything you develop in the bank's time and on the bank's systems belongs to the bank.'

'Nope. It did when I was an employee. Also, everything that was on the bank's servers was bank intellectual property.'

Chivers clasped his hand to his forehead. 'So it's not on one of the bank servers and I'm assuming you're about to tell me you've refactored the code so it's no longer the same system.'

Tom grinned. 'You've got it in one and you've got the bank's IT department to thank for that when they forced us to shut down the version we had on an unofficial server under the desk. When I knew that Minerva was going to have to be moved, I re-wrote a big chunk of it – refactored it – so, as you rightly said, it's an entirely different system even if does lots of the same things. And don't forget that I paid for the other servers out of my own pocket. The change in ownership, the licence fee and one or two other clauses like that were all baked into my contract when I went from being an employee to being self-employed. Simple self-preservation really.'

Chivers looked at him intently. 'Either you've got the gift of the gab or this company has used some extremely stupid lawyers.'

'Bit of both I suppose,' said Tom with a smile.

Chivers remained impassive. 'Hmmm, I can't say I'm very happy with that and I don't want to continue under that arrangement, nor does Denise but we'll come back to that.'

Come back to it all you like, thought Tom, but until you pay David and me for Minerva, the intellectual property rights aren't going anywhere.

***

The Saturday after he returned from London Tom awoke to the sound of heavy rain drumming on the roof of le Mas des Oliviers. A strong southerly *Vent Marin* was driving low, scudding clouds across the coastal plain of the Languedoc and into the Minervois and it was clearly a day for catching up on work rather than getting out in the fresh air. He looked up from reading the new message that had just hit his e-mail inbox. 'Fancy a few days in New England, darling?'

'Sounds fun,' replied Sally. 'Another conference? Where this time?'

'Newport, Rhode Island, in September, "Fourth Annual Global Electronic Trading and Messaging Symposium" according to the e-mail, and the bank want David and me to do our double-act.'

'You won't be offended if I don't attend the nerdy bits, will you?'

'Of course not. You're formally excused everything except the...now where's the list of events? Ah, here we are, you'll like this: you're formally excused everything except the welcome cocktails on the Sunday, the tour of the Newport summer cottages and gala dinner on the Monday night, and the boat trip followed by a traditional clam bake on the Tuesday.

'You never know, if there's time you might even get time for some shopping too. We can spend a couple of nights in Boston and a couple more just sight-seeing – we could do Cape Cod, I've heard it's great and it'll be out of season so it shouldn't be too busy. We can fly to Logan and pick up a car from there. The conference lasts from Monday to Wednesday, so if I take some holiday, we could fly out on the Friday, say, and come back overnight the following Saturday-Sunday.'

It gave Tom enormous pleasure to take Sally with him on his travels whenever possible. First, it was precious time spent together, and secondly, her spirits seemed to rise as though the weight of what had happened to her that rainy winter's day in London was being slowly lifted from her shoulders.

Chapter Nine

Sam Bortoleski was not happy. It was four o'clock in morning and the phone was ringing. He angrily snatched the receiver from its cradle. Without any form of greeting he snarled, 'This better be fuckin' good.'

It was Chivers.

'Sam, it's Andrew, I need to talk to you.'

'You *are* talking to me, Andrew. It's four AM and to wake me at this hour, it had better be fuckin' good.'

Without emotion or any apparent fear of Bortoleski's wrath, Chivers explained what had happened, that it was urgent: an emergency in fact and that action was required.

'Get her on the next flight. I want that stupid bitch in my office today. And tell Lane that his team's not going anywhere.'

'No, Sam, listen to me.' Chivers' voice maintained its icy calm. 'The news will reach your office this morning through the normal channels – it has to and has to be seen to do so. Check your Blackberry but make sure read receipts are turned off. Lane is sure to have sent you an e-mail and, if he hasn't left a voicemail already, he'll be calling your office from seven AM Eastern Time, that I'm sure of. And as for getting anyone on the next flight for New York, that has to come from you too – remember, she was your idea.'

'Yeah, yeah, OK, Mr Smartass. I'll be in the office in an hour. I'll call you then.'

'No. Don't rush it. Go back to sleep and come in at the normal time – today is nothing out of the ordinary – all that happens is that you get a big surprise when you read your mails or Mandy checks your voicemails for you. Remember, Lane will be expecting you to respond but if you do so at five AM, although he may not pick that up as odd right now, he certainly will when he calms down. He's a smart guy so be careful.'

'Does O'Reilly know anything about this?'

'I don't think so. I don't think anyone else saw it coming, but

I'll try and find out if this was a solo effort or not. You, however, need to brief Matt before talking to anyone else and be sure he understands that because of the gravity of the situation, you are dealing with it personally, but want his input. He must be kept in the loop and must feel that he's part of the decision-making process. This is business as usual.'

'Yes, I'll do that too. Shit. OK, Andrew, I'll call you later. Oh, and Andrew?'

'Yes.'

'Good job. Thanks for fielding this one.'

***

'Mr Bortoleski's office, how can I help you?'

'Good morning, Mandy. This is Stephen Lane calling from London. Is Sam available, please?'

'Certainly, Mr Lane. I'll put you straight through.'

'Good morning, Stephen. I was expecting your call. I got your mail and your voicemail for which I thank you. Firstly, let me put your mind at rest. There appears to have been a misunderstanding somewhere and I can assure you that your team is safe and there are jobs for all of you.'

The tension and anger in Lane's voice crackled down the line. 'A misunderstanding? I'm not ten years old, Sam, you've known me long enough. That's bull... that's nonsense.'

'Stephen, please. I had no idea anything like this would happen, nor did Matt when I told him about it earlier. Denise is very good but she's new in the job. She's had to make some hard decisions when it's come to cutting costs. This time it's clear that she's made a bad mistake and has overstepped the mark – laying off a team like yours, which may I add, is very highly thought-of in this bank, was the wrong thing to do and I have personally reversed the decision already. She will speak to your team today, my office will issue a formal communiqué that an administrative error has occurred and that Transition Management maintains a core product within the World Wide Investment Bank.'

'Thank you, Sam. I very much appreciate your personal involvement, but I must tell you in all honesty that it's going to be very difficult from now on reporting into someone who…how can I put this delicately?…in whom I have no confidence and simply cannot respect as a fellow professional.'

'Stephen, listen to me.' The effort of playing the unaccustomed role of good cop was becoming too much for Bortoleski. 'You've made your opinion of her very clear, but she's the right person for the job and has my full support. You all have your jobs, you will have an apology, she stays. You got that?'

'Yes, Sam.'

'Good. Thank you, Stephen, and have a wonderful day.' He hung up and yelled through the open office door. 'Mandy, have you got that flight for Evans yet?'

'Yes, Mr Bortoleski. She just called again by the way.'

'Which part of "I'll speak to you when you get to my office" does she not understand? You make sure you tell her that, Mandy. Oh, and get O'Reilly in here would you?'

***

At nine twenty-five New York time, Denise Evans stepped out of the suffocating humidity of a Manhattan summer and into the cool of the air-conditioned glass and marble cathedral that was the reception hall of the bank's headquarters. They were expecting her. She collected her visitor's pass from reception and was also issued with piece of paper carrying the PIN code that allowed elevator access to the top floor. She had of course met Bortoleski before and had seen him shred his subordinates in public when the mood took him, but had never been summoned to his office. It wasn't an experience she was looking forward to – the combination of heat and fear were already winning their unequal struggle with her deodorant.

The executive floor receptionist showed her into the outer office: a discreet sign announced, "Samuel J Bortoleski, Head of Global Execution and Brokerage Services." Awaiting her were his secretary Mandy, and a uniformed female security guard.

'Miss Evans,' said the guard, 'would you please take off your coat, place your bag and your cell phone on the table here and stand with your arms outstretched, ma'am.'

She patted her down, airport security style, and then ran a hand-held detector of some sort over the visitor's body.

'What is this about?' said Denise, the catch in her voice betraying her nervousness.

'Routine security check, ma'am. Company policy for all visiting personnel to this office.'

'Are you sure this is strictly necessary?'

'Ma'am, if you do not co-operate fully or if you subject me to verbal or racial harassment I am empowered to place you in custody awaiting the arrival of the New York Police Department, who, under section 23-G of the....'

'OK, you've made your point. I am co-operating fully. See how co-operative I'm being, look, see me co-operate.' The sarcasm was entirely wasted.

She completed her scan of Denise's ample exterior. 'You may proceed, ma'am.' The guard left.

Mandy keyed the intercom. 'Mr Bortoleski, Miss Evans is here.'

'Send her in.'

Mandy released the intercom. 'Good luck, honey,' she said, pressed a button on her desk and the door to the inner sanctum swung noiselessly open.

Denise took a deep breath and walked in. Bortoleski remained seated behind his ornate wooden desk. The door swung shut behind her. The silence was deafening.

A chair stood in front of the desk but Bortoleski did not invite her to sit down, in fact he didn't speak at all but merely looked at her as a hungry spider might at a fat fly. His hooded eyes fixed her intently.

Leaving her standing in the middle of the oriental rug in front of his desk, Bortoleski got up and crossed to the window. The floor-to-ceiling glass gave a spectacular view over the Battery, the harbour and, off to the right, Liberty Island and Ellis Island where his grandparents had arrived in the Land of the Free. Next to the window were two sofas and, between them, a low coffee table. Bortoleski reclined on one of the sofas and ran a hand across his bald pate. He pointed at the other sofa and spoke at last. 'Come and sit down, Denise. Has Mandy offered you a drink – coffee, water, a soda? What would you like?'

'Er, just water thanks, Sam.' This wasn't what she'd been expecting at all.

He got up, crossed the room to the door, opened it and asked Mandy to fetch a jug of water and a diet Coke. He sat back down opposite his perspiring visitor.

'So, Denise....'

Here it comes, she thought.

'So, Denise, did you have a good flight? Hotel and everything else OK?'

His demeanour took her completely by surprise. 'Yes, Sam. Everything was just fine thanks.' The hotel was magnificent and the bank had booked her a suite overlooking Central Park. Instead of flying coach, she was booked first class both ways. None of this made one iota of sense to her.

'Good. Excellent. And it's very good of you to come all this way to see me at such short notice. Nice office, huh?'

She nodded. This isn't happening, thought Denise. Why isn't he shouting, why hasn't he fired me? Why is he behaving like everyone's favourite uncle? An image of Stalin flickered across her mind. Perhaps that was it.

'Know how you get an office like this?'

She shook her head.

'No? Give up? Good answer, it was a trick question and I was expecting you to say something about hard work. Nope. Hard work won't get you here. The guy who paints my house on Long Island works hard but he don't have an office like this. I'll tell you what gets you an office like this – being an asshole.

'This world is not short of assholes – the jails are full of them. They're the stupid assholes. The smart assholes work in banks, the stupid ones go to jail. That's the trick: to get an office like this, you gotta be an asshole, but you gotta be a smart one.'

'You sent for me, Sam.'

'Yes indeed, I did, didn't I? Ah, here's Mandy with the drinks. Thanks, Mandy. Cookies too, my lucky day.'

The door closed behind her and the oppressive silence fell once again.

'Now where were we, Denise?'

'You sent for me,' she said lamely.

'So I did. I take it you know what this is about?'

She nodded.

'So tell me, Denise. What do *you* think it's all about?'

'The Transition Management Team?'

'Right first time. The Transition Management Team. You haven't fired them again I take it?' He smiled, but the smile never reached his eyes.

Denise shifted uncomfortably in her seat. 'No, Sam.'

'Good, that's something at least. So perhaps we can start with an explanation of what the fuck you were thinking of,' he said, his earlier modulated accents now replaced by a street-fighter's snarl.

The abrupt change in tone finally dislodged Denise's fingertip grasp over her self-control, and she was aware of her eyes prickling as the tears welled up. She sniffed and swallowed hard.

'It was a simple matter of cost, Sam.'

'Go on.' Uncle was back.

'The Transition Management team come under an equities cost code, but because of the way they operate, their revenues fall across multiple product lines, and they're doing more and more work with the fixed income teams. Because of that and because of the fact that equity markets are flat at the moment, over half their revenue falls under fixed income. So I went to see Harry Wells.'

'Yes. He told me.'

'I went to see Harry Wells…'

'Yes, you went to see Wells with a reasonable request to alter the balance of cost and revenue attribution between his group and yours. Correct?'

'Yes, Sam.'

'Yes, Denise, but instead of handling it properly by doing your homework first and having the numbers ready, your facts straight and your line of argument worked out, you went in there, screwed it up entirely and pissed Wells off to such an extent that he threw you out of his office. Now that takes some doing. Wells is a nice guy and he's fair too; but you manage to piss him off so bad that he throws your ass out of his office and is on the telephone to me thirty seconds later asking who this obnoxious idiot is that I've hired. So did you tell O'Reilly? He is after all your immediate superior: head of equities, remember?'

She opened her mouth to speak.

'No, you didn't tell him, did you? So you couldn't ask his advice either, could you? And if he didn't know, then how could *I* know that you'd just pissed off the head of fixed income if he hadn't told me himself.'

'But, Sam,' she interrupted, 'I was wearing all the cost and less than half the revenue. The equities business is losing money by running a transitions team.'

'And so you decided to let them go?'

'Yes.'

'Without consulting anybody else?'

'Sam, you told me yourself that I was going to have to make hard decisions and that I'd have to take them on my own and would gain or lose, as you put it, on their success.'

'You really are a hopeless fucking case, aren't you? Every gut feeling, every instinct, every bone in my body is screaming at me to fire you for this. I take it you're aware that we've had to let people go from the equities IT world?'

'Yes, Sam.'

'In fact we've had to let IT people go across all product lines. And will you please stop that damn snivelling and pull yourself together,' he snapped. 'We've had to lose good people from IT, but it was done properly because my staff here know what they're doing. We looked at our IT cost base, we looked where cost fell across product lines, where we need development resource, where we needed support people, what skill sets we're going to need and so on. We spoke to the product heads – we even spoke to you, remember? We did an impact assessment, we looked at the individuals' performance, our likely future requirements, next year's budget, the whole damn works. Then, and only then, we decided who was to go and who was to stay. Know what that's called?'

'No, Sam.'

'Management, Denise. It's called management – management one-o-fucking-one. You are paid to manage.' His tone became softer again. 'Now get out of here, go home and start behaving like a manager and not like a stupid asshole.'

The door closed behind her. She picked up her belongings and prepared to leave the outer office.

'See, that wasn't too bad, was it, honey?' said Mandy.

Chapter Ten

Following the instructions from the hire car's sat-nav, Tom and Sally crossed the causeway from mainland Newport to the island where the hotel stood. From the outside it was unprepossessing and looked more like one of the buildings on the US Navy base further up the coast to the north. However, once inside, their concerns evaporated.

David Liebowitz had brought his girlfriend, Caroline, to the conference too. They had flown out on the Sunday, and straight after the conference were heading down to New York to visit Liebowitz's family.

All four of them had signed up for the tour of the "Summer Cottages" which was to take place after the conference sessions on Monday. Most were built during the latter years of the nineteenth and early years of the twentieth century as summer homes for the seriously rich. Set along the cliff top, with magnificent views of the ocean, each "cottage" seemed locked in competition to outdo its neighbours in terms of size, ostentation and, some might say, vulgarity. Although their oil baron and financial tycoon owners usually only used them for a few weeks of lavish partying and entertainment every season, they were truly immense constructions. The guide book told them that although some are still in private hands, most are now owned by the Preservation Society of Newport County.

Next to a black and white Tudor-style mansion, complete with half-timbering and barley-twist brick chimneys stood a copy of a French château; next to that stood an eighteenth century English country house in the Palladian style, which in turn was next to a vast, Lutyens-inspired Arts and Crafts manor. Thus the theme and mix of styles continued, on past other more restrained mansions – although, when talking of the Newport cottages, such terms as "restraint" are relative - such as "Rosecliff" (inspired by the "Trianon" at Versailles), "The Breakers" and so on, until they reached "Braemar" for the gala dinner and ball that was laid on for the conference delegates and their partners.

Braemar had been built in 1903 by an iron and steel magnate – which gave Tom his cue for a series of bad jokes – and was supposed to be in the Scottish baronial style. However, Scottish baronial had not travelled well and the outcome was at best transatlantic. Both inside and out, Braemar seemed to anticipate every movie castle from *The Ghost Goes West*, via *Sleeping Beauty* to *Shrek*.

They crossed the drawbridge into a vaulted entrance hall, hung with tapestries and decorated with animal trophies, swords and shields embossed with heraldic designs. To their left, in the fireplace, was a blazing log fire and opposite, along the other wall, stood a long oak table covered with a starched white cloth and from which uniformed staff were serving drinks. In the corner, next to the broad, sweeping stairway was a gleaming suit of armour.

From the hallway, they were ushered under a minstrels' gallery into the *belle-époque* ballroom, which in turn gave onto a broad terrace, decorated in the rococo style – no self-respecting Scottish castle should be without one. From the terrace, elaborate flights of marble steps curved down to the manicured lawns and formal gardens which fell away in tiers all the way to the cliff top. In the middle of the lawns stood a floodlit Italianate fountain.

Once the dinner was finished and the disco started up in the ballroom, Caroline and Sally were keen to stay. However, both men were insistent that this was a "school night" and wanted to make sure that they were on form for their presentations at tomorrow's conference session. They were jointly declared "a pair of old grumps" by the girls.

***

Liebowitz and Mansell were down to do five speaking slots between them over the three days of the conference: one each as solo presenters on two of the days, and one that they called their "double act." For the "double-act", which took place on the Tuesday, they had drawn the graveyard slot, the last presentation of the day when the speaker is effectively the only remaining obstacle between the delegates and the bar. However fascinating the topic, there is only so much information that the human mind can be subjected to in one day without switching off, and it was a credit to their presentation skills and the humour that they managed to work into what is a fairly dry and academic topic – "high-frequency trading and liquidity discovery" – that their audience followed their every word with rapt attention.

The other sign that a presentation has been well received is the number of people who come up to the speaker afterwards, either just to make contact and exchange business cards or, better still, to ask questions and to propose follow-up meetings. After the presentation the two men were surrounded by a large crowd: there was the usual mix of familiar faces and, most importantly for them, a number of potential clients who wanted to know how they too could tap into their expertise. Business cards and pleasantries were exchanged – the two were old hands at this game: don't let yourself get buttonholed by anyone because the person who gets tired of waiting to speak to you, gives up and walks away could've turned out to be a future big client or important contact. Never burn bridges, never miss the chance to talk to someone and be nice to them – next year they could be your boss. Finally, the crowd dispersed and the two were left sitting on the step of the conference room podium.

'Did you speak to those two guys from Noviprom?'

'No.' said Tom, 'I didn't even know they had anyone here, they don't normally get out much. Funny, I'm sure they weren't on the delegate list.'

'You'll never know what you missed. They were really strange. Kind of intense, really,' said Liebowitz, and showed Tom the two business cards he'd been given. 'These names mean anything to you?'

'Hmmm. Both MDs – they've obviously sent the highly-paid help this time but I don't know the names - wouldn't even try pronouncing them. Why d'you ask?'

Liebowitz shrugged. 'Oh, no real reason. They just seemed

incredibly keen to talk to us this evening. You'd have thought their lives depended on it, but they wouldn't say what it was about. If it was about starting up a trading relationship I'd have thought they'd have said so. It's not as if that's so desperately urgent that it can't wait till after the conference when we can sort things out properly.'

'Do you reckon compliance would let us take them on as a client anyway?' Tom said with a frown. 'There's some pretty murky stuff going on out there at the moment. According to *The Economist*, most of the Noviprom board are connected either directly or at one remove to the president of Nashyastan and his family. I'm not even sure I'd want the business.'

'Well,' said Liebowitz, 'If what they say in the press is true – and after all, half the world's heroin addicts can't be wrong – they sound like a bunch of regular guys.'

***

There were nearly one hundred and fifty delegates at the conference and the Liberty Belle was more akin to a small liner than a simple pleasure craft. The weather and the setting were perfect: it was about an hour before sunset and for mid-September, the notoriously fickle Newport climate had smiled on them with still, warm conditions, and the waters of Narragansett Bay were almost flat calm. Once on board, everyone made for the top deck and Caroline and Sally sat in the stern, basking in the sun and enjoying their cocktails while the two men circulated.

The Liberty Belle eased her way slowly between the yachts and small craft in the harbour and headed out into the sound, swinging northwest and picking up speed to head towards the Jamestown shoreline and the Newport Bridge.

Liebowitz returned from the bar clutching two cold bottles of beer.

'Hey, Tom. Take a look at Bert and Ernie in the suits over there. Those are the guys I told you about. Shit, me and my big mouth – looks like they've spotted us, and we're too far out to swim for it.'

They weren't hard to miss. Just about all the other delegates were in casual clothing, but the two thickset men who approached them were still in the same expensively-tailored suits that they'd been wearing for the conference sessions. Both sported close-cropped haircuts and designer sunglasses, giving them the air of B-movie gangsters. Tom was surprised to note that one of them, the taller of the two, whose blobby nose, single black eyebrow and residual tuft of dark hair did indeed make him look remarkably like Ernie from *Sesame Street*, was barely out of his twenties: young for a senior executive of a sovereign wealth fund in any country. The older man who looked as though he was approaching sixty and was almost as broad as he was high, removed his sunglasses and introduced himself.

'Mr Mansell, Mr Liebowitz, my name is Igor Kaliski and this is my colleague, Vladimir Ursk. We represent our nation's sovereign wealth management authority, Noviprom.' He turned to David. 'We spoke earlier, Mr Liebowitz, after the excellent presentation you both gave today.'

'Hello again. Very pleased you enjoyed it, Mr Kaliski.'

They spoke grammatically perfect, although heavily-accented, English but what Kaliski said after the usual introductory small talk came as a surprise.

'I will get straight to the point, gentlemen – we are very direct in my country and I will apologise in advance if this seems abrupt. We have been very impressed by the presentations you have given during the conference so far and we are looking forward to hearing what you have to say tomorrow. However, what has impressed us most is the performance of your company's alternative execution service desk over the recent months. You are not easy to detect in the markets, but we feel that we now have a good knowledge of how you trade and some knowledge of why you trade in that way. You are highly respected in our country.'

Looks like we've got ourselves a new customer and a new compliance headache, thought Liebowitz and Tom simultaneously.

'After long discussions with our board and with our minister of finance, we are honoured to invite you to come and work for Noviprom: both of you. You will be very rich.' He mentioned a colossal amount of money.

Tom was lost for words. Christ almighty, he thought, you're not hiring casual labour on a street corner, you know. This wasn't how you tried to poach a team to come and work for you. There were protocols; there were lunches, dammit; discussions; hints and so on. It was all about relationships and trust. These guys don't even know us, haven't even got our CVs for Christ's sake. It was supposed to be a courtship, not "get your coat, you've pulled." Full marks for directness, he thought, but this is how you pick up hookers, not how you hire professional trading teams.

Tom glanced towards the stern of the boat where the girls were sitting. The surreal atmosphere of the setting for the Noviprom approach was magnified by the presence of the chief conference organiser who was now in conversation with Sally and Caroline. In keeping with the nautical theme of the evening, he was wearing a large, white, Father Christmas false beard, an eye-patch, a captain's peaked hat with a nautical badge, and on his shoulder was a toy parrot. If Noviprom had invited them to come and sail with them as pirates it would've made about as much sense. Where do I start? thought Tom.

He cast a look briefly at his colleague and then back at the two men from Noviprom whom he steered discreetly by the shoulder towards the ship's rail. 'Can we just move over this way please, gentlemen, where it's a little quieter? I'd prefer not to shout.' He checked around him again to make sure they were not being overheard and then continued. 'Mr Kaliski, Mr Ursk, it's difficult to know where to start and I hope you'll forgive me if I seem a little taken aback by your offer. It's not that we're not grateful and extremely honoured by what you've proposed, it just came as rather a surprise. If I understand correctly, your company does not have a London office, is that correct?'

'Yes, that is correct.'

'So therefore, if we came to work with you we would be

based…?'

'In our capital, Novi Bar.'

'I'm sure it's a wonderful place, but in terms of a career move, it's not exactly what either of us had in mind, is it, David?'

'No, that's right. Neither Mr Mansell nor I really want to move away from, how shall I put this? – an established financial centre.'

'But Novi Bar is the established financial centre of the Nashyastan Republic. You would be extremely rich and pay no tax – I will see to that personally. Money will not be an issue, gentlemen.'

This is sheer bloody madness, thought Tom. We've got to get out of this conversation, and fast. 'Gentlemen,' he said, 'as you would expect, this isn't the first time that we've had an offer like this, although never in quite as direct a way, and never on a pleasure cruiser. And, may I add, although it's always a great honour, it's not the first time that we've turned one down. As I'm sure you'll agree, this is not exactly a private setting and I'm very uncomfortable discussing something as delicate as this in public. If anyone has overheard us, and I hope they haven't, then the rumours that will start won't do any of our reputations any good, so I really must insist, with the greatest of respect, that we stop this conversation right now.'

'I understand, Mr Mansell. We are a very direct people – some consider us rude – and English is not my first language, so please accept my apologies. I agree we should continue this conversation in private; let us say, when we get back to the hotel.'

'I'm sorry, gentlemen, I apologise if I wasn't clear earlier, but I don't think you've fully understood me. You say that you are very direct in your country, so I'm sure you'll understand if I myself am direct with you. Much as we are both extremely flattered, there is nothing further to discuss on this matter and we do not wish to join your company. Now if you don't mind, I'm going to join my wife for a drink. Please excuse me.'

They left the two Noviprom men on their own at the rail and headed for the stern to rejoin Sally and Caroline.

'Jeez. Which part of central casting did they get those two clowns from?' said Liebowitz. 'I know we're all whores in this business, but that was only one step away from "me plenty dollar, you me do jig-a-jig".'

Tom was now in fits of laughter. He had managed to suppress the attack of giggles that was rapidly gaining on him until the two men from Noviprom were out of sight, but now he was laughing so much, the tears were rolling down his face. 'So you don't fancy living in Novi Bar then?'

'Well, normally I'm a big fan of Soviet-era concrete, corruption, drive-by shootings and winters where it's minus forty for nine months of the year but, you know, my Elbonian is a little rusty these days and there are only so many yaks a guy can take care of, so I think I'll skip it this time.'

'Yeah, but, David, think of the cosy warm glow from all that nuclear waste. You'd never be cold even at minus forty.'

'Nah, still not convinced.'

The ship rounded the northern tip of Gould Island and swung south to follow the Newport side of the bay. As they passed the Naval base and crossed back under the bridge, it was already getting dark and a chill breeze now ruffled the water.

By the time they docked it was fully dark and the lights from the marquee where the clam bake was to be held reflected in the waters of the bay. Everyone agreed the food was excellent, but there was just too much of it.

After the main course, Tom went back to their room to fetch Sally's cardigan. On the bed was a surprise: one of the conference sponsors had obviously got the hotel room staff to do it, because in the middle of the bed, which had been turned down, was a present, wrapped in gold paper with a label bearing the sponsor's logo. He opened the parcel to find a very attractive pair of miniature binoculars, again, decorated with the same logo, but what brought him up short was the other package on the bed. It too was delicately wrapped and tied with a bow, but attached to it was a label bearing the same logo he'd seen on two business cards earlier: Noviprom.

What the hell is this? he thought, as he tore off the wrapping. Inside were two slim oblong boxes, about six inches long with the name of a very well known and very expensive Swiss watch manufacturer embossed in gold on the lid. He opened one and inside was a man's watch – he wasn't intimately familiar with the maker's catalogue, relying as he did on a cheap, plastic digital number that he'd bought from a catalogue shop, but this one he knew must be somewhere near the top of the range and must cost, he thought, about $50,000. That was without the gold and diamonds with which both the face, hands and case were decorated. In the other box was a lady's version of the same watch; equally gaudy, equally tasteless and equally ridiculously expensive. On the label was a handwritten message, "A small token of our esteem. Looking forward to continuing our discussions in London very soon." Esteem? fumed Tom. This is an out and out bribe and if I get caught coming back through customs with this thing round my wrist……

He took out his mobile phone. 'David? It's Tom. We've got a problem, a serious one. Can you please come up to my room now – it's 504 – but make it look casual. I'll tell you about it when you get here.'

'Wow, that's about two hundred and fifty thousand dollars worth of watch. And the lady's one can't be far off that either.'

Tom showed him the gift label.

'Oh, shit, what's the betting I've got the same package? I'll be back.'

Two minutes later he reappeared. Sure enough, same presents, same message.

'Shit! These have got to go back. What do you reckon, David – disclosed or undisclosed?'

The program trading analogy brought a smile to Liebowitz's face.

'Disclosed.'

'Done, and at five basis points! I don't care how much we piss them off, we don't want them as a client, especially not after this. And I think that doing it openly, but of course very diplomatically, sends just the right message. You ready?'

Liebowitz nodded. 'Fully disclosed it is.'

'OK, let's go.'

He wrapped the watches in Sally's cardigan to hide them from view and the two men returned to the marquee.

Tom folded back a corner of the material, holding it such that only they could see. 'Sally, Caroline, just take a little peek at what's in here.'

Caroline's big brown eyes went wide with amazement. 'Where on earth did you get those from?'

'They were a gift from some not very wise men from the east and they're going straight back. Now.'

Replacing the lids, Tom collected the four slim boxes, slipped them into his jacket pocket and stood up. Liebowitz made to come with him.

Tom put his hand on his friend's shoulder. 'It's alright, David. I'll do this. We don't want to rub it in too hard – I'm happy for the other people on their table to see, but it's not fair on everyone else if we start a scene.'

By this time, the party was beginning to break up and groups of people were heading back indoors to the disco which had just started, so Tom's arrival at the Noviprom table did not raise any eyebrows. He spoke softly.

'Do excuse me for interrupting, ladies and gentlemen. Mr Kaliski, may I have a quick word please? I believe these belong to you.' And with that he placed the four boxes gently on the table, turned and set off back the way he had come before Kaliski even had time to open his mouth.

'What did he say, Tom?' said Liebowitz.

'Nothing. I didn't give him time. I didn't make a fuss about it, just said that I thought they belonged to him and left it at that. If he's got half an ounce of sense, we won't be hearing from Mr Kaliski again. I'll report this to compliance as soon as we get back so that we're completely in the clear.'

'Tom, darling. What on earth is this all about?'

'I'll tell you later.' Engrossed in their own conversations, none of the other people on the table seemed to have noticed the small drama being played out in front of them, but he wanted to be sure that it stayed that way, '*Pas devant les enfants,*' he said. 'Anyway, what can you expect from a nation that doesn't play cricket? Present company excepted, of course,' he added, grinning at Liebowitz.

Chapter Eleven

Life in France was good for the Mansells. Sally had joined the local cycling club which helped to keep her both occupied and fit. It seemed to Tom that the memory of what had happened to her in London was at last beginning to lose its grip, and her fears of being followed appeared to have gone too. As for him, he'd got used to his regular weeks back in London, although leaving France was always a wrench. He had even turned out for the village rugby team when they were a man short on a couple of occasions, much to Sally's dismay; and also helped out with training the village junior team.

Tom had also managed to complete the necessary paperwork to get his pilot's licence accredited for use in France and had started taking lessons to polish up his rusty aerobatics. The local *aéroclub* had a couple of Cap 10 aircraft on its books and he'd been amazed at how quickly his instructor had moved him on from the basic loops and rolls to more advanced manoeuvres. These involved an uncomfortable amount of negative g, and he also learned to use the gyroscopic effect generated by the aircraft's propeller to carry out a manoeuvre known as a Lomcovak. The first time his instructor showed him one of these, Tom described it as like being inside a washing machine on a fast spin cycle.

It was now autumn: the pool was covered for the year, the leaves were turning and the tourists had all gone home. One crisp, sunny Saturday morning, Tom was working in the garden at Mas des Oliviers. Sally had popped into the village.

'Christ, what was that?' The crack of a high-velocity rifle rang out from nearby. The round slammed into the umbrella pine and brought down one of its lower branches. He'd been planting a shrub only about twenty feet away and was now very alarmed. Someone was shooting at him. This isn't possible, he thought and suddenly his mind raced with what Sally had told him about being followed. What if she'd been right all along?

Another bang, shouting, barking and crashing; and with that

an enormous wild boar burst through the hedge, tore across the garden, out through the open back gate, up the slope and into the scrubby woods beyond. He cursed, threw down his spade – he knew exactly what this was – and went out into the lane to remonstrate with whichever idiot had nearly killed him. A group of ten or so *chasseurs*, each with a high-velocity rifle was milling about in the lane and their dogs were snuffling about in the base of the hedge trying to work out where the boar had gone.

Every year, French enthusiasm for hunting overcomes firearms safety training and several people die, usually fellow hunters, walkers or mushroom pickers after being mistaken for game species, despite their absence of antlers, tusks or fur. The fact that boar and deer rarely, if ever, cycle, wear hats or high-visibility jackets, never seems to enter into consideration either. Hunters in France take their sport and themselves very seriously: they have a strict code of conduct; exams have to be taken before a *permis de chasser* can be obtained; none of which prevents the annual death toll, either from negligent firearm discharges or from blind drunk incompetents firing on anything that moves.

As he strode down the lane to confront them he noticed that they seemed to have no notion of basic safety. Even in the cadet corps at school and on the University Air Squadron, he had been taught never to point a weapon, whether loaded or unloaded, at anyone; but these jokers were swinging their rifles around as they chatted or called to their dogs, and on more than one occasion as he walked towards them he had the disconcerting experience of looking down the barrel of a loaded gun.

They greeted his complaints about their stupidity and lack of common sense with studied indifference. The general consensus seemed to be that this was all perfectly normal; they were hunting, they were shooting at a boar – the biggest one they'd seen all season – and how were they to know there was a house behind a tall hedge of cypresses? The inference was that if anyone was so inconsiderate and thoughtless as to build a house in an area where *les chasseurs* might at some stage fancy doing a spot of boar hunting, well that was their look-out. What do you expect?

In fairness, they did promise not to fire near his property again, if possible, and then asked – demanded would be more accurate – to be allowed through his garden to pursue their quarry. They seemed quite put out at his refusal but grudgingly admiring of the Englishman's ability to swear at them in their own language. Tom chased the remaining dogs out of the garden and returned to his digging. He'd talk to the mayor about these idiots on Monday.

***

Being in any big, crowded city on your own can be one of the loneliest experiences in the world, and London is no different. To Andrew Chivers it seemed as though he was surrounded by eight million antagonistic strangers whose sole aim was either to get in the way, keep him waiting, insult him or invade his space. He wandered aimlessly across Green Park from Piccadilly towards the Palace, in the vain hope that fresh air and exercise would clear his head and somehow bring inspiration. Sunday, he'd decided was the most depressing day of the week – why anyone in their right mind could wish for a month of Sundays was beyond him – from midday onwards it always had a big black cloud called Monday lowering over it.

His mood had not been improved by either of the two phone calls he had received. On Friday his lawyer had called from New York: Stacey had started a divorce action on the grounds of his alleged "cruel and inhuman treatment" and had already outlined an eye-wateringly expensive list of demands. He was at a loss to recall anything he'd done that was even vaguely "cruel and inhuman" unless you included not listening when she was shouting, or asking her to limit her spending. Now he came to think of it, he'd put up with a lot – all those get-fit obsessions of hers: she couldn't just play tennis, she had to have the best equipment, expensive lessons, membership of the best clubs; then it was gym equipment; then it was golf; then she had to have a sailing dinghy that she'd used all of twice. Cruel and inhuman treatment to my damn bank-balance more like it, he fumed.

He had no idea how this was going to end. Whatever the outcome, it was unlikely to be good and he now felt embittered and hostile towards her, something he had never done, even at the height of her tirades, or when she was off on one of her fads. This could cost him a fortune, most of his 401(k) savings plan and a big chunk of his pension, not to mention a half share of an apartment which was already worth less than they'd paid for it thanks to the crash in real estate values.

As if that wasn't enough, Sam Bortoleski had called while he was out walking.

'What do you mean, "nothing yet?"' snapped Bortoleski.

'I've asked him outright, I've tried appealing to his better nature, told him he should reconsider the offer – everything...'

'You call that "everything", Andrew? You're gonna tell me you tried saying "please" next. If this shit was easy, I could've got someone else to do it. You've got six weeks, starting Monday or you're gone. Got that?'

'Sam, this isn't a good time for me. Stacey's filed for divorce and she's out to ruin me financially.' As soon as he'd said it he realised that he'd made an error. He'd shown himself up as weak and was asking for pity – bad move.

'Andrew, my dog has piles and the vet's bills are killing me. Even the dog says it's a pain in the ass. Your personal life, however trying, is your own affair and not mine. Six weeks, Andrew, six weeks.' With that the line went dead.

It had come on to rain again, one of his shoes was leaking and he hadn't got a clue what to do about Mansell and that wretched system of his. He paused under a tree to shelter from the rain. A squirrel was watching him from its perch on the back of a park bench and holding an acorn in its front paws. He stooped down, picked up a stone and threw it at the animal in frustration. It missed and the squirrel skittered off out of range up the tree, scolding as it went.

A voice from behind made him spin round in surprise. He hadn't seen or heard the stranger approach. 'Mr Chivers? You don't know me but my name is Igor Kaliski.'

Chapter Twelve

Tom was deep in discussion with two representatives from a rival bank's program trading desk. The annual London meeting of Financial Information Exchange Protocol Limited, or FIX to its friends, was always a lively social gathering.

He felt someone touch him discreetly on the arm, turned, and saw a familiar if unwelcome face.

'Mr Mansell, what a very pleasant surprise.'

'Hello, Mr Kaliski. This is indeed a surprise,' said Tom, diplomatically. 'What brings you to London?'

'We are here visiting our London office. Did you know that Noviprom has opened an office in London and that we are now members of FIX Protocol Limited?'

'Yes, I'd seen that. Congratulations.'

The conversation Tom had been part of gradually closed ranks and drifted away. He was now alone with Kaliski. Where the hell was David?

'I apologise if there was any misunderstanding when we last met, Mr Mansell. It was never my intention....'

Tom interrupted him.

'No, Mr Kaliski, there was no misunderstanding. Even as a self-employed contractor with the bank, while I'm working for them, I cannot receive gifts over a certain value, particularly if the gift in question is an inducement to break my contract.' Help, David, where are you?

'How very English.' Kaliski's mouth smiled, but his eyes didn't. 'Listen, Mr Mansell, as well as being direct, I am, as you would say, stubborn. I can understand that neither you nor Mr Liebowitz wish to move to a country whose culture and language you do not know, but now that we have an office in London, that impediment is no longer there and I would like to renew my offer to you.' Tom was about to speak, but Kaliski held up his hand. 'Please hear me out, Mr Mansell. I understand that you are in the enviable position of owning the intellectual property rights to the

Minerva system that your bank uses to such good effect. I congratulate you. Therefore, as part of our revised offer, we will pay you an annual licence fee for the use of your software and we will double the salary we mentioned to you in Newport. If taxation is an issue, we are happy to pay for you to relocate anywhere you wish: Switzerland, Monaco, anywhere tax-efficient – it's entirely up to you. Now, I don't need you to give me an answer straight away: my colleagues and I are leaving shortly and we would like you to come with us so that we can introduce you to some of our friends who I am sure would love to entertain you.'

'Friends?'

'Lady friends, Mr Mansell.'

'Prostitutes, you mean?'

'I find that such a vulgar word, Mr Mansell. I much prefer "lady friends", it has a much nicer ring to it I always feel.'

Tom, fighting to suppress his fury, spoke clearly and deliberately. 'Mr Kaliski, please listen to me very carefully. You spoke earlier of cultures that people may not know. You are clearly incapable of understanding the cultural or ethical framework within which I choose to operate. In September, you offered me a job in very much the same way as I would imagine you recruit your "lady friends". When I said no, and very clearly at that, you then tried to bribe me. I returned the bribe at once and reported the matter to the bank's compliance department. Now, once again, you try to bribe me and to add insult to injury, you imply that I'm so feeble-minded that a quick, soulless fuck with some disease-ridden whore you happen to have in tow is going to influence my decision. What I want you to do now, Kaliski, is to turn round, go over there to the cloakroom, collect your coat and leave. The alternative is that I will physically remove you from here, which I guarantee will hurt, and I will then call the police. Have I made myself clear?'

'Oh, yes, Mr Mansell. Perfectly clear. You are a very foolish man; very, very foolish. Do not worry, I am leaving but you will hear from me again.'

Tom took a step towards him and Kaliski turned and scuttled

towards the cloakroom.

He found David sitting dejectedly on a seat at the far end of the room in which the reception was being held. 'You all right?'

'Not really.'

'Did you just get buttonholed by someone from Noviprom?'

'Yeah. It was that fucking asshole Ursk that we met on the boat.'

'But what did he say to you for God's sake, man? You look as though you've seen a ghost.'

'Nothing, it really doesn't matter. I told him to get lost.'

'David, tell me, what did he say? Where is he? I'll kill the bastard.'

'Leave it, Tom. It's over, he's gone. I don't want to talk about it.'

'You're probably right. It's not worth getting steamed up about a bunch of idiots like that. Did Ursk offer you hookers, by the way?'

David nodded.

'Yeah, me too. I guess that's how business get's done in their crummy swamp of a country.'

'A crummy swamp with almost half the world's oil reserves.'

'True – no one ever said life was fair though, did they? Come on, let's go and grab a curry, that'll cheer you up.'

David shook his head. 'No thanks, Tom. I'm just going to head for home, thanks.'

'OK. I'm going to have a quick catch up with the guys from the Deutsche Börse and then I'll head off too. See you tomorrow.'

Tom stayed longer at the reception than he'd intended and it was after nine o'clock when he set off down Bishopsgate towards London Bridge. A black Lexus with darkened windows swung out of Fenchurch Street. It continued slowly down Gracechurch Street, caught up with him just before he reached the Monument and then took the slip road to turn left into Eastcheap.

***

94

The following morning David Liebowitz seemed to be back to normal. If anything, was even more lively and full of ideas than usual.

'Ah, Tom. Morning. This is great timing. Put your stuff down, come with me…no, no, don't bother logging in. You'll like this, I think it's a great idea.'

They went into an empty office off the trading floor.

Liebowitz explained his idea. 'So what do you think, Tom?'

'I think that you should get a leather chair, a white cat and start planning world domination. It's a great idea provided we don't get sacked for it.'

'What can they sack us for? I've gone down the list and we're completely clean.' He ticked the points off on his fingers. 'They're not a client so we can't be accused of front-running them. There's no conflict of interest. We're not manipulating the market and we're not *really* mis-using bank assets. Hell, we'll make the bank money.'

'It's the "not really" bit that worries me,' said Tom. 'Who else have you spoken to about this?'

'The prop desk. They're up for it.'

'I'll bet they are. What about funding?'

'It'll go across the prop desk's books, they'll do the funding, they give us half of any profit they make.'

'And if we make a loss?'

'We won't, that's what I want to show you. Look.'

David slid his laptop out of its bag and turned it on.

'This is a simulation of how Noviprom trade. Watch the heat map on the left. It's speeded up but this runs through a week's activity against all the triggers and indices we have. They're slow, clunky and predictable.'

Tom watched the lines and surfaces of the heat map move, converge and diverge as the sequence played out on the screen. 'And you want to risk your job by taking them for the suckers they so clearly are?'

Liebowitz nodded in reply. 'Risk is minimal, don't worry.'

Tom continued his scrutiny of the Noviprom algorithm's

trading pattern with a frown on his face, 'Beats me how they got a man into space before the Americans. If this is the best they can do after all that time, their rocket must've needed a bloody great milk bottle to launch it.'

'How quickly can you write something to handle it?' asked Liebowitz.

'Day or so, call it two, I've got something that I can adapt pretty easily. Then I'll need a couple more days' data to back test it against.'

'I've got that.'

'Day after tomorrow then. Have you mentioned this to Chivers, by the way?'

'You kidding? He might say no, and then what?'

'I'll tell you the "then what" that worries me. We need to have our story ready for if and when this comes to light. I'm doing some tweaks to a couple of the algos we can use for this little venture anyway and if I was really to stretch a point, I could claim that this was live testing focussed on one particular market participant, which is true but not for the reasons anyone will think it is. I can also say we have proof that it didn't have a material impact on any of the bank's clients. I'm still not sure I like it, you know.'

'Come on, Tom. It'll be fun.'

They went live on the Thursday and the next day Tom flew back to France.

On Tuesday afternoon, Liebowitz called in a state of high excitement.

'*How* much?' asked Tom, aghast.

'Forty million US and they pulled out of the market this morning. We took a small hit when we unwound some of the positions, but I wanted that to happen so that they would be in no doubt as to who'd done it to them.'

'They won't send you a Christmas card, you know.'

Liebowitz laughed. 'So what does a good Jewish boy like me care about Christmas cards, already?'

'Does Chivers know about what's happened?'

'Don't think so. The jump in the proprietary trading desk's profit figures – and ours too, come to that – is going to take some explaining, but in all the years I've been working in this place I've never known anyone ask difficult questions about good profit numbers other than "how can I take the credit for stuff I didn't do?",' said Liebowitz.

'That is brilliant news. Tell the prop desk they owe us drinks: lots of drinks.

'While I remember, has Chivers been giving you any grief about how Minerva's hosted, where the intellectual property sits and so on?'

'He mentions it from time to time, but it's more of a background grumble about how stupid the bank was and that you should've accepted their offer and so on. Why d'you ask?'

'It's just that he phoned me the other day from the office – quite late too, it was after nine in the evening here, so just after eight UK time – and he kept on and on and on about it. Nothing heavy, nothing I hadn't heard before, just the usual violin music: emotional blackmail; appealing to my better nature; doing the right thing by the bank because letting me work from home was such a huge favour and so on.'

'You're not telling me you're suffering are you, Tom?'

'No, not in the slightest. I'm the luckiest bastard alive and I know it. I just asked him to explain to me how it was that work was only of value to an organisation if its workers suffered while carrying it out.'

'What did he say to that?'

'Nothing. He couldn't. No, I was just wondering if you knew what had prompted him to start on at me about ownership of Minerva again, that's all.'

'Perhaps he's seen the numbers and wants to revisit the idea of moving to the prop desk.'

'Don't think so,' said Tom. 'I think we all agree that Minerva should be a proprietary trading system rather than being used for client order facilitation, and your little scheme is proof positive. Rumour has it that the block on that move is coming from way above even Bortoleski's pay grade. I'm probably making mountains out of molehills, but it was just that Chivers seemed almost – I don't know how to put this – almost desperate somehow.'

'He's just weird, Tom. That's all.'

'True, and well done again for taking those bastards like that. It's true what they say about "a dish best eaten cold", but you still haven't told me what Ursk said that upset you so much.'

'I'll tell you one day, just not now. OK?'

***

Kaliski closed the door behind him and headed for the elevator. His conversation with the president about the $40 million loss had been one-sided and unpleasant. He loosened his tie – God, how he hated wearing those things – and shoved his hands deep into his pockets. One year to recoup what he'd spent so far on setting up the London office and to show an annualised ten percent growth. Great, just bloody great.

He stumped through the one working door onto the trading floor. More puddles, he thought, still not fixed that leak. 'Come in here, Ursk,' he shouted through the flimsy partition that separated their offices. 'I need to talk to you. We've got work to do.'

The younger man joined him and sat down on the hard steel chair in front of the desk. 'What's up?' he asked.

'Your uncle isn't happy.'

'Didn't think he would be. Forty million Dollars is a lot of money.'

'All right, point taken, I didn't ask you to come in here just so you could state the obvious. It's serious and it affects you too. The bad news is that we've got one year to recoup what we've spent so far and then show an annualised ten percent growth on top. The good news is that we've got outside help: we've been given free rein to increase staff numbers in the London office and your uncle has put a detachment of the NFSB at our disposal.'

At the mention of the feared military arm of the Nashyastan

secret police, Ursk let out a whistle. 'So what's the plan, do we get to kill them for this? I'd like to kill that little Jew myself.' His eyes lit up with joy at the prospect.

'Ursk, you don't get any brighter, do you?' Kaliski shook his head in despair. If it wasn't your uncle sitting upstairs in that overheated mausoleum of an office of his, he thought, you'd be plodding the streets giving out parking tickets for a living. 'No, if we kill either of them, then who creates the algorithms and who does the development? If Mansell is dead, how can he sell us the rights to Minerva? Do try and be sensible. We're just going to have to be a lot more intelligent about how we approach things and use our new resources in order to be a hell of a lot more persuasive. Now, do you follow me?'

'I'm looking forward to this,' said Ursk with a smile.

Chapter Thirteen

Tom was getting used to the regular trips to London but each time, the underlying sense of aggression, the crowds and the sheer foulness of the British climate came as an unpleasant shock as though he were encountering them for the first time.

He'd finished the coding he was doing for a new statistical arbitrage strategy and was reviewing the finer details of their new, successful and highly-targeted trading strategy that they had trialled a month earlier.

His concentration was broken by a familiar voice. 'You staying the night here or are you coming for a beer?'

'Tricky one, David. Give me two minutes and I'll be right there.'

They made an odd couple as they left the building and crossed the small landscaped area that separated the bank from the path down to the Thames: one was a tiny, bird-like figure who walked with a rapid, jerky pace in order to keep up with the long strides of the taller man next to him. The early flurries of snow had turned to sleety rain; the wind blowing in off the river was glacial and Tom, who just a few days earlier had been enjoying milder climes, wrapped his coat around himself to keep out the cold.

'I see you didn't invite Chivers, then?' said Tom. 'After our conversation a few weeks ago, he's barely spoken to me since I got here.'

'Nah, I've given up,' replied the smaller man. 'He won't socialise with any of us – he had lunch with Denise the other day, but that's as far as it goes. He's been in this industry long enough to know what's expected of you even if you don't enjoy it. Drinks with the troops is a duty, even an uptight, clean-living American like me knows that much. Look at Matt – complete asshole, but at least he knew the rules of the game – and Chivers is a Brit so he ought to know better.'

'So we're all drunks, are we?'

'Did I ever say that was a bad thing?'

After the chill of the evening air, the atmosphere of the Cock Linnet hit them like walking into soup.

They took their drinks to a corner as far away from the hubbub at the bar as possible. A group of secretaries were just leaving and the two men managed to grab their table.

Liebowitz continued his thread. 'Tom, I think you need to be very careful. I've been doing some research on our friend Chivers and I'm not hearing anything good. In his last job they called him the Prince of Darkness and none of the ex-Lehmans people I've spoken to have a good word to say about him – very good at his job they said and a very good trader, but a real smiling knife – stab you in the back anytime he thought it would be good for his career. Same deal at Citi apparently, but he'd have had the chance to learn from the best there.'

'A real charmer,' said Tom.

'I didn't want to say anything this morning because I wanted to be 100% sure of my facts. I had lunch with Malcolm Marshall today. We were at O'Connor together, and he knows Chivers from when they were both at Lehmans.'

'And?'

'Not good, Tom. Hatchet man, very political, smiling knife, doesn't trust him: all the same things I heard from the other guys. There were rumours that he was "invited to resign" from Citi but Mal said he didn't know why.'

'Do we know *anything* about him? Like where he lives, married, kids, gay/straight, hobbies, that kind of thing.'

Liebowitz shook his head. 'No. Nothing at all. Prefers tea to coffee, but that's about it. Asks lots of questions and you can have a perfectly sensible conversation with him so long as you stick to work-related stuff. But as for getting any sense of what he's really like: forget it. Not that there's necessarily anything sinister about that,' he added. 'There are enough borderline autistics in this industry without worrying about one more. Oh, yeah. Forgot to tell you, you know Graham Fleming?'

Tom knew him well and had been delighted when Fleming had been appointed head of equities IT.

'Sure I know him. Why?'

'Got laid off this morning.'

'Shit. You're kidding?'

'Nope. No kidding. There were five of them got let go.' Liebowitz mentioned the names, two of which were familiar to Tom. 'Couple of guys from the New York team went too. That makes at least fifteen since June. Looks like the usual cost-cutting crap: get rid of the good guys and bring in someone cheap and no damn good.'

'But you can't do that,' said Tom. 'Under UK law, if you make someone redundant because their job's no longer required, it's illegal to hire someone into the same role.'

'So it is in the States, but when did that ever stop them? There are a hundred-and-one ways round it and what can you do about it anyway? They've just given you one hundred thousand Sterling to go away – what are you going to do, Joe Schmuck, sue one of the world's largest financial institutions and play "let's see who blinks first" or do you take the money and go? I know what I'd do.'

'Yeah, suppose you're right. Never looked at it that way,' said Tom. 'At the rate they're letting people go there'll just be HR and the Diversity department left.'

At about nine o'clock, leaving David Liebowitz chatting to a group of colleagues, Tom left the bar and headed for the Canary Wharf Tube station. A fine drizzle had set in and he had the dockside path to himself. He noticed that one of the bars they sometimes drank in was closed and surrounded by scaffolding. He vaguely recalled a noise – the wind flapping a loose piece of plastic sheeting. A vivid flash of light exploded in his head and he was aware that he was falling, that he had hit the ground and that someone was kicking him in the ribs. Another rain of blows came and he put his hands up to protect his face. He struggled to remain conscious and was aware of a pulling, tugging sensation and the shoulder-strap of his laptop giving way. Running feet, rain on plastic sheeting. Then nothing.

Tom's head swam and the wooden decking he was lying on seemed to be turning on its own axis. His head hurt abominably and he felt sick. He tried to sit up but the pain in his right side forced him back into a lying position. He looked up. He was aware that he could see perfectly well out of his left eye, but that his right wouldn't open properly. In a funny sort of way, the drizzle on his face felt almost comforting and in his confused state he considered just lying there till this all went away.

Slowly, his head cleared and as full consciousness returned, the waves of pain became worse.

The bastards have taken my laptop, he thought. Of all the suits going home from the pub with their laptops, why for Christ's sake take mine? I have work to do, I do not need this. He sat up, rolled on to his left elbow and was violently sick. He got his mobile phone out to call the police but thought better of it. Get back to the pub and wait in the warm and dry, that's what I'll do. Must phone Sally. No, don't: she'll go frantic.

'Jesus Christ! What happened to you?' Liebowitz's eyes were wide with amazement.

The noise of conversation in the Cock Linnet stopped dead. Framed in the doorway was an apparition: bleeding from the nose and mouth, with a right eye closed by an ugly purple bruise and his clothes wet through, torn and covered in mud.

Liebowitz ushered Tom to a seat. The barman came running round from behind the bar to help.

With great care, the two paramedics guided Tom to the ambulance. They were efficient and gentle and Tom, in his groggy state, found the sound of the sirens and the reflections of the blue flashing lights vaguely surreal as though none of this had anything to do with him.

The paramedic sitting with him leant over and said, 'Sorry it's taking so long. Royal London's a bit busy tonight – must've started early – so we're just sorting out where they've got room for you. Thursday's when it starts getting busy you see, what with the fights and the drunks an' all. They'll probably need to keep you in overnight just to make sure you don't have an intracranial bleed.'

The accident and emergency department at St Edmund's

Hospital, on the edge of the City, was like a neon-lit war zone. It was only ten thirty at night, but a drunk was lying in the middle of the floor in the recovery position next to a pool of vomit. Others were propped up in plastic chairs, bleeding, ranting or comatose. An over-excited little man in a brown and white robe was shouting at a nurse in Bengali and waving his arms. The ambulance crew dealt with the admissions nurse, settled Tom in a seat, wished him luck, stepped over the drunk and left. The nurse re-appeared with her clipboard and asked him a series of questions – in the interests of simplicity he gave his address as that of Brian's grotty flat. He declined the offer of an interpreter, confirmed he was not a rape victim and gave his ethnic group as Eskimo. Shortly afterwards he was led into a cubicle by a doctor who asked him most of the same questions as the nurse, gave him a cursory examination, ran the basic tests for concussion and then informed Tom that he'd suffered a bang on the head and had bruised ribs – no kidding, thought Tom – and that he'd be kept in overnight for observation. The rest of the conversation was cut short by a commotion in the waiting room: the nurse with the clipboard had been attacked by one of the drunks and a policeman was now wrestling her assailant to the ground.

'How did the police get here so quickly?' he asked the doctor.

'Oh, that's simple, we have a police station on site. Did you see the grille on the other side of the waiting room? Well, that's our little police station and on Thursday, Friday and weekend evenings we have two full-time policemen here in A&E.'

After about half an hour back in the waiting room, a tired-looking policeman invited Tom to step into their office. Tom told him about the mugging and that his laptop had been stolen. From the line of questioning, it became clear to Tom that the policeman was more concerned about the fact that Tom had been drinking, and kept asking him about the extent to which he may have provoked his assailants and whether he had assaulted anybody. His head was hurting and he ached all over: he just didn't need this. He was given a crime number, but declined to make a victim personal statement and was returned to the waiting room.

Time wore on, more drunks and broken bodies arrived. It was now nearly midnight.

'Excuse me, nurse. Have you any idea when someone's going to be able to see me?'

She smiled at Tom. 'Oh, shouldn't be more than another three or four hours, we're very busy tonight and a bit short-handed you see and one of our x-ray machines is broken.'

'I thought there was something where all patients had to be seen within four hours?'

'Oh, but you were: when Doctor Oduba assessed you earlier. That's the end of the statutory waiting period. We're just waiting to try and find you a bed, but we're full at the moment. If you want to get your head down until we can get you in for an x-ray, you can sleep on a trolley if that's all right. Then we can see about getting you a bed.'

Her heart was so obviously in the right place and she was so clearly overworked that Tom simply said, 'No that's ok thanks, I'll wait for a bed.'

He waited until she had gone into one of the cubicles to deal with a shouting, vomiting drunk and then rose unsteadily to his feet and made his way towards the door.

He splashed through the hospital car park and limped out into the street. The traffic was sparse at that time of night and the earlier drizzle had turned into steady, penetrating rain. He had only been waiting there a minute or so when a taxi came into view: he couldn't believe his luck, the amber light on the roof was on. He stumbled out into the road, his torn, wet trouser leg flapping as he walked. He tried to flag it down but the taxi swerved round him and sped off.

Don't blame him, thought Tom.

His second attempt was more successful. He hauled himself painfully into the back of the cab and was aware that the driver was checking him over in the rear-view mirror. Tom gave him the address and they set off. The driver did not attempt small-talk and Tom was all too aware of what sort of figure he must have cut, staggering around the streets in torn clothes at almost one in the morning: just another bloody drunk starting the weekend a day early. At last, they arrived at the flat. He paid the fare and tipped generously.

'Night, mate,' said the cabby, 'you ought to see a doctor, y'know.'

'I tried,' slurred Tom blearily, 'but there weren't any.'

He was fumbling with the key to the outside door of the flat when his mobile phone rang. It was the police.

'Yes? What? Who?' He was aware of the rain running down the back of his neck.

'No. Clearly I'm not at the hospital.'

'Why? Because I didn't want to wait twelve hours on a filthy trolley in second-hand sheets on the off chance of perhaps being seen by a doctor who hasn't slept in the last twenty-four hours. Nor do I want to leave hospital with some foul disease that I didn't have when I went in.'

'Yes, I know I'm risking a brain haemorrhage, but that would be far preferable to spending the night in that hospital, believe me….yes, that is the address…eleven o'clock is fine and if I die in the night I'll call you. Goodnight.'

Fuck you. Fuck the bloody lot of you.

***

The laptop stood on the trestle table and the technician addressed the small group of men who stood around him. 'You will be pleased to know that we have the BIOS password and user account password. It's a dual-boot 64-bit machine with 8 gigabytes of RAM, Windows and Ubuntu, the usual Microsoft applications and a few opensource apps as well: .Net Enterprise edition with some interesting ASP projects, but nothing really usable for trading. The good news is that we have personal files, bank details, letters, bills, statements, details of savings, pension projections, scans of legal documents, property and business details in French, .pst files —everything we need. As expected, all .dat and other history files seem to have been cleared down and shredded; we found the usual remote access and VPN software, but no password generators, not that we need them anyway.'

'Is there anything you are missing?'

'No.'

'Excellent. Well done, all of you.'

Chapter Fourteen

Tom didn't wake until nearly half past ten the next morning. The consolation of being able to see out his right eye was immediately diminished by what felt like all the hangovers in the world happening at once. It was still raining, but as he opened his eyes, even the grey London morning light filtering through the cheap curtains of Brian's crappy flat seared into his head like an electric shock.

He eased himself painfully from the thin mattress of the sofa-bed and stumbled to the bathroom. Each footfall sent waves of pain juddering through his head and neck.

The sight that greeted him in the mirror was not pretty. His right eye was still partially closed and the swollen, purple bruise now had an unattractive greenish tinge to it. All his teeth seemed to be in place but his top lip was swollen and tender, he had a bruise like an egg on the back of his head from where he'd hit the ground and his neck was so stiff that he had to turn his whole upper body in order to look left and right. His ribs hurt like hell and there were bruises all over his arms from where he'd tried to defend himself. The little finger on his left hand didn't seem to want to work properly, but based on the experience from when he'd broken it playing rugby, he didn't think it was broken this time.

He felt a little better after a hot shower. Now for the hard part – better get on with it, the police are coming at eleven.

He made a cursory call to the office to let them know that he was still alive but wouldn't be coming in. He told Liebowitz about his experience at the hospital and why he'd discharged himself.

'Yes, honestly, David I'm fine; I've had worse playing rugby,' he lied. 'And thanks for your help last night. I owe you one. Look, I've got to go now – I've got to break the news to Sally and I know she'll go crazy.'

He was right. 'They didn't even give you an x-ray? Tom, for God's sake, go back to hospital and get checked out properly, you could die, you could……' Tom could hear the wracking sobs down the line. '…then please just come home. Tell them you're not coming to London any more. Darling, it's not safe…that horrible place, it's just not safe. I knew this would happen again. Just don't die, please don't die.'

'Die, my dear doctor? That's the last thing I shall do.'

'Tom, will you be serious for once. Please,' she sobbed, 'please, darling, go back to casualty and get someone to look at you, you've probably got broken bones. And then please, please come home.'

At just after eleven, the intercom sounded and Tom buzzed the two policemen into the flat. They looked slightly taken aback at the squalor that greeted them.

'Do come in, gentlemen. I apologise for the state of the place but it's not my flat. The owner's just gone back to Sweden.' That doesn't actually explain anything does it? thought Tom. Oh, stuff it, what does it matter?

They showed him their warrant cards and introduced themselves as Inspector Hill and Sergeant Willis: both wore civilian clothing. Hill was a spare, raw-boned man of about forty-five: he had short-cut grey hair that was receding at the front, small, close-set blue eyes and strong features with an aggressively angular jaw. His colleague was about ten years younger, quite short for a policeman, pudgy-faced and already running to fat. The walk up the three flights of stairs to the top floor of the block had left him blowing and red-faced.

The two policemen cleared a space among the magazines, empty crisp packets and socks so that they could perch on the edge of the sofa opposite Tom. They gave the impression of not wanting to put any more of their anatomy in contact with Brian's furniture than was humanly possible.

'Before we start, I must say that you really should go back to hospital, sir,' said Hill. 'I'm no expert on these matters, but I do know that any sort of head injury can result in a bleed and that can be fatal. And it's no respecter of sex or size either.'

'Yes I know, inspector - you're quite right. I've played a lot of rugby and I've heard enough stories about people twice my size who've been concussed, tried to laugh it off and failed to wake up in the morning. What I did wasn't big or clever and I took a stupid risk – I just couldn't face another minute longer in that hospital.'

'I do sympathise, sir, and I know what casualty can be like after the pubs turn out, but I wouldn't be doing my job if I didn't warn you of the risks. I'm not being entirely altruistic: you would cause me even more paperwork if you died,' he smiled.

After what had happened to Sally and the behaviour of the police then, Tom was extremely wary of them: even the ones like Hill who at least seemed to be concerned, understanding and, to a degree, friendly. Still wouldn't trust you bastards any further than I could throw you, he thought.

'That's ok. I appreciate your concern and it's very good of you to come out to see me.'

'For cases as serious as this, it's standard practice.'

'I'm glad the police are taking mugging so seriously. It was a different story when my wife was attacked a while ago. You remember, surely? The Sally Mansell affair. It was on the front page of the red-tops on and off for several weeks. We'd only been married eighteen months.'

Hill remained impassive. If he had views on the case, he kept them to himself. 'I'm sorry to hear that, sir, and yes, I do remember the case – foolish of me not to make the connection. But that's the whole point: in your case we're not sure it was just a mugging,' said Hill.

Tom looked perplexed.

'I know that may sound a bit odd, but let me explain. Sergeant Willis and I are from the City of London Financial Crime Unit – we were set up just over a year ago - you may have heard of us?'

Tom nodded. Each of the policemen proffered a business card.

'Normally we deal with non-violent serious financial offences such as money laundering, fraud, theft of information, hacking, cybercrime, that kind of thing. And from what we've been told by the Met, we're more than a little concerned that the theft of your laptop wasn't just street crime.'

'Certainly felt like it to me,' said Tom.

'I'm sure it did, sir. Now before you tell me I've been reading too many detective novels, let me explain why we think that. The Canary Wharf complex has one of the tightest security set-ups anywhere in the country. Private vehicles aren't allowed onto the site unless the driver can prove he has legitimate reason to be there; there are CCTV cameras everywhere; the banks have security staff and Canary Wharf has its own security people who patrol the site twenty-four hours a day. Next, unless you're on foot, there are only two ways in or out for someone coming on to the Isle of Dogs: the DLR and the Tube – I'm leaving the buses and black cabs out of this, they don't make the best of getaway vehicles – so if you're a nasty bunch of little yobboes looking for someone to rob, there are plenty of easier places to start, and where you won't stand out like a sore thumb. Finally, why take on a fully-grown man and steal a laptop – which I'm sure you'll find galling to know has virtually no value as stolen goods – but not touch his wallet, mobile phone or watch?'

'Now you put it like that, it doesn't make much sense,' said Tom. 'And it makes it all the more bloody annoying because it stops me doing my job. But why me of all people and have you looked at the CCTV tapes yet?'

'We have, sir. As you'll recall it was raining and the stretch of footpath where the attack took place is opposite a building that's being renovated and has had its CCTV cameras removed – we don't think it was a coincidence that the attack happened there, by the way. At the moment, all we've got to go on is a group of four men who arrived at about the right time, in the right area, in pairs and from different directions – they're the ones we'd like to speak to. The problem is that because of the rain, they all had umbrellas up which did a very good job of hiding their faces, and when we do see what we think is them again on camera, they've split up and each one is on his own. But we think, and I stress think, that we've got two of them on CCTV from the Tube and two from the DLR cameras, but we can't even be completely sure it's them because they're not even in pairs any more.

'All of them appear to be typical Canary Wharf workers: white males who could be anywhere from thirty to forty years old and all were reasonably smartly dressed. Not a hoodie or pair of incontinence jeans in sight. That's why it all seems so odd and so far removed from a run-of-the-mill robbery.'

'Perhaps you can help us make some sense of events, sir,' said the sergeant. 'Do you know of any reason why someone would want to steal your laptop rather than anybody else's and to take such a risk in doing so? An enemy or a business rival for example?'

Tom shook his head and wished he hadn't because it hurt. 'No. I don't have any enemies that I know of. As for the job I do, it's subject to the usual client confidentiality rules and so on. My work sometimes gives me access to potentially price-sensitive information but none of that is kept on the laptop, and would only be of use for a very short period of time anyway. I have access to systems that our competitors would like to know about, but although our industry has a bad name for ethics and there's no love lost between us and the competition, I don't think mugging people in the street is their style – far too unsubtle.'

The sergeant made a note of this and then looked up again at Tom. 'Please go on, sir.'

'So, even if we assume that one of our competitors or anyone even vaguely connected with banking were trying to get hold of confidential information they'd be bright enough to know that stealing a laptop wouldn't achieve anything. The BIOS password protection on laptops is very strong and anyway, if you're going to get into our systems, you need a log-in, a password generator and all sorts of other odds and ends. If you've got the right access and the right communications software, you can get in from an internet café for Christ's sake, you don't need to steal some poor sod's laptop and hit him on the head. And why risk being caught and having your company put out of business just for something like this? Correct me if I'm wrong, inspector, but your suspects are four white blokes in suits aged between thirty and forty? They should stand out like sore thumbs in Canary Wharf. I can just see the headlines, "Ten thousand men are helping the police with their enquiries".'

'Not suits exactly, but I do take your point, sir, I agree that this whole case is full of inconsistencies and we very much need your help if we're going to solve it. Tell me, what is it exactly you do at the bank?'

Most people who work in wholesale financial services hate this question and Tom was no exception. 'Well,' he said, 'if you really want to know I can give you the edited highlights. It's mainly a technology role bound up with the design of algorithmic trading and arbitrage software. With me so far?'

The pair of them nodded and Tom continued. 'Good. In practice, what that means is that I take advanced mathematical ideas and turn them into usable software so that we can trade more efficiently, thus making more money for our clients and therefore more for the bank.'

'So you don't trade for the bank's own account?' asked Hill.

'No. If we tried to do both, we'd run into conflicts of interest. All I do is write the software and if that's enough for someone to want to mug me for my laptop, I'd be very surprised.'

Inspector Hill considered Tom's reply at length and said, 'I know it's going to be difficult for you to see it like this, sir, but let's just suppose for a minute that you hadn't been attacked and we just look at the list of people and organisations to whom knowledge of the inner workings of your systems would be useful. Can you tell us who they are and why it might be useful to them?'

'If you're going to look at it like that, I suppose the easiest thing would be to list the people who we consider our competitors, both in terms of getting the best price in the market and also of getting the biggest share of client revenue.'

'And they would be?'

'The most obvious competitors for client order-flow are the other major investment banks and brokerage houses.'

'Is that all?'

Tom pondered for a moment. 'There's the hedge funds of course. And that's about it: Colonel Mustard, under orders from the other banks and hedge funds, outside Canary Wharf, with the lead piping.'

'Nobody else you can think of, sir?'

'Nope.'

'Can you think of any other motive, Mr Mansell?'

Tom gingerly shook his head. 'Not really. But even the idea of a competitor is crazy. Nobody in our industry, however big a psychopath, is going to risk jail for mugging someone.'

Hill sucked the end of his pen. 'Doesn't leave us with much then, does it, Mr Mansell?'

'The only thing I can think of, if it wasn't just an addict stealing something to fund his next fix, is that there are enough people out there who hate bankers – and by default, anyone who works in Canary Wharf is one of those – that they decided to take it out on someone, and that someone was me. I happened to have a laptop on me and so they took it, either as a blow against capitalism or to use in their plans for world domination by unwashed, lentil-eating half-wits. I don't see it as anything more complicated than that.'

'It's possible,' said Hill. 'But if that's the case, it would be the first in a pattern of attacks because we haven't seen anything like this so far: we can only wait and see if it happens again. Just one last question, sir, and then we can leave you in peace. Can you tell us what was on the machine in the way of software, files and so on?'

Tom gave him a run down of the software on the machine, the files and its security safeguards.

'Could whoever's got it gain access to your bank's systems?'

'No, inspector, absolutely not. The remote access software is there but you'd need the password generator and for that you'd need my right index finger for the fingerprint reader, so no.'

'I know this must be tiring for you, Mr Mansell, but I just want to find out if there's anyone else who might have a motive of any sort to want to harm or frighten you,' said Hill. 'I know you say you don't have any enemies, but surely somewhere along the line you will have crossed swords with people in your line of work, maybe professionally or even personally.'

Tom smiled: smiling hurt too. Bugger. 'No. On the trading floor people shout and swear at each other, but it's never personal.'

'What about people from outside the firm?'

'Oh, I'm sure we've put lots of people's noses out of joint,' said Tom. 'But market professionals in our industry don't beat people up and steal their laptops just because their *amour propre* is offended.'

'Indulge me, sir: who's "we" and whose noses have you put of joint?'

'"We" are my colleagues on the desk and me. I work very closely with a chap called David Liebowitz. He's our ideas and maths man and what he's done is to show a lot of the self-appointed market gurus out there that they're not as clever as they thought. And there are some people with fragile egos who don't like David for that, and resent the success we've had.'

'And is your system really that far ahead of the pack?' said Hill.

'We like to think so.'

'So you can predict the lottery numbers?'

'Yes and no,' said Tom. 'Talking about the lottery implies gambling which is exactly what we don't do. Without going into too much detail, David's models use a branch of mathematics called non-linear dynamics that allows you to predict how certain variables are likely to behave when they are subject to the simultaneous effects of literally thousands of other variables which in turn may affect each other to a greater or lesser extent, sometimes immediately, and sometimes with a time-lag.'

'If you'll forgive me, sir,' said Willis, 'how does that help us work out who might dislike you?'

'It doesn't, but it'll give you more of an idea of why we've ruffled a few feathers along the way. David and I get invited to speak at financial conferences and sometimes that involves introducing ideas that go against the conventional wisdom. On occasions there are people in the audience whose careers and reputations have been built on just the ideas that we're challenging. The business guys are usually ok about it, it's the academics who are worst by a mile – that said, I've yet to hear of gangs of pissed-off academics attacking people outside pubs because they don't like their ideas about the nature of interference patterns in phase space.'

Inspector Hill narrowed his eyes and looked intently at Tom. 'Given the success of what you do, you must have firms trying to head-hunt you?'

'Yes we do. It happens a lot less than it did before the sky fell in, but we still get the odd call.'

'And is there anybody out there, either head-hunters or the firms that hire them who might be upset because you've turned them down?' asked Hill. 'And I do appreciate that I'm clutching at straws now.'

'No, it doesn't work like that. Sure, firms get pissed off when entire teams get lifted but it's all part of the game, nobody whacks anyone over the head about it.'

'And you've never been tempted to move?'

'Sure I've been tempted but now I'm working from home, nothing could ever shift me.' Tom paused and smiled to himself. 'That's reminded me, and this was really funny. The oddest approach we had was from a sovereign wealth fund in one of the former Soviet republics. Does the name Noviprom mean anything to you?'

At Tom's mention of the name, Hill's eyebrows rose, 'Yes, sir, I've heard of them. The Nashyastan Government Investment Authority.'

Tom continued. 'Yes, they're the ones. They've become quite a serious player of late and to give them their due, they've gone from a standing start to being a reasonable outfit in no time flat. They offered David and me a ridiculous amount of money to move. Neither of us fancied moving so we told them no and thought that was an end to it. The hilarious thing was that they wouldn't take no for an answer, they offered double the money, sent us expensive watches and got very miffed when we gave them straight back. Then later they tried to bribe us, offered us hookers, all sorts of things. I just don't think they're used to people turning them down, and in the end they got quite ratty about it. They finally got the message and left us alone: it was water off a duck's back to me, but along the way they said something to David – I've never been able to get him to tell me what it was – that really got under his skin and so he decided to have a little bit of fun at their expense.'

Hill's face wore a look of concern. 'What did you do?' he asked.

'Don't worry, it was nothing illegal,' replied Tom. 'Just like most of the other operators in the market, they weren't as smart as they thought they were, and David and I were able pretty quickly to reverse-engineer how their algos worked. So when we were testing some changes we'd made to the Minerva system prior to actually putting client trades through it, we took them, quite legally I should add, for several tens of millions of dollars for three days running until they cottoned on to the fact that they were being arbed. And just to rub it in, we let them know, very subtly, who was on the other side of their losing trades. Funnily enough, we've not heard a peep out of them since. They're still active in the markets of course, but they seem to have got a lot smarter since then.'

Hill made to speak but Tom held up his hand and the inspector fell silent. 'Now, listen, gentlemen, I'm not feeling well and if you don't mind, I'm going to have to ask you to call it a day. I'm not back for about three weeks, but here's my e-mail address and contact details in France if you need to call me.'

'Thank you, Mr Mansell, you've been most helpful. If we have any news, we'll contact you straight away.'

Chapter Fifteen

Not far to the west of Saratoga Springs in upstate New York, a woman was cycling towards the village of Connor's Brook. She'd been climbing for the last four miles and was now standing on the pedals as the gradient toughened towards the summit. The speedometer told her that she was now below 10 mph and she dug in again to make one last effort. Nearly there, she thought, another half mile or so and then all down hill.

The weather was perfect. She'd deliberately kept away from the main roads and so there was little traffic to bother her out here. Better still, she hadn't seen a single semi truck all day: those were the ones she really hated, especially when they overtook too close. That awful gap between the rear wheels of the truck itself and the back of the trailer seemed to want to suck you in.

An old Toyota pick-up with a gun-rack went past. As it did so the driver gave her a cheery wave and called out an encouragement but she couldn't make out what he'd said.

A little further on, a dark brown delivery truck overtook her, once again giving her plenty of room – thanks, guys – and stopped a short distance up the road. A man got out of the passenger seat and examined the name on a mailbox at the edge of the road – the properties were few and far between in this rural part of the State and were all set back, out of sight of the road, at the end of long private drives. She dug in once more, only a few more yards and she'd be there, checked behind her and started to overtake the truck. As she drew level with the cab, the driver's door flew open and a man's arm tried to clothesline her round the neck. She ducked instinctively and his arm bounced off her cycling helmet, and although the impact sent her wobbling into the middle of the road, she just about managed to stay upright and continued going the same way, trying desperately against the gradient to put as much distance between herself and the truck as possible. In sheer terror, she checked back over her shoulder. All manner of horrors flashed across her mind: murderers, rapists, crazies – who were these people? Why pick on me?

It hadn't moved yet but she could hear raised voices and slamming doors. Then she heard the revving of an engine and the sound of wheels scrabbling for traction in the roadside gravel. The hilltop was only yards away now. Push legs, push. Don't let them hurt me, please don't let them hurt me. She'd find a car, any car going in whichever direction and make them stop. There must be someone coming along soon, there has to be, please.

Her breath was rasping as she crested the rise. She could see Connor's Brook nestling peacefully in the valley below and beyond the village, and could clearly make out the hills that rose up towards the distant Adirondacks. But where is everybody? Somebody help me. Somebody make this stop. She looked back again. The truck was now only about fifty yards away and gaining fast, but the road was downhill now and steep. Maybe a bike is more agile, maybe I can keep ahead of them until I find help, she thought.

Compared with cars and trucks, bikes have lousy brakes, and at the first hairpin, they nearly caught her, but she managed to stay ahead by being able to get round the corner quicker than the cumbersome truck. She checked over her shoulder – a fifty yard lead but they'd swallow that up on the next straight. She was in top gear now and pedalling as hard as she could: the speedometer touched 40 mph. A car came up the hill in the opposite direction, but she saw it way too late to try and attract the driver's attention and was past it in a flash. She threw herself into the next bend and nearly ran off the road – just how far can you lean on bike tyres? She didn't know, she was a careful, risk-averse cyclist, this was what crazy kids or those mad guys in the Tour de France did, not Miss Sensible Stacey. Just stay in front of them, please don't let them catch me. The gradient steepened again and she stood up on the pedals coming out of the corner in an attempt to accelerate as hard as possible, but still they came. Another corner, 42 mph - too fast, now brake, brake hard, and as she did the front wheel locked on a patch of gravel and went from under her. She put one hand out to try and break her fall. It did, but the impact snapped her collar bone.

The bike continued to slide and tumble and she followed after it, aware the road was tearing the skin from her knees and elbows, aware there was no pain yet, aware of passing clean underneath the crash barrier. Then the sliding stopped. That must be good, but no, she was falling, falling.

The delivery truck slowed and the driver pulled out to avoid the tangled bicycle that lay in the middle of the road. Ten feet further on lay the body of a woman clad in cycling clothing. The drop from the bend above was a full sixty feet. She was dead. A simple accident. They hadn't even needed to touch her.

***

The news threw Chivers into a state of turmoil. He'd almost forgotten the conversation about the divorce. Hadn't even meant to talk about it, it just kind of came out in conversation while they were talking about why he was in London. And when Kaliski had said, "we can help you", he'd made the natural assumption that he'd meant financially or with a hot-shot lawyer, not like this. Never. He'd wanted her back. Not dead, he'd never wanted her dead. He'd never had dealings with people who did things like this, and when he stopped to consider what the price for this unwanted favour might be, it made his blood run cold. For a moment he considered going to the police and making a clean breast of what had happened, and sat with his head resting in his hands, desperately working out what to do.

People who could carry out a murder and successfully make it look like an accident were unlikely to take kindly to his going to the police. Most likely, he would end up as the prime suspect or dead – probably both. Then his thoughts returned to the quid pro quos that would shortly follow – better to take the risk of going to the police than face a lifetime of being at the beck and call of murderers. That was the logical, sensible thing to do, that's what he'd advise anyone else to do. Calm down, he thought, it was probably just a coincidence – lots of people sound off to anyone who'll listen about the shortcomings of their partners, past and present – doesn't mean that what he said had got her killed, that's just fantasy, story book stuff. It was just a coincidence, a tragic accident – simple as that. Moments later when the shrill, metallic nagging of his mobile cut short his reverie, all his worst fears were confirmed.

It was Kaliski. 'Please accept my condolences, Mr Chivers. That said, I am sure your grief will be tempered by the knowledge that you no longer face the prospect of expensive legal bills and worse.'

'Kaliski, that's the most callous, bloody awful thing I've ever heard. When you offered to help me I thought you meant financially or legally, but not like this. Never.' He paused. 'You've made my mind up for me, do you know that?'

'How so?'

'I didn't want to believe that you were behind this, but now that I know, I'm going to the police…' Kaliski cut him short.

'That would be a very bad decision. We have very skilfully edited recordings of your conversations, your fingerprints, DNA, records of cash deposits, photographs of you talking to certain people, and more. All of which would be more than sufficient to convict you for complicity in your wife's untimely death, should you choose such a foolish course of action. The good news for you is that we have no interest in seeing you sent to jail, and so all that we ask in return is that you provide us with information when we need it, and help to facilitate our purchase of certain items. That is all. Not your immortal soul nor a pound of flesh,' he laughed. 'Now, Mr Chivers, I'm sure you have a lot to do, including attending your late wife's funeral, so we will be in touch when you return. Goodbye, Mr Chivers.'

With his head still spinning, Chivers made a brief call to work and then booked himself on a flight to the US. At Newark airport he hired a car and headed through the gathering darkness for the small town of Doversfield, just to the west of Johnstown in upstate New York. Facing her family was going to be hard. Harder still was facing up to the reality of what he'd done and what he'd got himself involved with.

***

Having spent the night at a small motel just outside the town, the following morning he was on familiar territory as he swung the car into Church Lane. Everything looked the same: the neatly-tended lawns running down to the road with its row of plane trees on either side; discreet, well-spaced and freshly-painted houses set back among tasteful gardens. Everything may've looked the same, but for a small universe of people, his ill-chosen words and rash acceptance of a vague offer meant that their lives had changed for ever.

Stacey had been close to her parents and had gone back to stay with them after she'd walked out on him. For her it was the natural place to go: her bedroom was still the same as the day she'd gone off to college nearly twenty years earlier, a comforting sameness that always gave her a sense of permanence and security each time she went back to see them.

The funeral, which took place the next day, was a torment for Chivers. It was a fine early summer's day, the puddles from the night's rain were drying, everything seemed picture perfect, and the evocative scent of burning charcoal and roasting meat from other families' back-yard barbecues that caught his nostrils as they filed into the simple white-painted wooden chapel seemed horribly incongruous. Passing along the aisle to the sound of muttered condolences from the bowed heads of strangers, he was touched to see how many people had turned out to say farewell to Stacey. Sitting in the front pew and avoiding the baleful glare of Stacey's father, he felt utterly alone and distraught. Every word the young priest said seemed to carry a secret reproach aimed directly at him. It was the kindness and sympathy that was hardest to bear, but whichever way he looked at it and however much he wished her back, there was no escaping it: all this was of his doing and his alone.

Her high-school principal was there. After the service he

introduced himself. 'She was a fine young woman,' he said. He was stooped now and his voice held a tremor, but his handshake remained firm and the steady gaze of his pale blue eyes held Chivers rooted to the spot. 'Whatever happens, be sure you'll always be among friends here. We don't say things like that lightly in this town and we stand behind our word. Remember that, young man, it's not an empty promise.' And with that he handed him a business card. 'I'll leave you now, Andrew, forgive me if I've intruded on your grief.' This was too much for Chivers who mumbled his thanks and, turning his back on the mourners gathered around the porch, moved away to stand alone among the yew trees and gravestones. No tears came, just an overpowering sense of his wretchedness in the midst of such goodness.

Being left alone with her parents at the family home after the service and the interment was the worst. 'Andrew, darling, I just wanted you to know that Stacey's father and I do not blame you for what happened and that we will always consider you as one of the family. Please promise us that you'll keep in touch and come and see us again, won't you, dear?' She moved the black veil from her eyes and dabbed with a small white handkerchief. 'George and I were both in relationships when we first met, so we do understand that the best of marriages can go wrong without it being anybody's fault.'

The last of the funeral cars had left, the caterers were packing up and getting ready to go too and the room was hot and stuffy.

'That's really good of you and I do appreciate your kindness, Paula, but there wasn't anybody else – not for me and not as far as I know for Stacey. We had a row – lots of rows – one too many I suppose. She walked out on me and that was it. Maybe I deserved it: I know I'm not always easy to live with. After that, as you know, she wouldn't take my calls and three weeks ago I heard from her lawyer that she had filed for divorce. I can't stop blaming myself for the fact that if she hadn't wanted to walk out, she'd still be alive.'

Stacey's father, George Montgomery, sat opposite them saying nothing. He and Andrew had never got on and it was clear from his demeanour that his wife's offer of forgiveness and kinship did not meet with his approval. *If you hadn't given her* cause *to walk out, you mean, our baby would still be alive,* he thought.

Chivers shifted uneasily under the older man's gaze – it was as if he knew somehow. *Don't be stupid, how could he?* Nevertheless, he felt desolate, uncomfortable and out of place. He'd wrecked these people's lives, watched them bury their only daughter – there wasn't even the consolation of grandchildren – and now he was going to make a feeble excuse and just walk out of their lives for ever, to leave them sitting alone in that airless room, alone with their loss and the gathering darkness. *It was done; he would never see them again. Just say your goodbyes and leave. You may well get over it one day, they won't. Just go.*

He had a few more legal formalities to sort out back in New York and the day before his flight left for the UK he went into the office.

Sam Bortoleski was sympathetic. 'Andrew, I'm really sorry about what happened. If you want to take some vacation, just get away for a few weeks, that's fine – I'll sign it off. And in case you're worrying, don't even think about what we discussed the other day. Go get some down time and when you come back, then I can think about being an asshole to you again.' He put a bear-like paw around his shoulder. 'Now, listen to me, Andrew, because you know I don't say stuff I don't mean and don't follow through on, if you need anything, doesn't matter what – if you need anything, you call me. Got that? If I find out afterwards that you were in a hole and didn't get in touch, then I *will* get mad at you. None of this Limey stiff upper lip crap. OK?'

'Thanks, Sam. I do appreciate that, I honestly do.' He felt his eyes pricking. If only people would stop being so damn decent.

Chapter Sixteen

La Borda is one of the few genuine Catalan restaurants in London. It is tucked away on the northern edge of the City, not far from Smithfield Market, in a small courtyard that once formed part of a 17th century coaching inn. There is no shortage of tapas bars in London but La Borda is the real thing, a must for anyone looking for the genuine, hearty, mountain food that is so hard to find outside the Pyrenees. Its other advantage for the three men having dinner that evening, was that La Borda offers private dining rooms where conversation cannot be overheard, and unless someone comes and peers closely through the glass, it is almost impossible to see who is dining with whom. On this occasion, Tom Mansell and David Liebowitz were the guests of Greg Callaghan, head of the brokerage division of one of their biggest rivals. Discussions were going well.

'What about the rest of the team?' asked Tom.

'Our interest is in yourself and David. We weren't planning to make offers to anyone else.'

'Well, Greg, in that case I'm not sure we can accept.' Liebowitz kicked him on the ankle under the table. 'Our three traders and their assistants at least should come over too. We're used to working with each other, even our most recent starter has been with us, what is it, David, three years?'

'That's correct.'

'So you see,' continued Tom. 'These guys are good. We spent a lot of time and heartache over the selection process, we've invested a huge amount of effort into their training and now we've got a team that we know, trust and respect, we really don't want to have to start from scratch and build a new one. There's a moral aspect too, Greg. We might be the guys who do the high-profile stuff, but without our traders and their assistants, it's all just so much air-guitar.'

'I'm still not sure, Tom, I'm really not.'

'OK, Greg. I'll tell you what. You postpone paying the first one hundred thousand of my starting bonus – don't touch anybody else's – and if our traders are no good, then at the end of six months, you let them go and you keep the money. On the other hand, if after the six months, they're still there – and they will be, you'll be fighting to keep them on board – you pay me one twenty-five. How's that sound?'

Callaghan smiled and looked up at the ceiling. Remind me never to play poker with you, he thought. 'OK, Tom,' he said. 'You win, I'll live with that, just promise me that Denise Evans and Andrew Chivers aren't part of the deal.'

'Don't worry, Greg. You've no concerns on either score. We won't be sorry to say goodbye to either of those two.'

'So, gentlemen, we're agreed then? Excellent, let's sort out some dates. Tom, you're not back in the UK for three weeks, is that correct?'

Tom consulted the diary on his mobile phone. 'That's right. Let's see…I arrive on the Thursday, Friday I'm speaking at a conference in the morning, then I'm going down to Dorset to see my parents over the weekend, so really any time that following week. Does that fit in with your plans, David?'

Liebowitz consulted his Blackberry. 'I'm out of town till the Wednesday,' he said, 'So Thursday or Friday are best for me.'

'Thursday it is then', said Callaghan. That'll give me plenty of time to get legal to draft your contracts and also the contract that conveys the title in Minerva to us. I'll e-mail those to your personal accounts and, if you could give me any requests for change as soon as possible, then we can certainly turn that round in four weeks.'

'One last thing,' said Tom. 'We'll need to sort out something for the traders and their assistants. If we break the news to them now it'll leak, so we need to get our timing right. If we sign with you on the Thursday morning, say, and put our resignations in that afternoon, then you'll have to put the offer to them straight afterwards, David. I can't do it because of the non-solicitation clause in my consultancy contract. If I'm seen to encourage them to leave the firm, the clause can be invoked, the bank can terminate my contract for fault on my part and the intellectual property in the Minerva system reverts to them. Last but not least, Greg, there's the outside chance that they will invoke their right to match your offer for Minerva. I don't think for one moment they will, because without David and me there to keep developing it, it'll lose its value, but you need to understand that there's potential for delay should it turn into a bidding war.'

'That's fine, Tom,' said Callaghan, 'I fully understand. So, gentlemen, are we done?'

Liebowitz and Mansell both nodded. Callaghan shook hands with each of them in turn and then raised his glass. 'Here's to a very profitable future together and now that we've done the serious stuff, let's enjoy the rest of the evening.'

Outside in the yard, after taking off his headset and collapsing the hand-held parabolic antenna, a figure detached itself from the shadows and moved silently out into the street, turned left at the corner and walked a few yards along the left hand pavement of Candlemaker Lane. A black Lexus pulled up alongside and the man got in.

The following day Tom walked up to where Liebowitz was working and tapped him on the shoulder. He spoke quietly, 'Hey, David, you're never going to believe this. Can you step off the desk for a couple of minutes?'

They wandered outside across the pavement outside the office, past the ever-present little groups of smokers and into the small landscaped area beyond.

'What's up, Tom?'

'Chivers.'

'What about Chivers?'

'He's only invited me out to lunch. Bit of a coincidence, don't you think?'

'You reckon he knows about last night? How could he?'

'One of Callaghan's people?'

'Incredibly unlikely and anyway, how would anyone who wasn't completely familiar with the deal know to contact Chivers? The only thing I can think of is that someone saw us entering or leaving the restaurant and put two and two together.'

'But that doesn't work either,' said Tom. 'If that was the source then it would need to be someone who knew all three of us, where we work and what we do. Then they'd need to know a) that Chivers wasn't part of the deal and b) that he's the desk head.'

Liebowitz thought for a moment. 'OK, so perhaps he's decided to lighten up at long last. He's been very withdrawn after his wife's accident and maybe it's changed him somehow. It does happen sometimes. You know, bringing home the reality of your own mortality and your need to connect with others. Shit, what do I know? I don't do introspection, just anxiety and guilt. I reckon it's just lunch.'

It wasn't.

Chivers had booked a small private dining room at a very expensive seafood restaurant in Canary Wharf. During the five minutes or so that it took them to walk there from the office, the two men exchanged few words. Chivers waited until they were seated, the apéritifs ordered and the door closed.

'Tom, I'll come straight to the point. I understand you're planning to leave us. Please tell me whether that is true or not.'

'Andrew, with all due respect, what I plan to do is nobody's concern but my own until the day I put those plans into action.'

'That isn't the question I asked, is it, Tom? Please tell me whether or not you plan to leave us.'

'No.'

'As in "no, I don't plan to leave the bank"?' asked Chivers.

'No, Andrew, as in no I'm not telling you. I have all manner of plans. For all you know, some of them may involve what I'm going to have for dinner this evening. Others may involve plans to commit mass murder, but so long as they stay in my own head and don't involve conspiracy to do something illegal or something that will affect the bank, then they remain private thoughts and are nobody else's business but my own.'

'You ought to be a lawyer, giving replies like that, or perhaps an MP,' sneered Chivers. 'I don't have all day, nor do I intend going around in circles with you arguing over what do you mean by "what?".'

'So if I understand you correctly, Andrew, I am now required to defend myself. Am I allowed to know the charges?'

'Tom, stop trying to be a bloody smart-arse, it doesn't become you. You and Liebowitz had dinner with Greg Callaghan last night at a restaurant called La Borda. Shall I continue?'

'Feel free,' said Tom with an air of nonchalance that was nowhere near matching what he was actually feeling. 'Are you really labouring under the delusion that who I have dinner with is any of your business?'

'Interesting that you don't deny it then. Of course it's none of my business what you do out of work hours, but you know damn well that isn't the case when two of my key staff have dinner with the head of brokerage at one of our biggest rivals, don't you? That you discussed terms for their purchase of Minerva and that you plan to take the traders and their assistants with you on terms that put your own sign-on bonus at risk. And that's none of my business? That's solicitation, Tom. Contractor or full-time employee, if you do anything to encourage someone to leave the firm or suggest to someone else that they hire them, that's a sacking offence.'

Christ, thought Tom. This is very, very sinister. He took a deep breath. 'You want me to stop arguing like a lawyer, Andrew?'

'Yes, it would save us all an awful lot of wasted time.'

'It'll be my pleasure,' said Tom. 'Andrew, I will only say this once, so I'd be grateful if you'd be so kind as to listen carefully. Firstly, what I plan to do, what I think or even what I hope for remains my affair and nobody else's. Secondly, like I said, my choice of dinner companions is none of your business. If, in your capacity as desk head, you think that I have said or done anything that contravenes the contract I have with the bank, then grow up, be a man and have the balls to make the accusations. Oh, and when you do, get yourself a very good lawyer because I will take great pleasure in suing you into the stone-age. Got that?' With that, Tom stood up, threw down his napkin and, leaving his apéritif untouched, returned to the office.

Tom rushed on to the trading floor. 'David, I need to talk to you urgently.'

'I need to talk to you too. Callaghan's gone missing.'

Tom's jaw dropped. 'What do you mean, "missing"?'

'While you were out I tried to call him on my mobile to ask him about something that was in my draft contract. According to his secretary he didn't come in to work this morning, he's not at home, his car is at the station as usual and his wife has reported him missing.'

'David. This is getting nasty. Chivers just tried to grill me about last night. He knew every damn detail of our conversation…Shit, David, turn your mobile off, now! I know this sounds crazy, but that bastard knew everything we said, word for word. To have that level of detail, somebody must have overheard the conversation.'

'And you reckon someone has put a bug in one of our phones?'

'I've no idea how they did it, but he's got the conversation down to the last syllable. Come on, let's go outside. I'm locking my mobile in the desk drawer even though it's turned off and I think you should do the same.'

'OK, good idea.'

They sat down on a bench in the little garden outside the building.

'Look, David, I know this seems mad but let's consider the facts. Here are the options. One, Callaghan did this to wind us up and get us into trouble with Chivers and now he's faked his disappearance. Two, you or I told Chivers. Three, somebody else was in the room with us and overheard what we said. We can discount all of those, so what does that leave?'

'That somebody recorded the conversation. But that's impossible.'

'I hate to say it, but it's the only explanation that stands up,' said Tom. 'The question is, *qui bono*? Who stands to gain?'

'The only one is the bank,' replied David.

'And they couldn't run a bath, let alone organise electronic surveillance. Secret agent Denise Evans strikes again – doesn't sound right, does it? So who does that leave?'

David's expression was troubled. 'Bert and Ernie.'

Tom's face told the same story. 'That's what I was afraid you were going to say.'

'So, if we assume for argument's sake that it *is* them and that they're somehow listening to our mobile phones, how do we prove it?'

'God knows,' said Tom. 'I wouldn't know where to start. Look, I'm going back to France tomorrow and we need to keep in close touch, but no telephone and no e-mail unless it's totally banal work stuff. I'm going to set up a new Skype ID as soon as I get back – here, I'll write it down, you do the same – that at least should be safe from prying eyes and ears. When I get back, I'll call Callaghan's office again and see if they've got an update for us.'

***

'Mr Chivers for you, Mr Bortoleski.'

'Put him through, please, Mandy.'

'Sam, we've got a problem. Don't ask me how I know, but Liebowitz and Mansell have accepted an offer to go and work for Greg Callaghan.' For a moment there was silence from the other end of the phone.

'Shit. That's bad, real bad. Tell me, have they already signed a contract, have they resigned yet?'

'No. From what I gather, we've got between three weeks and a month.'

'Still doesn't give us much time. So what's your plan, Andrew?'

'The only thing I can think of is that Mansell persuaded Callaghan to include my three traders and their assistants in the deal. I've double-checked his contract and there's a clear non-solicitation clause in there that forbids encouraging or facilitating

131

our people to leave or aiding and abetting other firms to hire them. We could use the threat of ending his contract to get him to re-open negotiations about the system.'

'Or as an excuse to fire his ass.'

No, for God's sake, no. Anything but that, thought Chivers. Then everything just reverts to the bank and then….no, it wasn't even worth thinking about what they'd do to him if that happened. Time, we need time, that's all.

Bortoleski continued, 'That's not a bad start, but what proof do you have that he actually said what you say he did?'

'My source told me.'

'Your source? Bullshit. Stop playing secret agents with me, will you? Who's your source, Andrew?'

'I can't tell you, Sam.'

'Andrew….!' he growled.

'Sam, I really can't. Not now anyway, but I promise I will tell you, just not right now. OK?'

'So at the moment, the only proof we have is what a little bird told you. Is that right?'

'Yes, Sam.'

'And how do you know the little bird isn't yanking your chain?'

'I just do, Sam. Trust me, I am not making this up. I had lunch with Mansell earlier today and in my opinion his reaction confirmed everything. He was very evasive and when I put the details of what they'd discussed in front of him he told me to mind my own business and stormed off out of the restaurant.'

'Interesting. I think that answers your question beyond any doubt but remember, none of this adds up to an ounce of proof that any court of law would even so much as look at. It's still all just uncorroborated hearsay for now. Have you told Evans yet?'

'No. Do you want me to?'

'Shit, why not? We need as many people working on a way to stop this as possible. Christ, Andrew, I dunno, jam her fat ass in the doorway so they can't leave the office. I don't care how you do it. No, can that, this is a taped line. I don't care how you do it so long as it's legal.' A very large wink travelled down the line between New York and London. 'Give me a call on my mobile later.'

At almost the same moment that Tom's flight to France left UK airspace, the Evening Standard and the BBC were reporting breaking news.

"Top banker found hanged. According to Police sources, missing superstar banker Greg Callaghan was this morning found hanged near his home near Denham in Buckinghamshire. Reports say that the body was discovered by a dog-walker early this morning and that a formal identification has been made. Foul play is not suspected."

Chapter Seventeen

Chivers sat disconsolately on the same bench in Green Park and waited. At the appointed hour, the two men he'd been expecting came and sat down, one on either side of him. Kaliski he recognised: the other man he'd never seen before. The newcomer didn't introduce himself and kept silent throughout, paying far more attention to the passers-by than to the conversation taking place next to him.

'As an insider, Mr Chivers, you are not doing very well. I expected more of you – you should be discovering these things, not leaving it to me to discover them. How was your lunch with Mansell?'

'Not good, he – '

'He walked out of the restaurant, didn't he? I take it from his actions that you failed to persuade him. Two failures in the same week: not good. I suppose you have spoken to Bortoleski.'

'Yes and he in turn has informed Evans, my boss.'

'And what was their reaction?'

'They weren't sure what to do,' said Chivers. 'There was a suggestion of using the non-solicitation clause in Mansell's contract against him because of his insistence on bringing the traders and their assistants into the negotiations. But of course, that it doesn't help Noviprom's case if his contract is terminated for cause, because in that event, the intellectual property goes to the bank. However, after this morning's news, I think we have more time because clearly, all bets are off.'

'Yes, it must have been very sad for Callaghan's family that he decided to end his life in such a way.'

That's one way of putting it, thought Chivers.

'So we have more time but still Mr Mansell remains obdurate. Let me remind you, in case you have forgotten, in return for our help and past kindness we require you to deliver Mansell, Liebowitz and the Minerva system to us. Now, tell me, Mr Chivers, do you know Mansell's wife?'

***

Scary Mary tapped on the glass door of Denise Evans' office. 'Bihar Jalil to see you, Denise.'

She looked up from her screen to see a small, athletically-built man of about thirty. He had neatly-cropped dark hair and a short beard. His eyes flickered nervously about him as he came into Denise's office. As the recently-appointed head of trading systems IT he was still coming to grips with the fact that he was no longer a coder and a doer but a manager, and he was concerned that one of the many personality clashes that he'd had with his new charges since taking over in the role had finally gone up the ladder to Denise. His fear of her was enhanced because she had a hold over him.

It had happened about two years earlier when he was still working in systems support. It was quiet on the evening shift and nearly ten o'clock at night. He thought no one else was around and that he had the trading floor to himself. It is not uncommon for floor staff to leave a change of clothes in one of the many cupboards that are provided for just that reason, and when Denise found him, he was naked except for a borrowed pink dress, viewing a very questionable web-site and enjoying some fairly vigorous solitary sex at the same time. With the headphones over his ears so as not to miss any of the oohs, aahs and other delights of the soundtrack, he didn't hear her walk up behind him and wasn't aware of anything until the flash of the mobile phone camera. When their paths next crossed a couple of days later, all she said was, 'If at some time in the future I ask you for a favour, you will say yes, won't you, Bihar?'

He looked nervously at her. 'Come in, Bihar,' she said. 'And please close the door behind you – don't worry, I won't bite. Now, I want you to do me a very big favour and I do so hope you'll be good enough to say yes. When you've done it, I'll let you watch me delete that picture of you. Pink really isn't your colour, sweetie.

'Here's what I want you to do.'

***

Chivers answered his mobile phone. 'Andrew, it's Sam. I've got a solution for you. You've got first-hand experience of this shit, so tell me, how *do* you finger someone for front-running customer business?'

'I don't think that's a good idea, Sam.'

'Bullshit. It's a brilliant idea and I'm just surprised you didn't think of it first. We get him for front-running, we turn him in to the FSA, he's dismissed for cause and Minerva comes back into the fold for free. We come up smelling of roses. What could be simpler?'

'Are you really asking me to frame him for something he didn't do?' asked Chivers.

'Don't be so fucking naïve, Andrew,' spat Bortoleski. 'Do I have to spell this out for you? Is your memory really that short? Just do what you did at Citi, but make sure that this time it's got Mansell's finger-prints on it, not yours.'

'I really don't think it's going to be that simple, Sam.'

'Of course it is, you moron. We do agency programs, we do a lot of agency business for the transition management team – assuming that Evans hasn't fired them again – so just pick one of those and make sure it happens.'

'Well, I'll take a look, Sam, but I don't make any promises.'

'Fine by me, Andrew. A promise in this business ain't worth shit anyway. It's results I want: results or you go work someplace else. Simple as that.' Bortoleski hung up.

I only wish it was that simple, thought Chivers.

Chapter Eighteen

The heat of the day had faded and Tom and Sally took a bottle of wine and a blanket up to their favourite spot on the hill behind the house in order to enjoy the sunset and the calm of a rare windless evening. They sat in silence for several minutes until at last Sally spoke.

'Tom, are you seeing someone else?' she asked quietly.

'What? No! Are you bonkers? Why on earth would I be seeing someone else?'

'You've been back five days now. You've barely spoken a word to me, when you do I get monosyllables and grunts, you lock yourself in that office of yours all day, I only ever see you at mealtimes and you're drinking too much again.'

'But – '

'Let me finish, Tom. What worries me most, on top of all this, is that in the five days you've been back, you've not come near me, not laid a finger on me. Normally, as soon as you get back from the airport, you drag me off upstairs, which you know I love. Now it seems that all of a sudden you don't want me physically, you're clearly fed up with me and your mind's elsewhere all the time. So tell me, what other conclusion is there other than you're seeing someone else?'

He put his arm round her and she rested her head on his shoulder.

'Tell me it's not true, Tom.'

He stroked her hair and pulled her tighter to him. He loved the smell of her thick dark hair and the warmth of her body next to his. 'Look, you big silly, I promised you that I'd never cheat on you. I never have and I never will. There's nobody else but you: never has been, never will be.' He kissed her tenderly as she turned her face towards him.

'Are you sure, Tom? Really sure?'

'Yes, you great nelly,' he said with a smile, 'How many times do I have to tell you? I'll look – that's genetic, I can't help it – but

I'll never touch.'

Sally was smiling now. 'Like at Catherine's tits you mean?' she said with an impish grin. Catherine was one of Sally's girlfriends, an expat divorcée who lived in the next village in a tiny flat and house-sat for them when they went away. It was an arrangement that suited everybody: Catherine was able to escape from the claustrophobia of living in two rooms and Tom and Sally knew the house was in safe hands.

'Ah, well, ah, yes, no, I mean –' spluttered Tom. Catherine often popped round to see Sally and to use the pool and Tom would frequently come down from his office to find the pair of them sunbathing or swimming topless. The hedge round the property was at least eight feet high which meant that the pool and its surrounds were only overlooked by the ridge to the south east and that was over a quarter of a mile away.

'Aha, guilty as charged, you old lech,' said Sally. 'The last time she was here you couldn't take your eyes off them.'

'Well, she spent about ten minutes rubbing suntan lotion into them. What's a chap supposed to do?' he countered.

Sally gave him a playful slap on the knee. 'So you think they're nicer than mine, do you?'

'Hmm, I'll have to check.' And with that he tried to put his hand up her tee-shirt. She fought him off, although not in a totally convincing manner.

'Beast. Stop. What will the neighbours think?'

'They'll think that in a minute, we're going indoors and I'm going to fuck Mrs Mansell.'

'Why do we have to wait a minute before we go in?' she said, releasing his hands and allowing them to carry on their wanderings.

***

Later, as they both lay sleepy and contented on the bed, Sally reached over and poured herself another glass of wine. 'This is very decadent, don't you think?' she said as she leant over him to

138

refill his.

'That's not what you said earlier,' said Tom with a sly grin.

'Not *that*. God, you've got a one-track mind,' she laughed. 'I mean bringing a bottle of wine up to the bedroom.'

'Yes, we ought to do it more often. I'm a great believer in wickedness and sins of the flesh.'

'But you still haven't told me why it took you five days to remember that. I was beginning to think you'd gone off me. Is there something wrong at work? You would tell me, wouldn't you?' Sally's tone was serious once more.

'There's some weird stuff going on and I don't really know what it means if I'm honest.'

'What kind of weird stuff?'

'Where to start?' he said. 'I don't want to read too much into it and I'm probably making two plus two equal five – fifty more like – but you know what I said about David and I talking to Greg Callaghan about possibly going to work for him and that we'd agreed terms over dinner the other night and what all that was going to mean for you and me? Well, the move to Monaco or Switzerland is on hold, maybe permanently.'

'Oh no, did they change their mind?'

'It's a lot worse than that. Greg was found hanged in the woods near his home last week. They say it was suicide, although there doesn't appear to be any reason why he did it – happily married, couple of young kids, no money worries, no history of depression, nothing – so a complete mystery. Under normal circumstances, the fact that we'd been talking about coming to work for him would be something that you'd put down as pure coincidence and assume there was no connection between the two events. But what worries me is this. According to the police he hanged himself the day after David and I had dinner with him in London – just another coincidence you'd think – but earlier that very same day, Andrew Chivers confronted me with what was effectively a verbatim transcript of everything that we'd said in the restaurant. It was a private dining room, we said nothing in front of any of the restaurant staff, none of us would have any cause to mention it to Chivers – he wasn't part of the deal – so how the hell did anyone find out? I suppose you could argue that if someone who knew us saw the three of us leaving the restaurant together, then they could have had a reasonable guess about the content of our conversation. But what Chivers said went way, way beyond that.'

'So what did he say?' she asked.

'Scary, scary stuff. He'd obviously had sight of a transcript of everything we'd said, and the only way that can have happened is if the conversation was recorded without our knowledge: bugged in other words. As if that wasn't bad enough, whoever bugged us had to have prior knowledge of where we'd be that night – Callaghan's secretary booked the restaurant under his name, so we can probably rule that out, unless you assume that the same person who was bugging Greg was also interested in us – which, again, is highly improbable. So that leaves us with one conclusion, someone's been snooping on David and me. I don't know how, but I can take a guess at who.'

'I'm frightened, Tom. Who do you think it is?'

'Remember the boat trip and the clam bake at Rhode Island and those two idiots from Noviprom? I think it could be them.'

'I remember the funny-looking one who had one long eyebrow and a silly little tuft of hair on top. He looked like a Muppet and you two called them Bert and Ernie. They were the ones who tried to bribe you with those horrible, gaudy watches. Weren't they from Russia or something?'

'Nashyastan. Noviprom's the Nashyastan sovereign wealth fund. Noviprom is a new kid on the block and they're trying to do about twenty years' of catch-up in three. That's why they were so keen to get David, me and the Minerva system on board so that they could leap-frog the competition. The whole country is shot through with corruption and Noviprom's right at the middle of it – I wouldn't touch them with a barge pole but the buggers keep chasing me. I told you what happened at that FIX conference the other day when they really upset David, he still hasn't told me what they said, and I ended up threatening one of them. I thought we'd seen the last of them but now I'm not so sure, so maybe those buggers *are* the buggers so to speak.'

'Do you think they were the ones who stole your laptop too?'

'A week ago I'd have laughed at you for saying that,' said Tom, ruefully. 'But now I'm not so sure. Quite why they'd do it is another matter. There was nothing on there that would be of any use to anyone. I've changed all the user names and passwords on every account and log in I have and nothing was touched before I could do it. On balance I still think it was just a bunch of stupid kids, but I'm less sure than I was.'

'But the police said their suspects were four white, adult males.'

'Maybe they latched on to the wrong guys.'

It was now almost completely dark and she snuggled up next to him, 'I still don't like it, darling. Someone's gone to a lot of effort to find out what you're up to.'

Tom gave a deep sigh. 'Perhaps I'm creating a conspiracy theory out of nothing. Maybe it's the bank after all and maybe Sam Bortoleski's behind it.'

'No, Tom. You always say that they're a total bunch of incompetents. The people who bugged you, the people who attacked you – they have to be the same – they're professionals, they know what they're doing. Listen, when I was still practising I came into contact with people who were very clever at listening to other people's conversations, their phone calls, eavesdropping on their e-mails and so on. There's all sorts of very sophisticated equipment out there and a lot of it's not only cheap but available over the internet, so it would be dead easy for a government.'

'I know. But before we go down the James Bond route, there's the simple fact that the only person who seems to know about what we said is Chivers, which brings us right back to the possibility of this being something to do with the bank rather than Noviprom, because so far as I know Chivers has never spoken to any of their people.'

'But what's that got to do with Greg Callaghan?'

'Probably nothing. Greg obviously had demons none of us

knew about, which is why he killed himself. And it's probably pure coincidence that he decided to do so the day after having dinner with us. If it *is* the bank then my money is on Chivers. He's definitely a wrong'un. None of us knew he was going to take over from Denise, not even Matt O'Reilly if you ask me, and I reckon he was parachuted in by New York with a view to getting hold of Minerva, probably by Bortoleski or even someone higher up.'

'And now you think Chivers is following you around in a dirty mac and a trilby, listening at keyholes?'

'Don't see why not. He doesn't seem to have any friends, any hobbies, doesn't drink much, so maybe he needs something to do to keep him occupied of an evening.'

'So why don't you just confront him and ask him outright how he knows?'

'I had thought of doing that, but there are snags. Firstly, it would be tantamount to admitting that the conversation took place – I know it took place and so does he – but I don't want to do that because of what I said to Callaghan about making an offer to our three traders. Secondly, I don't think for one moment he'd tell me and I don't want to give him the satisfaction of knowing that I care about what he gets up to. Still, we don't have to worry about any of this for another three weeks, and you've got your trip to Orange to look forward to.'

In the twilit darkness of the room he could just make out her naked form against the light. He reached over and gently pulled her towards him.

'Tom, what are you doing? Not again, surely?....ooh, Tom, that's very naughty...what are you doing? Oh, Tom....please don't stop...'

***

The day before Tom's departure, as arranged, Catherine Farrell came round to see them. She pressed the button on the intercom and Tom opened the gates from the panel by the front door. He strolled out to meet her as the battered green Renault came into view round the curve of the drive.

'You might as well put it straight under cover, Catherine, you'll boil if you don't get it in the shade.' Tucked around the side of the house furthest from the village was a range of outbuildings that had once sheltered farm machinery, but was now ideal for leaving cars out of the sun. Failure to park in the shade during a Languedoc summer can have painful consequences.

She returned clutching a bottle. 'Hi, Tom, I've brought some rosé. It's still cold so I'll put it straight in the fridge if you don't mind.'

'That's fine and thanks very much for bringing it. Sally's in the kitchen getting the salads ready. If you go and find her I'll get the barbeque lit.'

Catherine had moved to France only six months earlier following an acrimonious and messy divorce from her alcoholic, violent husband and was renting a tiny flat while she worked out if this really was the life she wanted or whether, like a large number of expats in France, she was simply running away from reality – a reality that has a nasty habit of catching up with you. Of a similar height to Sally, she had shoulder-length dark hair and regular, unremarkable features – not that many men noticed her features anyway since most of them were unable to tear their eyes away from her figure: "like the best of Page Three rolled into one," as one wag had put it. She had plenty of suitors in France but Catherine had decided in her words, "to have a gap-year as far as men were concerned", and they all went away disappointed. As Sally had noticed, even Tom couldn't keep his eyes and his mind from wandering, especially when she wore that little red bikini.

Later, as they ate under the shade of the canvas awning that shaded the terrace outside the kitchen, Sally outlined her plans for the trip to Orange. As for Tom, rather than spending his usual four or five days in the UK, this time, he would fly out on the Thursday because he had client meetings on Friday morning. He then planned to spend the weekend at his parents' house in Dorset before going back to London for the following week. To coincide with his absence, Sally had arranged a trip with three of her

French girlfriends. The plan was on Tuesday to go down to Le Lavandou where Mathilde's parents had a holiday home, spend some time down there by the sea and then come back up to Orange for one of the annual *Chorégies* concerts that were held in the old Roman theatre. Since Tom didn't like beaches and couldn't stand opera, the timing was perfect. While they were both away, Catherine had agreed to house-sit.

Chapter Nineteen

Bihar Jalil tapped on the door of Denise Evans' office and let himself in. 'I think we're nearly there,' he said. 'From what I can see in their pre-trade system, the transition management team have a big equities-only rebalance to do and it looks ideal. There are plenty of illiquid small caps and the volatility numbers are the highest they've been in the last six months. As soon as they've created their trade list and it looks like they're ready to go, I'll put in an offsetting pre-hedge that will look as though it's come from Minerva and that'll create the front-running opportunity. I've written a little app that sits on the data bus to listen for the real trade going through and then I've got another little routine that works out what to allocate and where. It also adds the right user names to the log files so this will all look like user input.' He paused. 'You still haven't told me why you want to do this, Denise.'

'No, and I'm not going to. I've told you that already. If you do as you're told and you don't do anything clever to try and implicate anyone else, particularly not me, then I'll delete your picture. This is a very simple little favour and I'm sure you can manage it, can't you, Bihar?'

Chapter Twenty

That morning Tom had meetings with two of the bank's hedge fund clients in the West End. The first client's offices were in St James's, and since it was such a gorgeous day and he had plenty of time in hand, when the meeting was over he decided to walk to the next meeting which was to be held near Berkeley Square. St James's park and the Serpentine were glorious on a perfect June morning like this and he could have cheerfully spent the day just sitting in the sunshine watching the world go by. At a gentle amble, he crossed the footbridge and turned half left to head for the south east corner of Green Park. The time he'd spent with Sally in France had recharged his batteries, and although there was still a nagging concern, it had also pushed the worries about the aftermath of the meeting with Callaghan to the back of his mind.

Crossing The Mall, he wandered slowly into Green Park. The horse chestnuts were in bloom and the world looked fresh, green and new. About halfway across the park he saw something that made his blood run cold. On a park bench, two men were in conversation: a third sat next to them without speaking. Chivers was in animated discussion with Vladimir Ursk from Noviprom. It didn't look as though they'd seen him. Trying to remain as nonchalant as he could, he turned away from them and, taking as circuitous a route as possible, made for the Piccadilly side of the park, quickening his pace as he went. What the hell does this mean? he thought. This is just about as bad as it gets. If Chivers is in bed with Noviprom, then maybe it wasn't him who'd bugged their dinner at La Borda, and if that was the case, maybe Greg Callaghan's death wasn't suicide and maybe…no, that's ridiculous. This is twenty-first century London. Reality, not the plot of some supermarket penny-dreadful. Far more likely that they've given up on David and me and now they're trying to use Chivers as leverage. Yes, that's bound to be it.

Despite repeated attempts to convince himself that what he'd seen was perfectly innocent, he wasn't wholly successful, and those lingering, stubborn loose ends refused to go away. He could barely concentrate on anything during the meeting and once it was over he didn't head straight back to Canary Wharf. He needed time to think: time to work out what the hell to do. He wanted to call David but he was in New York where it was still six AM. Still deep in thought he took a roundabout route and meandered in the general direction of Green Park Tube station. For no particular reason he stopped and looked briefly in the window of a second-hand bookshop, and while marvelling at the eye-watering prices of the goods on display he was aware that he had company.

'Good morning, Mr Mansell, what a lucky coincidence.' It was Kaliski and this time he wasn't alone. He was accompanied by what Tom took to be two of his security people. Both were well over six foot four and looked as though they spent most of their life in the gym. They were huge. Neither of them spoke.

'Funny how we keep running into each other, isn't it, Kaliski?' He resumed his walk towards Green Park but at a quicker pace. Kaliski fell into step beside him while the other two remained a few yards behind.

'I would like to talk to you, Mr Mansell. Our offices are only just round the corner, so perhaps it isn't that surprising that our paths should cross again. I think it is fate.'

Fate, my arse, thought Tom and lengthened his stride so that the smaller man was almost running to keep up. 'I thought I'd made it perfectly clear to you that we have nothing to say to one another, now, if you will kindly excuse me – '

'Mr Mansell, I fear your life may be in danger.'

Tom stopped dead in his tracks and swung round to face Kaliski. 'Listen to me, you obnoxious little shit, if this is some kind of audition for a part in a third-rate gangster movie, then well done. Fucking bravo, you've got the part. Let me make this perfectly clear for the very last time. I do not want to work for you, I will never work for you and I do not ever want to see you anywhere near me again. If your last comment was supposed to intimidate me then please be assured that it didn't. If you so much as come anywhere near me or any of my colleagues, I will report you to the police. Now, kindly crawl back under your flat stone and die.'

Kaliski smiled. 'Of course, Mr Mansell, you have the right to do whatever you want. If you like, we can end this conversation right now and I guarantee you will never have to speak to me again, but before you take that decision, I'd like to show you this.'

He handed him a photograph. The colour drained from Tom's face and his mouth fell open. 'Where did you get this, Kaliski?'

'All in good time, Mr Mansell. If you please.' And gently took it from Tom's hands. 'Come, Mr Mansell. Let me buy you a coffee.'

The four men went into a branch of one of the high street coffee shops. During the late-morning lull, only a few of the tables were taken and Kaliski led them to a quiet corner where they were partially hidden by a wooden partition. All the casual observer could see of the four men was from the shoulders up. 'What would you like to drink, Mr Mansell?'

'Nothing. I want nothing from you. Where did you get that photograph?'

Kaliski said something in his own language and one of the gorillas went to the counter to order. The other kept a very close eye on Tom.

'All in good time. Let us be patient.' They waited in silence for the order to be completed. 'Ah, here is my colleague with the drinks.' The gorilla returned and sat next to Tom: uncomfortably close. 'As for the picture,' continued Kaliski, 'let us say that a friend of mine took it. And quite a few more. Here, take a look, but please don't think you can take them with you. If, as you insist, you want nothing from me then so be it, I will keep the photographs.'

There were about twenty of them, all of Sally in France. There were shots of her out cycling, shopping in town, driving the car, pottering in the garden, walking on the hill behind the house, and each one was marked with a date, time and a precise latitude and longitude. There was even one of her sunbathing topless by the pool. Kaliski smiled. 'Your wife has magnificent breasts. It would indeed be sad if anything were to happen to them, or to her for that matter.'

Tom's fists bunched with rage. 'You miserable, creepy, little pervert, I'll kill you for this.' He had barely moved when his arm was seized in a vice-like grip that held him pinned in his seat. On a command from Kaliski, who had by now retrieved the photos from the table, the grip slackened and Tom shook himself free.

'Mr Mansell, I have been very patient with you, but in return you have been extremely stubborn and, may I say, more than a little rude. However, I am also a tolerant man and I will explain matters to you. I will also explain what I expect you to do… no, please do not interrupt. When I have finished, you will do me the kindness of running along and explaining things to the little Jew also.

'On more than one occasion my colleagues and I have offered you very generous terms to come and work for Noviprom. Not only have you not understood just how generous we have been, nor the concessions we have made in making you several offers – most people receive but one – you have compounded your error – forgive me, I take it that "compounded" is the correct term?' Tom ignored the conceited attempt to fish for compliments, but continued to stare unblinkingly at him eye-to-eye. 'You compounded your error by agreeing to an offer that was made to you and your Jewboy friend by the foolish, and may I add, late, Mr Callaghan and for far less money than *we* offered you.'

Tom was frightened now: adrenalin was taking over from reason. 'You really are about as intimidating as a – ' He was cut short. At a nod from Kaliski, Tom's arms were efficiently and brutally pinned behind his back while the other man seized his knee and began dislocating it. The pain was appalling and Tom gasped for breath. Kaliski nodded again and they released him. He was now bent almost double over the table, grasping his knee.

'Shall we continue, Mr Mansell? But I warn you, even *my* patience has its limits.'

'What is it you want, Kaliski?' spat Tom.

'That's better. I knew you'd see sense in the end if matters were explained clearly enough. Our offer remains on the table. Nothing changes. You are to accept the offer and you are to make sure that the Jew Liebowitz accepts the offer too. Of course, you are to give us the source code for Minerva as well. After that, you can continue working from your lovely home in France, or anywhere you like for that matter, and the only thing that changes is that you will become a lot richer. In return for your agreement, we will even overlook the matter of what you did to Noviprom in the markets a few months ago. It cost my government a good deal of money which was bad enough, but the way in which it was done has drawn your names to the attention of some very influential people whom it is not a good idea to upset. You might think that you were very clever – believe me, you were not. Now, let us look at the alternatives should you or your colleague be so foolish as to refuse this final offer – I did mention that this was our final offer, didn't I? When we spoke in the street earlier, I may not have been strictly truthful with you. I said your life was in danger, whereas, if you think about it, we have every reason for wishing you to remain alive. After all, a dead programmer is not much use to us. The fact is, Mr Mansell, that if you do not accept our offer, we will harm that which is nearest and dearest to you and in ways that you would not wish to contemplate, believe me. Do you know why your friend Callaghan killed himself?'

Tom shook his head.

'We showed him some video clips of what we do to people who offend us, or our friends come to that, complete with the sound track of their begging and screaming. These were only excerpts of course. Thanks to advances in medical science; transfusions, blood clotting technology, antibiotics and so forth, our doctors can keep people alive for several days, weeks even, while we are killing them. We make no distinction between men and women in these matters, something I find personally distasteful but necessary, and, may I add, extremely successful *pour encourager les autres,* as I believe they say. Why do you think so many of the Americans' "rendition" flights landed in our country? Both the CIA and your MI6 continue to owe us a great debt of gratitude, we have excellent diplomatic relations with your government so just think about those facts before you talk about running off to the police.

'We explained to Callaghan that he had a choice: he and his family could be in a crate on the next diplomatic flight to Nashyastan and have a starring role in the next set of video clips or, we would provide him with the wherewithal to commit suicide and we would stay with him to make sure he went through with it. He needed our encouragement, shall I say? But let's say he made a wise choice. If you wish, I can show you some of our latest clips of what may await your dear wife should you refuse.'

'Fuck you, Kaliski.'

'I'll take that as a no, shall I? I should also mention that if you still prove obdurate, we are quite willing to move your place of work to Novi Bar where there will be plenty of room for your wheelchair – provided of course that you know how to use a wheelchair when you've only got one arm. You have forty-eight hours, Mr Mansell. I know it's early in Manhattan but I suggest you call your little Jewish friend right away because our kind offer extends to him too, and of course the offer of starring in one of our videos to his dear and currently pretty friend, Caroline.'

Tom stood up to go.

'Sit down, Mr Mansell, I haven't finished yet. I must warn you that should you be so foolish as to go to the police or to breathe a word of our conversation to any of your other colleagues apart from the little Jew, then we will take that as a refusal of our terms and I hope you've understood what that implies. Good day to you. I look forward to receiving your acceptance.' He placed a business card on the table. 'You can contact me on this number.'

The three men stood up, left the coffee shop and turned towards the Nashyastan embassy. Tom was left trembling with fear and close to tears. He must call David. Limping out into the street, his knee throbbing and tender, he took out his mobile and dialled.

David Liebowitz's voice was muzzy with sleep. 'Christ, Tom, do you know what freakin' time it is?'

'David, this is a matter of life and death and I am not joking. Is Caroline within earshot?'

'Yeah, she's right next to me. Why?'

'Go somewhere she can't hear you and then call me back. This is serious.'

Liebowitz called back two minutes later.

'Tom, you sound frightened. What's going on?'

'David, I am terrified out of my wits. Here's what's just happened.' Tom outlined the conversation with Kaliski in all its detail. 'We also have to assume that they're listening to what we're saying now.'

'So what do we do?'

'I'll call you on my standby Skype ID later. Just look out for me to come on line. About half an hour or so. Good luck, David.'

'You too.'

Tom took the Jubilee line from Green Park back to Canary Wharf. His knee was swollen and really hurting now. Bastards must've damaged the ligaments, he thought. When he got into the office, Chivers was already back at his desk but didn't so much as look up as Tom sat down. Neither man spoke to the other. He tried to do some work but could barely think straight, let alone write code, and was still shaking with fear. When Chivers left the desk to go to the lavatory, Tom picked up the phone and called his friend Alan Jones at HSBC.

'Alan, I need a favour.'

'Sure, Tom. What is it?'

'Do your client meeting rooms still have wireless access?'

'Yes.'

'Can I come and borrow one for half an hour or so?'

'Sure. I'll book a room then head down to reception and see you when you get there.'

'Thanks, Alan.' Bloody good egg, thought Tom. He knows full well that I've asked for something weird and wonderful and he doesn't ask one single question, just does it. Solid man.

Jones met him at reception and Tom picked up his visitor's pass. 'You hurt your leg?' asked Jones as they made for the lifts.

'Oh, it's nothing much, think I must've twisted it playing rugby or something,' lied Tom absent-mindedly.

'In summer?'

'Oh, it's an old injury. Comes and goes, you know.'

Jones led him to the meeting room and left him on his own. 'Give me call when you're done and I'll come and get you,' he said.

Tom started his new laptop and waited for the wireless connection to come up. He followed the instructions that Jones had left him and logged into his new Skype ID. He pinged Liebowitz a chat, confirmed he was ready, put on his headset and started the call.

'Christ, David. Where are you? Sounds like an echo-chamber.'

'I'm by the indoor swimming pool at the hotel. I reckoned it should be pretty difficult for anyone listening in to pick up a conversation with all this background noise. Can you hear me OK?'

'It's not great but it's workable. What the fuck do we do, David?'

'The only thing I can think of is that we stall for time by telling them we'll accept, but wait until the deadline. In the meantime, we try and get someone who they haven't got hooks into to go to the police on our behalf and then go in to hiding with the girls.'

'The trouble with that is that they're clearly watching the house in France and I'm stuck in the UK. For all I know they may even be able to listen in on our phone. The other thing I didn't mention earlier, and which makes things ten times worse, is that I saw Chivers talking to Ursk. I don't know how it happened but we have to assume that they've got to him too.'

'Shit! You're right. That just made things a whole bunch worse. How about you call the French police or get the British police to contact them, that's a better idea?'

'It's too much of a risk. If I have to put my own life in danger then so be it, but I'm not going to do anything that puts Sally at risk. I can't see anything else for it – I'll call Kaliski this evening. I'll break it to Sally as best I can when I get back.'

Tom packed up his laptop and called Alan Jones from the phone in the meeting room.

'Success?' asked Jones.

'I guess you could say that,' said Tom. 'And, Alan, thanks for coming up trumps on this one. It was very important.'

'I thought it might be, which is why I didn't ask,' he replied with a smile.

When he got back to the office, Chivers had gone but Denise Evans was buzzing about the trading floor as though she had work to do. You're not fooling anyone, you know, thought Tom.

At about six o'clock he left the office and headed back to the flat. Let's get this over with, he thought, and dialled the number on Kaliski's card.'

'Noviprom, Kaliski speaking.'

'Kaliski, it's Mansell. I've spoken to David Liebowitz and we will agree your terms as discussed and within the timeframe you proposed.'

'Yes, I know.'

'What do you mean, "I know"?'

'You made a VOIP call, I presume to Liebowitz, from HSBC this afternoon. I cannot imagine for one moment the two of you would have been so foolish as to try and trick me. Remind me, what was the name of that friend of yours at HSBC again?'

'Harry. Harry Starkers. What's it got to do with you anyway?'

'Starkers? Hmmm, I am sure that is not the name of the deceased gentleman that your wonderful Metropolitan Police are currently retrieving from the Thames. I'm sure it was something like Jones. Still, never mind. I must be mistaken. I look forward to having the pleasure of your company again soon, Mr Mansell. You will be contacted and told where we will meet. Until then.'

Tom hung up. His hands were shaking. He rang Sally on her mobile. No point in frightening her with the details now, that would have to wait. He could hear giggling, the clinking of glasses and Catherine's voice in the background. Neither of them sounded terribly sober. 'Darling Tom, we're having such a lovely time, it's so hot…beep, beep, beep…oh, bugger, I'm running out of juice. Call me tomorrow. Love you…beeeeeep.'

He wandered back disconsolately into the living room and turned on the TV. There was a loud bang at the door. Who the bloody hell was this, and how had they got past the external door anyway? There was no chain so he opened it a crack and peered round. The door exploded into his face and sent him flying up the hallway before coming to a halt in a heap at the foot of the stairs. 'Armed police officer, keep still or I fire!' Despite the warning he turned his head slowly and looked up. There were at least four armed policemen who had their weapons trained on him and a further four or five behind who had crammed their way into the hall. Given their well-earned reputation for being trigger-happy, he kept the rest of his body stock-still.

'Don't shoot. You've got the wrong address,' said Tom with as much politeness as he could muster. They forced him to lie on his face with his arms and legs outstretched while they searched him and then repeated the process with him lying on his back.

'Suspect clear,' shouted one of them. The armed policemen stood back a little and a voice from behind them barked, 'Stand up!' The voice seemed vaguely familiar. He got to his feet and the ring of firearms moved aside. He knew who the voice belonged to now. It was Inspector Hill, in uniform now, complete with stab-proof vest and side-arm.

'Thomas James Mansell, I am arresting you under Section 41 of the Financial Crimes Act 2009 and under the provisions of the Counter Terrorism Act 2008. You do not have to say anything – '

'Just a minute, Hill.' Tom was livid. 'If you want to speak to me, you have my telephone number, you know where I work, where I stay when I'm in London, so why the hell do you have to go through this idiotic pantomime rather than giving me a call?'

'You are resisting arrest.'

'Balls.'

A policeman grabbed Tom's arm and twisted it hard behind his back causing him to cry out in pain. Other unseen hands held the other arm and soon both wrists were handcuffed behind his back.

'Now, where was I?' said Hill. 'Oh yes, you are under arrest for assaulting a police officer, resisting arrest, for offences contrary to the Terrorism Counter Terrorism Act 2008 and the Financial Crimes Act 2009. You do not have to say anything....'

Tom's arms were held tight by the policemen either side of him and they stayed glued to his side all the way to the car. There were four police cars and a van, complete with a riot shield to protect its windscreen, all with their blue lights flashing.

***

'He's come out of the flat. I couldn't see clearly, but the police were in a protective huddle around him in such a way as to prevent a clear shot from anywhere but well above. He must have told them that his life is in danger. They're leaving now.'

'Thank you, good work. He will pay for this act of stupidity. Kill the Mansell woman. Mansell himself and the other two I want taken alive. Let me know how quickly you can get a team to New York.'

Chapter Twenty-one

'Did he say what it was about, Mandy?'

'No, Mr Bortoleski, Mr Smith just said it was extremely urgent and that he wanted you to come to his office right now.'

'OK, tell him I'm on my way.'

Mike Smith was head of the global corporate and investment banking division and two up the hierarchy from Sam Bortoleski. For those who worked for him, when he said "jump" the only question was, "how high?"

Bortoleski was worried. He was well aware that the schemes he and Chivers had discussed went way beyond the very elastic boundary of what counts as unethical in the banking world, and were now deep into the realm of illegality. Maybe Chivers had ratted on him. Who knows? We've said nothing illegal across a taped line, there's no document trail, nothing that would stand up in court so nothing to worry about. Just keep calm – probably wants to tell me what a great job I'm doing. Yeah, that'll be it.

He breezed into Smith's outer office, trying to give the impression of a master of the universe who hasn't a care in the world – this one or any other world you care to mention. 'Hi, Tracie. Mike said it was urgent. Could you let him know I'm here, please?'

'Just go right on in, Sam, he's expecting you.'

Smith's expression was grave as he rose to meet Bortoleski. He closed the door behind them. 'Have a seat, Sam. We've got a big problem in London, it's potentially huge. I've just had the director of the SEC on the line and he's told me the CIA may have to get involved in this too. We only have sketchy details at the moment, but I want you to take charge of our response because the problem is right bang in the middle of your division.'

For once, Bortoleski was lost for words. 'W-what do you want me to do, Mike?'

'I'll get to that in a minute. Let me explain. Yesterday, a report was sent to the Financial Conduct Authority in London about the activities of our alternative execution service desk there. From what we can gather, a guy called Mansell, who I believe is one of your traders cum tech people, has been systematically front-running customer business to the tune of several millions of dollars over a period of several months. We haven't got the numbers yet but it looks as though it's in the region of ninety mil.'

'Jeez, that's huge.' Bortoleski went pale.

'Quite. That in itself is not the problem though. The problem is where the money ended up. The British are working on the exact destination and who the players are – they're keeping pretty tight-lipped about who's investigating what and you can draw your own conclusions from that. But it looks as though he's also managed to get round the compliance procedures for account opening, and the money has been diverted to customer accounts he's set up for his own purposes. Now, here's where it gets worse still: those accounts have been traced to a company that the British believe to be linked to known Islamist terrorist groups.'

Why the fuck didn't Chivers tell me he was going to pull this? thought Bortoleski. I'll wring his scrawny Limey neck for him. 'Shit!' he said aloud.

'Exactly that, Sam. The bank's reputation is on the line here. If one guy, working on his own can run rings around our systems security and compliance procedures, we are going to get torn apart. If we get our response to this wrong, I will lose my job, you will certainly lose yours and so on right down the line. There is a very high probability, depending on what we find, that we will have to shut the entire London brokerage operation down. It could potentially bring down the entire investment bank. Now, here's what I want you to do. First, this must not leak. The British police have arrested Mansell, and because it's a terrorist-related arrest, they can hold him incommunicado for forty-eight hours under their new legislation. From what I've been told, the only people who know the full story are Denise Evans, Chivers who runs the AES desk, the head of prop trading – what's his name again, Sam?'

'Wood.'

'That's it, Wood. He knows, as does the head of compliance. Second, the other people on the AES desk may or may not be involved. It'll be your job to find out and in doing so, you'll need to put the fear of God into them about what'll happen if they breathe a word about this to anyone. You will set up an internal enquiry to find out what happened, when and who did what. You'll also be responsible for making sure that it can't happen again. Anyone who was anywhere near this and so much as forgot to wipe their feet before coming into the office I want you to fire. We have to be seen to be coming down hard even if we don't know what we're coming down hard on. With me so far?'

'Yes, Mike.' Bortoleski's Adam's apple bobbed up and down like a cork in a stream.

'Good. Third, you're going to have to work with the press office to make sure that when the story breaks, it's our version that hits the press and nobody else's. Finally, you have whatever resources you need: anyone who gets in your way, you let me know and they'll be out sweeping the streets within the hour.' Smith handed Bortoleski a thick sheaf of paper. 'Take this and guard it with your life. It's a numbered copy of the initial report and gives details of all the information we have. Ask Mandy to get you on a flight to London this evening. Any questions?'

'Just one, Mike. Who found all this crap and how?'

'It was Denise Evans. Seems she was reviewing some of our systems audits a while back and decided to get them updated. When she did, guess what fell out of the closet? She ran straight to compliance, Peacock took one look at it and nearly crapped himself. He did the sensible thing and called the regulators. At this stage it looked like just another trading scandal, but when they dug a bit deeper and found the terrorist link, that's when it really hit the fan.'

If there had been a prize for the most relieved man in Manhattan, Sam Bortoleski would definitely have been on the top step of the podium at that moment.

He nodded sagely. 'Interesting, and well done Ms Evans. She had a bad start and I thought I'd appointed the wrong person to succeed Matt, but I'm glad she's come good,' said Bortoleski. 'I'll get Mandy on the flight bookings and go pack a bag. I'll call you when I get to London.'

'Thanks, Sam, and good luck.'

Bortoleski paid off the taxi and took the elevator up to his apartment. As soon as the door was closed, he called Chivers on his mobile.

'Andrew, what the fuck is going on? Did Christmas come early or something? How the hell did you swing it so that Evans picked up the front-running, and what's all this Islamic terrorist shit?'

'Sam, thank Christ you called, I thought it was all *your* doing.'

'What are you talking about, Andrew? Are you trying to tell me you didn't know anything about this?'

'Nothing. Absolutely nothing. I told you I thought the front-running scheme was a bad idea and that I was working on some other ideas of my own. When it all kicked off I got called in to Denise's office and there were a couple of suits there who said they worked for the Treasury – not that they were anything to do with the Treasury if you ask me, and that it was all very hush-hush because there was a terrorist angle. When they mentioned terrorism, believe me, I was calling you some names right then, I thought that you must've gone crazy. So if it wasn't you, then either Christmas has come early and he really did do all this shit or, someone else had the same idea as us and beat us to the draw to put him in the frame.'

'I don't think it's Christmas, Andrew. Mansell could walk out tomorrow, set up his own hedge fund and make a small fortune within a year. And the other thing is the Islamic terrorist link. Does he strike you as a religious fanatic?'

'I don't think I've ever even heard him mention religion. He drinks, I've seen him eat a ham sandwich and from the picture on his desk he doesn't make his wife go round wearing a sack with eyeholes in it, so it must be some new branch of Islam that we don't know about if that's the case.'

Bortoleski paused. 'So what does that leave us with?'

'I really don't know, Sam. If we assume that he's been set up, it must've been by someone internal to the bank, but who else but us would want to do that and who else would overdo it by adding mad mullahs to the story? It just doesn't make sense.'

'OK, well keep digging. Mike Smith's asked me to go to London to find out what happened and to run a damage-limitation exercise. I'm leaving tonight and I'll be with you tomorrow morning. We'll talk then.'

Chapter Twenty-two

Tom was bundled into the back of the van, made to sit down with his handcuffs attached to a shackle. The van had a small row of darkened windows right at the top of the side panelling which let in a little light but made it impossible for anyone to see in. A policeman sat either side of him holding his arms and two others sat opposite him with their batons drawn. Nobody spoke.

He tried to work out where they were going by the turns they took through the London streets and the time they spent going in a certain direction, but he very quickly lost track and gave up. After about twenty minutes, the van came to a halt, reversed a short distance and the driver stopped the engine. From outside he could hear raised voices, the clanking of machinery and what sounded like a metal shutter closing. The back doors were flung open and Tom blinked in the unaccustomed brightness as he was led out of the van, his hands still cuffed behind his back.

He was inside what looked like an over-sized garage or workshop, about thirty feet wide by sixty long. It had a green-painted concrete floor, white breeze-block walls and was dazzlingly lit from overhead. All around the van were armed police: there were even three dog-handlers present, each with an evil-looking Alsatian. He was led through a metal door set in the far wall and up a flight of concrete steps. Heavy metal rods slammed home as the door thudded shut behind them, their footfalls echoing eerily around the stairwell. But still, nobody spoke to him.

Tom suddenly had the horrifying thought that these people were not police at all, but were all part of some hideous subterfuge got up by Kaliski, and that shortly he was going to be playing the leading role in one of his revolting snuff movies. The situation was so unreal that Tom would not have been the slightest bit surprised to meet a white rabbit in a waistcoat examining its pocket watch. At the top of the stairs, they passed through another heavy metal door which also was locked behind them, and then turned right down a corridor flanked with metal doors down each side.

'In here.'

He was shoved into the cell and would have fallen had not one of his escorts held him up. Unseen hands undid the handcuffs, which by now had become excruciatingly painful, and he tried to massage some life back into his hands and wrists. The cell was about ten feet by six. Along one wall was a bed made from a single, smooth piece of stainless steel and covered by a thin mattress encased in shiny waterproof material. There was a wash basin, a metal lavatory with no seat and that was it, no windows, no other furniture, just white paint and white light. Hill came into the cell. 'Right, remove your clothing. All of it.'

'What?' Tom said.

'Are you deaf as well as stupid? Remove your clothing. Now!' Hill stood aside and a man wearing a white coat came in. In his confused state, Tom began to wonder whether he was a doctor or merely a cricket umpire who had got lost on his way to Lord's.

He did as he was told. His clothes were taken away in a bag and he had to undergo a full body search: latex gloves and probing fingers taking away his last shreds of dignity. The men who had escorted him to the cell stood watching and jeering in the doorway while the search took place.

A parcel of clothing was tossed on to the bed. 'Put these on and wait.' The door slammed and was locked shut. He was alone. Where he was and why he was there, he had no idea.

Tom undid the bundle. Inside was a new pair of underpants, several sizes too big, a pair of socks, a tee-shirt and a pair of overalls. For his feet there were a pair of cheap slippers which he was amazed to find fitted him rather well.

He tried desperately to make sense of what was happening to him. It was clear that the arrest wasn't a case of mistaken identity: they knew who he was all right. If he'd done something at work then surely he would have been called in to see Denise, she would have called compliance and even if he'd done something so utterly horrendous that it warranted arrest, such as swindling the bank to line his own pockets, then they wouldn't have sent a fully-armed goon squad to break down his front door.

Then, his fuddled memory of the last hour began to clear. Hill had said something about offences under the terrorism act so that had to be it. But if someone had implicated him in both financial crimes and terrorism, then for Christ's sake who? Clearly nobody at work so that only left Kaliski. But that made no sense either: the last thing Kaliski would want, mused Tom, is me in the hands of the police and in a place so secure that even he couldn't get at me. It just doesn't make sense.

***

'Caroline, I don't like this. I can't raise Tom. His phone is going straight to voicemail and he's not up on Skype. He was showing as on-line just after lunch, so about seven their time, and now he's disappeared.' Liebowitz paced up and down the hotel room as he spoke.

'We have to go to the police, David. It's our only chance.' She was crying again.

'We can't. We have no proof, no evidence, nothing. We walk in with a story like that we'll get treated like a couple of UFO conspiracy fantasists. And besides, if Kaliski's people find out then I dread to think what they'd do to Tom and Sally. We just have to play along with it for now and then find some way, somehow to get out.'

'Shouldn't we warn Sally?'

'I don't know. What if he's just left the phone on silent in his coat pocket and the internet connection in the flat has gone down, or he's turned his laptop off or something like that. We're going to scare her to death – she's been as twitchy as hell about Tom going back to London and we don't want to make it worse.'

'You don't have to frighten her, just say that there's something you wanted to ask him, he's not answering his mobile and if he calls, please ask him to call David.'

Liebowitz dialled the number.

164

The voice that answered was loud and more than a little slurred. 'Hi, David. How are you? How was the conference? Catherine and I have just opened another bottle by the way. Cheers!'

'Hi, Sally. Cheers! Conference is going fine thanks and Caroline sends her love. Hey, listen, that old soak of a husband of yours has obviously gone out and left his phone on silent and I need to ask him something. Has he called this evening?'

'Yes, he called about two hours ago. Why?'

'Oh, it's nothing. It's work-related stuff and just in case he hasn't noticed that I've left him a voicemail I was going to ask you to get him to call me if he calls you, but since he already has, don't worry about it and I'll leave the two of you to your party. Thanks. Bye.'

'Bye, David. Byeee!'

'She says he called two hours ago which tells us nothing.'

'So what do we do?'

'Sit tight. Nothing else we can do. If we go to the police, we have to assume Kaliski will know somehow. If we run, there's a chance they'll harm Tom and Sally. And anyway, where would we run to – next door to Elvis and two down from Bigfoot? I'll send him another e-mail about some technical crap and ask him to contact me urgently. If he doesn't respond by tomorrow, then we'll have to make some big decisions. We're due to sign in forty-eight hours. Shit!'

Chapter Twenty-three

Tom lay on the hard, unyielding metal bed. The mattress was thin and offered little in the way of padding. He put his hands behind his head and stared up at the ceiling. From time to time he was aware of an eye at the small grille in the door. From somewhere down the corridor came what sounded like a high-pitched repetitive keening. One of the gaolers hammered on the door and told the inmate to shut up. At least I'm not the only one caught up in this nightmare, he thought.

He must have drifted off to sleep because the next thing he knew, the door was being unlocked. Hill and two others came into the cell. 'Sit on the bed and put your hands together out in front of you.' They cuffed his hands again. This time they also cuffed his ankles: the manacles were joined by a short length of chain that allowed him to walk but only at a slow shuffle. 'Now stand up and face the wall.' Tom obeyed and a pillowcase was put over his head. Hands grasped his shoulders and steered him out into the corridor.

The shuffling procession made its way along the corridor, round various corners, negotiated another flight of steps until they reached what Tom took to be a larger room, from the sound of a number of voices. He was pushed down on to a chair and the pillowcase removed from his head. In front of him was a long table behind which were seated Hill and two men in plain clothes. Other officers, some of them armed, stood guard over him. On the table was what he took to be some kind of recording device. The room itself was like a bigger version of his cell: white walls, concrete floor, bright overhead lighting and no windows. The air conditioning hummed monotonously in the background. The door behind them closed with a solid thump.

Hill spoke at last. 'I take it you know why you have been arrested, Mr Mansell.'

'No idea at all, but I'm sure you're going to tell me.'

'No, Mr Mansell. Wrong answer. You're going to start by

telling me what you know about Mughal Holdings Limited and why you carried out illegal trading activities in order to provide them with funding. To save us all a lot of time and yourself from considerable physical discomfort, we know exactly what you've been doing and who your accomplices are. What we're interested in is why. We have a list of names, we know all the facts so I suggest that you co-operate with me. If you don't, you are very likely to spend the rest of your life behind bars. Co-operate and you could be out in ten years.' Hill nodded to one of his colleagues who switched on the recording device.

'Believe me, Hill. I haven't the faintest idea what you're on about. All I can think is that you've been the victim of a very elaborate leg-pull. Also, and far more importantly, there are people who need to know that I've been arrested and I would like to see a solicitor.'

'All in good time, Mr Mansell. You are being detained under the Counter Terrorism Act 2008 and because of the amendments that were made to it this year the normal provisions governing detention do not apply for the first forty-eight hours. We don't want your accomplices knowing who you're talking to, do we?' Hill opened a box-file on the table in front of him. 'Show him these. At ten twenty-six PM the prisoner was shown the system print outs marked as exhibit A. Take your time, Mr Mansell and explain to me what you see.'

Wearing handcuffs, it was difficult for him to leaf through the hundred or so A4 sheets that he'd been given. 'If you want me to try and make sense of this, Hill, could you please free my hands? It's not as if I'm going to get very far with these things on my legs.'

Hill nodded to one of the guards who unlocked Tom's wrists.

Tom studied the print-outs intently. He was back on familiar territory. The first twenty or so pages were activity log files and, according to the header on each sheet, were from his desk's program trading system. He scanned the dates, times, trigger events and against each one was either the name of the automated process that had generated it or the user's user ID: his own. At the sight of this, his hands began to shake, and he braced them against the tops of his thighs so that Hill would not notice. He continued, struggling to regulate his breathing in order to hide the rising tide of panic, deliberately taking his time in order to see whether Hill's patience would crack. For now it held.

As Tom worked his way through the print-outs, the story became clearer. A client order was received – quite a big program trade by the look of it – and against each security was a corresponding series of executions, so far so ordinary. Then there was a series of price and traded volume "tick data" for some of the securities in the program. I know what's coming here, thought Tom, some bastard's trying to make it look as though I've been front-running an agency program. He flicked through the pile of paper and, near the bottom, found what he'd been looking for: the bookings for each execution. As expected, all the favourable prices had been allocated to one set of accounts – the account number didn't mean anything to him – and all the less favourable prices to another, presumably the accounts belonging to the client on whose behalf the program was being executed. To make it look convincing, whoever did this would probably have provided a decode of the account number and he was fully expecting to see that an account in his name had been set up. In fact, whoever had tried to frame him had been a little more subtle. There was a name next to the account number, but it was Mughal Holdings Limited: a UK company with an address in Bradford. A log file showed the various steps in the automated account opening and approval process and the user IDs of everyone who'd updated or approved the account and Tom's was all over it. He smiled.

'Something in there you find amusing, Mr Mansell?'

'Yes, there is actually,' said Tom and left it at that. That should get his curiosity going, he thought. Taking great pains to make sure that he understood the entire story that the print-outs were trying to weave, he spent another ten minutes poring over them, not only to make sure that no last detail had escaped his scrutiny, but also to goad Hill's impatience. The crucial piece of evidence was missing, however. That meant one thing: either his antagonist had been very clever or unbelievably stupid. He wasn't sure which. Tom rearranged the papers, leaned forward and placed them on the table in front of Hill. Then he sat back in the chair and waited.

'Well then, Mr Mansell. Pretty conclusive isn't it?'

'Yes. Couldn't agree more.'

'So you admit that you set up accounts in the name of Mughal holdings into which you diverted the proceeds of illegal trading activity with the aim of aiding and abetting terrorist acts?'

'No.'

'But Mr Mansell, the evidence is clear, you've seen it yourself, and as a seasoned industry professional with first-hand knowledge of the trading techniques and systems involved, your involvement is beyond any shred of doubt.'

'Do you know what you've got there, Hill?'

'Evidence of your guilt, Mr Mansell, that's what I've got there.'

'What you've got there is a fairy story. Please don't get me wrong. I don't doubt that these trades may've taken place and that funds could have been siphoned off to unauthorised accounts, but it's a fairy story none the less.'

'What do you mean?'

'I mean that anyone with half an ounce of systems knowledge, with the right access and rudimentary programming skills can not only modify user IDs but also over-write time-stamps and amend system-created records. For example, I never set up trading accounts nor do I approve them, so whoever messed around with the account opening log files made the basic mistake of trying to make their story look too good. I've been warning the bank about this kind of system vulnerability for years. Clearly they've still not got round to doing anything about it. There are other, slightly more sophisticated ways of proving that this is all an elaborate fake too.'

'So what are they?'

'For now I refuse to answer that question. Not on the grounds that it might incriminate me but on the grounds that I do not trust you personally and the police in general not to be colluding with whoever did this. However, because I'm a law-abiding individual who wants to go home to his wife, I will now tell you something that's far more interesting than anything cooked up by whoever produced the nonsense in your box file. It also happens to be true.'

Tom then started to tell the police about everything that had happened with Noviprom and Kaliski. As soon as he'd begun, he realised that he'd miscalculated badly. Not only did they refuse to listen to what he said, nor to his insistence that his wife's life was in danger, accusing him of being a serial fantasist, but they kept dragging the questioning back to their original line of front-running and terrorist funding. This is getting nowhere, he thought, so at well after midnight he folded his hands in his lap and said quietly, 'Gentlemen, I see that it's now twenty to one in the morning and way past my bed-time. May I request that we call a halt for the evening and that we resume tomorrow, ideally starting by you listening to what I have to tell you, rather than asking me the same silly questions. Then please check with the French police that my wife is OK and let me go home.'

Hill went white with rage. 'Mr Mansell, we will decide when this interview is over, not you. Let us go back to the day you opened the Mughal Holdings account. Tell me how you gained access to the account opening system.'

Tom broke eye contact with Hill, tucked his hands under his thighs and looked down at the floor. They'd had a lecture about this when he'd been on the University Air Squadron. Let's see if it works, he thought. 'I cannot answer that question, sir,' he said quietly.

Hill was once more beside himself with anger. 'What did you say?' he bellowed.

'I cannot answer that question, sir.'

'Don't you try that with me. How did you get access to the account opening system? Tell me.'

Tom paused about fifteen seconds: it seemed like a lifetime.

'I cannot answer that question, sir.'

And so it continued for another hour as they took it turn to question him – whatever they asked, he waited for a varying length of time and then gave the same response, 'I cannot answer that question, sir.' In the end, Hill made a comment into the recording machine to the effect that despite being cautioned that it could harm his defence, the prisoner refused to answer any further questions. Tom's hands were cuffed again, the pillowcase was placed on his head and he was led back to his cell. First, they unshackled his ankles, then his wrists but they left him standing blindfolded for about ten seconds. Then the pillowcase was yanked off his head and the door slammed shut.

With the cell brightly illuminated at all times, he lost track of time. He was frantic with worry about Sally. He had to warn her but what could he do?

Despite the brightness of the lighting in the cell and the difficulty of trying to get comfortable on the thin, nylon-covered mattress, he managed fall into a fitful sleep. The sound of the door being unlocked woke him up. He had no idea if he'd been asleep for minutes, hours or even days. Time no longer had any meaning – that's the idea of course.

'Right, get up. Time for breakfast. You do want breakfast, don't you?'

Tom nodded. His back hurt abominably from where they'd hit him during the arrest, he felt dirty, clammy and his mouth was like the bottom of a parrot's cage. The door swung open again and a uniformed policeman handed him a tray on which was a bowl of cereal, a carton of UHT milk, a mug of stewed tea, a rather stale cheese and tomato roll and some plastic cutlery.

'Thanks,' said Tom and made a start on the unappetising offering in front of him. He realised that he'd had no supper last night and since they'd only given him water to drink since his arrest, he was ravenously hungry.

A while later they returned. He was given a towel, a basic washing and shaving kit and a black bin bag. 'Get undressed, put all the clothes in the bag and come with me.' Tom wrapped the towel around his waist and set off down the corridor, one officer in front of him, another close behind. After the shower, he still felt gritty-eyed and desperately tired, but at least now he felt clean. When they returned to the cell, another surprise awaited him. The clothes that he had been wearing when they had arrested him had been freshly laundered, pressed and put into a neat cellophane wrapping. Next to them on the bed were his watch and wallet. After he'd dressed he was handed a clipboard with a piece of paper on it and a pen. 'Sign here to acknowledge return of your belongings.'

'Where's my phone, my laptop, my passport and all my other things? Your people took far more than that from the flat and none of it's on this list.'

'You're signing for the stuff we're returning to you now. A full list of anything else that may have been removed will be given to you at a later date.'

'Do I have a choice?'

The policeman put his head on one side and looked at Tom with utter disdain. 'Course you do. You can carry on wasting my fucking time if you like. In which case we will beat the shit out of you, purely in self-defence you understand, and because we can.'

Tom signed and returned the clipboard.

'Put the towel in the bag with the clothes, leave the washing kit on the bed and come with us. You're going on a little journey.'

Tom's hopes rose. 'Are you letting me go home?'

'Think we've got a fucking comedian here, Kev.'

His colleague laughed. 'Nah, you're going to Buckingham Palace for lunch with the Queen, what did you think? Stupid prick. You're off to Paddington Green, mate.'

This time there were no manacles and no blindfolds; just the same maze of corridors, stairwells, armoured doors and white-painted concrete. Eventually they reached somewhere he recognised: they were back in the over-sized garage where the van had stopped the night before. This time, there was no police van, but in its place was what looked like a security van, bearing the markings of a private company. Two men in the uniform of the company stood chatting and smoking with a group of policemen. On a bench against the opposite wall sat a small, forlorn figure clutching a tatty plastic carrier bag.

'Stop, that's far enough.' Tom felt a hand on his shoulder. 'Right, come over here. Sit down and listen to what I'm telling you. See him over there?' The policeman nodded in the direction of the figure on the bench. Tom nodded. 'Know what he is?'

'No,' said Tom.

'A fucking nonce, that's what he is. A filthy, slimy, fucking nonce, and you are going to do us a big favour. Instead of putting cuffs on you and sitting holding your hand on the little journey you're both going on, we're going to put the two of you in the back of the van together, all on your own, real cosy like. Depending on the state of our little pervert friend when they open the doors at the other end, my colleagues will either be very sympathetic to you or make you wish you'd never been born. Do you understand me?' He winked at Tom.

'Er, no, I'm sorry. I don't understand you at all. What's a nonce?'

The policeman tutted and rolled his eyes in despair. 'What's a nonce?! You posh twat. A nonce is a paedo. Someone who messes around with little kiddies, a child rapist, the lowest of the fucking low. Read about that little girl in Portsmouth last week?' Tom shook his head, 'Six years old – raped and murdered, so just use your imagination. And it was him. So if when you get to see my friends, they have to remove what's left of that little piece of shit from the back of the van with a mop and bucket, then they will be very nice to you. Now do you understand?'

'Yes,' replied Tom. 'I do now.'

'Good. Now, you're a big strong lad, so don't let us down, will you?'

Two escorts grabbed the nonce and put him in the back of the van. Then it was Tom's turn. Inside was a security cage made of steel mesh. This time there were no windows, just internal lighting. The driver shut the cage door, locked it, shut the back doors of the van and locked them too. Tom sat on a bench that ran down one side of the cage, his fellow passenger sat opposite, their knees almost touching. He heard the same mechanical clanking noises as last night, the van's engine started and they set off.

For the first five minutes Tom said nothing to his companion who was white-faced and trembling with fear. Eventually he spoke. 'I know who you are and what you are,' said Tom with an air of menace.

'Yes, they told me.' The man had a high, reedy voice.

'Do you know what I'm going to do to you?'

The man started crying. 'Please don't hurt me, please don't.'

Tom looked at him with contempt. 'All right, I won't hurt you, but in return I want you to do something for me. I want you to memorise a telephone number. Then, when you get access to a solicitor I want you to tell him to call that number and pass on a message. It's extremely urgent and can't wait, not even a few hours. Now, just in case you think you can forget all about this the moment you get out of this van, then you're wrong.' OK, thought Tom. Big lie told with lots of confidence, just pretend you're the Prime Minister. Deep breath. 'My wife is a solicitor in London and believe me, she has a very extensive network of contacts. When she returns from her business trip next week she will be able to find out if you've done what I asked you. If you haven't, I will tell everyone, the police, the press and the TV about what you told me in the back of this van about the little girl in Portsmouth and how you bragged about it and how you thought it was perfectly normal. Do you want that?'

The nonce was sobbing now. 'Please don't do that, please no. You mustn't.'

'All right, calm down. Do as I tell you and there'll be no need. Now listen carefully, we'll do the message first, it's very simple so there's no need to worry. You are to tell the solicitor to contact a man called David Liebowitz – I will give you his mobile phone number and a little trick to help you remember it – to tell him that his life is in danger because Tom Mansell has been arrested. That's all. He'll know what to do.'

'David Liebowitz's life is in danger because Tom Mansell has been arrested,' parroted the nonce. 'Is that it?'

'Yes, very good. Now for the mobile phone number.' Tom

made sure he had it by heart. The nonce had stopped snivelling.

'So where was that place?' asked Tom.

'You really don't know?'

'No.'

'That, mate, was none other than the National Counter-Terrorism Detention Centre.'

'But I thought you were a n…' Tom hesitated. 'A paedophile. So why were you there, that's got nothing to do with terrorism?'

Now it was the nonce's turn to look at Tom with contempt. 'Christ, you really are green as grass aren't you? Any time the police want to keep someone under lock and key for any reason, but they haven't got enough evidence to charge them, they arrest and charge under the Terrorism Act. One of the coppers explained it to me. Because of the way the way the law was changed last year after that suicide bombing in the West End, there's no solicitors, no tape recordings when it suits them, nobody there but the police and God knows who else. So they've got forty-eight hours to get a confession out of you pretty much any way they choose.'

They swayed as the van rounded a corner and Tom had to brace his foot against the opposite bench to stop himself being thrown forward. Then the driver hit the brakes and they were flung sideways. An enormous bang and a violent acceleration threw him back against the side of the cage, a muffled explosion and then all around him went white. He was falling, floating, losing all sensation – all white, nothing but white.

Chapter Twenty-four

Languedoc, southern France

'Do not lie to me, you little imbecile. Your two little bum-chums have told me exactly what you did. You killed that woman because she saw you trying to break into the house, didn't you?' Adjutant-chef Monti of the *Gendarmerie départementale* towered over the terrified youth who was now on the verge of tears.

'I didn't touch her, please believe me.'

'How old did you say you were?'

'Nineteen, sir.'

'Nineteen, eh? Do you know what happens to little prats your age when they're banged up in *Les Baumettes*? Let me tell you. A nice piece of young, untouched arse like you will be buggered senseless about ten times a day for your first six months. They'll be queuing up to screw you. Won't that be fun, eh? Like it up the arse, do you? No? So how about telling me the truth? If you mess me about, be very sure that I will pin this on you and your mates and if that means there are three less scumbags out on the streets, whether you did it or not doesn't interest me one bit. So start talking.'

The youth choked back a sob. 'I was working on a house that's being built at Mirepech. You can see a lot from up the scaffolding. Just down the road there's this big house – bloody English again, it's always the sodding English, driving up the house prices and behaving like they own the place.'

'Cut the crap and get on with it,' snarled Monti.

'All right, I'll admit, me and my mates have done over a few houses. I move from site to site, wherever I can get work and I'm never in the same place for more than a few weeks, or a month or two at the most. Gives me a good excuse to have a snoop round, see if there are any houses worth doing and watch for patterns – you know, when do people go out, when they come back and so on.'

'And then you fence it on. I'll need details of who your fence is.'

The youth started babbling, unable to get the story out fast enough. 'I've got a mate who takes the stuff at a good price so we just go in quick, jewellery mainly, stuff we can put in a rucksack or a carrier bag, nothing big or heavy and then out.'

'So why did you kill her? Threatened to call the cops did she? Stop lying to me you little shit.'

'No, it's all true. I promise. I never touched her.'

Monti noted the rising panic in the youth's voice with satisfaction. He'd got the little bastard. 'I'll believe you for now. Go on,' he said.

'I'd been watching the house for about a month and it was obvious that Tuesday was their restaurant day – car would go out about eleven and come back around half two, three o'clock. I'd done a bit of a recce and one side of the electric gates was easy to force and from what I could see from the scaffolding, they don't seem to close their shutters – so when we saw the car leave today, we decided to give it a go. And that's when we found her. She was just sitting there, propped up on the sunbed, but with no head – it was horrible, horrible, but believe me, we didn't touch her. Please don't send me to prison. Please,' he sobbed.

'Keep an eye on him,' barked Monti to the two Gendarmes in the interview room, and strode off down the corridor to his office. He made two brief phone calls. 'All right, my office when you've finished.'

After five minutes he was joined by two other Gendarmerie NCOs. 'Same story from mine too,' said one. The other nodded in confirmation. 'And mine.'

'Makes sense,' said Monti. 'Firstly, I don't think they did it. Why would they? Secondly, I'll bet forensic don't find any firearms residue on them and thirdly, why blow someone's head off and then ring up to tell us? Get statements off them, call their parents, but keep them here for now.'

The senior *médecin légiste* – police forensic surgeon – from the Toulouse laboratory was unimpressed at being called out just as he'd started a pleasant family lunch by the pool at his daughter's house near Montpellier. I'm supposed to be on holiday, he fumed, this had better be something worthwhile.

By the time he reached le Mas des Oliviers, he was still in a foul mood. However, as soon as he ducked under the tapes surrounding the area where the body had been found, he realised straight away that he wasn't dealing with a simple murder. His hopes of getting away quickly that afternoon had just evaporated.

The seriousness of the case sent it ricocheting up the command structure of the *Direction Centrale de la Police Judiciare* (DCPJ) who now took overall charge of the investigation.

In less than an hour after the police surgeon's report had been received, a Mystère 50 from the Armée de l'Air's ETEC 65 squadron was airborne from the Base Aérienne 107 at Villacoublay. On board was a forensic team from the Gendarmerie's *Institut de Recherche Criminelle de la Gendarmerie Nationale*, or IRCGN for short. The aircraft was met by a helicopter at Béziers airport which took them the last few kilometres to Mirepech.

Capitaine Henri Gatinois was relieved. The local boys hadn't made a mess of things for once. Under the command of a captain from the local brigade who was in charge of the investigation, they had sealed the site off, had kept the public away and didn't seem to have trampled over too much of the evidence. His trained eye took in the crime scene, and for Gatinois, who during his career had seen just about every possible variety of cruelty that human beings can inflict on one another, it was pretty obvious what had happened. He introduced himself to the captain and then turned to Monti who had driven back from the *gendarmerie* to Mirepech to meet him.

'I take it you've checked with the neighbours and with the rest of the builders working on the site?' asked Gatinois.

'Not one of them saw a thing.'

'Did anyone report hearing a gunshot?'

'Nothing. The three lads that we've nicked are certain they heard nothing either.'

'That's interesting,' said Gatinois. 'It's clearly not a shotgun wound and to do this much damage, the round either had to be going very quickly or be very big – both of those normally imply a gunshot that you'd hear several kilometres away. Do we know who she is yet?'

Monti looked at his notebook. 'We're pretty sure her name is Mansell. Sally Mansell. English. We think her husband's away on business somewhere and we're trying to find him. My boys are trying to find anything that looks like a flight booking on the PC in the office upstairs but we can't get past the bloody password. We'll need a formal identification of course but I'm certain beyond any doubt that it's her.'

'That's one less question to answer then', said Gatinois. 'Tell your people to touch as little as possible and to keep out of the other rooms. Find out if she's registered with any of the local doctors and if she is, get the doctor down here to make a provisional identification. I think we can forget dental for now.'

'Capitaine.' A voice interrupted them. 'Come and have a look. I haven't found the round itself, but I was getting a large amount of what seem to be fragments, and then I found this.' In a pair of forceps, Adjutant Lafarge, Gatinois' deputy, showed his boss a small, deformed piece of metal that had a distinct curve to it. Gatinois took out a magnifying glass, took the forceps from Lafarge and examined the object. He let out a low whistle.

'If this is what I think it is, we've got a big problem. Take it back a second, would you, Lafarge?' Gatinois went to his bag and got out a micrometer. 'Just hold it steady …here we are. Damn, I was right.'

'What is it?' asked Monti.

'Just a second, Monti. Lafarge, take your detector and see if there are any traces of fragments embedded in the sunbed or in the torso of the victim.'

'Yes, boss.'

'I don't get it,' said Monti.

Gatinois frowned, deeply concerned. 'I don't want to be alarmist, but what Lafarge found looks unpleasantly like part of a

12.7 mm Russian-made, high-explosive sniper round. A STs-130PT to be precise.'

'What's one of those?' asked Monti.

'It's a very nasty piece of kit. They've used some very clever technology to produce a subsonic round, with low drag and an exceptionally high twist rate so that it stays stable in flight. And all that with a muzzle velocity of only around 300 metres per second. A normal round comes out of the barrel at around 700 to 800, in other words at around twice the speed of sound, and that means things going bang, very loudly for two reasons: firstly, the amount of explosive charge in the cartridge to give it the required amount of energy, and secondly, because of the shock wave from the round itself. This one you'd barely hear being fired, but what you would hear is a slightly louder bang as it hits its target and explodes inside it.'

'Inside it?' Monti shuddered at the thought.

'Yes, this type of round has a standard centrifugal safety and arming device and a simple deceleration fuse that detects impact with a target and then, depending on the exact bullet type, anti-personnel, anti-vehicle, incendiary and so on, there's a variable time delay to allow the round to penetrate before detonating. And that's what took Madame Mansell's head off. The nasty thing about them is that they're effective out to about 600 metres, which is about fifty percent further than most subsonic rounds can manage and still remain accurate. From what's left of the poor woman and the distribution of remains on the wall and on the ground, it looks as though the round was fired from the hill opposite the house, so get your men to seal the ridge off. It'll have the advantage of keeping nosey press cameramen away too. Once we've finished here, we'll try and get up there later if there's enough light left.'

Lafarge returned. 'You were right, sir. Fragments in the shoulder and neck area and I think also in the sunbed. Difficult to say too much about how much is embedded in the wood because there are all sorts of screws, fittings and other bits of metal holding it together.'

'Monti, this is nasty,' said Gatinois with a shake of his head. 'It's not my place to tell you how to do your job, so please don't take this the wrong way, but I'd get your boss to make a report to the *Commissaire de Police* straight away. The *Préfet* needs to be kept updated too. Oh, and let the mayor know as well if he's sober, and for heaven's sake tell him to keep it quiet. Whoever did this knew what they were doing – up till now we thought that only specialist units of the Russian FSB had access to weapons like this – and we need to find out what the Mansells are mixed up in that caused someone to want to do this. Oh, and for Christ's sake, keep the press and TV away from it as long as you can. Right, I'm going to suit up and take a look round the house. Any questions? No? Good.'

Chapter Twenty-five

If this is what being dead is like then it's very odd, thought Tom. All around him was white, he could hear voices but they seemed muffled somehow and far away. And for some strange reason he was swaddled in what felt like a slowly deflating balloon. He pushed the material away and crawled towards the sound of the voices. It was lighter in that direction too. He pushed the last shrouds from in front of him and realised what had happened. The van was on its side, both the door to the cage and the van's rear doors were open and what he'd been wrapped up in must have been a series of airbags. He crawled on, blinking into the daylight and was helped to his feet by a couple of well-wishers.

'Are you all right, mate?' one of them said.

'I'm OK, but there's someone else in there and I don't know whether he's been hurt.'

'Don't you worry, we'll get him out. You won't run off, will you?' And with that they crawled into the van and disappeared under the collapsed airbags.

'It's all right,' Tom called after them. 'They were taking me to be released.' There was a muffled reply from inside the van but he didn't catch what was said.

The accident had drawn a considerable crowd and Tom joined them to try and get a better idea what had happened. What he saw was a ghastly sight but one that made him realise how lucky he'd been not to be badly injured or worse. The front of the van had been obliterated and now lay under the front of a vast articulated lorry; from the writing on the side of its trailer he could see that it was Polish. There was no sign of the two men who'd been in the front of the van and he preferred not to look any further.

He checked that his wallet was still in the back pocket of his jeans and set off at a slow walk away from the scene of the accident without any idea where he was or where he was going. If they had been on their way to Paddington Green, and assuming the place he'd been held last night was also somewhere in London, then he'd be bound to see a street sign or something he knew.

Next he stopped at a cash dispenser and, using his platinum card, he withdrew £500. Using his other card he took out £250. Knowing that he'd been in the area from his card usage wouldn't tell anybody where he was going, not that he had much of an idea himself. Then he crossed the road and went into a newsagents to buy a phone card. As he came out, he spotted the two things he was looking for: a London Underground sign showing the way to Baker Street Tube station and an un-vandalised phone box. He tried to call Sally; there was no reply. He hung up and dialled a different number.

It was just after six AM in New York and Liebowitz's voice had that pissed-off snarl of someone who's just been woken up. 'Yeah, what is it?'

'David, it's Tom. Listen to me. Someone has framed me for illegal trading and terrorist funding and I was arrested last night.'

'Yeah, I got a call from Mike Smith saying you were in deep shit and that he was going to London to try and sort things out. I've been ordered back to London too.'

'Listen, David, I've managed to escape from the police. No, don't ask questions, I know it sounds stupid, just let me finish. We have to assume that Kaliski and Chivers know what happened and will assume I've told the police everything. That means you and Caroline are in danger and so is Sally. I'm stuck in London, Sally's in France and we need to warn her, but neither number's answering. You've got her mobile number as well as the landline, haven't you?'

'Yes.'

'Good. If she's at home, tell her to call you straight back on Skype. She'll have to know the truth however much it frightens her. Then tell her to go and stay with friends, anything, just get away from the house, keep the car out of sight and call the police. I'm going to try and get to France – tell her that – God knows how, because the police will be watching the ports and airports for me, plus I haven't got my passport. I'll explain why later, but the police think I'm a terrorist. Now, wherever you are, after you've spoken to Sally, get the hell out. OK, I've got to go. Bye.'

Tom set off at a brisk walk, mind racing in an effort to think of a solution. He came to an abrupt stop, turned round and ran back towards the phone box. That's it, he thought. I know what I'll do, I'll call Hutch, he'll help me, I'm sure he will. He re-inserted the phone card and called one of the horrendously expensive directory enquiry lines. 'Hutchinson. Richard Hutchinson, Manor Park Farm, Littleham Road, Coolham, Sussex. Oh, right, OK thanks.' He hung up. 'Bugger!' he said aloud: Hutch was ex-directory. I'll just have to turn up on the doorstep, that's all there is for it, he decided.

Forty minutes later Tom emerged from the shop. He was clad in lycra and pushing a bicycle with a small rack on the back to support the panniers that held his clothes. He'd also bought a cycling helmet and a pair of sunglasses which would act as a very effective disguise. For everything he had paid cash. He'd never cycled in London and never used pedals with under-sole cleats before, but there had to be a first time for everything. Crossing the Thames via Vauxhall Bridge, he stopped and bought some supplies: a change of clothes, packs of underpants and socks, a notepad, a pack of ballpoint pens, washing kit – shaving was off the menu for now – a towel and some food.

After Croydon, and an hour or so into the journey, he headed towards Wallington and Banstead. Tom was fairly sure that if anyone was looking for him they'd start with the trains and buses and he hoped that no one would give a cyclist a second glance. That's assuming I don't get killed by a lorry, he thought, that would be too ironic. He was on familiar territory now and after a roadside lunch stop near Dorking, he continued on to Betchworth – resisting the temptation to drop in and see how the people who'd bought their old house were getting on – through Leigh and along the Surrey lanes to Broadbridge Heath in Sussex.

Although he was fit, he found cycling much harder work than he'd expected. The saddle seemed to have been designed to inflict as much pain as possible, despite the padded shorts, and he now found that at each rise in the road his legs felt weak and didn't want to work. The speedometer that the man in the bike shop had offered to him for free was telling him that he'd averaged 13 mph so far – just about half the speed that the *peloton* average during the Tour de France, mountain stages and all – but it wasn't far to go now: Brooks Green 2 miles, according to the signpost he'd just passed. Nearly there.

Tom turned off the main road and into the lane that led to Hutch's place. His legs were like jelly now and he'd covered just under sixty miles in a little over four and a half hours. He closed the five-bar gate and cycled up the long drive to the farm itself. Propping the bike against the wall of the barn, he rang the doorbell and waited. Nothing. Bugger, they must be out. Please come back soon, Hutch, I've got to get to Sally. He waited but still Hutch didn't return so he cycled back into the village to buy some more food in case he didn't come back till much later. When he returned there was still no sign of anyone. The weather was turning chilly now, and the heat of the day had given way to a blustery west wind and gathering clouds. Spots of rain were falling. While in the village he'd tried to call Sally from a call box: he knew it was a risk. Worryingly, the call to her mobile had again bounced straight to voicemail. The phone at le Mas des Oliviers still wasn't answering either.

It was getting dark. Suppose they were on holiday. What was he to do then? Only one thing for it. He took the tool roll from under the saddle and went round to the lean-to workshop at the far end of the barn. To his relief, the fanlight still didn't close properly and, using the screwdriver from the tool kit, he easily levered it open, reached inside and opened the window. He climbed through, dropped to the floor, crossed to the door that led to the barn and turned on the workshop lights. Luckily for him, the key was still in the lock and he quickly whipped the door open, pausing only to turn on the lights in the barn itself and scampered across to the alarm panel, which was already emitting its regular warning beep at one-second intervals, and keyed in a four digit number. Please let it still be the same code. It was: the alarm fell silent.

The room above the workshop had been used in the past as temporary accommodation. There was a bedroom which smelled of damp and a small, grubby bathroom with a shower cubicle – not the Ritz but it would do. The windows of the workshop faced open countryside so there was little chance of anyone seeing a light, but Tom wasn't taking any chances, so after he'd cleaned himself up and finished the leaden sandwich that he'd bought in the village, he settled down to sleep as best he could.

When he awoke the next morning, he could barely stand, his legs were so stiff and painful. The saddle seemed to have inflicted irreparable damage too and he felt as though he'd been hit on the backside with a club. After taking a hot shower he went back down to the house to see if there was any sign of life. Nothing. They could be away for weeks, he thought, and I've got to get to Sally. Hutch may well kill me for this, but it's my only option, I just hope to Christ I don't damage the bloody thing. He went back down to the workshop, tore a sheet out of the notebook he'd bought in London and started writing a note to him.

Chapter Twenty-six

Languedoc, southern France

Gatinois started with the upstairs of the house. Nothing out of the ordinary caught his eye as he checked the bedrooms. Everything was neat and tidy. One thing was odd though: at the far end of the house from the master bedroom, one of the guest rooms showed clear signs of occupation – clothes hung on the back of a chair; women's make-up and toiletries on the sink top in the en-suite; a small suitcase, half-unpacked, lay on the floor and, on the bed, which hadn't been made, was a woman's handbag. It didn't make sense. Where was the visitor? He continued checking the rest of the house. There was nothing to suggest that anything untoward had happened, no signs of a break-in or a struggle, just simple domestic ordinariness.

Holding a sealed plastic bag in gloved hands, Gatinois ducked back under the blue and white tape that was stretched across the door to the house and walked back into the garden. He pulled back the hood of his white forensic suit and went back over to where Monti and his boss were standing. 'Monti, did any of the three lads you've nicked mention seeing anyone else here?'

'No, sir. From what they said, when they saw the car leave they were sure the Mansells had gone out to a restaurant and that the coast was clear for them to break in.'

'Makes sense, but we need to know who was driving and where they've gone. What's bothering me is that the main bedroom, which from the stuff on the bedside tables and so on looks like it's the Mansells', is completely tidy whereas the guest bedroom at the other end looks as though there's a woman staying in it: clothes, make-up, handbag etc. There's even a half-unpacked suitcase in there. Have you managed to get hold of the local doctor?'

'Says he's on his way, sir. Should be here in ten minutes. Do you think the visitor, whoever she is, might have something to do with the murder?'

'It's possible, I suppose, but I don't think it's likely. If the visitor was implicated, she wouldn't run off and leave all her belongings behind. I just want to know who the visitor is. I've taken the handbag from the room and bagged it up. I'll take a look and see if there's a driving licence or a *carte bleue* with a name on it.'

Monti's boss chipped in. 'That's a good point. Monti, get your lads to check all round the property and at the back of the house just to make sure we're not dealing with a multiple homicide. Whoever was staying in the guest bedroom might be a victim as well. Check again with the traffic boys to see if they've got any details on the Mansells' car.'

Replacing his hood, mask and protective goggles, Gatinois opened the handbag and took out a small leather wallet. Inside was a British driving licence and a series of credit cards. They all bore the same name.

Chapter Twenty-seven

Tom took the keys to the main doors and walked round to the front of the barn. He undid the heavy padlock and slid each door fully back. Now for the fun part.

Returning to the workshop, he found what he was looking for: another set of keys. He turned one of them in the lock and eased back the canopy. So this was Hutch's new pride and joy. He'd only had it a couple of months and Tom had never seen it before. He reached in and flicked the battery master switch on. There was the familiar electric whine of systems starting up and the sight of needles flickering in their dials: a warning panel to the right lit up with a series of red and amber captions. Scanning the aircraft's instrument panel, he found what he was looking for: the tanks were three quarters full – more than enough. After turning the battery back off, he jumped down, checked the chocks and then climbed back up to release the parking brake. To do this he had to sit in the seat and depress the footbrakes by pressing the top of the rudder pedals while releasing the brake handle. He then removed the chocks and set about pushing the aircraft backwards out of the barn, a task that required multiple stops and starts to make sure that the wingtips would clear the sides and to try and persuade the nosewheel to stay in the alignment he wanted. After about ten minutes of concerted effort, it was done. He re-applied the parking brake and stopped to get his breath back, his mouth dry at the thought of what lay ahead.

At university, Tom had been a volunteer member of the University Air Squadron and had amassed over seventy-five flying hours in those three years. Severely bitten by the flying bug, once he'd started work and was earning enough money, he completed a private pilot's licence course and always made sure to log enough flying hours every year to keep his licence current. Just before leaving for France, he had added an instrument rating to his qualifications.

Hutch was ten years older than Tom and had been his desk

head when Tom had been a young trader. Hutch's ambition had always been to give up the City as soon as he could afford it and live the life of gentleman farmer, an ambition which he had now fulfilled. Just like Tom, he had the flying bug and could afford to run a light aircraft which he flew from the strip at Manor Park Farm. When Tom was living in the UK, he and Hutch would fly together at least once a month and shared the cost of the fuel. Hutch had phoned him a few months earlier to tell him about the new toy; a top of the range, single-engined, German-made four-seater – fully aerobatic, glass cockpit and all the latest navaids – that he was planning to fly down to France to come and visit Tom and Sally. For Tom, it was a very different proposition from anything he had ever flown before.

He checked all round the barn and the workshop but there was no documentation: no pilot's notes, no performance manuals, nothing. In the cockpit was a checklist – that was a start – and a standard 1:250,000 scale aviation chart of the southern UK. But no maps of France and no approach charts: better work out how to use the GPS, thought Tom. Packing his belongings into the baggage compartment, he set about working out how to get his bike into the rear seats. Taking great care not to get oil on the new upholstery he eventually got it in by almost completely dismantling it, but it was in, that was the main thing. After padlocking the main doors and re-setting the alarm, he climbed out of the workshop window, closed the fanlight and left things exactly as he'd found them, all bar the fact that he was about to make off with a very expensive aeroplane that didn't belong to him. The words of an extravagantly gay flying instructor he'd once met came back to him, "Do try not to crash, won't you, my dear?"

He finished the pre-start checks: parking brake on, fuel pump on, mixture fully rich, RPM to max, throttle set, fuel to "all tanks," he turned the key. The starter motor whined, the three-bladed, constant-speed prop turned and with a cough, the engine burst into life. Following the check-list carefully, Tom completed the after-start checks and was pleased to see that the artificial horizon in the glass display was now visible, as was the combined compass and navigation display directly beneath it. He flicked the switch on the side of the screen and the GPS display came to life too: he had no idea how to enter waypoints or destinations, but it showed a map, complete with an overlay of controlled and restricted airspace, so that would be more than adequate. He sat and waited for the cylinder head and oil temperatures to come up into the green sectors, opened the throttle slightly and released the brakes. The aircraft rolled forward and he dabbed the brakes again, just to make sure they were working correctly – even if you're stealing an aircraft, there's no excuse for letting your standards slip.

The wind was still coming from the west and the windsock showed that it was blowing almost straight down the grass runway – no crosswind take-off so one less thing to worry about. As he taxied, he checked the instruments were working correctly: turning right, horizon erect, needle right, ball left, compass increasing, standby compass increasing, headings aligned. He lowered half flap, turned on the pitot heat, the anti-collision lights and completed the rest of the pre take-off checks. Finally, just short of the runway, he stopped, turned the aircraft into wind and carried out a power check. Controls full and free, moving in the correct sense, all was well, now for it. He released the brakes and smoothly applied full power. The tendency to yaw during the take-off roll was easy to hold with a gentle squeeze of rudder and he noticed that it accelerated a lot quicker than Hutch's previous aircraft: no sooner had he raised the nosewheel than it was airborne. He retracted the flaps and reached down to the lollypop-shaped handle to raise the undercarriage: it wouldn't budge. Tom had no idea what the gear limiting speed was on an aircraft like this so he maintained 100 knots in the climb, which seemed reasonable, while he tried to sort the problem out. The next thing he knew he was entering cloud at around 2,000 feet so he transferred his attention to the artificial horizon from which he scanned out to the airspeed indicator, altimeter and heading, always coming back to the artificial horizon before scanning the next instrument – selective radial scan, his instructor had called it.

Although he knew that he was, strictly speaking, below safety altitude, he reduced power, lowered the nose and came back out of the clouds. He looked down and found the trouble; he'd forgotten to retract the undercarriage safety lock that prevented inadvertent raising of the gear handle on the ground. He pushed it aside and raised the handle: the three green indicator lights turned red and then went out as the gear locked into place with a satisfying clunk. Using nothing more than feel and guesswork, Tom leaned off the mixture slightly, reduced power to what he assumed was a sensible cruise setting, set the transponder to 7000 + mode C, trimmed the aircraft so that it would fly hands off and let it settle into a cruise at 2,000 feet, just below the cloud base – 150 knots, not bad, he thought.

As he coasted out near Birling Gap, the weather seemed to have improved slightly and he adjusted course to the east to head for Cap Gris Nez in order to keep the over-sea part of the journey as short as possible. He'd considered trying to file an airborne flight plan but he couldn't remember the procedure, plus there was the embarrassing possibility that French air traffic might turn him away and then if he continued they might consider him a threat. He changed to the French visual flight rules VHF frequency of 123.5 and, as a safety measure, he made sure that the radio was also set to listen to the VHF "guard" emergency frequency.

As Cap Gris Nez appeared out of the haze, he turned south to follow the coast, remaining just far enough offshore to avoid upsetting Le Touquet's air traffic control. The cloud base had lifted to around 3,000 feet, but the visibility was only just over 5 kilometres and there were a number of heavy showers around: this was going to make getting anywhere near Orange very difficult. Clearly, he didn't have enough fuel to make it all the way. Going east around the Massif Central still meant negotiating high points like Mont Pilat which went up to six thousand feet, and furthermore, he didn't want to risk drawing attention to himself by inadvertently flying into the controlled airspace round Paris or Lyon. He weighed his options. The only one that made sense was to stay to the west and head for somewhere like Bergerac, cycle to

Bordeaux and get a train from there. Just after Dieppe, he crossed the coast and set a heading that, according to the GPS would take him to the north of the military base at Evreux. His plan was then to skirt to the west of Châteaudun and then get as far south as he could. It all felt horribly surreal.

It was just as he was passing Le Mans that trouble struck. Although Tom's French was fairly fluent, he wasn't used to using the radio in the language and was completely ignorant of their air traffic procedures, but what he heard, he was pretty sure, was meant for him…

"…*sur garde…avion non-identifié…à dix nautiques à l'ouest du Mans….cap deux cent-dix…altitude trois mille pieds….transpondeur sept mille…identifiez-vous…je répète, identifiez-vous…*"

A few moments later the next transmission left him in no doubt.

"…*calling on guard…unidentified aircraft…ten nautical miles west of Le Mans…heading two one zero degrees…altitude three thousand feet…squawking seven zero zero zero…what is your callsign? I say again, what is your callsign?*"

Tom decided to press on. On the assumption that what he had heard was coming from a ground radar station, he was safe for the time being. He vaguely knew that the French Air Force's air defence bases were in the east of the country, a legacy of the Cold War, and it would take them at least half an hour before they got anyone airborne and into his vicinity. And besides, if the worst came to the worst, he'd be treated as lost rather than as a terrorist threat, wouldn't he? Then the doubts began to creep in. He'd already been arrested as a terrorist once in the last forty-eight hours. What if the British authorities somehow knew he'd stolen the aircraft and had told the French? Perhaps it might just be better to land. He looked down. The countryside was wooded and slightly hilly and there wasn't anywhere that he'd really like to try and land an aircraft that he was flying for the first time.

He was still considering his options when he heard a strange growling sound in the headset, shortly followed by a radio transmission. It was clear that someone was still trying to contact him on the emergency frequency; he didn't recognise the callsign and it could've been a ground-based radar station, but it was equally possible that it was a military aircraft, and in an era of post 9/11 twitchiness he didn't want to take unnecessary risks. His French wasn't good enough to catch it all but what he could make out was enough and even as he translated as best he could, he realised he was in trouble. With each succeeding transmission it sounded unpleasantly like a conversation between two military aircraft. Clearly, one of the pilots was double-transmitting because Tom was picking up what one of them was saying via the guard channel.

'Coton Alpha leader, contact bears 330, forty miles, heading two one zero. Low level. Contact is squawking 7000, speed now 120 knots. Getting propeller modulations on the radar. *"Tagazou"'* Tom didn't understand this last transmission, nor the French aviation slang term for light aircraft.

He had to land and quickly. Had he but known, two Mirage 2000 aircraft from the elite EC 02/005 fighter squadron that had just finished air-to-air refuelling, were being vectored from their air defence training mission and had been handed over to a civilian approach radar controller who was now giving them updates on the position of the unidentified light aircraft.

Tom spotted a likely field. He still hadn't worked out what all the buttons on the GPS did, but from the difference between his heading and his track, he worked out that the wind was blowing at about 15 knots from 290 degrees at 3,000 feet, so call it westerly-ish at 10 knots at ground-level. The field was into wind and looked reasonably level. He closed the throttle, overbanked and started to spiral down. In the cockpits of both fighters, the pilots saw the message "PSIC" flash in the Head Up Display. This was to warn them that their radars' discontinuous track mode could no longer resolve the difference between the Doppler shift from the radar returns of Tom's aircraft and the shift from the returns reflected from the ground. Despite thumbing the little mushroom-shaped button on the left-hand side of their aircrafts' control column to put the radar into single target track, both pilots lost contact as their radars unlocked, leaving a yellowy-brown *"plot fictif"* on their radar screens that continued to show an estimated position for the target based on its last known heading, height and speed. Tom heard the growling sound again.

'IFF contact only, three one five, thirty miles. Evading.'

Shit, thought Tom, they're tracking my IFF. He reached down and hurriedly turned the transponder off. He was down to eight hundred feet now and had managed to get the speed down to 100 knots as he turned onto an easterly heading to the south of his chosen field. He lowered half flap, set the RPM to max, mixture fully rich and checked that his harness was tight and locked and that the canopy was closed. As he rolled into a continuous left hand final turn he lowered full flap and increased power slightly: he had no idea of what the approach speed should be but decided that seventy knots over the hedge would probably be about right.

At about three hundred feet he was fully lined up with his field when an audio warning went off, accompanied by a flashing amber attention-getter on the cockpit coaming. He checked his instruments for the source of the problem and saw to his horror that a warning flag marked "U/C" was flashing across the air speed indicator. The undercarriage! He'd forgotten to lower the undercarriage. He frantically pushed the handle down and the three red lights came on as the gear unlocked. 'Come on, damn you!' he urged. As the aircraft crossed the hedge, one green mainwheel light came on. As he closed the throttle and gently raised the nose into the landing flare, the other came on. The nosewheel light was still red as he touched down. He was going fast now across damp grass and he needed to get the nosewheel down to be able to start braking. The far hedge was approaching rapidly. Green! He lowered the nosewheel and started to brake hard, pulling the stick back as he did so in order to weight up the mainwheels and prevent them locking. The aircraft didn't want to stop. Despite his efforts, both brakes were locked now and he was sure that Hutch's pride and joy was going to end up in a heap in the hedge. He closed his eyes and waited for the impact.

It never came. A small up slope just before the hedge had saved him a lot of explaining to his friend. The aircraft had stopped just yards from it. Taking a deep breath, he quickly added a handful of power and, applying full left rudder, swung the aircraft round. As he did so, two Mirage 2000s passed just to the west, the leader only a few tens of yards from directly overflying him. He hoped they hadn't seen him, but it wouldn't take them long to turn round and come back for another look, he thought. Hugging the western hedgerow of the field, he taxied up to an open-sided barn that was mid-way along the field; if he could get the aircraft in there, at least it would be safe from the elements and prying eyes. He taxied the aircraft up alongside it, applied the brakes and went through the shut-down checks. The barn was in a fairly neglected state and some of the straw bales stacked inside had started to sprout with weeds.

He jumped down from the wing to assess the situation and as he did so, with a deafening roar, one of the Mirages screamed back over the field from the west at 420 knots and about five hundred feet, causing Tom instinctively to duck. If they came back the other way, they'd be sure to see him. Scrabbling frantically at the bales, after about half an hour he had managed to clear just enough space to manhandle the aircraft under cover. Then, after removing his belongings, including the bike, he set to work building a protective wall of bales in an effort to hide it from view. His mind raced. What to do? Spend more time to make sure the aircraft was fully concealed or get on the move quickly before the police turned up?

Tom scanned the sky continuously and allowed himself a brief feeling of relief when there was no further sign of the Mirages. The relief was short-lived when he realised that they'd probably left the area having got a precise GPS fix of where he'd landed and that pretty soon he was likely to have unwelcome company. With the fear rising in his throat, he redoubled his efforts to hide the aircraft.

After about half an hour, satisfied he'd done what he could, Tom returned to the aircraft and used its GPS to confirm the exact latitude and longitude, which he then carefully wrote down. He turned the battery off, slid the canopy shut and jumped down from the wing for the last time. Next, he changed into his cycling gear, wheeled the bike out into the lane next to the field and set off in what he hoped, according to his last check of the GPS, was the direction of Le Mans. Like many country lanes, although this one started going in the right direction, it very soon veered off at a right angle and he feared he was doubling back on himself.

He pressed on and after about 10 minutes the road took him into a small town. Although it was a calculated risk, he stopped at a bank and withdrew as much cash as his French card would allow. Next, he bought a phone card, a series of Michelin road maps, stamps and a packet of envelopes from the *tabac* and some food from a down-at-heel village shop. To all appearances he was just another British tourist. He posted an apologetic letter to Hutch in which he recorded the GPS latitude and longitude of where he'd hidden the aircraft. He phoned Sally's mobile: still bouncing to voicemail. He called the house, still no reply. Then he tried David's phone – it bounced to voicemail. "David, it's Tom again. I've managed to get to France but I still can't get hold of Sally and all I know is that she's somewhere on the south coast: near Cannes I think. I'm going to head for Orange because she's due there on Saturday for some opera thing. I'll keep checking in with you as often as I can just in case you get through to her before then. Love to Caroline and keep your head down, mate. Talk soon." He retrieved the phone card and shoved it into the rear pocket of his cycling jersey. As he left the town, heading for Le Mans, an awful griping fear took hold of him. Maybe the reason Sally's phone wasn't responding was because he was already too late to save her.

From his experiences cycling in the Languedoc, he'd soon realised that with very few exceptions, French motorists are far more patient and considerate towards cyclists than their British counterparts, and those he met on the way to Le Mans were no different.

Tom had been cycling for about twenty minutes. The road was

narrow and with a stream of traffic coming in the other direction, the car behind him had no choice but to slow down and wait its chance to overtake. Unfortunately for Tom, on this one day when he couldn't afford any more hold-ups, the exception proved the rule and the driver's impatience got the better of him. The first thing Tom knew was when he caught sight of the car in his peripheral vision and felt rather than heard its approach, followed by its wing mirror missing his left elbow by inches, causing him to swerve into the gutter to avoid the impact. He braked hard but it was too late, the front wheel dropped off the surface of the road and into a narrow concrete drainage channel, sending him over the handlebars in a graceful somersault onto the grass verge. The impact knocked the wind out of him and for a moment he lay still, trying to get his breath, not daring to move in case something was broken. At last he gingerly sat up. The car was out of sight and he'd had no chance even to see its number plate. Nothing but silence, broken only by the birds singing from the hedgerows and the clickety sound of his back wheel as it spun slowly round.

He stood up and made his way over to the bike. He pulled it upright but it was clear that something wasn't right: the handlebars were at an odd angle and the front wheel wouldn't turn – he saw to his horror that the forks were twisted and the front wheel was buckled beyond repair with several spokes having come adrift at the point of impact. He was loath to abandon his sole means of transport, so, using the saddle tube as a lever, he twisted the forks more or less back into alignment. He replaced the saddle tube and found that by removing the front brake calliper and by applying some fairly crude twisting and bashing to the rim, he was at least able to get the bike into a state where he could wheel it along in a more or less straight line. Sadly, there was no question of its being able to bear his weight and as he set off, just to add insult to injury, it began to rain.

He'd been going for about a kilometre and was considering taking shelter from the elements when a white van went past him. It pulled into a lay-by a little further up the road and stopped. As he approached, the driver stuck his head out of the window. 'You alright? Need a hand?' The man's French was heavily accented and barely comprehensible but Tom got the gist.

'Thanks,' said Tom, 'I need to get to Le Mans, it's really urgent.'

'Well, I'm not going that far, but I can take you to St-Georges-du-Bois if that helps.'

'Is that nearer Le Mans than here?'

'Course it is, otherwise I wouldn't offer to take you there, would I? Put the bike in the back. I've got some deliveries to make on the way so it'll be a while. Jump in.' During the brief conversation, the remains of his cigarette had remained attached to the man's bottom lip. Tom slid the side door of the van open, stowed his bike among the sacks of cement, window frames and other building materials and, ignoring the smell of cigarettes and the even worse stink of the elderly Jack Russell with whom he was forced to share the ride, clambered into the cab. His rescuer spoke quickly and Tom didn't catch everything he said. 'Got four building sites on the go at the same time – not bad eh?' Tom nodded in agreement.

They set off and the van rattled over a level-crossing causing the driver's large belly to wobble up and down in sympathy. 'Nice bike you've got there. Used to do a lot of cycling myself,' he said. 'Too much work now of course. Weekends too.' From his appearance, too much food, too much wine and too many cigarettes seemed nearer the mark, but Tom made no comment. On closer inspection, what he'd earlier taken for premature greyness and a sickly complexion turned out to be a coating of cement dust that covered the inside of the van, the owner, his belongings – everything but the Jack Russell it seemed. 'So what happened to you then?' he asked. Tom explained that he'd been forced off his bike and that the front wheel and forks were ruined.

'On holiday then, are you?'

'Yes,' lied Tom. I'm on a cycling holiday and I'm on my way to Le Mans to get the train to Paris.'

'Paris, eh?' he said, with an air of disdain as though Tom had just mentioned a word that shouldn't be uttered in polite company.

'We get a lot of your lot over here – English that is. Got a couple of English clients that I've done some renovation work for. Good payers but God knows why they insist on spending a fortune doing up old places when they could have a nice new house for half the money.' He looked sideways at Tom. 'Bet you've got a house in France, haven't you?' he said, with what could have been a smile or even possibly a sneer – Tom wasn't sure.

'Yes we have actually, but it's in the Languedoc.'

'So what are you doing up here in the rain?' As he laughed at his own joke, the belly under the once white tee-shirt bobbed up and down in time with the cigarette on his bottom lip.

'Oh, I don't know, just a change of scenery, visit a part of France I've never seen, easy to get to from England, no real reason.'

'So you don't live in the Languedoc full-time?'

'No,' said Tom. He didn't want to give too much away about himself to this stranger, however kind he was. 'We live near London which is where I work.'

'House in the Languedoc, place near London, very nice too.' No smile this time. He slowed the van and turned off the road down a narrow track. 'Here, this is the first site; you can give me a hand unloading.'

At the approach of the van, what had seemed like a deserted building site suddenly sprang to life. As if from nowhere, a group of five men, four of whom were of north African origin resumed their work at a frantic pace as though they had only left off a matter of seconds ago. 'Lazy bastards,' said the driver. 'They think they can fool me that they've been working, but I know full well they'll down tools at the slightest excuse – drop of rain like this never hurt anyone. Come on, give me a hand.'

Tom jumped out of the cab and straight into a puddle. He squelched round to the other side of the van and, jumping in to the cargo space, retrieved his waterproof jacket from the bike's panniers and began helping his rescuer unload. Despite the man's bulk and his lack of inches, Tom was impressed at the way he swung the twenty-five kilo bags of cement around as though they were seat cushions.

Once the unloading was complete, the driver joined his workmen for a cigarette break under the eaves of the half-built house: he didn't introduce Tom nor did he invite him to join them, so he took shelter from the rain with the flatulent Jack Russell in the cab and wound down the window to get some air. From inside the van he could make out bits and pieces of the conversation and on occasions was none too sure that he wasn't the butt of some of the laughter that was coming from the group. By the time they'd finished their cigarette break and put the world to rights, the rain was falling as a steady downpour and as the van reversed to turn back up the lane, the builders made no pretence of renewing their work. 'Right,' said his companion – he still had no idea of the man's name, 'Couple more sites to visit and then I can drop you off.'

A few kilometres further on they came to a small village called La Croix sur Gée. It may've once been a one-horse town but the horse had left long ago. They pulled in to a scruffy, pot-holed car park in front of a row of shops comprising a *Tabac* a, bakery and a dingy bar called "Café de la Paix". 'Just going to get some cigarettes,' said the driver. 'Got any cash on you, I've only got a fifty euro note? Bloody cash machines.'

'Yes, but it's in the back with my things, I can get it if you like.'

'No, that's ok, don't bother,' he said and stumped off into the rain followed by the dog. After a few minutes the duo returned and the tangible quality of the fug in the cabin was now enhanced by a miasma of soggy clothing and wet dog. For another twenty minutes they continued, sometimes following signs towards Le Mans, causing Tom's hope to rise, and on other occasions turning frustratingly in the opposite direction. Finally, they pulled up in front of a tall hedge, beyond which Tom could just make out the outline of a roof, rendered barely visibly by the condensation on the van's side windows. 'Do me a favour would you,' said the driver. Go and ask for Mohamed, he's my foreman on this site, and tell him to bring his lads out to unload, I can't get the van any closer than this.'

Happy to get out into the fresh air, Tom zipped up his waterproof, shut the van door behind him and made his way towards the house. The gate in the hedge was rusted almost solid so it took him a couple of hefty shoves to get it open, and making his way through the rank growth of the neglected garden that almost hid the path from view, he approached the house. The roof had been replaced and the windows gaped open to the elements, obviously waiting for Mohamed and his boys to fit the new frames he'd seen in the back of the van. There was no front door so he went in. The house had been gutted – no stairs, all the render hacked off the walls and half of the upstairs flooring joists repaired, but where were the builders? Continuing into the kitchen there was still no sign of life. Tom called out: no reply. He felt almost relieved in a way, standing there in a half re-built house miles from nowhere, in the middle of a downpour and shouting for Mohamed made him feel extremely silly. He continued his search, but clearly Mohamed and his boys had done a bunk and, by the sign of things, a long time ago too. There were none of the usual signs of activity: no tools, no scaffolding, no bricks, no building materials. Nothing. Mr Fatboy Builder would not be happy, that was for sure. Retracing his steps, Tom pushed through the foliage, getting a good drenching as he did so, and back to the lane to report the sad news that the Marie Celeste had been left half-renovated. He was trying to work out how best to phrase it in French and was perplexed to find that on prising open the reluctant garden gate, there was no sign of the van. His assumed that his new friend must have parked somewhere further along the lane or gone to turn round, but as time wore on and there was no sign of anyone, he began to worry. Walking first one way up the lane for about five hundred metres and then the other, the horrible realisation sank in. He'd been taken for a rich, mug tourist and his would-be rescuer had made off with two prizes: a valuable bike needing only new forks and a front wheel to make it saleable and, worst of all, his wallet, complete with his credit cards and cash. All he had left was the clothes he stood up in and a half-used

French phone card in the back pocket of his cycling jersey. Great, just bloody great.

With no idea where he was, Tom decided to walk back the way they'd come in order to get back to the main road where at least he had a chance of hitching a lift. The afternoon was wearing on and his chances of getting to Paris before nightfall now seemed remote, whereas the probability of spending a night sleeping rough grew with each step. None of this was getting him any nearer to Sally.

After about forty-five minutes, he reached the main road and turned to walk in the direction of Le Mans. There was no pavement and he was forced to keep to the long, wet grass on the roadside to avoid getting run over, his attempts to hitch a lift producing nothing more than a soaking in dirty spray from each vehicle that thundered past. After about a couple of kilometres he came to a lay-by and decided that he might have more luck there. It was just after a series of quite sharp bends so the traffic wouldn't be going too fast, it gave any potential good Samaritan somewhere to pull in rather than risk being tail-ended by a heavy lorry by stopping on the long fast straight he'd just squelched along and, best of all, it was partially sheltered from the rain by trees. Tom's optimism was short-lived: nobody stopped, nobody so much as made eye contact for the best part of an hour and he was just considering the options of completing the ten or so kilometres to Le Mans on foot when a small white hatchback slowed down and pulled up next to him. The passenger window wound down, and the driver, a man in his sixties, leant across and called to him in French. 'Lost your bike?'

'Somebody stole it,' said Tom.

'That's dreadful. Do you need a lift?'

'Yes please. But I'm absolutely soaked and probably don't smell too good. Are you sure it's ok?'

'Don't you worry about that, young man,' said the man's wife. 'You just get in, and tell us where you want to go.'

As he climbed into the back seat, the sheer pleasure of being back in the warm and dry was overwhelming.

'So where are you going?'

'I'm trying to get to Le Mans to get a train to Paris.' As he said the words, Tom realised that he had no way of paying for his ticket; not only that, but no way of buying food or putting a roof over his head either.

'That's where we're going too so we can drop you at the station,' said the driver. 'You're English, aren't you?'

'Yes. Is my accent really that bad?'

'No, your French is excellent and it's a charming accent,' he said as they set off, 'I always wanted to learn to speak English, but when I was at school I never got the chance so I'm afraid I don't speak a single word and neither does my wife. But anyway, tell me what happened to your bike.'

'It was stolen along with all my belongings. I fell off and broke the front wheel. A man in a builder's van offered me a lift but in the end he just drove off with my bike, my clothes and my wallet, leaving me by the roadside.'

'But that's awful. We must call the police at once.' He turned to his wife. 'Use your mobile, darling, and call them straight away.'

'No please don't do that,' said Tom. 'I've no idea of the man's name, I didn't get chance to take note of the registration number of the van and I haven't got any proof of what he did.' Tom could see the man eyeing him suspiciously in the rear-view mirror. 'Besides,' he added, 'I've got to get to Paris tonight – it's desperately important – and if I have to stop at the police station to give a statement, I may be too late.' From the brief exchange of glances between driver and passenger and another quizzical stare in the mirror, Tom was aware that his credibility was waning fast. 'Look,' said Tom, 'I desperately need to make a call to Paris. I've still got my phone card and so if you could stop in the next village where there's a phone box, I can do it from there.'

Eye contact in the rear-view mirror. 'You don't want to talk to the police and you're in a big hurry to get to Paris you say. Are you in some kind of trouble, young man?' The tone was not unfriendly, but tinged with more than a hint of steel.

'No, but I will be if I don't get to Paris tonight.' Tom could almost hear the raising of eyebrows in the front seat.

'Very well, who do you need to call?'

'He's a colleague of mine – name's Vincent Deschamps.'

'Here,' said his wife. 'Use my mobile. If you really are in a hurry, you won't want to waste time stopping to use a pay-phone.' She turned round and fixed Tom with her large brown eyes. 'I don't think you are telling us the whole truth, but for some reason, I at least trust you. I am taking the risk that the English have better things to do than stand around in the rain in the hope of robbing or harming people like us.' With that she handed him her mobile.

Tom didn't know Vincent's direct number so he called the bank's reception and asked to be put through: four rings, five, but still no reply. The panic was rising, surely there must be someone still on the Paris program desk, it wasn't even five o'clock yet – for Christ's sake, answer will you. After what seemed like an age, he heard Vincent's familiar tones on the line. Tom spoke to him in English. 'Vincent, it's Tom Mansell, I'm in a lot of trouble and I need your help, I haven't got time to go into detail because it would take too long and I'm using a borrowed mobile. I'm in France, on my way to Le Mans, I've got no money....' He was brought up short by the sound of Vincent hooting with laughter.

Tom finally managed to get him to listen. 'No, Vincent, this isn't a joke, I'm serious. Sally's life is in danger; David and Caroline's too. My bike's been stolen, I'm cold, wet and a very kind French couple are taking me to Le Mans station, they don't speak English and they seem to be coming to the conclusion that I'm either a criminal or an escaped lunatic, so I don't want them going to the police on the basis of what I've just told you. No, don't interrupt, this is for real. Just tell me, if I can get a train from Le Mans to Paris later this afternoon, can I stay at your place?'

Vincent laughed again, but replied in English this time. 'A pleasure, Tom. It'll be great to see you again, call me from the station to let me know which train you're on and I'll collect you from Montparnasse. Then you can tell me what this is *really* about.'

'Look, Vincent, there's one last thing, I don't have any money or any form of ID, if I hand you over to the people I'm with, can you tell them that you'll repay them the cost of my ticket. Oh, and please make sure you give them your mobile number.'

'Sure, Tom, I'll make sure everything's ok. You're sure this is for real?'

'Yes, it's for real, Vincent.'

He handed the mobile back to the lady and waited while she spoke to Vincent. The conversation was taking far longer than Tom had expected. At first he put this down to his rescuers' natural suspicion that he was some kind of scam artist and they wanted to make sure that Vincent wasn't part of the scam too, but from what he could make out from hearing only one side of the conversation and after a series of exclamations of surprise from his elderly listener, Vincent was clearly spinning one of his tall stories. Tom could tell that even over the phone, his old friend had lost none of his ability to charm. Finally, after making a note of Vincent's mobile number, the conversation ended and she turned to Tom. 'Well, young man, I'm not surprised that you didn't want to tell us your real reasons for wanting to get to Paris in such a hurry.' Then she smiled and gave him a lascivious wink that would have shamed a woman half her age.

Vincent Deschamps, I will kill you for this, he thought.

Chapter Twenty-eight

Sam Bortoleski had taken over Denise's office and lost no time before turning everybody's life upside down. After coming in overnight from New York and having drunk too much Scotch on the flight, he had a sore head and was not taking prisoners. He assembled the heads of all the departments that were potentially affected by the scandal and made it very clear that they were going to be spending all weekend at the office. He grilled them as a group and left them in no doubt what would happen to them should anybody be foolish enough to leak to the press or to anyone outside the bank. Then he interviewed them one by one, looking for a story that didn't fit.

One of those he and Chivers grilled was Lydia Shaw, the bank's head of operations. What she told him only deepened the mystery, her assessment that Tom Mansell could not have circumvented the bank's controls in the way the log files appeared to show, was yet another problem for Bortoleski to overcome. Whoever was behind this stunt, an innocent Tom Mansell was the last thing he wanted. Shaw's final comment rubbed salt into the wound.

'And if even someone as slow on the uptake as Denise was able to spot something was wrong, well, it can't have been exactly sophisticated, can it? I'm sorry, gentlemen, but I don't think there's much more I can add. Was there anything else I can help you with?'

Chivers looked at Bortoleski who shook his head. 'No, I think that's it for now, thanks, Lydia.'

She left and the two men were alone for the moment with Scary Mary guarding the door. 'Andrew, please tell me for Christ's sake what is going on. You thought I pulled this, I thought you did and now it turns out that it was neither of us. Assuming Mansell didn't suddenly go mad, who else stands to gain by putting him in the frame?'

'I've honestly no idea.'

'Well, neither have I. I've got more people to speak to, but I am now one hundred percent certain now that this was a set-up. Sure, make it look like the guy's front-running and then blow the whistle on him, but this just looks like a pile of crap. If you were going to front-run client business, tell me how you'd do it. After all, you are the expert, aren't you?'

'That's not funny, Sam.'

Bortoleski wasn't smiling. 'It wasn't meant to be. Just tell me how you'd go about it.'

'Well...' he hesitated. 'I suppose I'd start small. You know, client with an "at market" or any sort of order to buy a single stock where we've got price discretion: pick a couple of those off a week. Then, if everything was going well, I'd try it with a small principal program and claim I was pre-hedging if I got caught, and then move up from there. What I wouldn't do is draw attention to myself by getting operations to make free cash transfers of the proceeds to an account that had "bad guys" written all over it. Whoever did this to Mansell was trying way too hard to make it look convincing.'

'Agreed. So, motive and opportunity, Andrew. Who fits? At the moment, we're expected to believe that Mansell somehow got access to the account opening system, bypassed the "two pairs of eyes" checks to open up an account for a client that was guaranteed to set every alarm bell in the bank ringing in thirty seconds flat. And that he then got access to a SWIFT terminal and bypassed all the security fail-safes in order to make payments from it. That is the biggest, steaming crock I have ever heard in my life.'

'Yeah, I see your point, Sam.'

Bortoleski wagged a finger in Chivers' face. 'Whoever did this has to be on the IT side or at least have system knowledge. This is my call, Andrew. I hate to say it, but much as we both want Mansell out so that the system reverts to the bank, we cannot do it on the basis of something as badly put-together as this. If whoever's behind the scam had used one iota of intelligence and cooked up something credible then we could've looked at all the evidence – not too closely mind you – found Mansell solely culpable and win-win all round. But now we've got a problem. We have to find out who's behind this and nail them instead. We have no choice. The downside is that Mansell is now in a position to sue the bank for millions and will probably walk off with Minerva under his arm into the bargain.'

'It buys us time, Sam.'

'And what use is that?' snorted Bortoleski. 'You heard what that woman from operations said. I like her, by the way, she's intelligent. That's a quality I admire. She said that none of it made sense and that system records must have been tampered with, and I don't think she's saying that just to cover her ass either. Someone from the business who, on the other hand, is not very bright has got together with someone from IT who is probably bright but doesn't know the business. Any names spring to mind.'

'That covers practically all our staff, but nobody with a motive that I can think of.'

'So, we keep getting them in here one by one and twist their arms until we get to the truth. We'll carry on with the desk heads, then the directors and move on down from there. You know what this means, Andrew? What this makes us?'

'No.'

'The guys in the white hats, Andrew. We're now the good guys. Ain't that just too damn funny? And you Brits say we can't do irony. Hah!'

Bortoleski heaved his bulk out of the chair and opened the office door. 'Mary, get Evans in here, please.'

While they were waiting for Denise to appear, one of the girls from the PR team came into the office and handed Bortoleski a piece of paper. 'You need to see this, Sam. When you've had chance to take a look at it, give me a call and we'll start putting a story together.'

Bortoleski read. 'Shit!' he exploded. 'That's all we need. The press has got hold of the story and to make matters worse, Mansell has escaped.'

'What?' The colour drained from Chivers' face. 'But that's

not possible. He can't have.'

'Says here that the security van he was in was hit by a truck, the safety devices triggered the door locks and he just walked out.'

'Does it say where he is?'

'No,' replied Bortoleski, 'Just says that the police are watching the ports and airports for him. It's now a major terrorist alert. Just what we don't need.' He handed Chivers the piece of paper.

The phone rang and Bortoleski picked it up. 'OK, right thank you. Yes, we'll make the necessary arrangements.' He turned to the ashen-faced Chivers. 'Things just got a whole bunch worse, Andrew. The police are here.' He gestured aggressively at Denise Evans who had just appeared outside the office to come in.

'You wanted to see me, Sam?'

'You said everyone was accounted for, so where is Liebowitz, Denise?'

'I don't know, Sam. He was in New York, but I passed on your message that he was to come back straight away.'

'Well have you checked? I asked you to check if anyone was missing and you told me there wasn't. Did he book a flight through one of the secretaries in the New York office? You haven't followed up, have you? Now get out and do as I tell you. Remember what we discussed in my office?' Denise went bright red and left.

'She was your idea, Sam.'

'You say that once more and I will pin this whole damn thing on your worthless ass.'

Chivers smiled weakly.

'That wasn't a joke either, Andrew.'

Chapter Twenty-nine

On receiving Tom's call from London, David Liebowitz did exactly as his friend had recommended. He called reception at once and ordered a cab to take them to the airport. Then, after flinging their belongings into their suitcases, they rushed downstairs to the lobby where they had the frustration of having to wait an eternity to check out behind a group of Chinese businessmen who were contesting every item on the bill, line by line and in broken English. Finally, once they'd paid and gone outside, they at least had the consolation of seeing that a car was waiting for them. 'Kennedy Airport, please,' said Liebowitz.

As they made their way along the west side of Manhattan, prior to crossing the city, the car slowed to a crawl in traffic. When it cleared, the couple noticed that the hooting of horns was becoming more insistent than usual and was coming from immediately behind them. The car wasn't moving. 'Is there a problem?' Liebowitz asked the driver.

'Yeah, I think it's the transmission, it's done this before,' he replied and switched on the hazard warning lights. Seconds later, both rear passenger doors burst open and two men shoved their way into the car, pinning them into their seats. Liebowitz opened his mouth to protest but found himself looking down the black muzzle of a semi-automatic pistol. 'Do anything stupid and I will kill you.' He couldn't place the accent but it sounded eastern European or Russian. Simultaneously, Liebowitz and Caroline let out a gasp of pain as their captors drove hypodermic needle into their legs.

Liebowitz came round first. They were in a cold, airless room that had no windows but was lit by a single bare bulb hanging from the ceiling. The concrete walls ran with condensation and were clammy to the touch. On the floor were two mattresses, each covered by a blanket, and on one of which lay Caroline. He tried to stand up but, fighting the waves of nausea, found that his legs wouldn't work, and as his head spun, the floor seemed to pivot sideways and slam into his side. He tried again and managed to get to a kneeling position: that at least was something. Steadying himself on all fours, he managed to half crawl his way across the cold, bare floor to where Caroline lay. To his relief he found she was breathing. Still unable to stand, he crawled over to the door and tried to open it. The handle moved down, but the door was locked so he crawled back and lay next to her. Lying down stopped the room spinning and he reached into his pocket for his mobile phone: it had gone. So had his wallet.

Liebowitz must have drifted back into unconsciousness because the next thing he was aware of was the door being opened and two men entering the room. For the second time that day he found himself staring down the muzzle of a semi-automatic pistol. At his side Caroline was starting to regain consciousness and began to groan.

'Who are you people and what do you want?' said Liebowitz.

'We're friends of Mr Kaliski. He's not very happy with you. Your stupid friend Mansell went to the police.' The man shook his head in disgust. 'And after everything we'd told him too. By doing that he has put your lives in danger.'

'Look, whoever you are, Caroline's got nothing to do with this,' said Liebowitz. 'If you've got a problem with me, fine, I can explain. But just let her go, please.'

'And have her go straight to the police just like Mansell did?' he laughed. 'As for you, Liebowitz, you are going to work for Mr Kaliski whether you like it or not. Your flight to Nashyastan leaves in a few days and it is up to you and the degree to which you co-operate with us whether it's a flight for two of for one. Now, tell me where Mansell is.'

'I don't know, I really don't and that's the truth.'

'You are lying.'

'Listen, we'd agreed to sign your stupid contract and then Tom was arrested by the police. He said that somebody had framed him for illegal trading, the police had taken him but he'd managed to escape. He was somewhere in London, that's all I know.'

'How very convenient. I will tell you what really happened: Mansell went to the police of his own accord and afterwards claimed to have been arrested to try and get out of the obligations he has to Noviprom, it's as simple as that. And now, what a surprise, he has made a miraculous escape. How utterly childish. Now you are going to tell me where he is.'

'All I know is that when he called me he said he was in London,' said Liebowitz.

Caroline was beginning to come round and was sitting up on the mattress, trying to make sense of the images flooding her drug-addled senses. 'David, what is this? I feel sick.'

Before he could answer, Liebowitz once again saw the pistol being levelled at his head. 'Go and sit on the other bed. Move.'

He staggered and half-crawled across the small room where he flopped down on the other mattress. The pistol was turned on Caroline.

'Now, Liebowitz,' he spat. 'You at least are of some use to my employers for the moment. Your pretty little friend isn't.' Liebowitz heard the safety catch click off. 'Now for the last time, tell me where Mansell is.'

'All right, all right, for God's sake don't hurt her, please. I'll tell you what I know, just put the gun down.' The man lowered the gun and re-applied the safety catch. 'He said he was going to try to get to France because he couldn't get hold of Sally. That's all I know. That really is the truth. He said that neither the house phone nor her mobile were answering and that he wanted me to keep trying to get hold of her.'

'And?'

'And to tell her to get to safety. To call the police. To go into hiding with her friends. Tom was really worried that he couldn't get hold of her. That's all I know,' he said desperately.

'He has good reason to be worried. Very good reason, and so have you if you don't tell me the truth. This is your last chance. Where are they?'

'I don't know, please believe me,' said Liebowitz.

'Very well, we will show you something that I think will

persuade you to remember.' The door slammed and they were left alone. Caroline crawled groggily across the floor and clung on to him as tightly as she could, burying her head into his neck.

After a few minutes, the metal door crashed open and the two men returned, one of them holding a laptop which he put on a chair with the screen facing the two captives and slotted a DVD into the drive.

'Watch closely. This is what will happen to you if you do not co-operate.'

What they saw displayed on the screen before them was an unbelievable scene of horror and suffering. Neither of them would have guessed in their darkest moments that human beings were capable of committing such appalling acts of cruelty on their fellow man. What made it worse was the sound-track of non-stop screaming and pleading. Liebowitz looked away and Caroline did the same, putting her hands over her ears in a vain attempt to blot out the awful noises coming from the tortured victims on the screen.

'I said watch!' said their captor, cuffing them about the head, an act he repeated each time either of them tried to avert their gaze from the horrors on the screen. After half an hour of the most dreadful, sickening images of mutilation, the film came to an end. Caroline was in floods of tears and Liebowitz clung to her in despair.

'Let me add that, thanks to the skills of our doctors in keeping people alive during such punishment, it has been known for some of our guests to take three weeks to die. Just think of that next time I ask you a question.' With that, he gathered up the laptop and both men left the room, locking the door behind them. A few seconds later, the lights went out and the couple were plunged into pitch darkness. From outside, all that could be heard was a low, continuous sobbing.

***

In a smoke-filled office in London, Kaliski looked up from his

214

computer screen as the door opened. It was Ursk. 'I think we've found Mansell,' he said.

Kaliski stubbed out a cigarette in the already overflowing ashtray. 'Good work, Ursk. Where is he?'

'France. The US team just called. Wish I was there – sounds like those boys are having fun with the Jew's girlfriend...'

'You can tell me about that later. I want to know about Mansell.'

'They said that Mansell phoned Liebowitz from London shortly after he got away from the police – that was from a payphone – and now he's just called him again from another payphone, but in France.'

'Any idea where in France? It's a big place.'

'Not yet, but from the code it's somewhere in the north west, near Le Mans where they have the motor race....'

'Spare me the travelogue,' snapped Kaliski. 'Is he still there?'

'I don't know, they didn't say. But the good news is that we know where he's going. His wife was supposed to be going to a place called...' He consulted the transcript of the call, '...Orange. She was due in Orange on Saturday and he's headed there to try and find her. He left a voicemail on the little Jew's mobile phone and said so. He'll have a nasty shock when he finds out she's dead.'

'Where the hell's Orange?'

'I've looked it up. It's north of Marseille – about a hundred and twenty kilometres.'

'That's a happy coincidence, isn't it? Make sure Kosov and his team stay put in Marseille and as a precaution get an airborne extraction team down there to join them.'

'I've already done all that.'

'Well done, Ursk. We'll make something of you yet,' said Kaliski. 'Now, to get to France, Mansell must have had help. Someone must have got him across the Channel, someone must be funding him, so he may not be travelling alone.'

'So why's he using payphones? If he's got the kind of friends who can spirit him out of the country with the police watching the ports and the airports, you'd expect him to have access to a mobile phone and then why Le Mans? If he's headed for Orange, it's an odd choice of route.'

'I agree, but we might be reading things into that that aren't there. As a precaution, get on to Novi Bar and get them to send us the latest phone subscriber lists for France and the UK, mobile and landline – and make sure they use the embassy's secure FTP site.'

'Done that too.'

Kaliski looked at his colleague with unfeigned admiration. 'Good lad, nice to see you using your head at long last. Trouble is, I still think this whole story looks all screwed up,' he said, picking up a copy of the Evening Standard from the shambles of paper on his desk and waving it at Ursk. 'Have you seen this? According to the paper, those clowns watching the flat were wrong. Mansell didn't go to the police voluntarily. He was definitely arrested and they're now saying he's involved in financial fraud and using the proceeds to fund an Islamist terrorist cell. Does that strike you as likely? You've met the man after all. A fanatical Muslim? A terrorist? Ready to risk everything for the Jihad?'

'It doesn't seem likely, I admit.'

'No, it doesn't.' Kaliski blew a cloud of smoke up at the ceiling. 'So let's take a look at the options,' he said. 'Either we got Mansell completely wrong and he's been acting a part, very effectively I might add, in order to hide what he's really up to, but now he's been caught. Or, he *did* make the first contact with the police after all and the whole arrest thing was cooked up to make his disappearance into custody look genuine. But if *that's* the case, why stage an accident that sets him free so we can get at him again, and that kills two security guards into the bargain, not twenty-four hours after they first "arrested" him? That's not how they operate over here, they're a little bit more subtle than that.' He paused and lit another cigarette from the dog end of his last one. 'D'you know what I think? I think he *has* done something wrong that they've arrested him for, but the police aren't letting on what it is.'

'Such as?'

'Such as using Minerva to piggy-back his own personal trading onto what the bank's been doing and taking a nice fat cut. If that's what happened, then all the crap will come back and land on the bank's doorstep for not stopping him – the press would have a field day. You can see the headlines, "Banks still not supervising their rogue traders" – the media can't get enough of that kind of story. That gives the bank or even the regulators a very good motive to spin this as a one-off crime carried out by an evil individual – and to the British psyche, you can't get much more evil than a swivel-eyed Muslim fanatic, particularly a white, middle-class, swivel-eyed Muslim fanatic – a traitor to his caste no less. And that's why I think the terrorist angle is just a smokescreen – whoever came up with that one has overplayed a good hand by my reckoning.' He smiled at Ursk and his irregular yellow teeth gleamed dully through the smoke. 'However, whatever he's done, our friend Mr Mansell is in a lot of trouble which is going to make him much easier for us to find. A little trip to France for you and me, Ursk, I think. Tell the protection team they're coming too.'

Chapter Thirty

Approaching the town from the south west, the small white hatchback carrying Tom and his new friends came into the outskirts of Le Mans to be greeted by a familiar French townscape. Anonymous industrial estates composed of clumps of identikit grey aluminium hangars plastered with gaudy advertising signs, slowly gave way to a belt of drab, concrete council housing where France dumps its social problems. As they approached the centre he noticed that a considerable amount of money must have been thrown at the town: bright red trams scooted busily about and a business park, a low-rise version of Canary Wharf, had been built just opposite the station to which he was headed. Even the station was a high-tech glass and steel structure. To Tom, it was far cry from the litter-strewn, vandalised hell-holes that the UK offers the travelling public.

The trio left the car in the station car park and walked to the booking office. Dressed in soggy cycling clothes, but with no bicycle, Tom felt as out of place as a submarine captain in the desert.

The couple who had picked him up from the roadside now clucked about him like a pair of benevolent mother hens. The husband handed him a train ticket and tore out a "RIB" bank details form from his cheque book which he also handed over. 'Give this to your friend, Monsieur Deschamps and he'll be able to refund us the cost of the fare.' He took the mobile from his wife's hand and dialled Vincent's mobile number. 'Hello again, Monsieur Deschamps, your friend Tom will be on the 18:19 train which arrives at Montparnasse at 19:15. No, not at all, it's always a pleasure to be of service. Good bye, Monsieur.'

They took their leave and Tom was almost moved to tears by their kindness and the trust they'd shown in him. He shook the man firmly by the hand and his wife embraced Tom heartily, kissing him on both cheeks. 'And before you go, take these with you, I've bought you a coffee, some sandwiches and something to read, it's our local paper.' She gave him yet another conspiratorial grin and squeezed his hand. 'And good luck in Paris!' Waving away all Tom's protestations of gratitude, they said their final farewells and left him standing in the booking hall, damp-eyed and feeling once more very alone.

The journey to Paris was due to take just under an hour. Under normal circumstances he would have enjoyed the ride and the countryside, now lit by watery sunshine, but he was far too preoccupied with thoughts of trying to find Sally and, most difficult of all, what to do once he'd found her. Despite being dressed in cycling kit, no one gave him a second glance. He finished the coffee and sandwiches and turned his attention to the copy of *Le Maine Libre* that she'd given him and began flicking through the pages just to see what he'd missed over the last few days. The local news was the usual stuff and of little interest and he was about to discard it when a feature in the national news section caught his eye. What he read made his blood run cold.

"Gangland murder in the Hérault," ran the headline. *"The Police are investigating the murder of a woman in a small village near Béziers that took place on Tuesday morning. The victim is believed to have been of British nationality and in her thirties. No formal details or identification have been released, but sources close to the investigation have suggested that the murder bears all the hallmarks of a gangland killing because she was killed by a single shot from a large-calibre weapon, normally only found in military use. Police are trying to trace the owner of the house, believed to be an Englishman who has not been named, but is believed currently to be in Britain where he is said to have recently escaped from police custody, following his arrest on charges related to fraud and terrorist activities."*

Tom clutched at the seat back in front of him for support. He felt the tears welling up and an indescribable, wrenching feeling of loss and desolation. He was too late. Sally was dead. He couldn't bear it. The article continued and he forced himself to read on,

"...although the victim has not been named, it is believed that she was looking after the house during the owners' absence and

'That means… Oh, thank God,' said Tom aloud. Sally was still alive. But if it wasn't Sally, then there was only one other person it could be. Catherine. Tom felt wretched now. Oh, Christ, what am I saying? Poor, poor Catherine. The elation he'd felt when he'd realised Sally was still alive was overlain with something more complex as a hundred conflicting emotions collided in his head. This is all my fault. If I hadn't got the wrong side of those two bastards at Noviprom, none of this would have happened. An unbearable weight of guilt descended on him, a haze of misery so profound that he began seriously to consider turning himself in to the French police. I must be mad to try and do something like this on my own, he thought. What if I do find Sally before them, then what? He stared out of the window at the tranquil French countryside but no inspiration came, just a dull ache of sadness, fear and loneliness.

By the time he arrived, the clouds had cleared and Paris was basking in clear evening sunlight. Vincent was as good as his word and as Tom made his way through the crowds at the station he recognised the unmistakable patrician good looks, topped off by a shock of blue-black hair and the beaming smile which lit up at his approach. They shook hands and Vincent spoke to his friend and colleague in French once more, but one look at the bedraggled Englishman's face showed him that something was seriously wrong. His tone was uncharacteristically serious as he grasped Tom by the shoulders. 'Tom, you look terrible. What's happened to you?'

Tom had to force the words out. 'Let's get away from here and I'll tell you all about it.'

Vincent had left his Porsche in a taxis-only parking zone and the car had already been ticketed. A taxi driver leaned out of his car window and treated him to a tirade of abuse, so Vincent got back out of the driver's seat, gently removed the ticket from the pile and gently placed it under the taxi's windscreen wiper, pausing only to treat the driver to a flashing smile and friendly pat on the head – as he turned back to Tom, he looked every inch the caricature of an Italian matinée idol. Given that he was at least as tall as Tom and just as strongly built, the driver didn't pursue matters any further.

Even at this hour, the Paris traffic was dense and they inched along the Boulevard Pasteur in a nose-to-tail jam. 'So, Tom, tell me what this is about,' said Vincent. Tom explained the whole story, from the first approach by Noviprom right through to Catherine's murder. By the time he'd finished they were crossing the Pont d'Alma en route to Vincent's flat in the 16th Arrondissement just to the west of where avenue Kléber crosses rue Boissière. Tom was once more close to tears and he slumped forward in the seat with his head in his hands.

'So now you know as much about this whole mess as I do,' said Tom, looking up. 'I'm so scared I can't even think straight. From what it said in the paper they've had one go at killing Sally and ended up shooting one of our friends instead which is bloody ghastly. And I don't think for one minute they're going to leave it at that. They'll certainly go after Sally again and they're probably going after David and Caroline as we speak, but I haven't got a clue what I can do to other than warn them and at the same time try and find Sally before someone with a gun does. I can't go to the police because I'm wanted on all manner of trumped-up charges in the UK, including assaulting a policeman, front-running client orders and funding terrorism.'

'You *have* been busy since I last saw you,' said Vincent with a smile.

'It's not funny, Vincent. I'm sure it wasn't Noviprom who set me up, but that means that someone else wants to get at me but I've no idea who or why.'

'It's a horrible situation, Tom, but what exactly do you want me to do to help?'

'I'm not altogether sure myself if I'm honest, but for now, I'd like to have another try at calling Sally.'

'No problem,' said Vincent, passing over his mobile. Tom dialled. His face fell: there was no reply.

'Why don't you try David again?' asked Vincent.

'I will, but I'd prefer to do it from a payphone.'

Vincent scoffed at this. 'You've been watching too many movies, Tom.'

'I'm serious, Vincent, either these people are very lucky or they're very good at finding anyone they want. I really don't think it's a good idea. I've no reason to think they know Sally's mobile number so a call from another French mobile would mean nothing to anyone, even them, but they sure as hell know David's and I don't want them knowing yours – I've dragged enough innocent people into this affair without adding you to the list.'

'Rubbish, I'll be fine. I'll call him now.'

'It's your decision but I think you're taking a hell of a risk. You got his number?'

'Of course.' He dialled: voicemail. He left no message and rang off.

Paris was radiant and the plane trees along the side of the wide boulevards of the city cast long shadows in the early evening afterglow as its last rays lit up the handsome stone facades of the buildings. Tom stared mournfully at the groups of strollers and at the couples sharing an early drink outside the bistros and cafés: their carefree world could have been another planet so far as he was concerned. The car crawled along in more solid traffic until they came to a halt at the lights at the right turn off Avenue du Président Wilson at the Place de Iena. Vincent waved a hand around at the twilit panorama in a theatrical gesture. 'You see, Tom. No reply and no bad guys.'

'I still don't think that was a good idea,' he replied quietly.

The traffic was thinning now and as they crossed the rue de Lubeck and continued along rue Boissière, the events of the day started to take their toll and Tom's eyes began to close. He was jolted awake as the car bumped over the ramp and into the courtyard of the *hôtel particulier* where Vincent lived – the four kilometres from the station had taken nearly half an hour to cover. The high, wooden electric doors closed silently behind them and, after parking in his numbered slot, Vincent led the way up the three marble steps into the brightly lit hallway from where they took the elevator up to his flat which formed the top floor of the building. The opulence was staggering and Tom felt like a scruffy intruder as he passed under yet another chandelier and into the elegance of the living room with its panoramic views south over the Trocadéro and the Eiffel Tower. He paused to admire a series of portraits and landscape paintings, all executed in subtle, almost faded colours.

'Nice, aren't they?' said Vincent. 'Know who they're by?'

'No idea.'

'Corot – and they're not fakes either. I take it you've heard of him?'

Tom nodded. 'Yeah, I had poster of *Ville d'Avray* on my wall at university just like everyone, but these must be worth a fortune, and this flat too. Have you taken to robbing banks in your spare time?'

Vincent laughed. 'No, like the apartment, they've been in the family for years – those portraits are of my ancestors by the way, and they liked his work so much that they bought some of his other paintings too – but for generations they've been passed down as being by "an unknown provincial artist in the style of Corot" and therefore, no problems with inheritance tax and wealth tax. For every genuine Corot in circulation, there are about four or five fakes so that suits us down to the ground because we'd never sell them. Anyway, I'll show you round the flat when we get back because we really must get a move on.

'If you want to get cleaned up, the guest bathroom is through there to the left and your bedroom is opposite. There should be a shaving kit and a new toothbrush in the cabinet but if there's anything else you want, just shout. I'll put some clothes out for you, they should be a reasonable fit. Give me that RIB and I'll make a payment to the couple who paid your train fare.'

After the day he'd had, to be clean again was like heaven and Tom felt that he could easily have spent the next hour in the shower luxuriating under the hot water if it hadn't been for Vincent yelling at him through the bathroom door.

'Come on, Tom. Get a move on or everywhere will be closed.

I take it you do want to eat tonight?'

'Hold on, give me five minutes.' Wrapped in a clean, soft, white dressing gown, Tom made his way through to the guest bedroom, the sensation of the expensive rugs under his feet bringing a welcome feel of luxury after his recent privations. When he opened the door he saw that Vincent had set out clean clothes for him as promised and despite the fact that the sports jacket was not only a bit garish for his tastes but a size too big, everything just about fitted, including the highly-polished black loafers – Lobb according to the label. Nothing but the best for our Vincent – the Paris desk must be doing well, he mused.

His host had showered and changed too and wore a black cashmere jumper under an expensively-tailored dark blazer. At Tom's approach he put down his glass of scotch and looked up. 'You're in luck, Tom, I've got us a table at a fantastic restaurant I know right near le Sacré Coeur.'

'Montmartre? But that's a god-awful shithole of a place, Vincent, it's all hookers, backpackers and drug-dealers.'

'So it is, but it's also home to one of the best seafood restaurants in Paris, as you'll see. Don't worry, it'll only take us about ten minutes at this time of the evening. Trust me, you'll love it. Rumour has it the chef's up for a Michelin star. It's called *le Homard qui Chante*, by the way.'

'The singing lobster?'

'That's what it's called.'

The restaurant was everything Vincent had promised it would be. Tucked away on a side street between the Boulevard de Clichy and the foot of the hill on which the Sacré Coeur is perched, it was a delight. Each table was set in its own private wooden cubicle and the subtle décor, set off by the soft glow of the wall lights gave the place a restrained elegance far removed from the over-priced tourist traps that cluster in the narrow streets to the west of the basilica. A waiter, dressed in black with a starched white apron, placed two glasses of Kir in front of them on the immaculate table cloth. Little beads of condensation ran down each glass. 'Good to see you again, Monsieur Deschamps,' he said to Vincent and then nodded politely to Tom. 'Très heureux, Monsieur.'

The meal, as predicted, was stupendous. Vincent chose a Chablis, with just the right balance of fruit and acidity to set off the food to perfection. After just a few sips, Tom found himself once again struggling to keep his eyes open. Vincent chose a dozen Leucate oysters to start but Tom, faithful to the rule of the "r" in the month, chose the sautéed baby octopus.

They ate in silence, held in awe by the food. Vincent chose lobster for his main course and Tom went for the grilled hake with a delicately-spiced tomato and coriander salsa, a combination which, to him, was little short of divine. 'So what do you think of my favourite restaurant, then?' said Vincent at last.

'I think it's perfect, even if it has got a silly name.' Tom paused. 'Sally would love it here,' he said wistfully.

'Well, the next time you both come to Paris, you are to stay at my place and I'll bring you here as my guests.'

He looked up into his friend's dark brown eyes. 'Thanks, Vincent, that's a very kind thought, I really appreciate your confidence. There've been times in the last couple of days, particularly since I read about Catherine's murder, when I've felt like giving up.'

Vincent regarded him gravely from under his dark curling locks. 'Don't worry, Tom, we'll find her before they do – you'll see.'

'No, Vincent, there's no "we" involved here, I'm not dragging you into this as well. These people are vicious bastards and I don't want anybody else hurt because of me. I've caused enough damage as it is.' Vincent made to interrupt but Tom cut him short. 'Listen, they killed one of my friends from HSBC just because he helped me make a call to David – he wasn't in their way but he was dead within a matter of hours. They didn't have to do it, but they did just to show me what they were capable of: that's the sort of people we're dealing with. Just lend me the price of a train ticket to Orange and a few euros spending money and I'll look after myself, thanks.'

Vincent's mood became serious once more and his brow

knitted into a frown. 'Tom, if these people are capable of such things then you won't stand a chance on your own. I've offered to help you and I will, it's as simple as that – I'm not James Bond, but I'll do what I can. Anyway, the markets are flat at the moment, we're doing no business to speak of and I can take the time off without any bother. You never know, it might even be fun.' At the sight of his friend's pained expression, he quickly corrected himself, 'I'm sorry, Tom, I didn't mean that to sound insensitive – I mean at the end of it when we've got Sally safe and sound, we'll look back on the affair with a sense of achievement.'

'When in a hole stop digging,' Tom said in English. He smiled ruefully at Vincent's look of bewilderment and switched back to French. 'Please, please, you must understand what you could be getting yourself into. This isn't a game. They've already killed people and if you do come with me and don't take things seriously, then you'll end up getting us both killed. I know it sounds callous, but much as I don't want you to get hurt because of the mess I've got myself into, I'm not having you coming along just for the ride and getting me killed into the bargain – that won't help Sally one bit and I'd sooner take my chances on my own if it comes to that.'

'You can trust me, Tom. You can be sure of it,' said Vincent, waving a lobster claw as he spoke. Tiredness was winning now and Tom's French was beginning to fail him, so he passed on speculating aloud about how long Vincent could take anything seriously.

Vincent continued. 'So I'll ask you again, Tom. What is it you want me to do?'

'Like I said, I have no idea. All I can think of is that you help me find Sally before they do and then we can turn ourselves in to the police – unless you've got any better suggestions of course.'

'We could always steal an aeroplane…'

'You see,' said Tom, throwing down his napkin. 'That's you all over. Two minutes and you're already not taking it seriously. I'll go on my own – just drop me at the Gare de Lyon and I'll take my chances from there.'

'I'm sorry,' said Vincent. 'I thought that the famous English sense of humour…. well, you know…'

'No, you're right. I'm just tired, confused and my nerves are in pieces. I'm the one who should be apologising. I was being petulant. Sorry.'

Vincent caught the waiter's eye and made the "please bring me the bill" sign. 'OK, Tom, let's get you home and to bed, we can work things out in the morning. I'll just have another try at calling David.'

'I'd still be happier if we used a payphone…'

'Don't worry it'll be fine…' He took his phone out and was about to dial when it rang. He answered. 'No, there's nobody at the flat. I'm ten minutes away in a restaurant on the other side of town…Yes, please get someone there straight away, I'm headed there now myself.' He rang off.

'Problems?' asked Tom.

'That was the company that monitor the alarm system in the flat and it's just gone off. It's probably another false alarm, but I want to get back before they call the police.'

It took them just under ten minutes to make the return journey, and as they turned into rue Boissière and neared the flat, to Tom's relief there was no sign of the police. Vincent stopped the Porsche and waited to make the left turn through the gates which were opening in response to the remote control which he now replaced in the centre console. A further short pause to let two cars go past in the opposite direction and then he began to turn. As he did so, two men came down the steps from the hall and into the courtyard.

'Stop!' shouted Tom. Don't go in, just get the hell out of here now. Go!'

Startled, Vincent stopped the car half way across the road, blocking the oncoming traffic, much to the annoyance of a fat man in a red Skoda who was hooting his horn and shouting abuse. He looked across at Tom in disbelief. 'What's the matter?'

The two men advanced on them at a steady walk. 'Just go, Vincent,' he yelled. 'I recognise one of them from London. They're the people I was telling you about. For God's sake, go, will you.' Vincent's eyes were wide with fear. With the traffic backing up, he was only able to reverse a few yards and, just as he selected first and raised the clutch, the man whom Tom had recognised levelled a pistol at them.

Chapter Thirty-one

Vincent floored the accelerator and spun the Porsche round in front of the stranded red Skoda. Events unrolled in slow motion and Tom watched in horrified fascination as the gun barrel tracked their progress. He braced for the impact but it never came, the gunman's colleague pulled his arm down and, turning back to look over his shoulder, the last Tom saw of them, they were running back up the road in the opposite direction. The reflection of flashing blue lights behind them showed him the reason for their flight.

It wasn't until they were back on the other side of the Seine, heading east that either man spoke. 'I hate to say this,' said Tom, 'but I did tell you that they were good at finding people, didn't I?'

'But who are they?'

'I don't know their names but when I last saw the one who pointed the gun at us, he was trying to dislocate my knee in a London coffee shop.'

'And these guys all work for Noviprom? The same people who killed your friend in Mirepech?'

'Yes.'

Vincent's face was ashen. 'But they had us cold. I can't believe they didn't shoot.'

'That's the irony, Vincent, they need me alive. You they'd kill without a second's thought, you'd better understand that.'

'So what do we do now?'

Tom managed a half smile. 'I guess the question of whether it's "we", or not, just kind of resolved itself back there, didn't it? I still don't know what "we" do, but the first thing *you* do is to switch off that damn mobile of yours.'

'You think they can track it?'

'Probably not, but I'm sure they know David's number and so when you called him, assuming they've got the right technology, which clearly they have, you gave away your number and I suspect that someone at your mobile phone provider has done the usual and sold a subscriber list to someone, who in turn has sold it to someone else and so on until it washed up on a desk somewhere at Noviprom. Once they had your address, it was simply a matter of paying you a visit, which they did. Lucky for us that they triggered the alarm – they're good but they're not infallible. The downside is that they now know you're with me, they know what you look like and they know what you're driving.'

'I need to make a call. D'you think it's safe to make one more?'

'No, but equally you're probably not going to start taking my advice after all these years, are you?'

'I'll make it quick.'

From what Tom could make out from listening to Vincent's side of the conversation, it sounded as though the person on the other end of the line was not pleased to hear from him and that a fair amount of invective was being directed Vincent's way. Vincent pleaded, he wheedled, he charmed, but none of it seemed to be having the desired effect and after about five minutes, the call ended and he slid the phone back into his jacket pocket. 'We're in luck, she says we can stay.'

'Who says we can stay?'

'Sophie. We used to go out together.'

Tom smiled at Vincent's choice of words. 'Used to go out together?'

Vincent nodded ruefully.

'Don't tell me, and then she caught you screwing someone else?'

Vincent's expression was one of genuine shock. 'But how could you possibly know?' he said, his eyes wide with naïve amazement. Tom just shook his head.

They continued in silence along the Boulevard Saint Germain, crossing into the 5th Arrondissement, and as they drew parallel with the Cathedral of Notre Dame, Vincent turned off the main road. Tom soon lost his bearings as they twisted and turned through the back streets of the Latin Quarter. They stopped in a small cobbled square, surrounded on three sides by restaurants that were still teeming with life even at this late hour. Vincent made another quick call and they continued, turning off the square into a lane barely wide enough for one car. About half way along, a young, dark-skinned woman was waiting for them. As they approached, Tom saw that in her hand she held a remote-control device which she used to open the up-and-over electric door of a garage, and without waiting for them or making any gesture of recognition, turned and went back through the blue door next to the garage.

'Wow. Is that Sophie?' asked Tom.

Vincent nodded. 'Her mother's Moroccan and her father's half-French, half-Vietnamese. Pretty, isn't she?'

'She's a stunner. Why the hell were you screwing around when you had her to come home to?'

Vincent just shrugged and said nothing.

The garage door closed automatically and the two men passed through a side door to the stairs leading up to the first floor of Sophie's apartment. Vincent led the way.

'Sophie, this is a friend and colleague of mine, Tom Mansell.' They shook hands. He was captivated. She was tall and willowy with smooth, coffee-coloured skin and long dark hair that was tied back from her delicate, high-cheekboned face.

'Very pleased to meet you, Mr Mansell,' said Sophie in impeccable English.

'It's all right, he speaks French,' said Vincent.

Ignoring him completely, she continued in English. 'So you are friends as well as colleagues? Tell me, what made you choose a person like *this* as a friend.'

'Er, we worked together in London,' replied Tom lamely.

'Would that you had kept him there. Vincent tells me you need help but I must tell you that, given my position, if you are in trouble with the police then I will have to ask you to leave.'

'Your position? Do you work for the police?' asked Tom.

Sophie laughed. 'Tell him, Vincent,' she said in French.

'Do you have satellite TV at Mirepech, Tom?'

'Only Sky. Why?'

'Sophie's a news anchor for a satellite news channel. She moved from one of the national channels a year ago and took over 50% of her viewers with her according to the statistics. And you're telling me you've never seen her on TV?'

'Vincent, you're embarrassing Monsieur Mansell. I don't expect everyone to know who I am. All I need to know is that if you bring people to my house, are you putting my reputation at risk by doing so?' She fixed him with the kind of stare that women teachers use to wither recalcitrant male pupils. Vincent shifted uneasily from one foot to the other. Tom noticed that she hadn't invited either of them to sit down. 'You can explain, Tom,' he said.

'Alright, I'll spare you the details,' Tom said, switching into French once more. 'I've been accused of something I didn't do – a financial crime. I was arrested in London, but now I'm once more at liberty,' – his well-chosen use of *"on m'a libéré"* skilfully blurring the truth about his escape. 'My wife's life is in danger too which is why I have to get to Orange. I presume you reported on the shooting of that woman in the Hérault?'

'Yes I did. It was mistaken identity, wasn't it?…but hold on, if you're who I think you are, then you're wanted for terrorist funding and being linked to organised crime.'

'That's me,' said Tom. 'But none of it's true. Someone's framed me and someone else is trying to kill my wife.'

'Sit down, please, both of you,' she said. They sat. Sophie remained standing with her hands on her hips. 'Someone's framed you and someone else is trying to kill your wife? That's either one hell of a coincidence or you're telling me a pack of lies. Now, whose version of events am I supposed to believe? That of the Republic's law enforcement agencies or the version of someone whom they believe to be a dangerous criminal and, to make matters worse, associates with the likes of Vincent Deschamps?'

Tom continued, 'Look, Mademoiselle… sorry, I didn't catch your last name…'

'Just call me Sophie.' She folded her arms and continued to fix Tom with a look that was anything but friendly.

'Sophie. If I was guilty, I wouldn't be here.' God, I'm struggling, thought Tom. This must sound pitiful. He continued, 'Anyone with a conscience or a scrap of decency would turn me in if any of this was true – and that goes for Vincent too. The allegations in Britain were an attempt to frame me – why, I'm not sure. The people who are chasing me and have tried once already to kill my wife are trying to get me to part with a software system that I've built. I can't go to the police because by the time I'd proved my innocence, my wife would be dead and other colleagues harmed.'

She remained standing, gazing at him intently as through trying to read his thoughts. 'I'm still not sure I believe you. Give me one reason why I shouldn't call the police right now?'

'Your public profile and value in the market.'

'My what?' Sophie cocked her head on one side and looked at him with a puzzled frown on her face. 'My public profile is at risk simply by having you under my roof. If anyone finds out that I've helped a dangerous criminal then my "value in the market", as you so charmingly put it, will be zero. And I'll have confirmed every negative racist stereotype that this country has about people like me. What do you mean?'

'What I mean is are you willing to take a risk?'

'Listen,' she said with mounting irritation. 'I've known you for all of five minutes. You're a friend of Vincent's, probably a criminal, and now you're talking in riddles. Believe me, I've already taken a risk by letting you through that door, and you need to understand that I'm not in the least bit convinced by what you've told me so far.'

'What I'm telling you is true, not that I expect you to believe it – in your position I wouldn't either. However, if you take the risk of helping me, I may be in a position to help you.'

She put her hand on the telephone. 'Offer me stolen money and I'll have the police here in five minutes.'

'I take it that you were trained as a journalist before moving into TV?'

'Correct.'

'Then listen to your journalist's instinct,' said Tom. 'Take that risk – I assure you that I'm innocent. Help me by letting us stay here tonight and if I get to Sally – that's my wife's name – and get her to safety, then I'll give you the biggest scoop of your career and no one will know that we've ever met.'

'Vincent will know,' said Sophie. Tom was about to say something about being able to trust Vincent, but thought better of it.

'That's all part of the risk,' said Tom. 'But just think of your ratings.'

Sophie shook her head and smiled. 'That's the worst piece of advocacy I've ever heard in my life…I must be completely crazy, but ok, I don't know why, but I'll trust you, you can both stay. Tom, you can have the spare room. Vincent, you can sleep on the sofa.'

'There's just one more thing,' Tom said. 'Can we leave Vincent's car in your garage until he gets back?'

'What's wrong with my car?' he said, clearly offended.

'It's too conspicuous. We keep this simple – tomorrow morning we take the Métro to the Gare de Lyon, we get a train to Avignon where we can hire a nice, sensible family hatchback and we drive to Orange, just like any other tourists.'

'Yeah, ok, I guess you're right,' said Vincent.

'Hold on just a minute. I haven't said yes yet…and don't you do your puppy-dog eyes routine on me, Vincent Deschamps, I won't fall for that again in a hurry. Yes, you can leave the car here, but only on condition that you give me the keys – I think I'll take it on one of those track days while you're away.'

Vincent's face was a picture of horror and Tom was dying to play along with the game, but there was simply too much at stake. 'I don't think that's a good idea, Sophie. These people know the car and if you're seen in it there's a very real risk that they'll harm you. Please don't drive it, promise me that.'

'All right, I won't.'

'One more thing,' continued Tom. 'Please don't call Vincent's mobile phone, that's likely to put your life in danger too. There's already one person in London who helped me and has been killed as a result – I don't want you added to the list. Finally, if you think you're being followed or if anyone other than the police contacts you asking questions about me, then you must go to the police. You can tell them I had a gun and forced you to help me.'

She remained silent, a look of deep concentration on her features. Once again she fixed him with that gaze. 'You know, I think you may've been telling me the truth all along,' she said. 'Please forgive me for doubting you.'

Early the following morning they took their leave of Sophie – she and Vincent were back on speaking terms – and set off on foot for the Métro. In a straight line it isn't far from the heart of the Latin Quarter to the Gare de Lyon, but the journey requires three changes in a very circuitous route. They were booked on the 09:16 departure under false names: TGV ticket inspectors rarely ask for ID to validate the name on the ticket. Arriving with over half an hour to spare, as they made their way up from the Métro towards *"les Grandes Lignes"* they had to battle through a sea of commuters headed into the city to start the day's work. Everyone, it seemed, was on the move and that was how Tom spotted them. Like rocks in a fast-flowing stream, they stood out as they deflected a turbulent current of grumpy humanity to either side of them. He grasped Vincent's arm and pulled him around to retrace their route, but a shout from behind confirmed his fears. Their about-turn had come too late. They'd been seen. At least they had a head start. Vincent took the lead, 'Where to?' he shouted over his shoulder to Tom. 'Shall we make for the street?'

'Safer than staying down here. Let's go.' They elbowed their way through the crowds to one of the escalators. The tradition of standing on the right isn't strongly observed in Paris, so they had to shout and barge a painfully slow path up the left hand side, opening up a clear road for their pursuers to gain on them. They had just cleared the top of the escalator and were heading towards the street exit when Tom again grabbed Vincent's arm. 'No good, there's another one over there and he's seen us,' and they ran flat out towards the down side of the escalator they'd just come up.

Luckily, the two men chasing them were still a few paces short of clearing the top of the up escalator and weren't able to cut them off.

'Follow me,' shouted Vincent and pulled Tom along with him towards the entrance to the Métro. 'Police officers, stand aside!' he yelled at the startled RATP staff as he vaulted over the ticket barriers with Tom following behind. The new tactic seemed to work – shouting "Police!" cleared a path like magic. Tom checked back over his shoulder. There were now four of them as far as he could make out – well-prepared and coming through the barriers using tickets rather than taking the airborne route. However, this slowed them up, the delay giving their quarry a further twenty metres advantage so that Tom and Vincent were almost at the bottom of the escalator just as the gang reached the top. 'Police, stop,' shouted Vincent again and to his surprise, three youths about five metres in front of them took off in panic, scattering commuters as they went and sending a visible ripple of confusion through the dense press of people. Vincent shouted again and then pulled Tom over to the right behind a ceiling-high plywood barrier that jutted out into the tunnel to surround some maintenance work that was going on. 'Right, don't run, act normal and follow me,' Vincent panted.

Gasping for breath, it was as much as Tom could do to get the words out as they turned into the side tunnel against a stream of commuters all coming the other way. 'Where are we going? This says "no entry".'

'Just follow me,' he said. 'Act normal and keep walking. We have to hope they follow those kids for a while. There are no signs visible to people coming the other way – for all they know this is two-way.' He checked nervously over his shoulder but there was no sign of pursuit. 'By the time they've worked out they're chasing the wrong people we'll be well away from here.'

Tom's brow was running with sweat and Vincent's borrowed shirt felt glued to the small of his back. He got his breath back enough to speak coherently. 'Thanks, Vincent, I owe you one. But where do we go now?'

'We'll get the 14 line to *Pyramides*. It'll be busy and the line's driverless – makes it harder for those sods to interfere with it.'

Chapter Thirty-two

Kaliski banged the table causing the Nashyastan Paris embassy's second-best china to rattle alarmingly. He ground out the cigarette that he'd just lit into the dregs at the bottom of his coffee cup. 'What do you mean, lost them? How could you lose them, you idiot?' he bellowed. Ursk, who was sitting next to him flinched – this was going to get ugly. The object of his rage stood on the other side of the table, trying not to make eye-contact with his chief. 'I've a bloody good mind to send you back to Novi Bar…on three separate flights. Do you get my drift?'

'Yes, sir, and I'm sorry, you see…'

'I don't want excuses, you clown. *You're* sorry? I'm sorry you were ever fucking born. You're supposed to be a team leader and you've let these two amateurs get away from you twice – make it three times and you're a dead man. Three separate flights – got that? Good, now, sit down. I want facts and I want to know what you're going to do to retrieve the situation. Tell me what happened and if you try and bullshit me…three flights, just remember.'

The team leader swallowed and tugged at his over-tight shirt collar. 'Well sir, last night we traced the mobile that'd been used to call Liebowitz's number to a colleague of Mansell's from their Paris office. A man called Vincent Deschamps. When we got to his apartment we let ourselves in to wait for him. I thought we'd disabled the alarm but it went off – that was entirely my fault, it's a dual channel system with the pressure pads wired independently of the movement sensors and I missed it.'

Kaliski waved this away. 'Mistakes happen. Learn from it. What happened next?'

'We went downstairs. I told the concierge we'd come to see Deschamps – told her we were colleagues from the Moscow office, but that when we'd got to the flat the alarm was going – it seemed as good a way as any to make it look as though we were bona fide visitors. She didn't ask any awkward questions and it gave us a good excuse to hang around chatting until they got back, which they did about ten minutes later. The car was about to turn in and I think Mansell must've recognised me because they turned round and drove off. Neither of us had a clear shot without risking hitting Mansell, and because the police had just turned up we decided to clear out.'

'Give me strength,' said Kaliski. 'You people haven't got the sense you were bloody well born with, have you? So then what did you do?'

'By the time we'd got back to the car there was no trace of a signal from the mobile and they were nowhere in sight. We thought they'd head straight out of the city and make for the autoroute, but the embassy guys called us a couple of hours later to say that they'd picked up a signal again somewhere the other side of the river, near the Sorbonne, but they couldn't get a decent fix. A kilometre radius was the best they could do – and after that they lost it altogether. From that, we figured they'd gone to ground for the night and, because the fix wasn't far from the Gare de Lyon, it was a fair bet they were going to try and get a TGV south this morning. As a precaution, we got Kosov to send a couple of his boys up the autoroute from Marseille to a service area near Valence to watch for the Porsche. By this morning, they still hadn't seen the car so we took the gamble of putting all our resources at the station.'

'All very sensible and workmanlike,' said Kaliski. 'Provided of course that they hadn't already left town in a hire car. We also have to assume that Mansell knows that his wife is still alive, otherwise he wouldn't still be trying to head south. I take it that coloured your thinking as well?'

'Er, yes, sir.'

'Bollocks it did,' snorted Kaliski. 'Turns out they didn't hire a car so you got lucky, that's all. So how did you manage to fuck things up this morning?'

'We'd planned to wait for them up at platform level, but the place was crawling with armed police so we decided to move back down a couple of levels nearer the exits from the Métro. It was swarming with people down there and we stood a very good chance of missing them if we'd tried to stay behind cover. I went up to the taxi rank and stayed up there just in case they came in that way because I didn't want to risk Mansell spotting me again. From what my lads told me, they were only a matter of feet away when they just turned and ran. They bolted back down the escalators and the boys said it sounded like they were shouting at someone in front of them, but it was so packed they couldn't see a thing other than a couple of people barging through the crowd ahead of them. By the time we got to the exits, they'd vanished.'

'Vanished?'

'Yes, sir.'

'Balls. People don't vanish. I know exactly what happened – you didn't cover the station exits properly and your goons spooked Mansell and his friend by looking like exactly what they were – not carrying rocket launchers or flame throwers were they by any chance?'

'No, sir.'

'You surprise me,' spat Kaliski. 'You have an hour. When you come back I want a thorough appraisal of the situation and a detailed plan of what you intend to do. Get it right and you and your family might still be breathing unaided this Christmas.'

Chapter Thirty-three

At the table farthest from the window in a nondescript café, just off the rue Saint-Honoré and less than a mile from the Nashyastan embassy, Tom and Vincent were taking stock. 'So now what?' said Tom – his hands shaking as he clattered his cup back into its saucer. 'We can't risk the railway stations, if we hire a car that means using your credit card and someone putting your licence details into a database.'

'We could take a cab,' said Vincent.

'To Orange? It's a seven or eight hour drive.'

'No. We get a cab a good long way out of town to somewhere that's got a station and then we get a stopping train to somewhere like Dijon and then get a fast train to Avignon.'

Tom shrugged. 'We can always give it a try.'

As ever, the traffic was snarled all the way out of town and the journey to Melun took an hour and a half. They stopped in La Place Gallieni opposite the station where Vincent paid the sullen, north African driver in cash.

'This is going to be painful, Tom,' said Vincent when he returned with the tickets. 'The booking clerk thinks I'm crazy. He says that the quickest and cheapest route to Dijon is to take the RER back to Paris and get a fast train from the Gare de Lyon – he wouldn't sell me a ticket to take the slow trains and change, said it wasn't allowed – so I've got us a couple of tickets as far as a place called Montereau where I know we can get a local service with only one change to Dijon. It'll take us the best part of all day but at least it's safe.'

'I hope you're right,' said Tom. 'By the way, I thought you played a blinder back there in Paris, pretending to be the police – that was a stroke of genius.'

Vincent shrugged, 'Just luck, I guess.'

They found an empty second class compartment and settled themselves down. Five minutes out from the station, Tom heard a sound that made his blood run cold: Vincent's phone was ringing.

'Don't answer it! For God's sake, don't answer it, Vincent.'
He calmly pulled the phone from his jacket pocket and looked at
the screen. 'Number withheld. Hmmm.' He rejected the call and
put it back in his pocket.

'Turn it off, turn it off now,' said Tom, glaring angrily at
Vincent. 'How long have you had it switched on?'

'Since we left Paris. You don't seriously think they can track
it, do you?'

'I don't know, but until I'm sure they can't then you must
keep it switched off. Please.'

'OK,' said Vincent. 'But I still think you've been watching too
many spy movies.'

At Montereau there was an hour and a half before the
connection to Dijon and they had time to enjoy a good lunch at a
small bistro opposite the station. The platform was almost
deserted, and to their relief, only two other passengers, both
elderly, got on the train to Laroche – Migennes. The journey
passed without incident, leaving them only a short wait for the
train that would take them on the last leg of the trip to Dijon.

Lulled by the gentle rocking of the train and the warmth of the
afternoon sunshine Tom had dozed off and was only vaguely
aware of Vincent speaking to him. He sat up and rubbed his eyes.
'Where are we?' he said.

'Tonnerre. No more stops after this and we should be in Dijon
in an hour.' There were more people on the platform this time, but
they'd given up taking any notice of their fellow passengers. The
train set off and trundled slowly through the gently rolling
Burgundy countryside. The sound of a raised voice coming from
somewhere behind woke him up again. Vincent had nodded off
too and so Tom shook his friend's knee to wake him. 'Wake up,
Vincent, it's the ticket collector.' Roused from his slumbers,
Vincent looked around him for a moment as though trying to work
out where he was.

'What did you say?'

'I said wake up, the ticket collector's here.'

Vincent stared past him as though still trying to work out

where he was. 'Shit, Tom, and look who he's talking to. No, don't turn round, just very carefully, get up and go through to the next carriage like it's the most natural thing in the world and I'll join you as quickly as I can. No, I said don't turn round, there are four of the fuckers.'

Tom slowly got up from his seat and made his way to the interconnecting door, bracing himself at every moment for the shout that would mean he'd been recognised. All he could hear were snatches of conversation between the ticket collector and one of the four men – it sounded like an argument was brewing.

'Halt, police!' Vincent had been spotted. Tom spun round in time to see Vincent come charging through the doors to join him. The ticket collector was lying motionless on the floor as the four climbed over him. A woman was screaming. Again the cry went up, 'Police, stop those two men.' They continued running towards the front of the train and through the buffet car. To the consternation of the lady behind the counter, Tom grabbed the refreshments trolley and jammed it across the corridor. In the next carriage, Tom stopped and pulled the emergency handle which, after a second's pause, caused the driver to slam on the brakes, throwing the two of them forward against the next set of connecting doors. Looking back, he could see that the sudden stop had now jammed the refreshment trolley even more firmly in place and that their pursuers were having to try and climb over it. 'Right, follow me,' yelled Tom and, pulling the emergency door release, swung the train door open and jumped down on to the ballast next to the rails. With Vincent in his wake, he sprinted across the tracks, up a low embankment and scaled a low wire fence. He paused to help his friend over and the two of them ran, lungs bursting, into a small copse bordering the railway line. Keeping the copse between them and the train, they ran across a field under the impassive gaze of a herd of cows and into a larger wood. For the second time that day, Tom was gasping and wheezing for breath. Vincent was in no better state and stood, bent over, with his hands on his knees, trying to get his breath back. Tom moved cautiously to the edge of the wood – the copse was about 100 metres away. 'I can't see them, but we need to get the hell out of here in case they change their minds and come after us. How the hell did the police get on to us anyway? D'you think Sophie had a change of heart?'

Vincent looked grim. 'That wasn't the police, Tom. It was your friends again. I recognised one of them from the Gare de Lyon this morning. Thank God for that poor ticket collector.'

'I didn't see what happened.'

'I was half asleep and I heard him arguing with them. I didn't take any notice at first but when he said something about not believing they were policemen, that's what spooked me. I don't think they noticed you when you got up but they spotted me all right. When they came after me, the ticket collector tried to stop them and they… they stuck a knife in the poor sod.'

'Christ, not another one,' said Tom.

'I'm afraid so.'

Tom sat on a fallen tree and put his head in his hands. 'I'm so sorry, Vincent. I should never have dragged you into this. Everybody who helps me winds up dead or injured, I don't think I can carry on any more.'

Vincent put a consoling hand on his friend's shoulder. 'Come on, Tom. You've got to see this through for Sally's sake. It's way too late to think about backing out.'

'You're right,' said Tom. 'Sorry. Anyway, where are we?'

'Somewhere north-west of Dijon. Orange is a bloody long walk from here. I think in the circumstances it's safe to turn my mobile back on.'

'What good will that do?' Tom asked.

'GPS – it'll tell us where we are and where the nearest town is.'

It took them half an hour to walk across the fields to Montfort-sur-Tille and they arrived, hot, thirsty and dirty in its quiet, dusty streets. They found a down-at-heel convenience store and Vincent bought two large bottles of water and four packs of ready-made sandwiches. At the bar opposite they tracked down the village's one taxi driver who was well into what was probably at least his third large glass of Pastis and didn't seem overjoyed at the prospect of an expensive fare into Dijon.

The ancient Mercedes taxi jolted into the outskirts of the town and past a newly-built shopping centre. Vincent clapped the driver on the shoulder. 'That'll do, over there,' he said. 'The *Darty* car park will do fine.' For the second time that day he handed over a large wad of euro notes to a taxi driver. The car set off in a cloud of diesel smoke, leaving the two men standing alone.

'What are you doing?' asked Tom. 'I thought we were going to the station.'

'We were, but I've had enough of trains to last me a lifetime, they're too dangerous. We're hiring a car. There's a vague possibility, if we're really unlucky, that they can track my credit card or somehow find my driving licence details – that's a risk I'm willing to take. However, I reckon if we go to the station, we'll find a welcoming committee waiting for us. We'll hire a car, get ourselves a change of clothes and make our way down to somewhere the other side of Lyon for tonight and then take a look at Orange on Friday…and, yes I'll keep my phone switched off.'

***

They stopped in the small town of Baumes-sur-Isère and booked in to one of the standard chain hotels. 'It's half past six now,' said Vincent. 'Let's meet in reception at quarter past seven and go and get something to eat in town. I'm just going to see if I can find somewhere to park the car and I'll see you later.'

On the way to the restaurant, they tried to call David again from a payphone – once again, there was no reply. Sally's mobile didn't answer either – just the same metallic recorded message saying that the number was unavailable.

As the evening wore on, the events of the day caught up with Tom and he found himself almost falling asleep in his food. Conversely, Vincent seemed invigorated by the excitement and wouldn't stop talking. 'That Mercurey was superb – shall I order another bottle?' he said.

245

'You can if you like, but I've had enough for one night.'

'That's not the Tom Mansell I remember,' said Vincent with a laugh.

'No, you're right, I think he got lost along the way somewhere.'

'Still, how about a *digéstif*? A glass of *Calvados* will bring him back.'

Tom reluctantly agreed and while he toyed with his glass of clear amber liquid that he really didn't want, Vincent drank at least five. So by the time that Tom finally managed to persuade him to stop for the evening and come back to the hotel, he was quite unsteady on his feet. As they neared the hotel the unmistakable bass thud of dance music announced the presence of a nightclub and as they drew level with the entrance, Vincent was all for going in. 'Come on, Tom, it's early. It's only just gone eleven – we needn't stay long.'

'No, Vincent. I want to make an early start tomorrow and if we do run into trouble again, I don't want be hung-over and knackered. Besides, places like that are my idea of hell at the best of times.'

Vincent was still chuntering about wanting to go back to the nightclub when they reached the hotel. As they came into the small, garishly-lit lobby, the receptionist looked up. 'Good evening, gentlemen. Does either of you own a car with this number plate?' He handed Tom a piece of paper with the registration of their hire car on it.

'Yes, that's ours. Why?'

'Oh, it's just that the police were in here earlier looking for the owner, that's all.'

Tom's face fell. 'The police? Did they say what they wanted?'

'No. There were four of them, came in about an hour ago – said they were looking for the owner, that's all. Is something wrong?'

'No, nothing at all, just curious,' said Tom, trying and failing to sound convincing. In the meantime, Vincent noticed that the barman was locking up for the night and set off to try and grab a last order before the grille came down. Tom thanked the receptionist and ran to catch up with Vincent. 'We've got a problem.'

'What do you mean, a problem?' he was slurring and clearly drunk now.

'Four policemen, or people claiming to be policemen, were in here an hour ago asking about our car.'

'Four policemen, eh?' said Vincent at the top of his voice, causing the barman and the receptionist to turn and stare at him. 'If it's those four arseholes from earlier on, I'll kill them with my bare hands…'

'Not so loud, you're making a spectacle of yourself,' hissed Tom, pulling him into a corner. 'You are *not* Cyrano de Bergerac and you're not going to kill anyone. Now, tell me where you parked the car, give me the keys and in case I need cash, give me one of your credit cards – what's the code for this one?' Vincent told him. 'Give me your mobile too. Leave your drink on the bar and go to your room. If there's trouble, I'll call you and you call the real police. If it's Noviprom and I'm caught, I don't think they'll kill me – they'd kill *you* for certain. Now tell me where you left the car.'

After several false starts, Tom eventually prized the information he needed from Vincent. 'Now, go to your room and if I'm not back in an hour, get the hell out. Got that?'

Vincent nodded glumly. His patrician features had the same look of chastened schoolboy that they'd worn under the icy gaze of Sophie. 'Why is it that every time I have a drink, everyone around me turns into sodding Hitler?' he said, wobbling unsteadily towards the stairs.

The receptionist had retreated into his office and was watching television. Tom collected a map of the town from the rack on the counter, studied it carefully to try and relate it to Vincent's description of where he'd left the car and, stuffing the map into his pocket, slipped out past the kitchens through the back door of the hotel and into the night.

A blast of hot, greasy air from the kitchen air-conditioning welcomed him into a narrow alley at the end of which was a residential street lined with parked cars. There were no other pedestrians about so, keeping away from the pools of light under the streetlamps he made his way past the backs of the shops and restaurants that formed part of the same block as the hotel. At the end of the road he turned right up another side street, crossed the main road and made his way gingerly towards La Place Voltaire where Vincent had said he'd left the car. Stopping briefly to get his bearings, he crouched down behind the cover of a parked van and took another quick look at the town plan – from what he could make out he was on the other side of the square from where the car should be.

The middle of La Place Voltaire was taken up by a small garden, tastefully landscaped and densely planted with trees, shrubs and, thought Tom with a shudder, no doubt knee-deep in dog shit just like every other public space in France. He smiled to himself at the sheer bloody incongruity of worrying about treading in dog crap at the very moment when he was potentially about to meet four people whose sole aim was to ruin his life.

No fear now, just resignation that this had to be done. Avoiding the footpaths and keeping to the shadows, he made his way across the garden. Then he froze. Voices. He couldn't make out how many but there were at least two if not three men in hushed conversation barely yards from where he was standing. He crouched down but still couldn't hear what was being said and so, going as carefully and slowly as he could, he stood up and inched forward through the undergrowth.

'Who's there?' Suddenly, Tom was blinded by the light of a torch being shone directly into his face. He stood rooted to the spot: too late to turn and run, he was paralysed with fear. 'Stop fucking about in the bushes and come out here.' Tom shielded his eyes and took a step forward. Dark blue uniforms – it was the police.

He stepped over the low railing surrounding the park, brushed the leaves and twigs from his hair and stopped on the pavement in front of the two policemen. They looked at him in disgust. 'Who the hell are you and what do you mean by creeping up on us like that?'

'Somebody told me that someone was trying to break into our car so I came to take a look, that's all,' said Tom.

'So this is your car is it?'

'Not exactly, it's a hire car.'

'Well either way, you're parked in a disabled-only slot. You should be ashamed of yourself.'

'Yes, you're right, I'm sorry.'

'Bit late for that, isn't it? You've already got a fine and just count yourself lucky the tow truck hasn't got here yet or you'd be paying to get it out of the pound in the morning.' He handed Tom the "PV" from under the windscreen wiper. 'Pay it within seven days or it goes up. You're not a very good advertisement for the English, you know that, don't you?' Tom nodded submissively and made no reply. With heart thumping, he got into the car and drove off under the scornful gaze of the police.

As he walked back through the deserted streets he felt euphoric, almost drunk with relief. Kaliski's thugs hadn't found them after all and the world seemed at once to be a far better place, but when he returned to the hotel, everything looked the same – in the circumstances he'd somehow expected it to be different. The unforgiving glare was still highlighting the cheap, plasticky tawdriness of the lobby, the only difference was that the receptionist had now fallen asleep in front of the office TV which was now showing yet another idiotic game show, the fifth of the evening.

He took the stairs to the second floor. The door to Vincent's room was ajar so he let himself in. The lights were on and the same game show was bawling from the TV. As for Vincent, he was lying fully clothed across the bed, snoring loudly. Tom was going to wake him up and treat him to a detailed inventory of his shortcomings and fecklessness, but given that this man had saved his life more than once in the last forty-eight hours, he thought better of it and, after turning off the lights and the TV, Tom let himself out into the neon-lit corridor, softly closing the door behind him.

The following morning, when Tom came down for breakfast at eight he was surprised to see that Vincent had beaten him to it. The hung-over, rueful, bleary-eyed wreck that he expected was nowhere in sight and, on the contrary, he looked in excellent form. 'Morning, Vincent. How's the head?'

'Absolutely fine, Tom. We had an early night after all. So what happened to you?'

'It *was* the police – we've got a parking ticket. If you'd told me at the time that you'd parked in a disabled bay, then it might've saved me from nearly dying of fright.' Tom recounted his adventures of the previous evening which Vincent found hilarious. 'It wasn't funny at the time, I can tell you,' said Tom.

Vincent choked on his croissant. 'Oh but Tom, it's a brilliant story and I just have this wonderful mental image of you creeping about in the undergrowth and being caught by the police like that. They must've thought you were totally unhinged.' As he laughed and spluttered, the tears ran down his cheeks. 'Tom, you've made my day. That's the funniest thing I've ever heard.'

Chapter Thirty-four

Keeping off the motorway and using main roads as little as possible, they continued across the plateau of the Vercors, stopping for lunch at Vassieux, before turning south on the lower ground towards Orange. With time on their hands and no sign of anyone following them, the journey began to feel more like a gentle amble through some of France's most beautiful countryside rather than a prelude to anything sinister. After the terrors of the previous day, neither of them spoke about what might lie ahead and Tom was happy to listen while Vincent told him about the plans he had for the flat and how he'd like to get back together with Sophie.

Just after four Vincent decided to stop to refuel the car and to stock up on food. They parked, legally this time, in the square of an attractive hill town called Rochefort-en-Quint. 'One of the best-kept secrets in France, this place,' said Vincent as he manoeuvred the car into the shade of a plane tree.

Tom was thinking about Sally and not really paying attention. 'Oh really, why's that?' he said.

'Although we're miles off the beaten track, it's got some of the finest antique shops in the whole of France. You can pick stuff up down here for half the price you'd pay in Paris. There's a lot of overpriced tat of course, but if you know what you're looking for, it's a little goldmine. If you don't mind, I'm going to take a look round and see if there's anything I can pick up that would go well in the flat.'

'Fine by me,' said Tom, absent-mindedly. 'Just don't go buying anything we have to strap to the roof of the car. If it's ok, I'll use your credit card to pick up a few more clothes and get some cash – don't worry, I'm keeping a note of what we've spent.' Vincent waved his hand dismissively. 'Don't worry about it, Tom. I know you'd do the same for me. Anyway, I shouldn't need more than an hour or so – let's meet back here at four.'

Tom wandered aimlessly around the streets of the old town.

There was a castle, a "historic trail" around what was left of the town walls and a well-kept little museum next to the town hall. He strolled along the 17th century walls and stopped to lean on the railings. Below him, the old town of Rochefort seemed under siege from an encroaching sea of identikit modern bungalows and ring roads. At least up here he could pretend, just for a moment, that none of it existed. Under normal circumstances, he would have loved to spend the afternoon, ideally in the company of Sally, just mooching around the place and visiting all the sights. The weather was glorious, the setting perfect, but he couldn't tear his mind away from why he was there and where he was going. All this was just a picturesque way of prolonging the agony – at that moment, not knowing was worse than having his worst fears confirmed.

Tom was still a little early and so walked slowly, with a carrier bag full of clothes in one hand and an ice-cream in the other, back down the hill towards the car park. As he rounded the lower walls, he pulled up short in astonishment. Near where they'd parked was a crowd of people and several police cars, blue lights flashing. A red "SAMU" ambulance was leaving the scene and as it swept past where Tom was standing, the driver switched on the two-tone siren.

Tom threw down the ice-cream and hurried over to see what was going on. Deep down he knew, but couldn't bring himself to believe it. Just a coincidence, he kept repeating to himself as he strode across the car park, just a coincidence, that's all.

He elbowed himself to the front of the crowd. Their hire car was now surrounded by a perimeter of police tape and on the ground was an ugly dark stain and the shattered remains of what was once a stick-back chair. Both the local Police Municipale and the Gendarmerie were on the scene. He edged forward. A young, clearly distressed local policeman was talking to an older woman. Tom edged closer. 'Look, Mum, I'm on duty, I really shouldn't...'

'Nonsense, Michel, tell me what happened.'

The policeman looked nervously to his left. The Gendarmerie were busy trying to stop people taking pictures and to keep the crowd from pushing through the tape.

'Well, it was Madame Martin who saw it. She told me that she was coming back with her shopping to collect her car and saw an argument going on between the driver of the car and four foreigners. She wasn't sure, but she says she thinks that one of them was speaking English. Anyway, apparently it turned into a hell of a fight and the French chap belted one of them with a chair – from what the SAMU guys said, they must've stabbed him at that point – but Madame Martin waded into them with her shopping bag and they ran off: she doesn't like the English, you see.'

'So what's happened to the man they stabbed?'

He shook his head. 'They don't reckon he's going to make it.'

Tom turned away, ashen-faced. The pleasant afternoon idyll had been smashed. Reality had caught up far sooner than expected. Carefree, maddening, lovable Vincent – and now he too was either dying or already dead. How many more for Christ's sake? wondered Tom. In a state of shock he drifted slowly away from the crowd with no idea where he was going, nor what he was supposed to do. Presumably they were still in the area and still looking for him – he almost hoped they'd hurry up and catch him just to get it over with. He walked down the hill towards the new town and in a narrow street just below the walls he found a taxi office.

As the taxi left the town, Tom watched anxiously over his shoulder, but after a few kilometres it was clear he wasn't being followed.

The station at Crest was almost deserted and nobody paid any attention to the man with the pepper and salt stubble and a shock of unruly, mousy-brown hair. He bought a single to Valence and sat in abject misery, clutching his carrier bag like a security blanket as the train trundled its way across country.

Tom spent just over an hour in Valence before making his way back to the station to catch the train to Avignon. He'd decided that spending the night in Orange was too dangerous and that most of the hotels would probably be full because of the *Chorégies* anyway. At least they probably won't recognise me now, he thought. Once more he was pushing a bicycle and clad in brand-new cycling gear, topped off with a protective helmet and wrap-around sun-glasses.

The train pulled in to Avignon just before nine PM, dead on time as usual. Tom wheeled his new bike through the booking hall, avoiding the recumbent forms of the rough sleepers, backpackers and winos that are a permanent fixture of Avignon station. A wet nose bumped against his hand: the dog's master was asleep or unconscious and it was almost as though the animal had taken over his begging duties for the night. Tom got on the bike, coasted down the short approach ramp, crossed the ring-road and cycled into town to find somewhere to stay. In the end he chose a small place just off the Cours Jean Jaurès called l'Hôtel du Comtat, checked in and then chained up his bike in the underground garage. After a much-needed shower and a change into clean clothes, he decided that he'd have to take the risk of calling David again and so he took the stairs down to reception and set off into town to find a phone box.

The streets were empty and the Mistral was blowing litter around in little eddies. Away from the historic centre and the Palais des Pâpes half a mile further down the road towards the Rhône, Avignon can be grim and frightening after dark – he'd read somewhere that it was the delinquency and car crime capital of France. Continuing down the road and doing his best to avoid the incrustations of dog shit on the pavements, he eventually found a phone booth, partially vandalised, covered in tarts' calling cards and graffiti, but in working order. David's voice answered: he sounded edgy.

'David, it's Tom. Thank God you're ok, I was worried stiff. Have you managed to get hold of Sally?'

'No, Tom, I'm afraid not. Not yet anyway.'

'Listen, this is extremely important. Someone, and I've a pretty good idea who, has killed the woman who was looking after our house. I think they were after Sally. It's in the French press and on TV, so we've got to assume that Noviprom know too.

She's due in Orange tomorrow for the music festival and I'm going there to try and find her before they do. I can't go to the police or I'll get locked up myself so please, for pity's sake, keep trying her mobile. David, are you listening to me? David, are you there? David.'

There was a muffled sound that Tom couldn't make out and a voice speaking English with a heavy eastern European accent came on the line. 'Good afternoon, Mr Mansell, or should I say, good evening where you are. I am glad to hear that both you and your dear wife are in good health and my colleagues will be so looking forward to meeting up with you both in Orange tomorrow. Now there is something I want you to listen to – '

Tom heard a muffled sound followed by the sound of a woman's voice screaming, 'No, please don't. David, help me. No, no, no. Oh, God, no – '

Then a bang and the screaming stopped at once. 'At least your call has spared your friend Caroline any further discomfort. Until tomorrow then, Mr Mansell.' The line went dead.

With trembling hands, Tom replaced the receiver and, staggering away from the phone booth, was sick into the gutter. A few paces further on his legs gave way, and he slid down onto the dirty pavement, shaking and gasping for breath with his back against a shop-front. His mind refused to take in what he'd just heard. First Catherine, then Vincent, and now they'd murdered Caroline in cold blood. He shuddered to think what they had been doing to her and what they were likely to be doing to David. And all my fault, he thought. What the hell have I done? And what if they get to Sally first?

Tearful and distraught, he wandered unsteadily back up the road to the hotel, let himself back into the hotel room, flopped onto the bed in a heap and lay still, bereft of ideas. If Sally and her friends were coming to Orange from the direction of Le Lavandou tomorrow, then they'd probably take the *autoroute* and if he waited by the toll booths, they'd be bound to see him, but on the other hand so might Noviprom's people, and then what? But then there was the possibility that the girls would take a roundabout route and come on the back roads via Avignon or Carpentras which would bring them in on the other side of town. In that case he'd miss them for sure. Tom's other big problem was that whoever Kaliski sent to meet them would have a good idea of what he and Sally looked like, whereas to him, every stranger in a crowd was a potential assassin.

He tried to force his befuddled mind to analyse the options. Perhaps he should go to the police after all. No, that wouldn't work. It was midnight, the night shift would be on: anyone with the rank and brains to take a decision would be tucked up in bed. The following day was a Saturday and the police would be tied up with traffic and crowd control for the festival. He couldn't take the risk of being locked up on the spot with nobody willing do anything to help until Monday at the earliest. And that was assuming that they believed him and didn't just put him in cuffs on the next flight back to the UK and the tender mercies of Hill and his band of thugs.

He opened the book he'd bought at Valence station and tried to distract himself from the ghastly reality of what he had heard on the phone to New York. Reading – any activity would do, anything to make it go away, even for a short while. He started at the top of page eleven for the fourth time at least that day, but the printed words got no further than the back of his eyes. Exhaustion overtook him and the book sank slowly to his chest as he fell asleep, fully clothed and with the lights on.

Chapter Thirty-five

Bortoleski introduced himself to Inspector Hill and took him into the corner office. 'Come in, Inspector. This is my colleague, Andrew Chivers who heads up the desk on which Mansell works. I've asked my other colleague, Denise Evans to get you and your team set up with an office for the time that you are with us. Just let us know how we can help you; we're very keen to get this cleared up as quickly as possible.'

'So are we, Mr Bortoleski,' said Hill. 'We want Mansell caught too, you can be sure of that.'

'I don't think he did it, inspector.'

'I'm afraid our evidence suggests otherwise, Mr Bortoleski. I can understand that you want to protect the reputation of the bank and its staff, but this is not only an investigation into criminal trading practices but also, because of the destination of the funds, a terrorist matter directly affecting national security.'

'Have you spoken to Mansell, inspector?' asked Bortoleski.

'Yes.'

'And what did he say?'

'I can't go into details but he denied everything, claimed that he'd been set up and tried to spin us some ridiculous yarn about the Nashyastan sovereign wealth authority.'

'He *was* set up,' said Bortoleski.

'How can you be so sure?'

'Take a look. And this is only part of it.' Bortoleski handed Hill a large pile of printed paper. 'Know what that is?'

'Vaguely,' replied Hill. 'We've got something similar showing how Mansell got into your back office systems.'

'This is different. It's a FIX log. Know what that is?'

'No, I don't.'

'Shit. Thought you guys were supposed to be specialists. They pay you for doing this?' Hill ignored the barb. Bortoleski continued. 'Anyway, at my request, Mr Chivers has been following the systems audit trail and what you're looking at is a very big hole. Nearly all electronic trading is done using the FIX protocol, which in simple terms, is a collection of standardised message templates and workflows that allow one computer to understand what another one is telling it. For a trade like this there would be a FIX conversation between the system that generated the orders and the one that received and executed them, and the details of that conversation would be written to the FIX log. Only they're not there on the sending side. Whoever did this injected the orders mid-stream to make it look as though they were genuine, but forgot to create corresponding entries to the log on the sending machine. It's an elaborate fake.'

'That's exactly what Mansell called it.'

'Then he was right. Someone in this organisation has taken a lot of trouble to try and pin this on one man,' said Bortoleski. 'And when we find them I want you to lock them up for a very long time. I have better things to do with my time than sit and watch the reputation of this bank dragged through the mire by some idiot's personal vendetta.'

Hill cracked a reptilian smile, 'Oh we will, don't you worry about that. My question to you though, is who would want to do a thing like this, who would have the know-how and why Mansell?'

'No idea. But I'll tell you one thing. Find the person or persons with the right access to the relevant trading, account opening and payment systems and the right level of programming skills and you've got your answer. I think we should start with the IT department.'

'I'll be guided by you on that, sir,' said Hill. 'I'll need you both to sit in on the interviews to cover areas of specialist knowledge, but all I'd ask is that you leave the questioning to me.'

When Bihar Jalil's turn came, Hill used exactly the same technique that he'd used on everybody else.

Hill opened. 'So tell me, Mr Jalil, why would you want to have Mr Mansell take the blame for something like this?'

'I didn't.'

'You didn't want him to take the blame? Then who did want him to take the blame?'

'It wasn't like that.'

'What wasn't?'

'I don't have anything against Tom.'

'So who has?'

'You don't understand, it wasn't like that…' Jalil's eyes darted nervously around the room as though looking for something that would save him.

Hill continued. 'You're an IT specialist, is that correct?'

'Yes,' said Jalil.

'And in fact helped build some of the systems involved in these trades?'

'That's correct.'

'So perhaps you'd like to explain some of the holes in the case against Mansell and why you of all people didn't spot them when other people did.'

As the conversation moved on, Jalil became increasingly flustered and dug himself deeper and deeper into a hole. Chivers squirmed uneasily on his chair. Bortoleski remained stony-faced but was secretly loving every minute, happily storing away every aspect of Hill's technique for future use.

'You realise that you forgot to modify the FIX logs?' said Hill.

Jalil's mouth opened and closed but no words came out.

'Silly mistake, wasn't it?'

'But I didn't,' stammered Jalil.

'So you did remember to update them, then?'

'Yes, I mean no…'

Hill handed him the printouts that Chivers had collected earlier.

'Take a look, Mr Jalil. Big hole where the log events for those trades should be. Silly mistake. And you such a professional too: tsk.'

Jalil grabbed the printouts and frantically went through them. 'Look, they're here. See, just here.'

Hill raised an eyebrow. 'Mr Chivers, can you help us out here?'

'Certainly. The receiving system logs are there all right, but there's nothing on the sending side, that's where the hole is.'

The printouts slid from Jalil's grasp and fell to the floor. Hill left them untouched and continued his questioning. Jalil was babbling, almost frantic, contradicting himself at every turn. Hill was used to seeing people panic under questioning – in fact anyone who kept calm and poised was far more likely to draw attention to themselves – but Jalil was in a more advanced state than anyone he'd seen so far today.

'So you set this up then. That much is clear. What I want to know is who helped you and why did you do it. As a final piece of theatre he turned to Bortoleski and said, 'I think you can let the others go home, we won't need to talk to anyone else today.'

He then used another well-worn tactic: the very big lie. 'Mr Jalil, if you tell me the truth and help me get to the bottom of this, you will not go to jail.'

'But I didn't do anything.'

'All the evidence that we can put before a court suggests otherwise. You do realise that you're looking at thirty years if you don't co-operate, don't you? Now, tell me how you did it, who else is involved and why you did it. If you do that, I'll do my best to see that you're treated leniently.'

Jalil hesitated, then said quietly, 'Do you promise?'

'Of course,' smiled Hill. If Jalil had had his wits about him and looked at Hill's dead eyes as he spoke, he would have realised that he'd just walked into a cleverly-baited trap.

'I had no choice.'

The words came tumbling out. He told of how Denise had blackmailed him and how he came up with the idea of adding the terrorist element in the hope that it would appease her. The friends of friends who had links to Jihadists and the details of Mughal holdings. All he wanted was to get her to delete that picture.

'Stay here,' Hill said. He went outside and spoke briefly to his sergeant who went off to find Denise Evans.

He returned and continued the interrogation. 'Right, let's start from the beginning. Unless it was something involving children, in which case even I can't help you, then I'm not interested in what was in the picture. Was it kiddie porn?'

'No.'

'Good. That's something at least. Why did Evans want to frame Mansell?'

Jalil was close to tears and his words came out in one long tumble. 'She said that if Mansell got fired, then the company would get to keep Minerva and that would be good for her career. And mine too, she said. It was her idea to use front-running and to make it look convincing and to do that I set up a couple of accounts in the name of Mughal holdings and over-wrote the log files in the account opening system with Mansell's ID to make it look as though he'd created the accounts. There are some people I know who've been on training courses in Pakistan – they're not good people and I think they've been trained to do bad things – they tried to get me to go but I'm just not interested in that sort of thing, but they gave me the name of that company and said it was run by good Muslims and that they'd help subsidise the cost of the trip if I changed my mind. When I saw them again I told them I might be interested and they gave me details of who to contact and so on. That was why I set the accounts up in that name; I wanted to make it look as though Mansell was tied up with them in some way just to make sure that the police got involved and that he lost his job.'

'Go on,' said Hill. 'I'm listening.'

'Then what I did was look in the transition management team's shared drive for their system – it's a desktop application that they wrote themselves because there was no funding for an in-house build – until they'd got the right sort of transition in there that we could easily trade against to our advantage. There's no security on it so you just click and it opens up. You see, they usually create a dummy trade list on the day before they start to execute it so that they can do their risk analytics first. Once I'd got the trade list, I created my own trade list to look like a pre-hedge and I wrote a small procedure to send the orders for execution to the prop trading desk that made it look as though they'd come from Minerva. I still don't know why the FIX logs didn't update, I'll have to check my code. Anyway, when I created these dummy trades and also the trades to close the positions out, I put the account number of the Mughal Holdings account in the FIX order message in such a way that the middle office system would allocate them automatically and because no-one hardly ever looks at executions that are auto-allocated, there was very little chance that anyone would spot anything suspicious. I'd used settlement instructions from two of our in-house accounts so the trades all settled correctly, and then finally I injected payment instructions via the SWIFT gateway to pay away the proceeds.'

'So where did the money go?' asked Hill.

'It didn't go anywhere, I just flipped it between copies of two in-house accounts, both of which were set up with Mughal Holdings' names. It's the account number and the other numerical identifiers that are important: the account name only gets looked at if someone needs to process the instruction manually. I was worried that this was the weak link in the idea but obviously, nobody spotted it.'

'And all this for the sake of an embarrassing picture? You do realise what you've done, don't you?'

Jalil held his head in his hands and stared dejectedly at the floor.

'Yes, I think I do.'

'No, Mr Jalil, you don't know the half of it. You've wasted a huge amount of my valuable time and that of your colleagues. You've caused an innocent man to be arrested for offences that could've seen him go to jail for over twenty years and you've dragged the name of your company through the mud. You disgust me. Sergeant, get him out of here.'

The sergeant led Jalil away. Hill turned to Bortoleski, who had now gone extremely pale. 'Could you ask Ms Evans to come into the office please, sir. And if you'll both excuse me, I don't think I'll need you to sit in. Also, if you don't mind, we will make the initial press release...'

Chivers interrupted him. 'Before you do that, inspector, I'd like a word with you in private. Would you excuse us for a moment please, Sam?'

Bortoleski left the room. When they were alone, Chivers resumed. 'Inspector, I think I've inadvertently become involved with something deeply unpleasant that is going to put a number of people's lives in danger. Don't ask me how, but I think I know where Mansell is.'

Chapter Thirty-six

Tom slept badly. The room at l'Hôtel du Comtat was stuffy and airless and the mattress felt as though it had been stuffed with gravel. From the tiny, smelly bathroom, the sound of a dripping tap ticked away the restless hours. At least the water was hot, and after a shower he felt a little better, noting with satisfaction that after three days without shaving, his beard was coming along well.

Leaving his bike locked in the hotel's garage, he wandered into town in search of inspiration. Not wanting to arrive in Orange too early, he planned to set off mid-morning and arrive during the lunch-time rush.

Avignon's pavements had been washed down and shutters were being rolled up as the first shops began to come to life. He noticed with displeasure that the Mistral was getting up. That would make the ride up the Rhône valley to Orange even harder. The town was almost deserted as he made his way along la rue de la République. Serenaded by the high-pitched calls of the swifts nesting under the eaves of the *Hôtel de Ville*, he came to the Place de l'Horloge where he sat outside a café and ordered breakfast. The strong black coffee helped wake him up and the *pain aux raisins* got some much-needed sugar into his bloodstream, but still inspiration wouldn't come.

His reverie was interrupted by something damp bumping his hand. It was the same dog that had goosed him the night before, but this time its owner was awake. The man smelled abominably. He put his hand out and said something in French that Tom didn't catch. He quickly gave him a one euro piece in the hope that it would make the man go away, but unfortunately it had the opposite effect. The man sat down opposite Tom at the table – he'd clearly made a new best friend – and despite his protestations that he didn't speak French and miming for the man to go away, he stayed put and continued his rambling, slurry monologue. God, he wished he'd go away. In the end, Tom picked up his cup and plate and retreated inside the restaurant where the waiter prevented the tramp from following him. Draining his coffee, he went up to the bar to pay then, checking the coast was clear, he left the café and retraced his steps in to town where he bought some clothes and a pair of scissors.

After changing into his cycling gear, he checked out of the hotel and set off. Crossing the Rhône towards Villeneuve les Avignon, he turned north towards Roquemaure along the Languedoc bank of the river and into a Mistral blowing at a steady fifteen knots. With a stop mid-way by the banks of the Rhône, the journey took just under an hour and a half and he was so deep in thought that he hardly noticed the headwind.

Tom had been to Orange before. Then, the place had felt depressing, down-at-heel and somehow menacing, but now it had clearly received a make-over. The crumbling facades and rotting shutters had been replaced, many of the dirty, narrow town-centre streets were now for pedestrians only, and places that he'd remembered as dingy, smoky dives had been transformed into smart restaurants. Trying his best to look like a tourist, he cycled past as many hotels as he could find in the hope of seeing Sally, tried to look in every car that had a Hérault 34 number plate, but there was no sign of her. He wheeled his bike around the pedestrianised lanes and squares and on several occasions his heart leapt at the sight of a dark-haired young woman, but each time as he drew close, it wasn't her. At the same time he desperately tried to assess each passer-by as a potential assassin but it was no use. Every man under the age of fifty without small children in tow could be the one and he began to attract attention to himself by staring at people too intently. The mounting feeling of panic became overwhelming and the need to get away from the crowds became too much.

Retracing his route back towards the Cours Aristide Briand, he turned off and cycled up the steep, narrow lane leading to the top of the Colline St Eutrope, the wooded hill which overlooks the town of Orange and its Roman theatre where that night's performance was to be held. He sat disconsolately on a bench and ate the picnic he'd bought in Avignon: saucisson, bread, a couple of tomatoes and a bottle of fizzy water – hardly luxury but it would do. The early haze had lifted, even the Mistral had dropped: it was clearly going to be a glorious day. From his vantage point above the town he could see right across to the jagged ridge of the Dentelles de Montmirail and to Mont Ventoux beyond. Under normal circumstances, it would have been something to relish, but at that moment he felt very frightened, completely alone and very small.

For the second time that day he was accosted by a dog and this one was begging too, but for food this time. It was a scrawny excuse for a creature; a medium-sized, flat-coated, brownish sort of mongrel with no collar, protruding ribs and a tail with a distinct kink halfway along. Tom shooed the animal away but it was persistent. Whether it was out of a sense of fellow-feeling or because his appetite had gone he didn't know, but when he tossed it a piece of saucisson it had the same effect as giving the euro coin to the tramp in Avignon: he had a new best friend. Great, just what I need, he thought, a bloody dog that won't leave me alone.

Chapter Thirty-seven

After leaving the office the previous evening, Andrew Chivers did something he rarely did – got blind drunk. He'd gone into a bar, bought a bottle of red wine and finished it in under an hour: he then repeated the process, twice. How he made it back to his flat in Pimlico was a complete mystery, but what he did know was that he had a splitting headache and felt sick. Sitting up hurt too much so he lay back down and tried to go back to sleep: that didn't work either. From the amount of noise they were making, the people in the adjoining flat seemed to be involved in a furniture-throwing competition. It got so bad, he could have sworn they were actually in the same flat. Then he heard a slightly different noise, there *was* someone in his flat.

Despite the hangover, he jumped out of bed, pulled on his dressing gown and flung the bedroom door open. No sooner had he done so than he was pushed violently in the chest, leaving him winded, on his back among the debris of last night's clothes and the kebab he'd never finished.

Looking up he saw two heavy-set men: each one trained a semi-automatic pistol on him.

'Get dressed, you are coming with us.'

'You have no business coming in here like this. Get out.'

'Kaliski wants to talk to you. If you co-operate you will stay alive. If not, we will kill you now. Your choice.'

Chivers began to get dressed. Blind panic at the thought of what they might do to him rendered his efforts all fingers and thumbs and he had to have three goes at buttoning his shirt. He tried to slip his mobile phone into his pocket, but it was taken from him and crushed under the heel of one of the intruders.

He was shoved unceremoniously out of the door. 'Now move. Downstairs.'

Outside the door to the street a black Lexus with tinted windows was waiting.

'Get in.'

Chapter Thirty-eight

In a nondescript building on an industrial estate on the outskirts of Marseille ten men were crammed into a windowless room. Despite the air conditioning, it was becoming increasingly hot and stuffy. Speaking in Russian, but with a strong Ukrainian accent, the leader of the group addressed them for what he hoped would be the last time. He indicated the two photographs taped to the white board. 'Right, this is the final run-through, so listen in. These are your targets. Thomas Mansell, age forty, about one metre eighty-two, ninety kilos, light brown hair. He is on the run from the British police so we are not expecting him to have contacted the French authorities, but please be aware that because of the *Chorégies*, there will be an increased police presence in the town, so use your common sense and don't attract attention to yourself.

Sally Mansell, thirty-three, one metre sixty-five, fifty kilograms, dark hair, shoulder length. Mansell will be looking for her, but she does not know he is here. I cannot stress too highly that the orders of the people paying your wages are unequivocal, the Mansells are to be taken alive.

Once you've made the decision to move I want a confirmatory call: male taken, female taken or, ideally, both taken. If you miss for any reason, it is equally vital that you call me, so before you get into the town, for God's sake check your radios and mobiles. Once you have the targets, take them to RV alpha, the swimming pool car park on the south side of the hill – everyone clear where that is without looking at the map? Good. We're not expecting any interference up there – the pool was closed indefinitely last week because of a health scare and the car-park is closed too. They've blocked it off with road cones and movable barriers so there's no problem with vehicle access. There are three private houses which border the car park: one is empty because the owners are on holiday in Italy for another week, one is a rental property that's been empty for six weeks and the last one is owned by an elderly couple and we'll make sure their phone line is cut. Now, if anyone, and I mean anyone, is unhappy about the safety of the RV, don't wait for my decision, take it yourself, make the call and we will head to RV bravo. Again, everybody happy so far? Excellent.

'Helicopter team. Unless you hear from me that there is a timing change, you will lift from Plan de Dieu as briefed, hold off to the south of the town and await my call to head for the RV. I will confirm which RV is in use. All except the drivers will then board the helicopters with the two targets and you will be taken to an airfield where an aircraft will be waiting for us. Apart from the pilots, the rest of you do not need to know the name of the airfield because if you are taken, you will not be able to compromise the operation.

'Truck team at Plan de Dieu. Make sure that you are masked up when the helicopters arrive. Once they're secured, only the driver and number three – where are you?' A dark-haired individual sitting cross-legged on the floor to his right raised his hand, 'You will remain with the truck. Once the helicopters lift, proceed with your cargo to RV charlie. Any questions?

'Finally, the two drivers. For you, gentlemen, and anyone apart from the truck team who doesn't make the helicopters, the long way home. If we are able to take both Mansells together we will use one car and the other will be cleared to leave the area. Drivers, if your car is cleared, take the Avignon road and then take the Chateâuneuf turning; go two kilometres down that road wait in the lay-by as we discussed until you are finally cleared to leave. Everybody with me so far?'

Nodding heads all round. He continued. 'Good. Now, working on the basis that we will need both cars and you are at the RV, once you have delivered your crews and their target, wait on the RV until you are cleared to leave. And remember, whether you are clearing from the RV or the Chateâuneuf road, do not forget to switch to the diplomatic plates. I'm sure our Russian friends will forgive us for impersonating them.' A ripple of nervous laughter ran round the room. 'From there, you are both to proceed to RV charlie where you will stay out of sight and meet up with the truck team.

'Finally, I'm sure I don't need to remind you of the seriousness of what we're doing, gentlemen,' he said. 'Otherwise we wouldn't be paying you so much.' More nervous laughter. 'However, just let me make it doubly clear that your employers are extremely well connected and should anyone have the misfortune to get himself caught and then be foolish enough to talk to the police, I promise you that you will be removed from wherever you are being held – yes, we can even get you out of French prisons in case you were wondering – and that you'll have a starring role in one of those lovely movies we watched earlier.'

***

L'École de Pilotage Heli-Mistral based at Avignon airport had been hit hard by the financial crisis. The management had already laid off one instructor and the other two were reduced to part-time working. Chartering or learning to fly a helicopter is an expensive luxury at the best of times: fine in a rising economy, but when the cold wind blows, it's just another discretionary spend and easy to cut, so the prospect of two new clients on the same day was too good to miss.

Monosyllabic, charmless and rich. Russians for certain, thought the chief instructor as he surveyed his potential clients. Only ones with enough money these days. Still, business is business.

Both men paid in advance, by corporate credit card registered to a company in Nice, and each booked a preliminary taster lesson for later that afternoon. The instructor was delighted that they both wanted to fly the school's two AS 350 Squirrel gas turbine helicopters since the hourly rate was much higher than for the piston-engined Robinson trainers that they also offered.

'I'm happy to say, gentlemen, that we can fit you in this afternoon. You're lucky, normally we're busy flying customers to Orange for the opening performance of *les Chorégies*, but this year demand has been a little bit slow.'

'Yes.'

I'd ask the charm school for a refund, if I were you, he thought, but instead smiled at them and said, 'Looking forward to seeing you again this afternoon then, gentlemen.'

'Yes.'

***

After lunch, the two men returned and were greeted by their instructors who led them off individually for a briefing on the short familiarisation flight they were going to undertake. They ran through how the controls worked, what they could expect to see, what to do if they felt airsick and the procedures to be taken in the event of an emergency. Neither pupil asked any questions and every time they were asked, 'Do you understand?' they gave the same answer.

'Yes.'

The two aircraft lifted off from the "Charlie" parking ramp to the west of Avignon's 35-17 runway and, on getting clearance from the tower, turned onto a north-easterly heading to their usual operating area just south of Carpentras. They had barely crossed the A7 *autoroute* and were still in sight of one another when both passengers did the same thing. Each man levelled a pistol at his pilot's head and gave the same orders in faultless French. 'Do not touch the transponder. If you attempt to squawk 7500 I will kill you. Do not make any clever radio transmissions or I will kill you. I know how to fly a helicopter so I will not hesitate. Do you understand? Good, now, you are to transmit an amended estimated landing time to Avignon tower. Remember, anything clever and I will kill you. Fly to the airfield at Plan de Dieu where you will see a blue truck: land next to it.'

The two helicopters altered course to the north and following the instructions of the hijackers, the pilots settled the aircraft down next to a blue Renault van that was waiting on the disused airfield's runway 17 threshold.

'Reduce power to ground idle and unstrap. Do not get out until

271

you are told.'

Four figures, their faces hidden by ski masks, emerged from the van and two ran across to each helicopter's right-hand door. The two instructors were led away at gunpoint and their former pupils, both experienced Mi-8 pilots, got out and took their place in the right hand seat. They were joined by two of the men who had supervised the removal of the instructors, each one strapping in to the left-hand seat. They waited.

***

Meanwhile in Orange, as the afternoon wore on, the crowds increased. Parking in the town is difficult at the best of times, but an influx of an additional 10,000 people made it completely impossible and tempers began to fray in the heat. In the narrow streets and in the shaded squares a carnival atmosphere reigned: jugglers, souvenir sellers, the inevitable white-faced mime artists and tuneless buskers were all competing for the tourist euro.

Less pleasant characters were plying their trade too. An unsavoury beggar, with unkempt, short, spiky hair and accompanied by a dog on a length of string was making a nuisance of himself. On his back was a small rucksack containing his few possessions and from the smell his clothes were exuding, he obviously hadn't washed in weeks, nor had he shaved recently and his incomprehensible rantings at anyone who refused to give him money, coupled with his sizable frame caused the crowds to part as he approached. The dog didn't help either. Every time they went past a restaurant it tried to steal food from the tables outside, while its owner did the round of the customers as quickly as possible before the waiters chased him off. If the dog couldn't find any food to steal, then it would amuse itself by trying to fight or fornicate with every other dog it saw. The pair's activities began to attract attention and two policemen, armed with automatic weapons, started following them about five steps behind, which seemed to have the desired calming effect on the beggar's behaviour.

272

After a while, the two policemen lost interest and wandered off to look for something more interesting and so the beggar took the opportunity to close in on a likely mark by the fountain in the Place Clémenceau: a group of tourists were taking it turns to take pictures of each other. At his approach they instinctively recoiled and moved quickly away, but he ran after them and catching one of them by the arm, spun her round.

'Sally, it's me. Don't make a fuss, don't say anything. This is serious, just follow me but keep well back.'

She turned quickly to her girlfriends. 'Don't worry, it's my husband. I'll catch up with you at the hotel.' Then turning back towards the malodorous apparition who had accosted her said, 'Tom, what in God's name are you playing at? And what the hell have you done to your hair? And you stink, do you know that?'

He pulled her by the arm. 'Just shut up and follow me, but keep well back.'

He'd never spoken to her like that and she was in two minds whether to tell him exactly what she thought of having her pleasant, girly afternoon ruined by a husband who not only stank to high heaven but hadn't bothered to answer her calls for the best part of a week. Just you bloody wait, Tom Mansell, she thought as she dropped in behind him. Keeping up was difficult. It was all right for Tom; at his approach, the crowds parted like the Red Sea, but by the time she got there, they had reformed ranks and she had to elbow her way through as best she could. Finally, they reached the eastern edge of the square and Tom continued a few paces down the rue Caristie when he suddenly stopped. Sally stood on tiptoe to see what was going on and as she did so she felt something hard and metallic pressing into the small of her back and a hand tightly gripping her arm. A voice in her ear hissed, 'I am armed. Do not make any sudden movements or I will kill you.'

Chapter Thirty-nine

The beaten-up old Toyota crashed over another pothole and the driver cursed. In the back seat his two passengers sat cradling their automatic weapons in silence. In the boot, David Liebowitz's head was slammed against bare metal for the hundredth time during the journey, but for the first time he was actually aware of the pain and discomfort as the effect of the drugs began to wear off. It was pitch dark, the air was a foul mixture of exhaust fumes and neat petrol. He tried to move but his wrists and ankles were bound. Every attempt was defeated by the bodywork all around him and had no choice but to lie still, fighting the growing panic engendered by his dislike of confined spaces, and the increasing feelings of nausea brought on by the after-effects of being drugged, the fumes and motion sickness.

Once more he drifted into merciful unconsciousness, but the next time he came round, his head began to clear and through the pain and fear his thoughts turned to one person: Caroline. They'd shot her in cold blood right in front of him. He tried to close his mind, but the image was still there, above it all, the terrible, crushing feeling of loss. Nothing could ever be the same again. Nothing. And all of this because a few stupid, greedy men wouldn't take no for an answer. The words that Ursk had spoken to him at that conference in London – it seemed half a lifetime ago now – came flooding back. 'The one good thing the Nazis did for our country was to get rid of people like you. Nothing would make me happier than to see you put in a cattle truck and for you to disappear up the chimney like all the others. One day I will personally make sure we do that to you too.' Perhaps that's what they had in mind for him now. He was past caring.

They were nearing the airport. This late at night there was very little traffic and they had kept off the New Jersey Turnpike, instead cutting through residential areas, back roads and housing projects as they made their way towards Newark Airport and the cargo sheds that stood on the site of the old North Terminal. As they turned into Brewster Road to run alongside the chain-link fencing that separates the airport from the road, the driver looked again in his rear-view mirror. 'I think we're being followed. Get ready.' He slowed right down, inviting whoever was following them to overtake, but they slowed down too. 'What do we do?' asked his front seat passenger.

'We have to keep going, nothing we can do…Shit!' Just before the right-hand turn into the cargo area they saw the roadblock: several marked police cars were in position and the road was lit up by pink flares and flashing lights. The driver slowed, swung the wheel hard over, hauled on the handbrake and, tyres squealing, executed a perfect J-turn to point the car back in the direction from which it had come. The driver accelerated as hard as he could, but the heavily-laden Toyota was slow to respond and the car that had been following them was now sideways on across the road, blocking their escape. The man in the left rear passenger seat lowered his window, took aim at the car blocking their way and fired a long burst from his Austrian-made automatic weapon. There was no return of fire and the Toyota bumped up over the kerb, missing the blocking car on one side and a lamp-post on the other, both by inches. A few yards further on, another car was parked at the roadside and it too was treated to a fresh magazine of 9mm automatic fire. What they hadn't seen was the back-up team in the storm-drain on the other side of the road. Taking careful aim, the leader of the SWAT team fired a short burst at the approaching car, killing the driver and front seat passenger instantly. Other members of the team fired low in order to disable the vehicle's tyres.

Engine racing, the Toyota mounted the opposite kerb and ploughed into the perimeter fence. The two unwounded gunmen piled out with weapons raised but were cut down before they had taken more than a few steps. Cautiously, the FBI men approached the vehicle and with practised expertise, removed the driver and the badly wounded front-seat passenger before checking the rest of the vehicle. The second-in-command raised his hand. 'Stop, be quiet. I can hear something.' Sure enough, from the boot of the car came a banging noise and a man's voice calling for help.

Not only had the impact slammed Liebowitz hard against the rear seat but he had collected a stray round that had shattered his left tibia at about half height. He groaned with pain as they lifted him gently from the vehicle and laid him on a thermal blanket next to the car so that the team's Emergency Medical Specialist could begin assessing the extent of his injuries. As he examined him, he reported his findings into the boom mike he was wearing, 'Superficial head trauma requiring sutures, multiple abrasions and bruising, possible broken ribs on right hand side, gunshot trauma from low velocity round in right lower leg and probable associated open fracture of right tibia, no sign of major vascular injury.' Liebowitz winced as he probed the wound. 'Sorry about that, we're being as gentle as we can…no sign of exit wound. You're not an opiate drug user are you?' Liebowitz shook his head and then grimaced as the paramedic pushed the needle into his skin. He continued his report, 'Have administered 5 milligrams of intramuscular diamorphine. You're going to be ok, Mr Liebowitz, you're in safe hands now.' But as the injection took effect and he drifted into a semi-conscious haze, all David could think of was Caroline.

Chapter Forty

Tom's problem was not dissimilar to Sally's. Barely a yard in front of him a thin, weasel-faced man was pointing a gun at his sternum. Tom could see the weapon clearly, but the man had a jacket draped over his arm which hid it from the other passers-by in the busy street. The gunman reached into his pocket and took out a mobile phone. As he was about to dial, Tom felt the string holding the dog go tight. The animal clearly found something about the man very attractive. He sniffed his leg. The man ignored him. He goosed him and the man recoiled. Then finally, with a look of ecstatic delight, the dog set to humping the man's leg. He lowered the gun slightly and, using his other hand, tried to bat the animal away, but in doing so, dropped his mobile phone. The back flew off and the battery fell out. Momentarily distracted, he took his eye off Tom and the gun was now pointing downwards at forty-five degrees. Tom seized his chance and caught him with a scything right-hander to the cheekbone which sent him crashing into a shop doorway. To the appalled amazement of the jostling crowds, a semi-automatic pistol clattered onto the pavement, the large tramp who'd just thrown the punch picked it up and doubled back up the street, scattering people as he went. Several people took out their mobile phones to call the police, others to take pictures. In a shop doorway, a smaller man with a huge swelling on the left hand side of his face was lying on the ground semi-conscious while being vigorously humped by a skinny brown mongrel.

By the time he got back to the corner, there was no sign of Sally. He ran one way, then the other but still couldn't find her. This couldn't be happening. What was he to do? Turning back towards the square in blind panic, he saw the two armed policemen who had been following him earlier and went tearing up to them.

'Please, you've got to help me,' he panted. 'I'm not a beggar – this is a disguise. I know this is going to sound crazy but I've come here to look for my wife and she's been kidnapped. Her life's in danger – it's the same people who killed that woman at Mirepech, near Béziers on Tuesday. You've got to help me. Quickly.'

'What's your name?'

'Mansell, Thomas Mansell.'

The policeman rolled his eyes. 'For Christ's sake, why didn't you just come and tell us? We've been looking for you all day, Mr Mansell. We even have reinforcements here specially. At least we've found you, but you say they've taken your wife? That is bad. Just wait.' He said something into his radio that Tom didn't catch. Tom grabbed him by the arm. 'Come with me, I think I know where one of them is. He'll know where they've taken her.' The three men tore down the rue Caristie towards the Roman theatre, scattering the crowds as they went. They stopped at the shop doorway: the man had gone but at that moment, Tom caught site of a familiar crooked, brown tail disappearing round the corner of a side turning. 'Follow me!' he shouted. As they caught up with the dog, sure enough, just a couple of paces in front of it a small, slightly stooping figure of a man was making his way unsteadily along the pavement. On the left side of his face was a large angry swelling. 'Just stay here and wait for me, this won't take long. OK?' said Tom. 'And if you don't mind, look the other way, as what I'm about to do might be slightly illegal in your country.' The policemen shrugged at one another. That the English were mad had been fully confirmed for both of them that afternoon. Mansell was looking for his wife – fine – but dressing up as a beggar, stinking like the corporation rubbish dump and going around pestering people for money instead of just going to the police was sheer lunacy. There really was no hope – completely insane, the lot of them.

Tom caught up with the man and jammed the gun into his back. He tried to turn round, but Tom caught his arm and twisted it hard behind him. 'Right, come with me. What do you speak, English or French?'

'English.' As he half-turned to face him, Tom could see the

terror in his eyes.

'Right.' Tom marched him into a small alleyway leading off the street and forced him to the ground behind a row of dustbins so that no one could see them from the road. With his knee in the small of the man's back, Tom pressed the barrel of the gun against his neck. The weapon was cocked and ready to fire so he made sure the man heard the safety catch click off. 'You have ten seconds to tell me where your people are taking my wife or I will blow your head off. Understand?'

'Yes, yes. Understand. Please don't shoot me.'

'One, two…'

'OK, OK, I tell you. They take her to Colline St Eutrope. Helicopter come for us.'

'Don't try and be clever, the Colline St Eutrope is covered in trees, you couldn't get a helicopter in there…three, four, five….'

'No, no. Is true. Car park at Colline St Eutrope. Is where I take you.'

'…six, seven, eight…'

'No, please. Is true.' The man was practically in hysterics and Tom noticed that he'd actually wet himself with fear. Pulling him to his feet, he stuffed the gun into his pocket and marched him round the corner to the two waiting policemen. 'Says they're taking her to a car park on the Colline St Eutrope to be picked up by a helicopter. Does that make sense?'

'Yes, there's a car park by the open-air swimming pool. The pool's been closed down. There's certainly room to land a helicopter.' He made another quick radio call. Tom caught the last phrase but didn't understand it, '…*oui, l'OPO à la base de Caritat: faudra faire décoller l'alerte.*' He turned to Tom. 'I've asked for a team to meet us up there.' Leading the weasel-faced man back into the alleyway, the policeman handcuffed him to a drain pipe. 'You stay here and behave yourself. Try not to piss in your pants again,' he said. Turning back to his colleague and Tom, he said, 'Our car's just round the corner, follow me.'

They ran across into the square in front of the theatre, jumping into the police car and setting off, sirens blaring, through the western end of the square. 'Where were you when they took your wife?' the one driving said over his shoulder to Tom who was sliding around on the back seat and trying to hold himself steady. 'In the square where the town hall is, I don't know the name of it but we'd just come out on the opposite side to the town hall.'

'Place Clémenceau, we may be in luck. With the road in front of the theatre blocked off and with the one-way system, they've got further to go than us, more traffic and more lights.' He swung the car hard left into the little road leading up the western side of the hill, narrowly missing a stone wall as he did so. Thank God it's one-way, thought Tom. Flat out up the straight, touching 130 kilometres per hour, the high walls on either side making it seem even faster, then hard on the brakes, two more sharp left turns and they were there. The engine screamed as they accelerated out of the last corner and Tom's head bumped hard against the roof as the car left the metalled surface of the road and dropped onto the bare earth of the car park. Ahead of them, he could just make out a single car and figures getting out of it, their faces hidden behind ski masks, but then all was obscured by huge clouds of dust being kicked up by a landing helicopter. As they raced onwards, there was a loud crack, a hole appeared in the laminated windscreen and something smashed into the rear door pillar, inches away from Tom's head. Cursing as he did so, the driver slid the car round to the left and stood on the brakes. They slithered to a halt against a scrubby hedgerow of pines and broom: luckily, the cloud of dust they had created with their emergency stop was just enough to spoil the aim of the gunmen who were now directing a steady stream of fire at them. They piled out of the car and took cover in the woods.

Tom lay in a shallow ditch while the two policemen edged slowly forward, moving from tree to tree and ducking down each time a stray round came their way. With a tremendous roar, a second helicopter came in low over where Tom was lying and swung into wind to land next to the first. Now the entire group at the other end of the car park was hidden from view. His stomach in knots, unsure whether he trusted his knees to keep him upright, let alone run, he realised this was going to be his last chance. Getting to his feet, he sprinted across to the opposite side of the car park. The distance can't have been more than fifty metres but, as he ran, it felt like a nightmare where the nameless horror is closing in but he could no longer run. He made it to the other side just as the dust cleared and vaulted a low fence into the garden of a private house. Just hope they haven't got a dog, he thought – had enough of dogs for one day. Nobody was shooting at him and the firing all seemed to be coming from the other side of the car park: what was worrying was that there was no sign of Sally. With armed police in the area, the people holding her couldn't risk making a move back to the helicopters, getting everyone aboard and airborne without the probability of getting hit. He made his way round the back of the house to see if he could get any closer to where she might be. So long as both helicopters were on the ground, then there was still hope. At the back of the property and in the direction he wanted to go, his progress was blocked by a high wall, topped with broken glass, so he retraced his steps. As he did so, to his horror he heard the turbine whine of a helicopter lifting off. He was too late, they'd managed to get her away: for a moment the despair at losing her for good this time was so overwhelming that he considered taking the gun and shooting himself.

The moment passed. No, he thought, not after what these bastards have done to Catherine, Caroline and now Sally. While she's still alive, I've got to see this through, he thought.

As he watched in abject horror, the helicopter stopped its climb at about a hundred feet and turned sideways on so that it was crabbing through the air but at a very slow speed. Perhaps they were going to throw her out and hope he was watching, just to rub it in. Not that, please not that. From his vantage point behind a child's Wendy house in the front garden, he saw why the helicopter had come into the hover. A second police car had arrived and was making its way towards the car park. From the way it was being driven, there seemed to be no sense of urgency and it was obvious that the driver had no idea how serious things were up ahead. As it eased between the barriers and jolted off the road onto the bare earth, a burst of well-aimed automatic gunfire from the left-hand door of the helicopter raked the car from end to end. It arced gently to the left and ploughed into a tree a few yards away from where the other car was parked. No one got out. The increasingly frantic radio calls from the car's controller went unanswered.

The helicopter's nose dropped and it swung into a continuous right-hand descending turn until it landed back next to the other machine. The whole episode had taken less than a minute. Again taking advantage of the dust kicked up by its blades, Tom was able to move forward another fifty metres before having to throw himself flat in the sparse cover of the ditch running the length of the car park. Sounds of gunfire were coming from the woods on the other side and he watched as a figure, its face hidden by a ski mask ran from the parked car to the helicopter. Some form of shouted conversation seemed to be taking place because the man with the automatic weapon unstrapped, got out and ran across to the woods, no doubt to help take on the two brave French policemen.

All eyes were on the woods now. Time was critical. It was becoming clear to the gang that they would have to make some sort of fighting withdrawal before the inevitable reinforcements arrived. Their leader, a hard-bitten, Ukrainian Red Army veteran, who had used his weapon to such deadly effect on the second police car, was worried too. Orange was not only home to a Gendarmerie barracks but, even though it was the weekend, it wouldn't take long to put together a squad from the 1er REC, the First Armoured Regiment of the French Foreign Legion, whose barracks were close by on the Avignon road. He set off towards the sound of firing. Who the hell recruited this bunch of amateurs? he fumed, dodging from tree to tree to join up with his three masked companions who were exchanging shots with the police. 'Start pulling back,' he ordered. 'Just fifty metres and get in behind that bank. I want to bring them on. Fire and move, remember your training.' With that, he left them and doubled back towards the helicopter, giving the wind-up sign to the pilot. If he had to leave some of them behind, so be it. His orders were clear: if all else fails, get the girl out.

Tom was almost within touching distance of the car now. A man in a ski mask sat at the wheel and in the back seat was Sally.

Pulling up on the collective pitch lever, the pilot lifted the helicopter off, enveloping everything around it in a cloud of dust. Taking advantage of the cover this afforded, Tom dashed forwards. All emotion had drained from his system and his sole focus was now on what he needed to do – no elation, no fear, no feelings, just a task to be achieved. Keeping low until the last moment, he pulled the passenger door open and fired three shots into the driver before reaching across and pulling the ski-mask from the twitching, dying man's head. Sally screamed. 'Shut up and don't move,' he shouted, which was a little superfluous because the cable ties round her ankles and wrists left her no other option. Pulling on the ski mask he applied the safety catch, returned the gun to his pocket and moved towards the other helicopter.

The tactics of the group's leader were now clear. His plan was to lure the police forward in pursuit of his colleagues and thus catch them in open ground where he would have a clear shot from the helicopter. He could see that his guys were sticking to what they'd been taught: fire and move, fire and move. Let's hope you boys are not wasting your ammunition, he thought. Single aimed shots at the centre part of the body exposed was the training: he hoped it had sunk in. Two of them were behind the bank now, leaving just one man up. The man fired again, broke cover and moved. No sooner had he done so than the leader saw him slump to the floor and lie still. Pity, but less weight in the helicopter and it'll bring them on quicker, he mused. Here they come, shit, only two of them after all that: hats off to you boys, but I'm still going to kill you. He raised the weapon and took aim.

Tom trotted the few yards to the right-hand side of the first helicopter which was still on the ground. At his approach, the pilot opened the sliding section of the Perspex side window only to be met by the muzzle of a 9mm pistol pointed at his head. He raised his arms in surrender and Tom motioned to him to get out. He forced the man to walk in front of him towards the car and when they were about twenty feet from the helicopter Tom shot him twice between the shoulder blades, pitching him forwards onto his face. The dust had completely cleared now and he realised that if anyone so much as looked his way then it was all over, so tearing off the hot, sweaty black ski mask he dashed back to the car where Sally was still sitting, trussed and unable to move. Now on the edge of hysterics, she was sobbing and screaming his name over and over again. Summoning all his strength, he pulled her out of the car, slung her over his shoulder and ran towards the waiting helicopter.

Two short bursts were all it took to end the valiant resistance of the French police officers. 'Right, land back on, we'll get everyone back on board and then lift. Got that?' In response, the pilot swung the machine round once more into a descending turn to land next to the other machine.

With butterflies massing in his stomach, Tom put on the pilot's headset and increased the power from ground idle. In response the gas turbine engine's RPM rose from 70% up to 100%, trimmed back slightly and then settled. It was nearly fifteen years since he'd tried this: three trips in the left-hand seat of a Gazelle at RAF Shawbury on a University Air Squadron summer camp all those years ago hardly counted as helicopter training, but it would have to do. With his left hand he tentatively pulled up the collective lever and as the aircraft lifted unsteadily off the ground he eased the nose round to face down the length of the car park. Then, as he pushed the cyclic pitch control gently forward in order to accelerate, the outside world disappeared in a dust-storm kicked up by his own take-off and by the other helicopter as it landed. Everything went brown. He'd never flown one of these things on instruments, let alone at twenty feet off the deck, so he heaved back on the collective to try and climb above it, almost over-torquing the aircraft's main gearbox as he did so. As he burst clear of the dust he saw to his horror that the aircraft was yawing wildly. Owing to his inexperience, he hadn't used enough pedal to counteract the torque of the main rotor and, worse still, he had thirty degrees of left bank on, causing the helicopter to drift rapidly towards the trees. He whipped the cyclic pitch control to the right, making the usual fixed-wing pilot's mistake of under-estimating the sensitivity of a helicopter's flying controls to even the smallest input. In response to his over-controlling, the aircraft now banked steeply to the right and began to descend back towards the dust cloud. With a good boot-full of pedal, another fairly agricultural heave on the collective and a slightly less vigorous application of left cyclic, the machine lurched into something nearing stable flight and climbed away, dragging its skids through the upper branches as it did so.

Two masked figures ran across from the woods towards the other helicopter as it settled onto the ground. After having dealt with the two policemen, the group's leader had seen something he didn't like, but fully expected. What took you? he thought grimly. Two convoys of vehicles, some with flashing blue lights, others of a distinctly military appearance were making their way up the two roads that led to the southern end of the hill. They had to get out, and quickly. 'Why's that bloody idiot lifted without waiting for orders? I'll have him shot. Wait here, I'll get the girl.' He motioned for the two men to get into the helicopter and then jogged towards the car. The motionless figure of the pilot, lying face-down in the dust and the driver of the car, sitting with his head flung back, eyes and mouth wide open, told him all he needed to know. Sprinting back to the helicopter, he jumped into the front left-hand seat and crammed the headset on. 'Lift,' he said. 'Quickly. Someone has taken the other helicopter and the girl. Mansell!'

The first of the vehicles were racing into the car park as the helicopter clattered over the top of them and out of sight to the south west.

Chapter Forty-one

At the French Air Force Base Aérienne 115 at Orange-Caritat, the OPO or Officier de Permanence Opérationelle put the telephone down and took a deep breath. Being duty ops officer on the weekend was a pain and at least he'd have Monday off, but this certainly wasn't in the script. Dry-mouthed, he picked up the direct line to the alert hangar where two fully armed Mirage 2000C aircraft and their pilots were always on duty, 24 hours a day, 365 days per year. A voice answered, 'Capitaine Pages.'

'Pages, confirm you are at readiness 10.' Air defence quick reaction forces are typically required to be airborne within 10 minutes if required.

'You're kidding me. A practice scramble on the weekend...'

'This isn't a practice, I've just had the duty air defence commander on the line. It looks like some sort of terrorist attack right here at Orange.'

'What, on the base?'

'No, in town. All they said is that a couple of helicopters have been stolen and now they're expecting a terrorist attack.'

'Shit. All right, you can confirm us at readiness ten. We can get both aircraft airborne in five minutes if they want. Tell them that.'

'I'll call them back now. The duty controller will call you direct on telebrief. I've got to get the MASA helicopter crew in too, there's some kind of fire-fight going on behind the Roman theatre. I'd come up to cockpit readiness if I were you. Both aircraft.'

***

Tom had no idea where he was going nor what to do next. Without a map in the helicopter he had a vague idea that to the south lay controlled airspace and the busy civil airport of Marseille-Marignane. The last thing he wanted was a collision with an airliner, so if he headed roughly south west, following the autoroute towards Nîmes and put the helicopter down near a town, then they could get help. He allowed the airspeed to build to 120 knots and, banking to the right, he followed the sound basics of his training by looking out into the turn to make sure there were no other aircraft in the way. What he saw brought all his fears flooding back. It was only a small dot over his right shoulder, but it was there all right: he could see that another helicopter was following him and gaining too. Not gaining fast, but gaining none the less. He'd heard the horror stories from the instructors at Shawbury about retreating blade stall where a helicopter can become uncontrollable if its airspeed becomes so high that, despite the automatic reduction in angle of attack, the retreating blades cease to develop lift and laminar flow gives way to turbulent over their upper surfaces. Whether or not it was possible to recover from such a stall, he didn't know, but he wasn't taking any chances by increasing his airspeed any more. He thought about making for Marseille airport: surely they wouldn't dare attack him if he landed at a busy commercial airport, but on the other hand, they'd been perfectly happy to engage in a pitched battle with armed police at Orange, so what was to stop them doing so again?

At the alert hangar on the Orange air base, the telebrief crackled into life. "Alert one, vector two four zero, climb five thousand feet, contact Rhodia radar on Lilas 2 scramble, scramble, scramble." Pages, who had been at cockpit readiness for the last five minutes, closed the canopy, gave the wind-up start signal to his crew chief, turned the battery master on, waited for the "BP" caption go out as he turned on the low pressure start switch, turned on both main low pressure fuel pumps, and, reaching down to the panel by his right hip, lifted the cover and pressed the start button. Then, as the RPM climbed through 10%, he clicked the throttle forward through the gate to ground idle. Seventh stage temperature coming up, below 950 degrees, dropping back to 610, idle RPM 50%, "Start" warning caption out, ALT1 and ALT2 out, inertial navigation selector to "Navigate," "VAL" selected. He waited to confirm that the Head Up Display was showing the correct symbology and the velocity vector was present, the inertial navigation system showing "Ready", temperatures and pressures normal, short automatic flight control check ok, all flight control captions out, no test of the emergency fuel system on a scramble start, radios confirmed on, radar standby, TACAN standby, IFF standby, IFF interrogator standby, radar altimeter on, standby artificial horizon uncaged, Head Down Display on, nosewheel steering on. Pre-taxi check: all captions out except for "PARK". He waved away the external power set and the chocks. 'Alert 1, taxi.'

The tower controller replied. 'Alert 1, clear taxi, runway 33, QFE 1019.' On a thumbs-up from the groundcrew, Pages applied a small handful of power, released the brakes, eased the Mirage 2000C out of the hangar and turned towards the threshold of runway 33 which was no more than 50 metres away. Taxi checks: TACAN on and tested, ILS off, Head Up and Head Down displays ok, IFF test ok, ECM and ESM standby, chaff and flares off, anti-skid caption out.

'Alert 1 take off.'

'Alert 1, you are cleared for take off, wind 330 less than 10. After take off, contact Rhodia on Lilas 2.'

As he turned onto the runway, he ran through the pre-takeoff checks: canopy down and locked, harness tight and locked, ejection seat safety pin removed, all captions out, audio warning on, radar to transmit, undercarriage safety lock clear. With the aircraft pointing down the centreline, he made a quick check of the heading in the Head Up Display, applied full dry power: RPM below 103%, temperature below 840 degrees, brakes holding. Brakes off, full afterburner, "FAN" caption on, fuel flow ok, the acceleration box in the HUD showing above .56 JX. One hundred and twenty knots came up in under 350 metres of runway and as he raised the takeoff symbol in the HUD to the horizon, the aircraft became airborne and he selected the undercarriage up. Raising the nose to give a climb angle of 30 degrees, he then overbanked to the left to maintain 5,000 feet and as the speed came up through 400 knots, pulled the throttle out of reheat and in full dry power let the speed build to a comfortable 450 knots. He rolled out on a wind-adjusted track of 240 degrees true, pressed the square PA button on the top left of the instrument panel just under the cockpit coaming and the button glowed green as the autopilot engaged. 'Alert 1 to Rhodia, Lilas 2.'

'Roger, Alert 1.'

He pulled in the lightly spring-loaded section on the front of the sticktop to take control back from the autopilot and adjusted his course slightly. 'Rhodia, this is Alert 1.'

'Alert 1, Rhodia, loud and clear, squawk 1543. You have two contacts bearing two two zero, range 30 miles, low altitude, slow. MASA procedures in force, you are to ensure that both contacts land and if they refuse, you are authorised to engage, I say again, if they refuse, you are authorised to engage. Alert 1, authenticate Foxtrot Lima.' Pages looked down at the authentication grid on his kneepad, checked the time and the crypto sheet in force.

'I authenticate Juliet. Rhodia, authenticate Delta Hotel.'

'I authenticate Mike.'

So this was it. Even an experienced pilot like Pages, a flight commander with over two thousand flying hours, was nervous at the prospect of actually opening fire on a live target. More than nervous if he'd care to admit it. He double-checked his switches. No room for screw-ups: get this wrong, boy, and you'll be famous world-wide and for all the wrong reasons, he thought. All sticktop safety catches safe. Good. Reaching down to the bottom left of the instrument panel, he double-checked that the red master arm switch was selected to safe too, selected the Super 530D missile system and immediately, the Head Up Display switched from navigation to air-to-air mode. He rocked the three-position selector on the front of the throttle to the outboard position: good, both Magic 2 infra-red missiles were indicating correctly and showing that their seekers were fully cooled down. He toggled the Head Down Display into 40 mile scale and there they were, two overlapping contacts at twenty-five miles range, a cluster of little, green v-shapes, the short line underneath each contact telling him that the returns were coming from the lower bar of his radar's two-bar raster scan.

'Contact, two one zero, twenty-five, low-level, slow: targets heading two four zero.' Thumbing the controller on the inboard side of the throttle, Pages looked in at his screen, moved the cruciform radar cursor over the targets and pressed the controller in. The cursor flashed as the radar attempted to lock. Target symbology came up in both head-down and head-up displays. Locked, no, bad lock, try again; no, still no luck, clear down the memorised "*plot fictif*" get in closer and try again. Because he was approaching very slow targets from astern, they were very close to the radar's main beam clutter notch where the doppler shift from the target and that from the ground are indistinguishable. To complicate matters further, in search mode, a pulse doppler radar often shows helicopters as multiple targets owing to the false returns generated by the main rotor blades as they effectively speed up and slow down relative to the radar that is looking at them.

'Confirm target. Identify and proceed as briefed. Check switches safe.'

'Alert 1 confirmed. Switches safe.'

Pages tried another lock. Got it this time. He flicked the radar into twenty mile range scale and altered the Mirage's heading to place the intercept steering dot central in the HUD, leaving it just below the steering circle.

Chapter Forty-two

Tom's hands were sweating and his mouth was dry. Every time he looked back over his right shoulder, there they were, gaining on him. Slightly out to the right, always on the same side, but now no more than 500 metres separated them.

The other pilot was an old hand, a veteran with thousands of hours of rotary-wing flying time, most of it in Mi-8 Hip helicopters – some of it in Afghanistan in the 1980s and other trouble spots where he'd served as a support helicopter pilot with the Soviet Army. However, brilliant aircraft handler though he was, he had no training in the wiles of air combat. Dogfights make for good movies but lousy tactics, and from the first air combats of the First World War right up to the present day, the same basic rule still holds true: a good fighter pilot will always try to approach unseen and kill without giving his adversary any opportunity to fight back. However, by flying at the same altitude as Tom and by staying offset to the right, he had thrown away all his tactical advantage because his adversary could see him coming – not that Tom could do much about it other than await the inevitable.

The city of Nîmes slid by to his left: no question of landing now, that would just make him an easier target – the thought of what had happened to that second police car was uppermost in his mind now. As they eased closer, he could even make out that there were two people on board. Almost level with him now, about 100 metres, slightly astern but closing, movement in the left-hand seat that he couldn't make out. Shit! Muzzle flashes then, simultaneously, two holes in the perspex just in front of him. Hyperventilating and sweating, he pulled the helicopter up sharply and turned hard towards the other aircraft in an attempt to get out of the field of fire, losing sight of the threat as he arced over the top of them in a continuous right turn. Then, he made a classic beginner's mistake.

Eight miles: Pages toggled the radar into ten mile scale,

rocked the weapons selector on the throttle outboard again and pressed the paddle switch on the front of the throttle with the middle finger of his left hand to slave the head of one of his Magic 2 infra-red missiles to the target. After a few seconds, a continuous tone in his headset told him that he had an IR lock and a dotted green triangle in the bottom left of the HUD showed that both the radar and the missile's IR seeker were locked on to the same target, but the dots meant that it was out of the HUD's field of view. Banking gently to the left, he closed the throttle, rocked back the airbrake switch with his left thumb and as the speed slowed towards 300 knots, the triangle changed from dotted to solid. Airbrakes in, power set. There they were, four miles away. 'Rhodia, Alert 1, tally two helicopters, manoeuvring.' The radar broke lock and the acquisition symbol in the HUD changed from a triangle to a circle showing him that although he had no radar lock, the infra-red seeker of his left-hand Magic 2 could still see its target.

Pages transmitted on the VHF emergency frequency, 121.50. 'Two helicopters at 3,000 feet, south of Sommières, manoeuvring, this is French Air Force Alert 1 calling on guard, you are to land immediately, I say again, you are to land immediately. If you fail to comply, your aircraft will be destroyed, I say again, if you fail to comply, your aircraft will be destroyed. Acknowledge.'

Please, no, I don't want to die, not like this, thought Tom. He pressed the button on the top of the cyclic in the hope it was a radio transmit button. 'No, please don't shoot, they're trying to kill me,' he shouted. But there was no side-tone: he wasn't transmitting. As the ground swung sickeningly towards him, he began to lose his grip on rational thought and his flying became increasingly ragged. During that first turn, he'd done exactly the right thing by turning towards the threat, but had then made the beginner's fatal mistake of reversing his direction of turn once he'd passed over the top of his pursuers. Straight away they'd taken advantage of this blunder to slot in behind him. Worse still, the other helicopter had forced him down to 1,000 feet and had him trapped on the inside of a left-hand spiralling turn. They had height on him now and so, each time he turned towards them to get away from the fire being directed at him from the left hand door, he had to pass underneath, losing more height with each successive crossing. His machine had taken several more rounds and it was a matter of time before one of them found something vital, if they hadn't done so already. He didn't even dare look behind to see how Sally was in case he lost control. He was down to 50 knots now and at this lower speed, his more experienced opponent was able to yaw his helicopter so that the left-hand door was always facing Tom. The figure in the left seat pulled his weapon in to reload a fresh magazine.

'Rhodia, Alert 1, neither aircraft is responding.'

'Roger, Alert 1. *Tir de semonce'* – fire a warning shot.

'Roger that.' Pages checked again that the sticktop safety catch was in the safe position, rocked the weapons selector inboard and, reaching down to the weapons control panel on the bottom left of the instrument panel, lifted the red master arm switch over its detent up into the live position. A quick check in the cockpit – weapons showing "RAP" for rapid fire, giving 1800 rounds per minute from each of the two 30 mm cannons, and the rounds counter in the HUD showing 125 for each side. Reducing speed to 250 knots, he closed on the spiralling helicopters, made a last check to make sure that his rounds wouldn't fall on built-up areas and, with his right thumb, flicked the safety catch to live.

Tom was down to below 500 feet and, as they spiralled, down he saw muzzle flashes spurt from the left-hand side of the other helicopter. At that moment he saw tracer rounds passing behind it and a grey delta-winged aircraft flash past. There was a loud bang from somewhere behind him and the helicopter began to vibrate. The engine RPM started to wind down and the rotor RPM warning sounded. He dumped the collective lever and pointed the nose down towards the largest open field he could see. It was only a matter of time before they killed him now.

After firing the warning burst, Pages made the sticktop safe and pulled his aircraft up into a steep wing-over. 'Rhodia, Alert 1. Neither aircraft is responding, confirm I am clear to engage.'

'Alert 1, Rhodia. I confirm you are clear to engage, I say again, clear to engage.' Three hundred and fifty knots, boresight radar lock on the nearest machine, one thousand metres and closing. The fall of shot predictor line streamed back from the fixed cross in the HUD like wriggling green spaghetti. Along its length, little groups of asterisks were travelling: known as "cyclists" they give the pilot a prediction of where a quarter-second burst of fire would fall. At the line's far extremity, with the 2 milliradian aiming point or "pipper" at its centre, the outer ring of the stadiametric aiming circle started to unwind and slowly creep up the screen as the range to the target reduced.

The last and only time that Tom had tried an auto-rotative landing had been twenty years ago and on that occasion he'd had a whole airfield to aim at. He had no idea what speed he should use and so picked 60 knots, more in hope than expectation. Auto-rotation is the nearest a helicopter can manage to a glide, and like a falling sycamore leaf whose action it is mimicking, the only way is down. As he approached, he saw that the field he'd chosen had a considerable down-slope with a row of solid-looking pine trees at the far end. He pulled the collective up and gently eased back the cyclic to initiate the flare but he was too low and now 10 knots slow, causing the helicopter to hit the ground with a jarring thump with the low rotor RPM horn shrieking in his ears. It bounced once and then landed hard back on its skids before slewing to a halt with rotors still spinning. Above them, another helicopter was circling. The muzzle of an automatic weapon appeared from its side window.

The impact of the burst was devastating. The tanks ruptured and fuel vapour met hot gas turbine and gearbox components, giving rise to a terrible explosion which engulfed the helicopter and blasted through into the cockpit. Other rounds found the main gearbox and rotor linkages, causing the rotor blades to scythe through the tail boom, detaching it from body of the aircraft. In the tangled, flaming wreckage its occupants perished instantly.

Pages thumbed the sticktop safety catch into the safe position, moved the master arm switch to safe and re-centred the weapons selector. He was hyperventilating and his stomach was full of butterflies. 'Rhodia, Alert 1. Fox-3,' he gave the NATO standard code for a guns kill. 'Splash one target, the other one has landed. Instructions?'

'Alert 1, Rhodia. Confirm switches safe, report exact position and ensure the other target stays on the ground.'

'Rhodia, Alert1. Switches safe. Wilco.'

Chapter Forty-three

Slowly, the dust settled, the rotor blades slowed to a halt and all was quiet save for a quiet sobbing coming from behind him. Tom jumped down from the helicopter and his legs went out from under him, sending him sprawling face-first into the dust. He was shaking and nauseous, now that he was able to think rather than just simply react. Getting unsteadily to his feet he went to retrieve Sally from the back seat. She hadn't been strapped in and the violent manoeuvring of the aircraft, followed by their sack of potatoes landing in the field had left her wedged between the rear seat cushions and the back of the front seats, totally unable to move. So, taking care not to hurt her, he eased the front seats forward on their runners, gently lifted her out and sat her down on the ground. A few hundred yards away in a vineyard, an angry column of thick, oily black smoke from the crash site was drifting on the wind.

From a nearby housing estate, people were running towards them and Tom, still shaking and clammy with fright, sat with his arm round Sally's shoulders, trying to comfort her while he waited for them to arrive. At his request, someone produced a penknife and he cut the cable ties that held her wrists and ankles. A thoughtful individual produced what they both needed most, a bottle of water. And a small group of older women began mothering Sally and asking aloud what sort of husband trussed his wife up with cable ties before throwing her in the back of a helicopter like a sack of turnips. But what can you expect from the English? Mad as hatters, the lot of them.

A few minutes later a police car arrived, bumping across the tussocky surface of the field. The growing crowd that now surrounded them drew back to let the two policemen through. 'Are you Mansell?' asked one. Tom nodded. 'An ambulance is on its way to take you Nîmes. You're safe now. You're going to be all right.'

'Thanks,' said Tom. 'It may be too late but I want you to

make a call for me. The same people who did this are holding a friend of mine in the US. His name is David Liebowitz. We're both fine but his life is in danger. Please contact the police in the States. Could you do it now, please?' The policeman put his arm round Tom's shoulder and gently led him towards the waiting car.

***

Although badly shaken by their ordeal, apart from a few cuts and bruises, Tom and Sally were physically unharmed and were cleared to go home by the briskly efficient staff at the Nîmes University Hospital. Two policemen remained with them at the hospital and stayed discreetly in the background.

Their escort went and sat in their car, still keeping an eye on them, and while Tom and Sally sat on the step of the air ambulance building waiting for the police helicopter to collect them for the return trip to Orange, he told her what had happened during the last few days: his arrest; the flight to France; the journey to Orange; the death of Catherine who'd taken a bullet meant for Sally; the irreplaceable Vincent; the murder of Caroline and finally, the events that had led to their nearly dying in a scrubby field just to the south west of the little town of Sommières a few hours earlier. As for David, he could be anywhere. For a few minutes, Sally sat in silence saying nothing. Then she said quietly, 'But why didn't you answer your phone, Tom?'

'The police took it off me in London along with my passport and laptop. Why didn't you answer yours?'

She looked down at her feet, embarrassed. 'I dropped it in Mathilde's swimming pool. I tried calling you on her mobile and from the house phone in Le Lavandou: I even went to an internet café to see if you were up on Skype. I was beginning to get really worried: the house phone wasn't answering, you weren't answering. I thought something had happened to you or you'd run off.' She paused. 'But instead you risked your life for me, didn't you? Were you frightened?'

'Frightened? No, not really,' he smiled. 'More like pant-

297

wettingly terrified from start to finish. I don't think I'm cut out for this sort of thing. There is one problem though.'

'What's that?'

'The two people I killed.'

'But that was self-defence,' she said.

'More like getting my retaliation in first,' he replied. 'What worries me most is how easy it was – I didn't even give it a second thought. Anyway, we'll find out soon enough what they'll do to me, here comes the helicopter. Reckon you can stand another trip in one of those things?'

Sally bit her lip and nodded; they waved a last goodbye to the two policemen in the car.

In the gathering dusk, the helicopter set down on the grassed area in front of the officers' mess at the Orange air base, where they were met by the base commander and a group of police officers.

The base commander shook them by the hand and addressed them in almost perfect English. 'Mr and Mrs Mansell, welcome to Orange. My friends from the police tell me that some of the people who were trying to harm you may still be at large so, in order that you can have somewhere safe and comfortable to stay, I would like to invite you to stay in the mess as my guests until we can be sure that it is safe for you to leave. Mrs Mansell, we have arranged for your belongings to be transferred from your hotel, I hope that is acceptable to you.' He continued. 'As you would expect, the police have a number of questions they wish to ask you, but they tell me that can wait until tomorrow when they come to see you at ten o'clock. You are free to come and go as you please, there is a telephone in your room if you need to make any calls and all I would ask is that you do not go too far from the area immediately around the officers' mess. Is there anything else I can do for you?'

'Yes,' said Tom, 'Could you please check with your colleagues that they got my message about my friend, David Liebowitz; his life is in danger and the US authorities need to be told.'

'Please wait and I will check.' He went over to the group of police officers and spoke to the captain in charge. 'Yes, Mr Mansell, I can confirm that your message has been passed on, but I have no other news.'

'Thank you, Colonel. There is one more thing, if you don't mind. I'd very much like to meet the pilot, the one who saved our lives. I'd like to thank him in person.'

'Certainly, Mr Mansell. Capitaine Pages is on duty till nine o'clock tomorrow, but after that I'll ask him to come to the mess.'

'Thank you, Colonel. There is a final favour I'd like to ask you. I don't usually go around dressed as a tramp and smelling this bad, is there any chance of getting hold of some clean clothes? I'll pay of course.'

'I'll have the duty storeman come over and see what we can find for you. It may be military uniform, I hope you do not mind,' he smiled.

'Not at all, that would be most kind. Thanks again.'

'My pleasure, Mr Mansell. Until tomorrow, then.'

'Thank you, Colonel. Good night.'

The duty barman handed them their keys and they went up the stairs to their room: spartan, simple, with two single beds and a small en-suite bathroom with a shower. It even had the obligatory dripping tap.

'Tom, I hate to say this, but you stink. Can you put those clothes on the window sill or somewhere outside? You can't have washed in weeks.'

'In fairness, it's not me, it's what I'm wearing. I got the idea from a beggar in Avignon and so I bought some clothes there, hacked them about with a pair of scissors – same ones I did the crew-cut with – and rolled them about in the dirt. Trouble is, after that they just looked like new clothes that someone had cut with scissors and rolled in the dirt, so I added essence of dead fish from the banks of the Rhône and fresh horse poo from Orange. I think I overdid the dead fish, though.'

'I think you did,' she said.

***

The following morning, the police captain whom they'd met the previous evening arrived at the mess to question them and to take a statement.

'Before anything else, Captain,' said Tom. 'Do you have any news about my friend, David Liebowitz?'

'Yes, and you'll be pleased to know that he is safe. I do not have all the details, but the US authorities stopped the car he was travelling in just outside the cargo area of Newark airport. There seems to have been an exchange of fire in which the men holding your friend were killed and he was wounded – we're told he was tied up in the boot of the car – but we understand that it's not serious and he'll make a full recovery.' He paused. 'I'm afraid there is no news of his friend Caroline.' Tom put his arm round Sally's shoulder and gave her a squeeze; she dabbed her eyes with a handkerchief but said nothing. 'The men who took your friends are believed to be from eastern Europe or one of the former Soviet Republics, but that's the only information we have.'

'There's another friend of mine who was murdered by them – Vincent Deschamps. Have you caught the people who did that?'

'I wasn't aware that anyone of that name had been involved. Excuse me while I make a phone call.'

A few minutes later the captain returned and placed a set of keys on the table. 'Our Gendarmerie colleagues in the Hérault have had new locks fitted to your house as a precaution.'

'Thanks,' said Tom. 'That was very thoughtful of them.'

The captain continued, 'And now I must ask you to explain what has been going on. We have an outline of events from our British colleagues and it seems that someone from within the bank attempted to frame you for misconduct; I shouldn't really tell you this, but they have arrested somebody called…' he checked his notes, '…called Denise Evans. Do you know that name?'

Tom's eyes went wide with amazement. 'Well yes, but I've no idea why she'd want to do that, no idea at all, unless…'

'Unless what, Mr Mansell?'

'No, it's nothing, just ignore me, I was going to suggest that she may have been given encouragement to do what she did, but I don't have any proof and if it's the person I'm thinking of, I'm very sure he won't have left any.'

'I don't understand.'

I understand only too bloody well, thought Tom. This has Sam Bortoleski written all over it. 'No it's nothing, really,' said Tom.

'As you wish, Mr Mansell. But you will be pleased to know that the City of London Police have dropped all charges against you.' He consulted his notes once more. 'Including that of escaping from lawful custody and various offences against the Air Navigation Order. However, what interests me is what happened here in France. Such as why a serious, paramilitary operation was carried out in this country in an attempt to kill or kidnap you. Some of the equipment we have recovered suggests a link with the Russian Federation. That ties up with the information we have so far obtained from the man who you knocked down, Mr Mansell; he is a Russian national and we believe that some of his accomplices were also Russian and Ukrainian. We have very little information beyond that because he is too frightened to talk to us.'

'Anyone from Nashyastan?' Tom asked.

'Not that we know of. Why do you ask that?'

'This whole affair started because Liebowitz and I refused an offer to go and work for Noviprom, which is the Nashyastan government's sovereign wealth authority. Find anyone who's even vaguely connected to them in France and you've got your answer.' Tom recounted the whole story of their dealings with Kaliski and Ursk, his arrest, escape from custody, right through to the threats to harm Sally and the kidnapping of Liebowitz and Caroline.

The captain looked grave. 'All I can say is that we are aware of Noviprom, who they are and what they do. However, at the moment, the only evidence we have against them is circumstantial. We believe what you have told us but so far it cannot be corroborated: nothing leads us to them at the moment but believe me, we are working on it. Nashyastan is a friendly nation and we have very close ties with them. Personally, I hope my government will review the diplomatic credentials of some of their people in this country and I hope yours will do the same.'

Fat chance of that, thought Tom.

'I have a question, Captain,' said Tom. 'Do you know whether my friend Mr Hutchinson has managed to get his aeroplane back from where I left it?'

The captain smiled. 'Thanks to the Mirage 2000 crews who intercepted you, we had an accurate location for the aircraft and found it later that day. I believe your friend is going to fly it back to England, if he hasn't done so already. There is some other good news. You may not know, but the two helicopters used in the attack were stolen from a flying school at Avignon. Two men posing as prospective students forced the instructors to land at the disused airfield at Plan de Dieu and then took over the helicopters. I heard this morning that the instructors have been found alive. Frightened but unharmed.'

Tom took a deep breath. 'There is something I need to tell you.'

The answer took him by surprise. 'Yes, Mr Mansell, we know,' he said gravely.

'The two men in the car park. The driver was carrying what we believe are fake Russian diplomatic papers and the car had false Russian diplomatic plates under its French ones. As for what happened to those individuals, it's as clear a case of *légitime défense* as we've ever seen. Self-defence, Mr Mansell, you have nothing to worry about.' Sally grasped Tom's hand under the table and squeezed it hard.

The questioning continued for the rest of the morning and just before lunch, the Captain was called away by one of his men. He returned with a broad smile on his face. 'I have some good news for you, Mr Mansell, your friend Vincent Deschamps is alive. He's still in a critical condition but his doctors expect him to live.' Tom beamed with delight.

They were joined at the lunch table by Capitaine Pages and his young wife.

Tom shook Pages warmly by the hand. 'We want to thank you for saving our lives,' he said.

'You were very lucky, Mr Mansell,' said Pages. We had no idea who was in the helicopters and, because of what had happened on the ground and the fact that policemen had been killed, my orders were simply to make both aircraft land and, if either refused, to engage. The orders were very clear.'

'You mean shoot them down?'

'That's correct. For all we knew, a major terrorist attack could have been underway. If your helicopter had been the nearest to me, I would have shot you down first. You were very lucky.'

'Twice in the same week then,' said Tom and recounted the story of his escape to France in Hutch's aircraft.

Pages smiled. 'That was me too, but you were in no danger of being shot down on that occasion. There used to be three squadrons here but we've been cut back to one and our main role, apart from providing the air defence quick reaction alert force, is to act as the Mirage 2000 training squadron. I was the instructor in the back seat of one of the aircraft that intercepted you near Le Mans; both were Mirage 2000Bs, that's the two-seater training version which doesn't have a gun and as neither aircraft was carrying live missiles, you were perfectly safe. To us, you were just another lost aircraft that wasn't in radio contact with anyone and hadn't filed a flight plan, a totally different situation to yesterday.'

'I was terrified that you were going to shoot me down,' Tom said.

'We were terrified that we'd caused you to crash,' replied Pages with a smile. 'That's why we kept looking for you.'

***

As the adrenalin slowly wore off, Tom puzzled over what had happened to him. It was clear that Denise Evans must have been given an incentive to frame him, but he couldn't understand why she had taken such a risk to do so.

303

Chapter Forty-four

That evening, a French Air Force Mystère 50 with Sally and Tom Mansell as its sole passengers took off from runway 33 at Orange and headed for RAF Northolt in West London. For the first half hour, neither of them said much: what more was there to say after the events of the last five days? Sally looked down at the French countryside unfolding beneath them. 'Tom, I don't think I'm going to be happy living in our lovely house any more. Not after everything that's happened. Poor, dear Catherine. They thought she was me. And Caroline too.'

'I understand, darling, I really do. I was expecting you to say that and I think I may already have a solution.'

She looked at him quizzically. 'What is it?' she said.

'It's one of my hare-brained ideas. You know, a bit like dressing up as a tramp and rubbing a dead fish into my clothes, only not nearly as sensible. It's risky and I won't tell you now in case it doesn't come off, but if it does, I think it'll make you very happy.'

At RAF Northolt, the aircraft taxied to the military ramp, on the northern side of the airfield.

They were met by the Station Commander, Group Captain Higgins, who drove them the short distance to the officers' mess. 'We'll get you on your way as soon as possible, but there are just one or two formalities to clear up, you know, the usual bumf. Chap from the Foreign Office wants a word.' Tom had no idea what the "usual bumf" was, but he and Sally followed Higgins through the front doors of the mess, along a corridor and into a small office near the bar that had "Mess Manager" painted on the door. 'I apologise for the setting,' he said. 'But at least it has the advantage of being discreet.' He knocked on the door and, without waiting for an answer, showed them into a cramped, overstuffed office which smelled of cooked cabbage. Waiting for them, sitting behind the desk was a small, downtrodden looking man in his late fifties – all that was missing was the black toothbrush moustache and he would have been the double of Mr Potato Head. 'I'll be waiting in the bar when you've finished,' said Higgins. To Tom, he seemed nervous.

Mr Potato Head stood up and shook hands with each of them in turn. He introduced himself as David Brown and gave them each a dog-eared business card. 'I apologise for detaining you like this,' he said in a high, adenoidal voice. 'But given what you've both been through, I've been asked to represent Her Majesty's Government and to explain a number of very important facts to you before you speak to anyone else – you do of course realise that your story has made headlines round the world and that your pictures are on every news channel almost twenty-four hours a day?'

'No,' said Tom and shot Sally a worried glance.

'Perhaps I should start by explaining what I do. As you'll see from my card, I work for the Foreign and Commonwealth Office as part of the Agencies Liaison team. What that means is that we liaise with other government bodies to make sure that we don't duplicate effort, or act in any way that's inconsistent with one another. Now, as I'm sure you're both aware, the people who have harmed your friends and very nearly killed you both are part of a powerful organisation. The British Government is aware of who they are and what they do. Now you must treat this information in the strictest confidence, but I can assure you that a full-scale investigation is underway into their activities and it's for that reason that we would be most grateful if you didn't speak to the media until we give you the word because we don't want anything to jeopardise the investigation. Of course,' he added hastily, 'we can't *stop* you doing so – this is a free country after all – but I'm sure you can appreciate that it will make it far more difficult to continue our enquiries if you do.'

'So to sum all that up,' said Tom. 'You mean you don't want us to mention to anybody that Noviprom is a front for government-sponsored organised crime.'

'Mr Mansell, I'm not at liberty to confirm or deny who's being investigated. It's just that if you could refrain from talking to anybody about what's happened until we give you the word, the Government would be most grateful for the reasons that I've outlined. Now, if you have any questions, I'll be delighted to try and answer them.'

'Not a poker player then, Mr Brown?' said Tom.

'Sorry, I'm not with you.'

'Nor are the people you work for I'd guess. Here's what I think. Either you work for the SIS or possibly you want us to think you do and that we've been very clever by working that out. As ordinary people who don't move in such circles, we couldn't fail to be impressed and excited that our case is being looked at as part of an MI6 or MI5 investigation – I can never remember who does what. You also made the not illogical assumption that we'd be more than averagely hacked off by what Noviprom has done and that if we thought it would help nail them, then we'd keep quiet until you gave us the word. The trouble is,' continued Tom, 'that the word would never come and by the time we realised why, the story would be ancient history or would've been spun into the long grass. No, the real reason is that the British Government is scared witless that the electorate will find out that for the last ten years or more it's been cosying up to a country that systematically tortures people and also acts as a conduit for most of the processed heroin and raw opium coming out of central Asia. I also think the fact that Nashyastan has the world's largest non-OPEC oil reserves could have some bearing on that, or maybe I'm just being cynical. What scares them even more is that someone will spill the beans about the "extraordinary rendition" to Nashyastan from the UK, the US and elsewhere of people whom the Government wanted "interrogated" and that it's still going on. That's why you want us to keep quiet; you and your employer want this whole thing swept under the carpet – you've no interest in bringing anyone to justice, far from it. All that'll happen is that the Nashyastan ambassador will be called in for a quiet word in his shell-like and be told to keep his boys under control in future. As for whether we talk to the press about any of this, that's our decision and nobody else's. There's no "full-scale investigation" and your job is to make damn sure there never will be.'

'Mr Mansell, I'm not an expert in the legal field, but I really would be very careful before you go around making wild allegations like that without any kind of evidence. Just friendly advice, you understand.'

'Oh but I do have evidence, that's the whole point.' Brown's eyes widened, just for an instant, but long enough to tell Tom all he needed to know. 'I have irrefutable, first-hand evidence from sources involved with the Nashyastan government that they have tortured terrorist suspects and that the resulting evidence – if you can call it that – has been used by UK Government agencies.'

Brown's face remained once more impassive. 'Fairy tales, Mr Mansell. You cannot have evidence of events that never happened – I wouldn't listen to every rumour that you happen to hear if I were you,' he said.

'You could always take the risk of calling my bluff if you like,' said Tom. 'Then we'll see who's telling fairy tales. On the other hand, you and your people could take a more sensible course of action. Stop trying to intimidate us and do some of your "agency liaison" stuff to make sure that Noviprom's operations are shut down in the UK and that those responsible for what they've done over the last few months are chucked out of any decent country we have links with. Now, we're both very tired and we want to go home and get on with our lives.'

Brown opened his mouth to continue but Tom and Sally got up and left him alone in the malodorous office, closing the door behind them. They found Higgins, sitting alone in the bar, nervously sipping an orange juice. 'Group Captain, we'd like to go home now,' said Tom.

Outside the mess, an unmarked police car was waiting for them. On the back seat were his laptop and a carrier bag containing the belongings that the police had taken when they'd arrested him.

The car stopped and started its way through the evening traffic towards the M25 and on to Sally's parents' house near Stowmarket in Suffolk. Tom noticed with satisfaction the two marked police cars in the lane as they neared the house.

Later that evening, Tom and Sally took a stroll around the garden before bed. They stopped to sit on a stone bench with their backs to the tall yew hedge that divided the garden from the orchard beyond and Sally rested her head on Tom's shoulder. 'You never mentioned you had evidence that the UK Government was using Nashyastan to torture terrorist suspects,' she said.

'I don't,' he replied. 'Everything I said is true – some of it Kaliski even told me himself – and although I may not have concrete proof to back it up, there's more than enough circumstantial evidence out there to point the finger at Noviprom and therefore at the Nashyastan Government. The more our side think I know, the more, I hope, they'll be keen to keep a tight rein on Noviprom. That was why I spun that line to Brown.'

'You need to be careful, Tom. It could backfire on us, and I don't think it's a good idea to antagonise them, that's all.'

'No, you're right. I suppose I hadn't looked at it that way. Still, it was worth it just for the look on Brown's face when I told him I had proof – won't hurt them to sweat for a bit. Anyway, it's getting cold, let's go in.'

***

Their first day at the house was spent taking it easy and, for Tom, making phone calls – he even managed to get through to Liebowitz's hospital room. His friend tried to sound upbeat and to make the right noises about soon being up and about and making a full recovery, but Tom could hear from the catch in his voice that all was not well.

Vincent wasn't well enough to talk yet, but the medical staff at Lyon confirmed that he was on the way to a full recovery.

As Brown had told them, the case had hit the media like a tornado. Speculation filled the airwaves and even the broadsheets carried wild invented stories. Despite their reporters' frantic efforts to find the Mansells, the Suffolk police did a good job of keeping the media at bay from both Sally's parents' house and the

Dorset force did the same thing for Tom's.

The following morning, leaving Sally with her parents, the police smuggled him out of the house in an unmarked van and drove him as far as Stowmarket station from where he took an early train to Liverpool Street and thence by cab to a small office just off the Gray's Inn Road.

After about three quarters of an hour, Tom's solicitor looked up from his notes. 'Well, Tom,' he said. 'I think you've got an absolutely water-tight case against the bank both in the UK and the US, because it was the actions of their staff that directly caused the problem. However, as for a case against the police, we can try, but I don't think you'll get anywhere. There were no independent witnesses to what they did to you, and, given the evidence they had at the time, they were within their rights to arrest you. On past performance, they'll close ranks, deny everything and say you were treated correctly, humanely and that everything they did was within the law. I hate to say this, but if I were you, I'd let it drop. Finally, and I'm sure you realised this already, despite what your friend from the FCO may've said, if you and Sally were to sell your story to the papers, you'd make a fortune. You'd probably bring down the current government as well and whether you see that as a good or bad thing is none of my business.'

Tom smiled at this. 'I'm not sure I want to spend the rest of my life with that responsibility hanging round my neck and believe me, fame is the last thing Sally and I want. Fortune I'll live with, but fame? No thanks. I think we may release the story one day, but we'll need to be careful how we do it to make sure that the right heads roll as a result.'

From the solicitor's office he took another taxi to Canary Wharf and was pleasantly surprised to note that his pass still allowed him through the turnstiles. When he got up to the equities trading floor and marched purposefully across to the corner office, a fuming Inspector Hill was waiting for him. At Tom's approach, Hill strode out to meet him. 'Mr Mansell, our meeting was arranged for ten o'clock. It's now half past eleven and there are still a lot of loose ends I need to tie up.' Tom ignored him, swept past into the office and sat down on what had been until recently, Denise's side of the desk. 'Come in, close the door, sit down, Hill, and shut up. After what I've been through, I don't care in the slightest that you have been inconvenienced.' Tom raised his hand. 'And don't interrupt. When it's your turn to say something I'll let you know, until then, kindly be quiet. Because of your deliberate refusal to listen to me when I told you about Noviprom, dear friends of ours have been killed and others badly hurt. Six brave French police officers are dead too, each one of them worth more than ten of you. Two helicopters have been wrecked and two flying instructors scared out of their wits. I have been beaten up, jailed, chased, shot at, my wife has been kidnapped and we both very nearly died in a helicopter crash, all because you preferred to toe the party line and were too stupid, cowardly and arrogant to do your job properly. Right, I promised you I'd give you an opportunity to speak. Yes-no answer, Hill. Are you going to do anything about Kaliski and Ursk in particular and Noviprom in general or are you going to carry on being party to this cover-up?'

'Mr Mansell, I can assure you there is no cover up. Our investigations are continuing, but my superiors have asked me to treat this with great delicacy, there are diplomatic niceties that you are clearly not aware of...'

He leapt to his feet. 'Out. Get out of this office now, Hill, or this time you really will have grounds to arrest me for assaulting a police officer, although I'm sure that my colleagues will close ranks just as tightly as yours do and lie just as convincingly when it comes to having seen anything.' With a look of determination on his face and his fist raised, he moved round the desk towards Hill who at his approach, got up and fled. Tom stood in the doorway of the office watching the retreating figure as it went through the automatic glass doors on the other side of the trading floor and down the escalators towards reception.

'Jeez, Tom. What did you say to him?' It was Mike Smith, head of the global corporate and investment banking division.

'Oh, hi, Mike. It was my delicately constructed and highly complex line of argument that did it.' Smith's eyebrows rose in query. 'I threatened to hit him,' said Tom. 'Anyway, Mike, what are you doing here and where's Sam?'

'Because of the gravity of the situation, I came over to take charge of things personally and I've sent Sam home to mind the shop over there. This whole damn thing is turning into a media feeding frenzy, Tom. It's the worst possible publicity for the bank.'

Pompous ass. Touched to see you're so concerned for Sally's and my wellbeing, thought Tom. 'We need to talk, Mike. Got a minute? It won't take long.'

'Sure.'

Tom repeated his tactic of taking the seat behind the desk. 'I'll come straight to the point, Mike. I've taken legal advice and this is how things stand right now. Because this was started by the bank's employees, in bank time, on bank systems, the bank is entirely responsible for much of what happened to me. The Noviprom side is the fault of the police and of people even further up the food chain, but that's another issue. Now, because this is currently the major news item on both sides of the Atlantic and because banks in general are at the top of everyone's hate list, this particular bank's failure to supervise its staff and put in adequate security provisions in place, coming right on top of its role in the economic collapse could, with a nudge in the right direction, give the SEC and the FCA all the ammunition they need to shut it down. If I were to take legal action in the UK courts and start a class action in the US, I reckon that would be a big enough nudge, don't you?'

Smith's expression hardened. 'Are you trying to blackmail me, Tom?'

'No, Mike, nothing of the sort, I'm offering you a deal.'

'I'm listening.'

'I've no interest in seeing the bank closed down,' said Tom. 'There are some good people here and if the bank goes, tens of thousands of innocent people round the world will lose their jobs: that would be vindictive. Also, if the bank does go down, however much the courts award me in damages, I won't be at the front of the queue of creditors, so I may not even get paid. I don't want to sue a bankrupt company: that would be stupid. After I took ownership of the intellectual property in Minerva, the bank tried to buy it off me but the price you offered was a joke. Make me a sensible offer and I will work with you to make it an even better proprietary trading system than it is already. David and I proved that it was possible to take Noviprom for forty million US in a matter of days. Now, not everyone is that stupid, you're not going to be able to do that to Goldmans very often, for example, but you could make five hundred mill per year for the next three years without breaking sweat. Agreed?'

'If anything, I think you're being conservative, Tom. But, yes, I know where you're coming from.'

'OK, Mike. Here's the offer, and by the way, if we haven't shaken on it when I leave this office then it lapses and I go straight back to m'learned friends. It's a one-time-only, take it or leave it deal. You pay one hundred million Sterling for the IP and the source code – seventy-five to me, twenty-five to David Liebowitz – and it's yours: I'll even throw in the servers for free. What's more, I'll carry on developing it for you and I'll only charge three thousand Sterling per day for my time.' Tom fixed him unblinkingly, eye to eye. 'What do you say, Mike? It's got to be a better deal than bye-bye, bank.'

Smith's face creased into a smile. 'Put like that, you bastard, I don't see I have a choice.' He extended his hand.

After Tom had finished talking to Smith, he wandered back to the AES desk and sat in his old seat. He still half expected to see David Liebowitz sitting next to him and his absence hit like a physical force – he was alive though, that was the main thing and the operation to mend his fractured tibia had been successful. The three traders and their assistants all swarmed round him, asking him how he was. How was Sally? Was it true that he'd shot down three helicopters single-handed? Sunk into the void left by the loss of his friends and the brave policemen he'd known so briefly, he barely even noticed their presence. His answers were non-committal and vague. 'Where's Chivers?' he asked.

'Didn't you hear? They fished him out of the Thames

yesterday morning. According to the papers he was in a terrible state. Must've been hit by a ship's propeller to do that much damage, they said.'

Chapter Forty-five

Tom and Sally took the elevator from the glass and steel atrium of New York's Mount Sinai Hospital to the orthopaedic department on the ninth floor. Passing along the light, airy corridors, they soon found Liebowitz's room where he was propped up in bed reading, surrounded by cards. Tom arranged the bouquet of flowers cack-handedly in a vase while Sally gave the patient a kiss on the cheek and a big hug; but when she stood up, Tom saw that they were both crying – he wasn't far from tears either and gave his friend a hug to hide his embarrassment. Liebowitz smiled at them through his tears. 'So how are you both? I hear you had one hell of a time in France, they told me you had a whole army after you.'

'We're fine thanks, David: I still jump ten feet in the air every time a car backfires,' said Tom. 'But it's you we're worried about – we're so sorry about Caroline, I just don't know what to say.'

'Me neither,' said Liebowitz. 'Not a clue – guess there *is* nothing to say. But I'll tell you one thing, as soon as this leg is fixed and I'm mobile again, I'm going after those bastards – I don't care how I do it or how long it takes me, but I'll find them.' He bunched his fists and bit his lip; Tom could see that he was on the edge of tears again, tears of rage, bitterness and frustration. 'You don't know what they did to her before they killed her and I'll never tell you, but I saw it with my own eyes and if I have to kill every single person in that godforsaken country of theirs to get at them, believe me I will.' Tom shot a glance at Sally. This wasn't the man they knew and loved. Such an ordeal would scar anyone for life, but what the Mansells saw that day in the hospital room in Manhattan frightened them. Gone was the funny, cynical wise-guy and in his place was something darker and harder; they could see at once that he was in deadly earnest.

'Thanks to you, Tom.' He reached up and grabbed his friend's hand. 'Thanks to your generosity, I can afford to spend the rest of my life tracking them down and that's exactly what I'm going to do. You remember how long it took them to catch Eichmann? I don't care how long it takes me, but I'll do it.'

'You'll need help, David. You can't do that sort of vigilante stuff on your own.'

'I know I will, but believe me I'm not going to ask for yours. I know you'd say yes, but I wouldn't do that to Sally. If needs be, I'll hire someone to help me.'

Tom shifted uneasily from one foot to the other and looked out of the window over Central Park. 'David, I don't want you to take this the wrong way, but this is crazy talk. If you do something, anything, in anger without thinking about it, firstly you could end up hurting another innocent person – I'm sure Caroline wouldn't have wanted that – and secondly, you could wind up spending the rest of your life in prison while leaving the real bastards to die in their beds of old age.'

'Yeah, maybe you're right. Maybe I shouldn't rush these things,' said Liebowitz. 'I've got a much better idea, I'll run for president and when I'm elected, I'll nuke their shithole country back into the Stone Age.' Tom smiled – maybe the wisecrack artist wasn't wholly gone, but the set of his friend's jaw and the way he bunched the sheets tightly in his fists said otherwise – Liebowitz wasn't joking. He looked up at Tom. 'I've had another couple of visitors too,' he said. 'Pair of heavies from the FBI telling me not very subtly to keep my trap shut about Noviprom and to let them go after the bad guys.'

'What did you say to them?'

'I told them to go screw themselves.'

'Now there's a coincidence,' said Tom. 'The guy who met us off the flight from France wouldn't let on exactly who he worked for, but I think I was supposed to jump to the right conclusions – that's the British way of doing things – and we had exactly the same conversation. I won't go into details here because walls have ears.' At this, Liebowitz's face looked grimmer still.

Sally perched nervously on the corner of the bed and tried to change the subject. 'So when are they letting you out, David? We'd like you to come and stay with us when you're well enough to travel.'

'The surgeon said I was lucky. Apparently I was probably hit by a ricochet and although it broke my shin, there was enough bone there to pin the two halves together and they don't think I'm going to end up with one leg shorter than the other. They've already got me waving the leg about and doing gentle lifts with it. I start rehab in a couple of days and they reckon that with all the metalwork in there I'll be able to get around on crutches pretty soon – the doc says that six to nine months from now I could be back to normal. It'll give me plenty of time to work out what I'm going to do and who I'm going to do it to.'

This wasn't going the way either of them had expected. 'We're thinking of moving to Switzerland full-time,' said Sally, trying once more to lighten the tone. 'We'd love it if you could come and spend some time with us there; you'd adore Lausanne, that's the area where we're looking anyway.'

'Sure, that'd be great,' said Liebowitz in a monotone and without making eye-contact. 'I've got plenty of unfinished business, but yeah, sure I'd love to come and see you when I get chance.' He shifted his gaze to look at Tom. 'It's bugging you, isn't it, Tom?'

'What do you mean, David?'

'What you're not saying. What you're trying to work out how to say. Tell you what, let me do it. I'll say it for you. You blame yourself for this, don't you?'

'Well, yes, I suppose I do,' said Tom.

Liebowitz turned to Sally. 'Do *you* blame him, Sally?'

'No, of course not.'

'And neither do I. This wasn't your fault, Tom, none of it. Nobody saw it coming and as far as you and I are concerned, nothing changes.' A heavy silence fell between them, one of those silences that only hospital visits can generate.

'We're here for a few days,' said Tom. 'Can we come and see you again tomorrow?'

'Of course you can,' said Liebowitz with a smile. And this time his eyes were smiling too.

Chapter Forty-six

With the Mas des Oliviers under offer, Tom and Sally moved to a small rented house just outside Lausanne until they found something to buy.

From their terrace, they had a perfect view over the town, Lake Geneva and the mountains on the French side of the water.

As promised, a fully-recovered Vincent Deschamps, now reunited with Sophie, had treated them to a wonderful long weekend in Paris, including the obligatory meal at Le Homard qui Chante. During their stay, Tom had a long conversation with Sophie about the promised scoop.

David Liebowitz was due to come and see them in three weeks' time, although Tom was concerned that his friend would cancel, such was his continued obsession with avenging Caroline.

One evening Sally was reading the UK news on-line. 'Hey, Tom, look at this. Denise Evans got twenty years and Bihar Jalil got fifteen.'

'Excellent, serves them bloody right,' said Tom. 'Only wish it was longer. You and I have still got to finish putting together a story for Sophie that the government won't be able to deny and that also shows what the Nashyastanis are up to. And that's not going to be easy.'

'You're right, Tom,' she said. 'But just not yet, it's all too fresh and raw right now.'

The coals in the Weber barbeque had turned to the perfect shade of light grey and Tom was just about to put the meat on when the phone rang. He put his beer down. 'I'll get it. It's probably David,' he said.

He heard a familiar voice, 'Good evening, Mr Mansell, I do hope you enjoy your barbeque. It is Kaliski here. I feel that we shall meet again very soon. We have unfinished business, do we not?'

THE END

COMING SOON FROM MAUVE SQUARE PUBLISHING

DEATH TO BANKERS

Chapter One

The young man stopped walking, turned and listened: no footsteps now, nothing but the distant swish of tyres on wet tarmac from the main road, and closer at hand, the ever-present sound of the river. Must be hearing things, he thought: get a grip. Peering into the darkness, he wiped the rain-streaked lenses of his glasses in an effort to see if there really was someone back there keeping pace with him, but the world beyond the little pools of light on the Thames-side path was lost in shadow. He smiled nervously to himself at the thought of someone following him. After all, why would they? And yet the nagging doubts remained; after all, it wasn't the first time.

The last time it had happened was on the way back from the Tube station a week earlier. He'd dismissed it as coincidence, at worst a mugger looking for an easy mark and put off by the chance appearance of passers-by. But now, once again, as he made his way home from the Waterman's Arms, and feeling a little unsteady on his feet, he'd heard footsteps close behind him. When he stopped, so did they: when he moved on they continued, sounding ever closer. This wasn't even his part of town, not somewhere he'd ever been before: to him, London was a city of islands, patches of firm ground, stitched together by the fine thread of the Underground and surrounded by uncharted waters such as these.

He set off once again, walking more quickly as the path followed the Thames in a wide loop around a turd-strewn patch of grass and weeds bordering the back fences of the houses which pressed against the river. Ahead was a stretch of boardwalk, better lit; and on a lamp-post was a sign pointing inland to the Tube station – another half-mile. Maybe I'll get a cab, he thought as he approached the fork in the path. Suddenly, movement in his peripheral vision caught his attention as a dark figure detached itself from the shadows: simultaneously he felt a hand gripping his arm. 'So you don't want to talk to me? You don't like me?' The man spoke with a continental accent – Italian, probably, he thought, turning to face him but making no effort to shake free. He'd heard the voice before. Their faces were now inches apart and under the stark light from overhead he recognised the man he'd spoken to briefly in the pub. He let out a sigh of relief. 'God. You made me jump, creeping up on me like that. What do you want?'

'You know what I want.'

'Look, I told you. I have to go home. I've got to go to work tomorrow,' he said to the stranger. Then lowering his eyes, 'We could meet again if you like. Maybe come to the Waterman's Arms again?'

'Yes, I'd like that,' said the Italian. 'But surely, just five minutes? There's nobody around.'

He released himself from the stranger's grasp. 'No. I told you. I'm going home. It's late, it's wet and cold. Not tonight.'

'Is true. You don't like me do you?' the stranger said, his tone becoming petulant.

'It's not that,' he said, raising his hand to touch the man's face. 'Let's do this properly. You know, another time. Somewhere comfortable, warm and dry.'

He felt the hand clamped round his arm again and heard the voice say, 'No. I want you now.'

The Italian jammed something into his ribs and when he looked down, saw to his horror that it was a semi-automatic pistol. He gave a nervous laugh: this has to be a joke. Play along with him. 'Look, there's no need for that…if there's somewhere we could go, but not here, not outdoors.'

'Good. Walk a little with me. By the river.'

'But you're going the wrong way, I need to get home –'

'I said I want you to walk with me,' the stranger's insistent tone once more backed up by a dig in the ribs with the pistol's muzzle. They walked on in silence through the persistent drizzle until they came to a gate in the fence and a sign saying "Gilmore's Stairs – Port of London Authority". The Italian released his grip. 'Stop here,' he said, putting his arms on the top rail and staring down into the black water. 'We should talk a little.' He slipped the gun back into his outside pocket.

The young man joined him, the rain on his glasses transforming the lights of the far bank into diffuse blobs and smears of brightness. 'What is there to talk about?' he asked, his nerves slowly calming and the fear caused by the appearance of the gun now replaced by a delicious frisson of anticipation.

'Your friend?'

'He need never know.'

'I am pleased,' said the Italian.

The young man remained leaning on the railings, and seemingly oblivious to the weather, for a moment turned away, gazing towards the distant lights of Canary Wharf, apparently deep in thought. 'He won't know,' he said once more. As he did so, the Italian slid his hand into a deep pocket, sewn into the inside of his coat, and his hand closed around the handle of a hammer.

He never knew what hit him, nor did he even feel it, so savage was the initial blow to the base of his skull. Ignoring the fine aerosol of blood that spattered his face, the Italian allowed him to slump to the ground and rolled the inert form face downwards. Six more well-aimed blows to make sure and the job was done. The Italian wiped the excess blood off the hammer on a patch of wet grass: the rain could take care of the rest. Then, opening the gate, he pulled the body down the stairs and into the darkness below.

***

The tide turned and began flowing against the current, stirring the grey-brown surface of the Thames into short, choppy waves. The action of the water bumped the white, puffy face of the corpse gently up and down against the muddy foreshore. Over his dead body stood an older man dressed in rubber boots and a faded parka, grimly clutching a long metal pole. He stopped what he was doing, put down the pole, waded into the shallows and tried to pull the body higher up onto the small patch of shingly mud that the low tide had exposed, but it was too heavy for him to move more than a few feet further inland; he knew that in a matter of hours the tide would reclaim the young man, possibly for ever.

The arrival of a Metropolitan Police patrol and an ambulance had its usual effect of drawing a crowd of onlookers. The Scene of Crime team came and went, the corpse was taken away and in the end, the last of the curious wandered off. All that remained at the site of the drama was a small area of South Bank footpath, cordoned off by blue and white tape. Two bored uniformed officers paced up and down, stamping their feet to keep warm and counting the time until their relief arrived. Ten minutes late, a police car pulled up and two equally unenthusiastic replacements wandered over to greet them. 'Anything exciting?' asked one of the new arrivals.

'Could be. Old boy mucking about with a metal detector found him this morning.'

He snorted. 'Metal detector? Must've been lots of lead in him then.'

'Nah. Nothing as exciting as that. Been whacked on the back of the head though. The doc reckons he'd been in the water about five days. Another banker.'

'No great loss then,' said the first, and his colleagues smirked dutifully in response to the gallows humour.

To be continued...